PERL

The Unearthing

MELISSA FLESHER

Paperback ISBN-13: 978-1-7354064-4-2

Cover design and illustrations by: Melissa Flesher
Map designs by: Erik Flesher
Printed in the United States of America

LOVE AND GRATITUDE

For my son Noah, my nieces Cora and Elena,
my nephews Oliver, Sebastian and Johnny,
and all the children who will inherit this world.

A special thanks to my parents Roger and Diana,
my brother Nick and his wife Katherine,
my brother Chris and his wife Jennie,
and to my sisters in this life Julie, Ursula and Marti.

And to my moon, my co-creator in this world,
my husband Erik.

To those with imaginative hearts
that hear the songs in nature,
connecting us to all life on Earth.

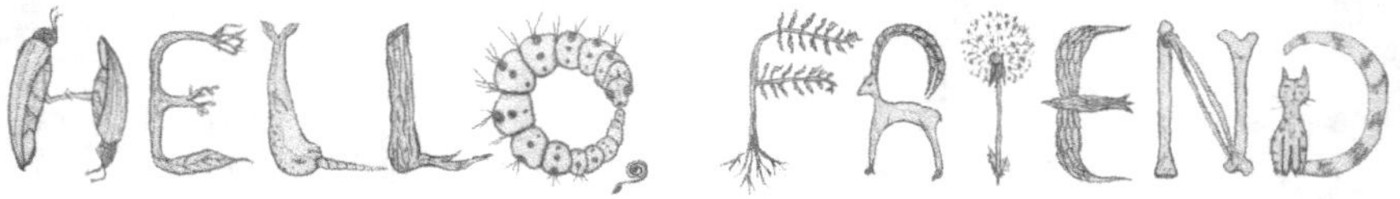

I am so grateful that you have been led to this book, yet, I don't believe that it was by coincidence. You and I are connected, as are all things on our Earth.

From my experience, there are two worlds—visible science and invisible mystery, and they merge in nature. My storytelling is rooted in this place of imagination. My hope is to pique your curiosity to look for the virtues of nature. To explore the hidden—be it in the seed pod, the bees' vision, the soil, or the human brain—and realize that you are a part of the greatest secret in human history. You are a masterpiece, as is all of life on this planet. Once you awaken to this, you'll see more and more the miraculousness all around you, and want to protect and defend it.

You can make a difference. You can change where the planet is headed for generations to come. You are capable of working magic.

Thank you for embarking on Perl's adventure. I hope it shapes your own adventures.

Love,
Melissa

This is where our first book, *Perl the Awakening*, left off,
as our story continues~

Perl completed Seeker training at Callowhorn in the Light Realm of Venusto. She has returned to her Earthly home with the monks on the island of Mont Michel. Perl is anxiously awaiting her reunion with her mother, Dianna, before beginning her next phase of training at Greenheart, which will advance her to the level of Seer. The balance of nature in the oceans has been restored, yet a new evil is rising; one more ancient and powerful than the Darkness that had been pursuing Perl and killed her father, Noaa. Humanity stands at the brink between an era of Light and Dark as the veil between the two Realms shifts with the Earth's climate now in flux.

Farewell,

I am the dissent from all rules ~
Every wish, every want, I transport desires
and understand the nature of people, old and young.
Step forward into another place, away from the moment,
exile from circumstances beyond your control.
Without judgement,
I hold up the mirror.

Let the voices in ~
listen,
you want all,
you deserve all.
Take.

~ The Ullen

~EVER~
NATURE PARADISE
VENUSTO
THE UNFORGIVEN
HALF~LIGHT REALM
PALO SANTO
EARTH
LIGHT REALM
DARK REALM
THE REALMS

1 HABOOB

The motionless desert air was crypt-quiet. A horned viper *(Cerastes cerastes)* sat coiled on a rock, too hot to strike, as three hooded holy men shuffled past. Their methodic steps crunched the desert sand like dry bread crumbs as they chanted hypnotically:

> "Eee-nu-rah, eee-nu-rah, eee-nu-rah, zay.
> Eee-nu-rah, eee-nu-rah, eee-nu-rah, zay."

Parched from the midday sun, they stopped to rest beneath an enormous saguaro cactus, the only bit of shade for miles.

"It's been forty days, and all we've seen is dune after dune and the occasional tumble weed, without a cloud in sight." Brother Sebastian unbuckled his sandals to rub his swollen feet. "Breathtaking as it is, this is a harsh and inhospitable place." A fisherman by trade, the monk was more at home on the salty sea. "I feel like I'm being baked alive."

"Agreed, it feels like I'm opening my oven door to turn the potatoes, yet the blast of heat never subsides." Victr, the head cook for the Brotherhood of the Quill, reached into a small pouch, handing his companions a stick of soybean jerky.

Brother Jonathan wiped his brow with a dingy rag. "It's official, we're roasted spuds."

"Ha! Yes, you do reek of garlic!" Brother Sebastian gave Jonathan a hearty slap on the back sending a waft of dust into to air. "Maybe even an onion or two!"

"Ha, ha, good to see you haven't lost your levity, young brother." Jonathon tucked his cloth back into his satchel.

"Oh, I'm not joking!" Sebastian chuckled, chewing with his mouth open. "Brother Victr could make a hardy broth from the likes of you!"

Licking his cracked lips, Brother Victr took a small swig of warm, flat water from a hollowed gourd that hung from a rope around his neck. "There will be no armpit stew on my watch! Let us refocus our energy on why we're here—to follow The Pilgrimage of the Truth and reconnect to our inner selves."

"None deny the enlightenment of our quest." Squinting, Jonathan pulled his hood over his eyes and sat down in the shadow of the cactus. "It's my outer-self that would like less of this burning sun."

Brother Sebastian interrupted, "Look there, the twentieth scallop!" He pointed to a shell on the ground. "We're halfway to Santiago." Being the youngest of the Brotherhood, this was Sebastian's first trek from Mont Michel through the Desertlands, and he kept an accurate count of each pathway marker they crossed.

"You see? A sign from Ever." Victr corked his gourd with a quick slap of his large hand. "Be like the lizard, Jon, old boy. Embrace what imposes you. Adapt to your environment."

"Yes, yes, making it my home." Brother Jonathan, the oldest of the three at sixty-eight, was having the most difficulty dealing with the unrelenting heat.

Brother Sebastian gave Jonathan a gentle tap on his shoulder, "Together we shall prevail."

A distant rumble echoed across the landscape, breaking the silence of the day.

"Dear Ever, was that thunder?" Jonathan hoisted himself up with his walking stick. His back cracked as he craned to look up. "Or am I hallucinating?" They heard another rumble.

"Praise be!" Sebastian sang out. "It has never rained here."

"It's no hallucination." Brother Victr, ever the anxious one, quickly packed up the snacks and tightened his robe belt. "Secure your belongs. Hoods up, and googles on, brothers."

Like angry giants stomping on the clouds above, the storm closed in fast. Dust devils swirled across the valley, whipping the monks' robes like loose sails on a ship. The men bunched together when they heard a loud trill from above.

"Fweet-ooo-eeee-oob!" A man was perched like a vulture *(Cathartes aura)* on top of the cactus. He was wrapped like a mummy peering through a pair of binoculars, whistling.

Brother Sebastian jumped at the sound. "What in the…has he been up there this whole time?"

The camouflaged man paused, craning his neck to listen, as a faint series of warbles returned from across the desolate canyon, "Fweeeeeeet—oy-oy-oy!"

"Did you hear that?!" Sebastian yelled over the increasing gale force winds. "Who is that? What are they doing?!"

"Talking!" Brother Victr hollered back.

"Talking?" Questioned Brother Jonathan. "Sounds more like the tweeting of birds!"

"It's Sfyria." Victr continued, "a whistled version of the spoken word. The sound waves travel farther than shouting."

Brother Sebastian wiped the sand from his dusty goggles. "Do you know what they're saying?"

The man whistled again, "Ssseeet-oooot-oooot! Eeeet!"

Victr thought aloud, "Some type of warning…vipers, perhaps? No, not vipers." He rubbed his chin, furrowing his brow. "Pirates, maybe…either way, a warning for sure."

"Come now, Brother Worrywart, you are beginning to vex even me." Brother Jonathan protested.

Lightening scratched through the clouds like electrified claws. Victr didn't need to hear any more. He could see the threat. "Haboob! Take cover!"

The downpour of rain evaporated midair, causing an enormous rush of cold air to plummet to the baked ground.

"A ha-oo what?" Sebastian dug his heels into the sand to steady himself.

"Dust storm!" Victr pointed east over a mountain of dunes. "There!"

Three thousand feet high and reaching ten miles across, a great wall of dirt was roaring towards them; a monstrous curtain being drawn across the landscape.

"Make way, monks!" A mob mounted on camels (*Camelus bactrianus*) stampeded past, nearly knocking Jonathan off his feet. "Are you blind, old man?"

The ramshackle herd moved off in a cloud of dust, continuing to swear at the monks, the clanking and rattling of pots and pans attached to their packs fading in the blustery wind. The nomads hunkered down with their nappy beasts amongst a shelter of boulders.

The storm-watcher whistled a final, "weeeeeet-weeeeeet," as he jumped off the thirty-foot cactus. Seconds before he hit the ground, a trapdoor in the sand swung open, swallowing him like a prairie dog.

"Brothers, did you see that?!" Sebastian yelled. "Hey! Let us in!" He brushed the sand off the heavy iron door, searching for a handle. "The storm is almost upon us! Open up!" He banged on the metal with his fist. "Please! Help us!"

From past pilgrimages, Brother Victr had not only learned to decode the Sfyria language, he also knew to be prepared for the worst. From a pocket inside his robe, sewn in there by Perl to carry extra jars of marmalade up from the root cellar pantry, the stout monk pulled out a blanket.

"Quickly brothers." Victr opened up the sheet. "Huddle in."

Sebastian and Jonathan each grabbed hold of a corner.

"It's spider silk, the strongest material on Earth. Sit! And tuck it under your bum!" Victr commanded.

The three monks sat knee to knee under the blanket as an avalanche of dust overwhelmed them. Seventy-mile-an-hour winds sandblasted the web from all sides, as walnut-sized hail pelted them from overhead. Desert birds, unable to escape, started dropping from the sky.

Sebastian bellowed, "It's not going to hold!"

Brother Victr began to chant softly, "Eee-nu-rah, eee-nu-rah, eee-nu-rah, zay."

The other two joined the hymn, "Eee-nu-rah, eee-nu-rah, eee-nu-rah, zay."

Completely engulfed in the cloud of suffocating haze, the cloth began to glow. Dimly at first, then beaming as brightly as a firefly. Brother Sebastian's eyes widened and Jonathan's mouth dropped at the miraculous sight.

"A gift from Ximu!" Victr shouted over the deafening noise. "The old spider monk thought it would come in handy!"

Their chants, a calling to the Light Realm for protection, along with the strength of the spider's web created a safe haven. They remained barricaded for what felt like an eternity as the haboob slowly dissipated. In reality the storm had blown by in less than ten minutes. However, the effects from this mammoth storm would be felt for months as outbreaks of valley fever would spread from soil-dwelling fungi. Overgrazing, deforestation and the depletion of water in the region had made these devastating storms an all-to-common occurrence.

The baying of wild dogs could be heard in the distance as the torrid heat returned.

"We should get moving if we're to make it to the oasis before nightfall." Victr stood gathering the webbed cloth into a ball, tucking it safely back into his robe. His hood blew back, exposing his scorched, bald head that shined like a crystal ball in the sun. "Keep your goggles on and scarves up. There's still grit and poisonous microbes in the air."

The monks looked around, seeing the lifeless birds strewn around them.

"Poor creatures," Sebastian muttered.

"As terrible as these storms are," Jonathan said, "they are part of a system that feeds the oceans and fertilizes our few remaining forests. In fact, they make up one of the greatest annual migrations on the planet, mineral migration."

"I'm constantly awestruck at how something we experience in one place can start from so far away." Agreeing, Brother Sebastian found a bit of pep in his step. "It truly is a wondrous force that ties our planet together."

Victr licked a bone-dry finger, clearing his goggles with what little saliva he had left. "Aha! There it is, Brothers! The oasis!"

After several hours in the searing late afternoon sun, they came upon an acre of water surrounded by towering palms.

"Thank the Light Realm," Jonathan leaned on his frayed walking stick.

Sebastian tapped a shell on the ground, "and we've reached the thirtieth scallop!"

"Ten more days, Brothers," Victr informed. "Tonight, enjoy the refuge and refreshment."

Footprints from man and beast dotted the landscape leading to the fertile pool in the middle of nowhere. As the monks approached, they saw caravans of rotters in makeshift helmets with spiraling tubes attached to oxygen tanks. Many of them pulled cages covered with tarps to shield their inhabitants from onlookers. The Desertlands were full of scavengers, thieves and murderers, but once inside the oasis there was an unspoken law to keep the peace. Even the hungry cheetah *(Acinonyx jubatus)* sat alongside the gazelle *(Gazella leptoceros)* in harmony drinking at the water's edge.

"Praise be to Ever, this feels incredible," Johnathan said as he dipped his raw, burnt feet into the pool.

Sebastian disrobed and dove in headfirst in only his undergarments. Coming up for air, he shook his shoulder-length black hair like a wet dog. "Incredible!"

"It floods once a year from an underground river." Victr filled his gourd to the brim, chugging the entire thing in one long swallow. "The aquifer generates tons of pressure below which allows the water to seep to the surface." Wiping his chin, he re-filled the gourd.

Drinking straight from the pond, Sebastian asked, "Are all these people going to Santiago?"

"Either going to or coming from. However, very few are on the path of The Truth. Much has changed in the fourteen years that I've been making the pilgrimage to check on Dianna, including the city's name. Ever since Prince Tobias and his brother Prince Névenoé took control, it has been known as The Under Kingdom."

"Don't get me started on those two heels," Jonathan said, picking up his sandals. "Shall we make camp?" He walked barefoot toward a pair of foxtail palms. "The sun is setting and I'm starved."

Sebastian cupped some water in his hands. "We can make a nice broth tonight, ala Brother Garlic and Onions here!" He gestured to Brother Jonathan. "Ha! How about you wash more than those toes, my friend?!"

In a burst of newfound energy, Jonathan dropped his sandals and ran full-bore into the water, doing a belly flop and drenching Sebastian. The three monks laughed harder than they had in weeks.

Lingering dust on the horizon painted the sky with streaks of orange and pink sherbet as the sun sunk beneath the dunes. A halo of campfires encircled the water's edge. Travelers settled in for the night, keeping a watchful eye.

The monks licked their rice porridge bowls clean, then prepared for their nightly prayer reading. Jonathan lit the charcoal and incense inside a small metal thurible, which hung from chains. From his robe pocket, Victr pulled out a small scroll tied up with a green vine.

"What else are you hiding in that robe of yours?" Sebastian teased.

"Tonight, we read from an ancient book of The Awakening." Victr untied the vine. "One that has never been uttered aloud."

"What book? I know every verse in The Awakening." Brother Jonathan's eyes were fixated on Victr as he slowly unrolled the old parchment.

"I was instructed to read from it once we reached the oasis." Victr held up the transparent paper inches from his face. He put on his glasses to read the incredibly small print.

Jonathan leaned in for a closer look. "Instructed, instructed by whom?" Plumes of billowy white smoke escaped the thurible, rising into the night sky like ghosts.

"Uriel." Victr raised an eyebrow.

Brother Jonathan bowed his head and clasped his hands together in reverence. "Begin."

Victr cleared his dry throat.

"The Codex of the Sacred Invisible, verses one through eleven…

Beloved, I am the silence that is incomprehensible.
As the dew to the morning grass, I come to thee continuously.
I am horse, hawk, bear, stone and tree.
You, my forgetful birds, have remained grounded too long,

flap your wings to rise and soar
with less need to land on the Earth for rest.
Prepare in this way to escape the snares of terra and become as one.
My light breaks through not as sun, nor fire,
but in the discourse of knowing
the secret mysteries of nature.
Now is the dawn of the Great Unearthing."

The monks sat back, momentarily contemplating the word of Ever as the dark orange sky pulled on its cloak of blackness. Sebastian's eyes sparkled, reflecting the stars that illuminated the sky above.

"Please, continue Brother."

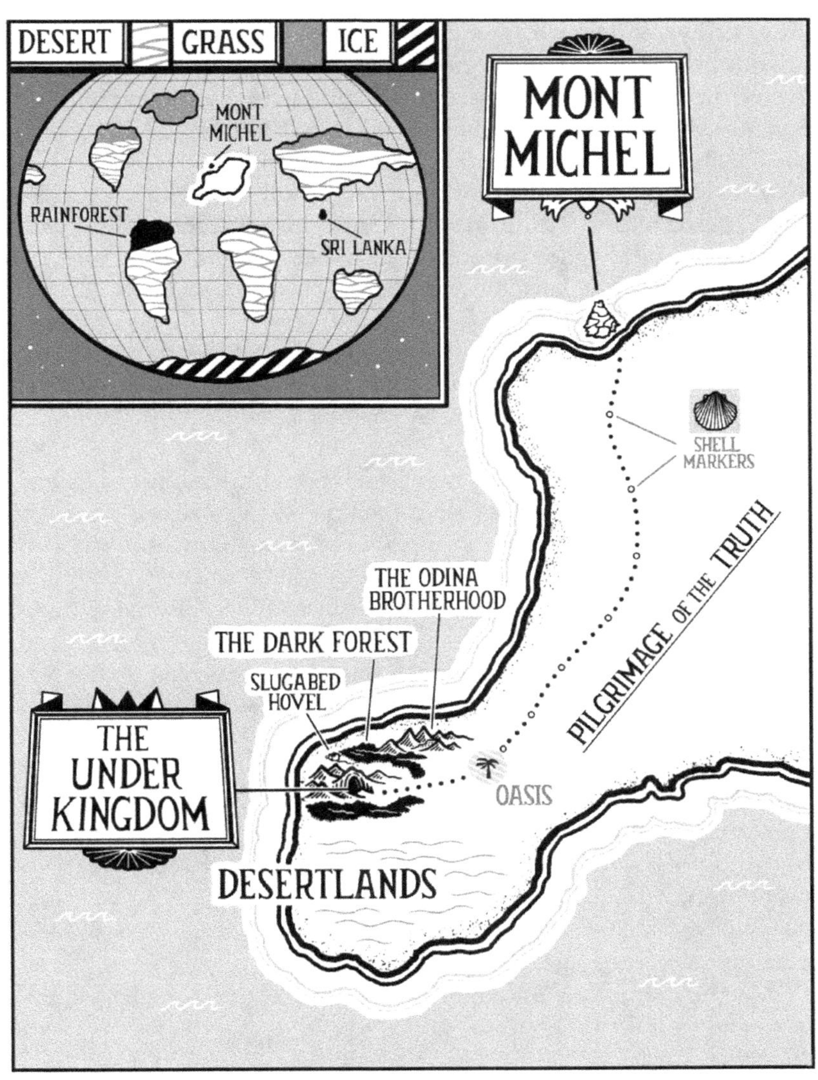

DESERT
GRASS
ICE
MONT MICHEL
RAINFOREST
SRI LANKA
MONT MICHEL
SHELL MARKERS
PILGRIMAGE OF THE TRUTH
THE ODINA BROTHERHOOD
THE DARK FOREST
SLUGABED HOVEL
THE UNDER KINGDOM
OASIS
DESERTLANDS

2 FOREST SISTERS

Fourteen years ago, on what should have been the most cherished day of Dianna's life, the day her first child was born, her husband Noaa was murdered in front of her. In order to save her baby from the killer, Dianna tucked the infant inside a barnacle on a great blue whale *(Balaenoptera Musculus)*, who delivered the child safely to the island of Mont Michel. Grief stricken and alone, Dianna sought refuge with the Forest Sisters of Elsewhere. Among these holy sages, Dianna found purpose and a reason to go on living. Her life became one of service, caring for the orphaned, the unfed, and the pilgrims seeking refuge in the Desertland city. To this day, she has remained hidden deep within the cells of the Under Kingdom, protected from her husband's murderer, Lophius, a Light Protector turned evil by The Ullen.

Like most sacred orders, the Forest Sisters lost their place in the high court and rebuilt their community under a veil of secrecy. Over the past decade, the monks of The Brotherhood of the Quill had checked up on Dianna, bringing news of her baby girl, the one they had named Perl.

Brothers Victr, Jonathan, and Sebastian were on the last leg of their journey through the Desertlands when they came upon a vast canyon. At the bottom was a forest with one opening in the wall of mangled trees. Tracks from all directions lead to the hole like a mouth swallowing up all who entered.

"The last shell marker." Brother Sebastian stomped his cracked sandal on the pathway. "We've arrived."

"Finally," Brother Jonathan added, feeling the sweet relief of gravity helping his aching knees as they descended down the dune, stopping where the edge of the desert kissed the woods.

"Look at these branches, they've melded together." Sebastian ran his hand over the bark. The limbs were knotted and twisted like pretzels.

"It's from the constant winds," Victr said, looking up at the canopy; all the trees bent to one side, their leaves pressed and matted down. "See? The entire thicket leans northward."

"I suppose it's into the mysterious forest we go, Brothers?" Sebastian asked with an air of nervous sarcasm.

"You know, some say the dark forest has an electromagnetic field that pulls in lost pilgrims if they venture too close."

"Brother Jonathan, your attempt to alleviate my worries is backfiring," Sebastian muttered.

"These woods are steeped in mysticism," Victr interrupted Sebastian. "Legend claims that it was once believed to be the end of the world. That when the sun disappeared beneath the trees, the veil between this world and the next thinned, opening the gates to the Light Realm."

I'll take that tall tale over the other more sinister one." Sebastian stepped ahead of his brothers into the shadowy mouth of the forest. "In we go, Ever guide us."

"The legend also says that the fortress within was constructed to trap demons," Jonathan added, "to keep evil from spilling out of the underworld and into the human realm."

Sebastian turned, giving the old monk a glare.

"Come now, Jon old boy, let's not condone such rumors. Young Sebastian won't sleep at night." Victr smirked. "But let us be on our toes nonetheless."

As they approached a turn, they heard a commotion. Where the trees opened up, the colossal entrance to the Under Kingdom came into view. Chiseled directly into the mountainside was a gateway barred with ten marble pillars. Above each column perched a screaming gargoyle, bright green smoke pouring from its fanged jaws. The strange facade looked like something out of a carnival.

Jonathan held his walking stick out, halting the other two. "It's that caravan from the oasis."

"Should we hold back?" Sebastian whispered. "They seem dangerous."

The monks looked on as a handful of the Kingdom's large, intimidating guards argued with the caravan of men. The bare-chested gatekeepers had chains bolted into their flesh, running up their arms and down their backs. Daggers, scythes, and other jagged blades hung from the chains. Wires weaved in and out of their skin, giving them an unsettling half-human, half-machine appearance.

"I was told I could take my cargo straight to the track," said an emaciated, sunburnt nomad from atop his camel.

"No offering! No entry!" snarled one of the burly guards. He swung a war hammer, striking one of the three covered cages they were pulling.

"These first two are promised to Prince Tobias," the nomad said, gesturing at the third cage, "but you can have your pick from the last litter."

"We take what we want!" A guard with black leather straps crisscrossing his goiter-covered head rocked the first cage. Something began growling and stomping inside.

"Careful! You know how expensive that beast is, you idiot—"

Another guard cut him off. "Shut hole or you disappear! And we take all." He slit the mesh on the middle cage. Fingers of several women reached through the bars. "Help us! Don't let them take us! My brother, he has money, please he'll pay you!" They begged, crawling over one another.

The nomad shouted at the guard. "Hands off the women! I said the last crate. Take one from there and that's our offering."

With a rusty metal hook where his hand used to be, the guard swung open the back door. A dozen children in rags scurried like mice to the far end of the cage. The guard licked his purple lips, smiling a toothless grin.

"Mmm…snacks." He hooked the pants of a small boy, pulling him out as the scared child kicked frantically. The guard threw the child head first into a smaller cage near the front gate. The boy snarled and cried, shaking the bars wildly.

"Open the gates!" the beastly man shouted.

At the top of the wall a robotic soldier stood at attention. The eight-foot-tall android wore an emerald green latex bodysuit, its head made of hard plastic like a mannequin. The skin around its mouth was gone, exposing its teeth and gums in a ghastly grin. It nodded and pulled down a lever, raising the gate.

"Heeyah!" The guards swatted the camels on the rear. "Git!" As swiftly as it opened, the heavy gate slammed shut.

Still hidden in the woods, the monks huddled together, shocked at what they had just witnessed.

"Women and children in cages." Jonathan said, shaking his head.

"We have to help," Sebastian added.

Victr started walking. "Come, Brothers."

"Victr, wait. We need a plan." Sebastian looked over at Jonathan, who shrugged.

Victr approached the guards.

"Good day, good gentlemen." Victr bowed dramatically.

"Give us your offering, monk!"

Brothers Jonathan and Sebastian quickly caught up and stood in Victr's shadow.

"What could we possibly have that they would want?" Jonathan muttered under his breath.

"Be quick!" The guard kicked the cage, rattling the frightened boy.

Victr took a step back. He was the strongest in the Brotherhood, but this guard towered over him like a sequoia, his bulging arms cartoonishly big. "I have a very rare pear elixir. One fit for the princes."

Jonathan shot Sebastian a look of surprise, "He does?"

"We do?" Sebastian whispered back.

The guard stomped over and stood inches from Victr's face. "Like hell you do!" Rancid breath and spit blew into the monk's face.

"Did we not come down the path of Truth? In fact, we work for Count Zell Graves as his personal brewers, making the finest ales in all the world." Victr said, proudly.

"Yeah, could be from da Mont," one guard said, "I seen monks like dis come through before."

Victr slowly removed a tawny glass bottle from inside his robe, presenting it on his sleeve like a sommelier. "I cannot give you all I have, but one of you may have a taste."

"You don't tell us how much!" The guard grabbed the bottle. "We all swig!"

The monstrous men fought over the bottle. "Give it here!", "I ain't done!", "My turn!"

"I recommend going easy. That's very strong," Victr said.

Back and forth went the booze until not a drop remained.

Victr feigned displeasure. "Now you've gone and done it! What will I tell Prince Névenoé when he requests his gift?"

"You'll say nuthin', monk!" The guard barked, stumbling back a step.

"Open the gate and we shall keep this little secret to ourselves. You have my word before Ever."

"Hic! Yeah, you'll be quiet or else!" Spat another guard, tossing the empty bottle into the woods. "Open da gate!"

The guardsmen were beginning to feel the alcohol's effects. One tripped and fell face first, giggling. While they were distracted, Sebastian sidestepped over to the small cage. He lifted the latch and stretched out his robe to shield the child.

"Go, go, now," whispered Sebastian. "Into the woods and don't look back."

But the boy didn't budge. He ducked under Sebastian's robe and clung to his leg. Sebastian looked around cautiously, then limped up to the gate's entrance.

A guard burped and squinted at Sebastian, trying to focus. "Get goin'!" The monks stepped through the gate as it slammed shut behind them.

"Hurry, men," Victr said, noticing the boy peeking out from under Sebastian's robe. "What few wits those guards have will be returning soon enough."

"What was in that elixir, Brother?" asked Jonathan.

"A little something extra from our friend Dimitri," Victr winked.

"Honestly, Victr, you have more secret pockets in your robe than Perl." Sebastian chuckled. The boy crawled out from under Sebastian's robe. He was skin and bones and covered in dirt, with big brown eyes that darted around the room.

Poor thing looks like a wild animal, thought Victr. He spoke softly to the boy. "What is your name, lad?"

The four-year-old looked at his feet. "Christopher." The boy's head had been shaved and tattooed with a crude scorpion.

Jonathan eyed the boy. "So what do we do with this little wildling?"

"He'll come with us. The Sisters will know what to do." Victr wiped a tear from the boy's cheek. "You're safe now, Christopher. Come with us, okay?" The boy gave a slight nod.

As soon as the four entered the tunnel, Sebastian stopped in his tracks. "Oh my."

Running along the length of the walls and ceiling were row after row of glaring neon lights. The lights threw off a harsh, disturbing glow, and the low hum of the tube's electricity was almost hypnotic. At various locations along the glowing corridor, large maps displayed the Under Kingdom's labyrinth tunnel system.

"The city is home to thousands of tunnels," Victr said, "connecting everything like a giant anthill."

"And only second to Mont Michel for being the world's most gaudy of destinations," Jonathan added, squinting against the annoying light show. "Yet second to none in its savage barbarity."

Victr waved them forward, "this way." He took a quick right turn down a tunnel illuminated with ruby red bulbs.

"Glad one of us knows the way," Sebastian said, holding Christopher's hand as they stumbled through the dizzying corridors.

"Watch out!" Jonathan swung his walking stick, moving Sebastian and the boy against the wall.

They froze as a squadron of the robotic soldiers in their emerald jumpsuits marched past. They looked like something from a nightmare, their gruesome mouths agape in silent screams under the blinding red light. One of them swiveled its head toward the monks. Sebastian noticed the things had no eyes.

"I'm beginning to believe there's some truth to your tale, Brother Jon. This place being a…" Sebastian covered the boy's ears, "…Demon trap. I mean, good Ever, what are those things?"

Victr shook his head. "The Royal Guard…and let's pray we never see them again. Keep moving."

At the end of the red tunnel, they came to a large arched entryway. Hanging above the opening were three rows of mounted taxidermy ram *(Ovis aries)* heads, thirteen in each row, their lifeless eyes staring down at them.

"Well, it certainly looks like the gateway to the underworld," Jonathan half chuckled, but deep down his heart raced.

An angry voice echoed from behind them. "Find those monks! They took our boy!"

"Move, like the wind, Brothers!" Victr commanded as they hurried through the threshold into the nerve center of the Under Kingdom.

The enormous main terminal was jam packed, bustling with hundreds of travelers. Moving neon sidewalks zipped pedestrians of all walks of life down color-coded tunnels. Others rambled about in bizarre vehicles made from junk parts, equipped with spikes, guns and the occasional rabid dog.

"It's chaos!" Sebastian shouted over the crowd.

"We want the blue line, there." Victr pointed. "Keep your heads down and follow me."

The monks hurried past a crowd of wealthy, well-dressed travelers congregating in front of a gold walkway, roped off and protected by armed footmen. Jonathan brushed too close to the rope, setting off an alarm.

"Warning! Warning! Step away!"

"Get back!" A guard yelled, hitting Jonathan in the head with the butt of his rifle.

The old monk fell to his knees, momentarily stunned as a trickle of blood ran down his cheek. "I've got you." Sebastian scooped Jonathan up under his arms, hurrying them to the blue walkway just as the burly guards and green sentinels burst into the station.

"Where are they?! Kill them all!" The guards yelled; their vision still cloudy from the liquor.

Stepping onto the blue conveyor belt, the brothers and the boy crouched down. Standing nearby, a colorful band of acrobats and circus folk peered down at them.

"You hooded boys the magic act in the arena tonight?" A heavyset clown with a tuft of sparkly orange hair smiled at the men.

"Ah, no, we're just visiting," Jonathan stuttered, holding his aching head.

"You, okay? You're bleeding…" A woman on stilts dressed as a pink flamingo asked. She noticed two guards sprinting toward them. "Those guards looking for you?"

The monks nodded.

The clown moved in front of the monks as the flamingo woman spread her wings, hiding them.

"Thank you kindly," Sebastian smiled as they pulled away from the guards.

Up ahead the conveyor belt forked into two lanes. "Stay to the left," Victr said as they parted ways with the circus troupe.

"How big is this place?" Sebastian asked, moving over to the far side of the belt.

"There are at least eighteen distinct levels that I know of," Victr said, "but it's been several years since I've been back. So much has changed." He rubbed his wrinkled brow. *"Worse than I remember"* he thought as they passed a ragged group of beggars looking for handouts. The sidewalks were fast and the monks were past them before they could even react.

Victr sighed heavily, "Poor souls."

Jonathan cut in, "I did some research before we left. It appears as though the entire city was carved from existing caves and underground structures that had first formed naturally from tuff, a type of volcanic rock."

"Keep left again," Victr directed as the passage diverged again. "This is not the only subterranean city in the world, but it is the deepest and largest one."

"It feels like we're going downhill," Sebastian added.

"Two hundred and fifty feet below the earth's surface." Jonathan steadied himself on his walking stick. "At least we're out of the broiling sun and hail storms." He chuckled softly.

The moving sidewalk whizzed by an open chamber. "Was that a well?" Sebastian asked, watching a group of women dressed in blue, pumping water into terracotta pots.

"It is. The inhabitants here have fresh water, stables, kitchens, bathhouses. It is a self-contained metropolis," educated Victr.

"How many people are down here?" Sebastian asked, looking back as the women disappeared out of sight.

"Close to thirty thousand known, but many are undocumented." Victr tightened his rope belt. "Get ready to hop off…now."

Leaping off the moving belt, the three followed Victr as he approached a heavy wooden door. Victr rapped three times on a door knocker shaped like a quail *(Coturnix coturnix)*. A peephole slid open above the bird.

"State your business," an old woman's voice crowed. A hazel eye with a split pupil darted around, investigating them.

Jonathan spoke up, "We've traveled The Pilgrimage of the Truth to deliver a message to Our Lady of the Woods."

"We were only expecting three of ya." The woman's voice cracked; her eye locked in on the boy.

"He seeks refuge. We had no other option." Sebastian half-begged, "Can you take him in?"

"What's your message for Our Lady, hmm?" She squinted.

"One of good news, of her daughter…and this." Victr held up the ancient scroll.

The peephole slammed shut. The men could hear her conversing quickly with others behind the door. She slid it open again. "I'll need the password to be sure. That scroll could be fake."

"Of course, my lady." Victr agreed.

The old woman put her lips to the peephole, "Awaken the divinity." She stuck her ear up to the hole.

"From the river of love," Victr responded. At that, the door unlocked.

"Welcome, Brothers. Sorry for the protocol." The old woman's tone softened. "One can't be too cautious this deep down in the earth, heh heh." She was short her back humped, yet it didn't slow her a bit as she slid off the stool she was standing on and hobbled across the room to where two women stood. Flatfooted, she was no taller than Victr's waist, with long grey hair that fell past her knees. "I am Sister Martha, head of this burrow," she said, turning toward the women flanking her. "This is Sister Ursula and Sister Betty." The two women appeared to be in their fifties. All three sisters were dressed head-to-toe in blue shirts, pants and long wraps.

"We're so pleased you've made it safely, Brother Victr," Ursula smiled.

"Thank you, yes, we have…blisters and all." Sebastian lifted his foot and wiggled his toes.

Victr cut in, "it's nice to be here." He bowed slightly, "This is Brother Sebastian and Brother Johnathan." The men nodded respectfully. "And this youngling is named Christopher." The small boy gazed up at the women suspiciously, keeping hold of Sebastian's leg.

"Christopher, are you hungry?" Sister Martha asked. The child's eyes widened. "Sister Ursula will see you to the kitchen."

"Go on, it's alright," said Sebastian. The boy released his grip, taking Ursula's hand.

Sister Betty gave the brothers each a cup of water. "You have a message about Perl? How is she? Has something happened?"

"She is well. Very well, indeed. Malblud…or rather, I should now call him by his Light Realm name, Lophius…has been defeated. The Brotherhood feels it is now safe for mother and daughter to reunite."

"Praise Ever! After so many years." Betty sat on the arm of a cozy quilt-covered couch near a pipe stove. "Come, all of you, sit."

"We wanted to wait a full year before coming here to share the news, just to make sure all was truly settled and to give Perl a break between her training." Victr sat down, feeling a bit more relaxed.

"Well then, this is a time to celebrate!" Sister Martha raised her glass and clinked it on Jonathan's cup.

"Indeed it is, for many reasons…including this." Victr held out the scroll. "I present to you the Codex of the Sacred Invisible."

"Goodness. I have only heard stories of its existence," Sister Martha said, balancing a pair of bifocals on the tip of her nose.

"The great Light Protector Uriel instructed that each house is to keep the book for a month, then pass it on to the next." Victr handed her the scroll.

"We shall see it done, Brothers." Sister Martha sniffed, wrinkling her nose and pulling her wrap to her mouth. "But first, you all smell as if…"

Sister Betty cut in, "you've been rolling in the pig's trough!" She giggled, almost falling off the armrest.

"Very much so!" Sister Martha said, shuffling over to a cupboard covered with carvings of flowers and doves. She placed the scroll inside, locking it. "I must insist you all bathe before meeting with Our Lady."

"I couldn't agree more." Sebastian downed the rest of his water.

"Most definitely," added Jonathan, "a bath would be just the thing."

"You may change into these." Martha handed them three light blue hooded robes from a trunk on the floor. "Afterwards, we will eat, toast, and plan for this glorious reunion."

In a warm pool at the bottom of a gothic grotto, the three monks joyfully soaked. Around them, centuries-old baroque frescoes adorned the ceiling and surrounding stone walls. Incense cones fragranced the air with the scent of myrrh.

Steam rose, clouding Brother Jonathon's spectacles. "Something smells delicious." He squeezed a sponge full of water onto his neck, the water running down his thin, scrawny frame. "We must be near the kitchen."

Candlelight flickered off of Sebastian's wavy black hair, which was in much need of a cut. "Mmm, warm bread. Finally, something to smell other than your foul pits!" He laughed. "Isn't that right, Victr? …Victr?"

Brother Victr was miles away, his eyes fixed on some distant point. Deep creases on his forehead formed like waves in the desert sand.

"Eighty days of food. Web blanket. Offering. Guards. Tunnels." Victr unconsciously fumbled with a sponge as he checked off a list in his head. "It's too much. It's not safe."

"Victr!" Sebastian raised his voice, rousing his elder. "Where did you go, Brother?"

Victr blinked his eyes but sat frozen like a deer in the headlights.

"Victr, what is it?" Jonathan asked, seeing the look on the man's face.

"How…how is Perl ever going to navigate this place on her own?" Victr said half aloud, half to himself.

"Ever will guide her, my brother. You must trust. This is the right time," Jonathan said, wiping his glasses to get a better look at his friend.

"I want to believe that. I do," Victr sighed.

"I will stay," Sebastian offered.

"What?" Jonathan cleared his spectacles again. "Stay here? With the Sisters? No. No. No."

"I will see Perl through," Sebastian confirmed.

"You are kind and brave, my young brother. But you've only been here once. I don't think it's—"

Sebastian cut Victr off. "I can do it. Perhaps with the help of whatever you have left in those mysterious robe pockets of yours," he added, trying to lighten the mood. "And with Ever's help, I will do it."

Brother Jonathan gave a heavy sigh, offering a slight smile. "You could be of great comfort. Not just to Perl, but to all here." Jonathan turned to Victr. "What do you say we give young Seabass this opportunity?"

A strong gust of wind blew in from the tunnel, vanquishing the votive candles behind Victr's head.

"There's our sign! The Sacred Invisible has spoken!" Sebastian chuckled.

"It would seem I'm outnumbered." Victr grabbed his fresh cotton robe from the rocky ledge. "Let's go see what plans our Forest Sisters of Elsewhere have to offer.

3 LICHEN

Dimitri's face was inches from the trunk of a maple tree. "Hiding, hiding, always hiding," he mumbled. The apothecary clipped a pair of pince-nez spectacles to the brim of his nose, leaning in for an even closer inspection.

Perl hunkered close by with a wooden tray of tools as Dimitri loomed just inches above the blades of grass.

"Tell me again what we're looking for today, Dimi-bee?"

Like her beloved spider-monks, Perl chose to see Dimitri not in his human form, but in his true essence; a man-sized, fuzzy honey bee *(Apis mellifera)*. No longer fearing him, Perl had given the scientist a new nickname. "Slaughterman" just wouldn't do.

Selecting a small knife and tweezers from the tray, the bee-man cracked a crooked smile, showing his missing front tooth, "Lichen."

"Lichen?" Perl set the tray on the ground. "The fungus and algae moss."

"The very same." Dimitri scraped the knife along a crack in the tree's bark. "Mostly the fungus we seek."

A year had passed since Perl returned home from Seeker training in Venusto, and after discovering Dimitri's true nature, they had become fast friends. Perl accompanied him on his daily excursions to collect samples and conduct experiments in his lab, always enjoying spending time with the curious character.

"Ah-ha! There you are, you lovely organism!" Perl smiled as she saw Dimitri's iridescent wings buzz with excitement.

Perl stood, pulling out her trusty narwhal sword, Fortis. "There's more over there." She walked over to a nearby tree, carefully scraping bits of lichen from off its thick, rugged bark. The green moss clung to the tip of her blade, which had turned a charred black color since her battle with Malblud in the Dark Realm.

"Yes, yes, here, there." The honey bee opened a glass jar and held it up.

Perl gently tapped Fortis on the jar, dropping in the sample.

"Marvelous." Dimitri screwed the jar shut, spun Perl around, and tucked it into her backpack.

"So why mostly the fungus?" Perl asked.

"Holds the key," Dimitri replied, staring at her through his lenses, his bee eyes even more magnified. "To unlock the world."

Dimitri had a stilted way of speaking, having lived alone for so long in his cave on Trash Island. Most thought it was odd, but Perl found it to be quite endearing.

"Okay, I'll bite. To unlock the world how?" She slid her sword into its sheath.

"Come, come to the lab," he said, swiftly collecting his supplies. "You will see."

Perl and Dimitri walked along the pathway toward Mont Michel's docks.

They made an odd pair; the young girl and the old man in his spectacles.

"So secretive." She said, smiling a big toothy grin. "What will I see?"

"Life is ordered, extraordinarily. Indeed." He nodded, as if agreeing with himself.

Perl stepped from a stone to a log to another stone, dancing along with the landscape. "So, you're saying there's order in chaos, then?" She loved to challenge the scientist.

"Most definitely," he retorted. "The structure of a cell mirrors the solar system."

"So? Maybe that's just a coincidence? Agh—!" Perl stumbled on a hidden root, her wild, unruly hair flying about.

Dimitri caught her. "Not by chance. Not coincidence. Order."

The Evensong bell sounded and the Brotherhood of the Quill's chanting could be heard echoing across the island of Mont Michel. Perl watched the honey bee flutter ahead, untying a small rowboat anchored to one of the wooden pilings.

"I suppose you're right." Perl hopped into the boat. "As usual," she said, rolling her eyes.

Dimitri paddled the boat across the channel to Trash Island, as Perl looked back on Mont Michel.

"So much has changed in a year. The beach is cleaner, rooftops have gardens, and the Ocean Conservation Coalition of Earthers and the Sisters of the Seahorse Initiative are actually working together."

Perl felt a twinge of pride as she watched a group of activists putting on snorkels near the shore. They were working on a project to revitalize the reef by attaching 3D printed coral models to the bleached coral. Perl recognized Princess Mik Graves and Gretar, the protester who had been so kind to her the night of the twin's ball. As the boat bounced over waves, Perl decided to shift her vision to see their essences. The Princess transformed into a red panda *(Ailurus fulgent)*, while Gretar morphed into a cute fuzzy quokka *(Setonix brachyurus)*.

"Makes perfect sense," Perl thought, leaning back on her elbows, letting Dimitri to do all the work.

Before long the boat came to a bumpy stop onto the shoreline of garbage. "I will never get use to this horrible stench." Perl pinched her nose.

While the efforts to clean up the main island were going well, the piles on Trash Island grew daily. Everywhere, heaping sentinels of rotten garbage teetered hundreds of feet high, surrounded by dark clouds of buzzing flies.

"Tie us off," Dimitri directed. He went over to a rusty manhole, kicking a rotten pineapple away from the lid. "Best we burrow, little Rabbit," he said, lifting the heavy lid and climbing down the metal ladder.

Dimitri had created a pet name for Perl as well. The girl was never without the hand-carved rabbit sculpture her best friend Javan had made for her. Perl had tied the pendant to a vine and wore it as a necklace.

As she leaned over the manhole, a lavender breeze wafted up. Perl inhaled deeply. "Ah, that's better."

"Hurry and close the lid!" Dimitri yelled.

The corridor was damp and dark. Dimitri flipped a switch on the wall, illuminating a strand of flickering lights.

"So, you still haven't told me," Perl raised an eyebrow at him. "How will this fungus magically unlock the world?"

"Hop this way, Rabbit." Dimitri cackled, turning down a side tunnel. At the end was a yellow, hexagonal door.

"What's this?" Perl ran to keep up with the quick-moving bee. "I thought I'd seen every room in your labyrinth?"

"Eyes don't always see a secret, you see?" he said, theatrically swinging the door open.

The room inside was a huge dome with faceted walls. A large circular glass table sat in the center, cluttered with bubbling beakers, microscopes, and clay pots growing all sorts of curious-looking plants. A portable ladder affixed to a track ran around the entire room.

"Whoa!" Perl's mouth dropped open. "Did you build this yourself?"

"Affirmative." Dimitri went straight to the ladder, sliding it around and stopping underneath a large cubby hole high up on the wall. He shimmied up the ladder and disappeared into the hole.

"I love it, Dimi-bee! It looks just like a honeycomb in here!" she shouted.

Dimitri emerged feet first out of the hole, carrying an armful of burlap bags, some slipping from his grasp as he clumsily made his way back down the ladder.

"Here, let me help you." Perl ran to him, grabbing a few of the drawstring pouches.

"On the table, over there," Dimitri gestured to the table. Like shuffling a deck of cards, Dimitri quickly organized the bags. "So many unlock, so many, so difficult to find just the right pattern. Lichen please, Rabbit."

Rifling through her backpack, Perl retrieved the jar and unscrewed the lid. As she did this, she heard a squeak. Two white mice *(Mus musculus domesticus)* scurried up the table leg, over the plants and jumped onto Dimitri's shoulders.

"Hello, Tick. Hello, Tock," Perl addressed the rodents. Each mouse nodded back, wearing a thimble hat with their names engraved on them.

The honey bee man loosened the strings on several of the pouches. Perl could see they were filled with different varieties of mushrooms. A woodsy scent filled the room.

"So, the key lies in the fungus," she said matter-of-factly.

"Precisely!" he said, grabbing the clump of moss. "Closer by the day now to finding what has always been." Dunking the spongy lichen into some spring water, Dimitri then squeezed it so that a few drops landed on a glass slide. "Clouds cloak the moon," Dimitri continued, as he looked down through the eyepiece. "Does not mean moon is gone." He placed the slide under the microscope to view.

"What has always been is hidden in the patterns of nature," Perl said as she hopped up onto an oak stool, pressing in beside the scientist, anxious to see. "It's in the chemical makeup of all living things."

"Fourteen-year-old eyes, yet very wise." Dimitri said, adjusting the microscope's focus. "Ever has placed it, science must uncover it. Look there." He pointed down at several latched doors on the dirt floor. "Middle one, go open."

Jumping down, Perl lifted the door and was instantly struck in the face with noxious gas. "Gross! It's just a bunch of disgusting muck."

Tick and Tock squealed from the stench, hiding their whiskers in Dimitri's fur.

"Look closer," he said, without raising his head from the lens.

Getting down on her knees, Perl examined the compost. "Mycelium?"

"Ah, yes! But not just! Plastic eaters." Dimitri looked up. "These fungi break down the plastic, making more fungi. From that, biomaterials…feed animals…generate antibiotics."

Perl looked at the bee, his antennae wiggled this way and that. "This is amazing, Dimi-bee. You could clear the landfills. Cure diseases. End world hunger." Perl's mind reeled at the possibilities.

"If! Could! Bah!" interrupted the scientist.

"What do you mean? You said it yourself." Perl pointed down at her muddy boots. "The keys to saving our planet are growing right beneath our very feet! So, no if's, and's, or but's!"

"If they listen. If they see. If they act." Dimitri returned to his microscope.

"Then we will make them," Perl slammed the compost door shut.

Dimitri was brilliant at whatever he turned his mind to, but he knew the truth. The world was ruled by an elite, secret society known as Under One's Heel, and that society only cared about their own. They controlled the drinking water, the food supplies, and the tech industries. Dimitri knew this because he was once one of them; a top scientist living in the upper tiers of Mont Michel, until the day he was cast aside a decade ago for secretly developing a vaccine for the underprivileged.

"A fire it will take, Rabbit. Keep the one in your belly stoked." He snorted out a laugh. "Come, come and see. We have a stowaway." He moved aside so Perl could look through the microscope.

On the glass slide sat a droplet of water. Perl peered through the lens. "It looks like a tiny Bear," she giggled, watching the microscopic creature's eight legs kicking.

"A water bear, yes, yes. Tardigrade. Hibernating in our lichen, ha!"

Perl was transfixed. "I didn't know they could live on trees." She felt a slight ache in her chest thinking of her friend and roommate from the Light Realm. She missed Bear's jokes, his sparring lessons, even the sloppy, disgusting way he devoured his meals. She longed to see all her friends from Venusto again, wondering what they'd all been doing since their adventures together.

Dimitri's voice brought her back to the present. "…Cryptobiosis! In this state a tardigrade can dry itself out like a raisin. In this mode they can survive, no oxygen. No food. Spring water reanimates them. Quite remarkable."

"And they are quite lovable and silly, too," Perl added, picturing roly-poly Bear juggling his favorite tarts.

"So say you, Rabbit." The scientist didn't always understand the girl when she spoke of things from the Light Realm. However, spending time with Perl had given Dimitri a new look on life, placing a feeling of hope in his heart that he'd never felt before. "I will return Mr. Bear back to his tree tomorrow."

Perl's face lit up. "I think I know how we can make the world see your discoveries. We should tell Princess Mik and Gretar. They have connections. They can help spread the word."

"Mm…" The bee shook his head. "Much trusting to do. Much testing to do."

"But we can't wait, we need to act," Perl said. "Let's show them. Time is running out."

"Great changes in the Princess since the loss of her twin, yes, yes." Dimitri wrung his thin hands together. "The boy Gretar. A leader. Mm. May listen to us."

Perl slid off the chair, hugging the round honey bee tightly. "Dimi-bee, you are brilliant!"

Dimitri's mice companions, Tick and Tock, held onto locks of his hair, clinging for dear life.

"Okay, yes!" Dimitri stood stiffly, not accustomed to human contact. "Princess and the boy will come. Witness the fundamental powers of fungi!" Dimitri let out a snorting chuckle. He pulled Perl's hood up, spinning her toward the hexagon door. "But home, home for you. Papa Ximu will give me grief for keeping you past supper."

"Oh, but we have so much to do," Perl reluctantly scooped up her backpack, pretending as if it weighed a ton.

"Next time, stories! I'll tell you about how Mont Michel was once called the City of Books…Enormous collection of sacred manuscripts." Dimitri teased, knowing the girl's desire for knowledge.

"You forget I live with monks, right?" Perl rolled her eyes. "There isn't a book I haven't read in our old, dusty library."

"Not all, smart Rabbit, not all." He winked back.

Dimitri dropped Perl ashore on the main island just as the Evensong bell sounded for the final time that day. She gave a wave while removing her vine lace boots, "See you tomorrow!"

The rowboat zipped back across the choppy waters toward the heaps of trash, now tall, lumpy silhouettes against the pink sky. Perl walked slowly in the direction of the root cellar, purposely sinking each brown, chubby toe into the cool evening sand. The bioluminescent spots on her knees began to glow as she pondered, *such potential in something so ordinary as a mushroom.*

4 KNEADING

"Ut-ut, come here, and wash those filthy paws!" Papa Ximu called to Perl as she tried to sneak past the kitchen doorway to get to her room. "I need help with these pot pies. I haven't a clue as to what I'm doing." Filling in for Brother Victr while he was on pilgrimage was turning out to be quite the challenge for the elder monk.

Perl had forgotten to bring her sketchbook to Dimitri's and was anxious to capture the day's lichen experiment in it, not help with cooking supper. Letting out a long, exaggerated sigh so that Ximu could hear, Perl sluggishly walked into the room, hanging her backpack on a hook next to the utility sink. After plugging the sink and sprinkling in some flakes of soap, she began pumping the handle of the old metal spout while inspecting the lichen caked under her nails. *"I wonder if there's a water bear in there?"* she thought, as salt water gurgled up then spat like a camel from the nozzle.

"Tell me of your day, Bumble." Perl glanced over at her Papa, his eight dark spider eyes blinking warmly. "What miraculous things have you been up to?"

"Saving the world is all," she boasted, cupping her palms and blowing sudsy bubbles into the air.

"Praise be!" Ximu opened a bag of flour, spilling most of it onto the wooden floor. "Oh dear! What a mess!"

Perl couldn't help but laugh, shaking her head of black curls. She dried her hands on her robe. "Looks like you're the one who needs saving."

"Yes, please."

She watched as the old spider tied his long white beard behind his head and floured the rolling pin.

"How does Victr keep the dough from sticking?" Papa Ximu muttered. "It sticks to the counter, to the pin, to the pan…"

"To you," Perl added, picking a clump out of his hair.

"To everything," Ximu said, slamming a ball of dough onto the cutting board.

"Here, I'll make the crust." She gave him a bump with her hip. "You do the filling."

"Good plan." Ximu scooted over to the stovetop and stirred a pot of simmering vegetables. "Now, what's this earth saving plan you've cooked up, chef?"

Perl picked up a handful of shiitake mushrooms. "The secret recipe is within these little fellows," she said, sprinkling them into the stew pot.

"Well, I eat those for my health. I didn't realize they were harboring such secrets." Ximu twiddled a claw playfully in front of Perl's face.

"Oh, but they are." She wiggled the rolling pin at him. "Some can eat polyester polyurethane. According to Dimi-bee, there are six million species of fungi. Imagine the mushroom goodness that is yet to be discovered!"

"Miraculous." Ximu studied a mushroom in his ladle.

Some minutes passed in silence as the two quietly went about their work. Eventually, the contents of the stew had thickened, filling the room with an earthy aroma. Perl carefully dumped the piping hot contents into the pie mold, briefly letting it cool. She gently layered the pie crust over the steaming filling, pinching the doughy edges around the pan.

"Did you know that fungi also contain a substance called chitin in their cell walls, which also is in the external skeletons of spiders and other arthropods."

"Hmm, no I didn't." Ximu held up a mushroom to his face. "So nice to meet you, brother shiitake."

"I wish I had a microscope of my own." Perl batted her long lashes at her Papa. "It's just so amazing looking into a magical world that exists that's invisible to the naked eye."

"For someone who has been to the Light Realm," the spider squinted over his wire-rim spectacles, "you shouldn't need a microscope to show you that other worlds exist."

"Oh, you know what I mean." Perl opened the oven door and placed the potpie on the center rack. "With a microscope, I could do my own experiments." She kicked the door shut with her foot. "Maybe Dimitri would let me borrow one?"

"You have learned much from your fellow bee." Ximu began chopping an onion. "I am happy that the two of you have had this time together. It has been good for you both."

"Why are you making it sound like it's ending?" She rolled out another ball of dough.

"Because it is."

"But why? Haven't I gotten all my chores done on time, and made all my deliveries with Regor? You said yourself that I'm learning things with Dimitri I'd never get from our ancient library."

"Easy, Bumble. You will be happy—"

Perl cut him off. "Happy? How would quitting science make me happy?" She began vigorously rolling the dough out.

Sensing the girl's growing frustration, Ximu placed his hand on hers. Perl saw her spider monk's fuzzy claw resting on her hand and stopped rolling, the dough now paper thin.

"If you will let me finish, Bumble, I was going to say that the time has come for the one thing you have been asking me for, for over a year now." He placed the onions into the steaming pot.

"Don't tease me, Papa." Perl turned facing Ximu. "Really?" Her bright green eyes were brimming with excitement.

"Yes. Truthfully."

"My mother?" Perl began to bounce on her toes.

Ximu stroked his beard and smiled. "Your mother."

She grabbed two of his spider claws. "I'm going to see my mother!"

"You're going to see your mother!" The pair spun in a circle singing. "I'm going to see my mother!" The flour on the floor wafted up around their feet.

Perl was beaming. One hundred-and-four-year-old Ximu paused to catch his breath. He had regained all the weight he had lost since being imprisoned by the Count and was back to what Perl called his 'jolly weight.' He wiped a tear away.

"Are you crying?" She smiled.

"It's the onions."

"The onions, huh?"

"Okay, they're happy tears," he admitted. "For you, and for Dianna."

"I can't believe it." Perl paused, "but why now?"

"A letter has come from Brother Victr. He has made it to The Under Kingdom."

"The Under Kingdom? I thought he was on The Pilgrimage of the Truth?"

"Yes, and that is where the journey ends," Ximu informed.

"But what does that have to do with seeing my mother?"

"She is there. That is where she has been in all these years, hiding from Lophius. And now that he is no longer a threat and we know you are both secure, well, you know our Victr. He wanted to see the conditions for himself, to make certain all would be safe for you to go. The Under Kingdom isn't the sanctuary it once was."

Perl wrinkled her nose. "Do you smell something burning?" She asked.

"Oh no! Our beautiful pie!" Ximu scurried over, quickly putting on oven mitts. He flung open the oven door; a thick cloud of smoke enveloped him. "Oh, dear me!" The spider waved at the fumes. "I shall take this as a sign. I need Victr back, toot sweet."

"So, what did Victr's letter say?" Perl fanned the smoke with a hand-carved cutting board shaped like a whale.

"It's on your bedside table." Ximu coughed. "Go. Go. I'll clean…" Perl was already bolting down the hallway. "…up." He grinned to himself.

Perl flung open the heart-shaped door to her room, dashing straight to the letter. Sitting on the edge of her quilted bed she read:

Dearest Brave Warrior,

I hope this letter finds you well and keeping a watchful eye over my kitchen. We have made it safely through the Desertlands to The Under Kingdom. It is called that for many reasons. The obvious one being it is underground, and the city is under the royal rule of Prince Tobias and Prince Névenoé. It is a place of many marvels, along with many dangers, and for that reason I have been very worried about you coming here. (Imagine your dear old Victr-worried!) However, after much discussion, the Forest Sisters of Elsewhere have assured me that you will have safe passage to your mother.

Dianna is simply over the moon to finally get to hold you. I see so much of her in you. You carry her imagination, fierceness and most of all her compassion. Promise me you will stay close to her and to Brother Sebastian, who is staying behind to guide you. He will be boarding with a trusted friend at the Slugabed Hovel, which is three stone throws down from the kingdom's portcullis.

Our other traveling companion, Brother Jonathan, has regained his strength, so by the time you receive this we shall be traipsing back to Mont Michel. I will see you back home after your reunion and before you leave for Seer training in Venusto.

Much love,

Victr the Victorious

P.S. Promise me you will not wander off to explore the kingdom alone…and you can have the jar of orange marmalade I hid under your bed. It will be our little secret.

"Mmm, marmalade!" Perl jumped off the bed. Reaching her arm under the bed as far as she could, her hand surfed back and forth through the piles of origami animals and drawings, like a shark in search of prey. "Where are you?" Her fingernail clicked on glass. "Ah-ha!" Perl pulled the jar out from amongst all the clutter. A note was tied to the lid. She read it aloud in her best Victr impersonation. *"Archeologist, you have uncovered the golden treasure from the forbidden pantry! Just don't eat the whole thing in one sitting! Hugs, V"*

Unscrewing the lid, Perl dipped her pinky in for a taste. Marmalade was a delicacy enjoyed solely by Palace royals, or for very special occasions. She closed her eyes, letting the sweet, citrusy jelly linger on her tongue.

Ximu appeared in her open doorway, his brown robe covered in flour. He cleared his throat to get Perl's attention, "What do you have there?"

"Nothing, nothing." She quickly buried her treasure in a pile of folded cranes. "Did you read this?"

"I skimmed it. There was a letter for me as well in the parcel." Ximu untied his beard from behind his head and stroked it as if he were grooming a cat.

"When can I leave?"

"Soon." Ximu said with a smirk.

"I'll be taking the pilgrimage through the Desertlands alone?"

"Not exactly." He twisted the edge of his curlicue mustache.

The hallway began to glow a bright lavender. The light silhouetted the spider monk as he stepped to the corner of the room. Through the doorway, an Amazonian woman entered, so tall she had to duck down so as to not hit her head. Her crystal blue cropped hair brushed along the ceiling beams. An exotic fragrance now filled the room like a floral garden, but with a sharp metallic tinge.

"Like a moth to my flame." Her ethereal voice filled the small root cellar bedroom.

"Uriel!" Perl jumped to her feet, straight into the arms of her guardian.

Uriel's floor length cape, decorated in tiny purple and yellow flowers, swept the ground as she lifted the girl up, the vines curling and winding around them as she moved. Perl hugged Uriel tightly around the neck, her feet dangling down. The spots on Perl's face lit up as she pressed her cheek against Uriel's smooth ebony skin.

"I have received all of your Hypercompe Scribonia messages," Perl said,

25

releasing her grip. "But it's so good to finally see you."

The Divine Protector gently returned the girl to her feet, pushing a curl out of Perl's eye. "I have missed you as well, young one." The leopard moth that hovered over Uriel's left eye fluttered. "I have been keeping close watch over you."

"You're coming with me to the Under Kingdom?" Perl stared up into Uriel's dark violet eye.

"After your good work here is complete." Uriel's chainmail clinked with every step she took. "Then I shall see that you arrive safely. And I'm afraid this visit is a brief one, and I must leave."

Perl looked at Ximu, who was trying to work his way around the towering Light Being. "Papa, you said the time had come."

He peeked around Uriel's tall frame. "I said, soon."

"But I have been waiting my whole life to meet my mother." Perl was getting anxious.

Uriel placed a hand on her shoulder. "Patience, Perl. Share your knowledge of the Pestalotiopis microspora, then I will deliver you to your mother."

"I do need to tell Gretar and the Princess about the fungi." Perl looked up at her guardian. "But shouldn't we just get the ol' spider balloon started ahead of time so we're ready?"

Uriel wiped a dab of orange marmalade from the corner of Perl's mouth. "No ballooning this trip."

"How long will I get to visit with her?" Perl's tongue searched her lips for any more of the sweetness.

"You will stay with your mother for a fortnight," Uriel answered.

"Only fourteen days!" Perl started to raise her voice, then thought better of it. "That doesn't seem fair."

"I am never unjust." Uriel sat on the corner of the small bed, lifting the entire mattress off of its frame. "A day for each year of your life."

"Well then, fourteen years would be fair, not days, right?" Perl asserted.

The hairs on Ximu's spider head stood on end. "Perhaps I'll go put on some tea," he said. "The two of you can catch up." He backed out, shutting the door quietly.

"Perl, Seer training begins in one Earth month. We must not be late to Greenheart. Besides, all of your friends have been missing you. In fact, all of Venusto awaits your return." Uriel knew Perl's heart inside and out, especially what motivated it.

"I do miss everyone." Perl took a small leap, landing the bed. "But I've waited so long…"

Uriel placed her hand on Perl's. "It is what Ever wants."

Perl smiled, too happy to argue. She snuggled up to Uriel, resting her head on the great Light Protector's shoulder, feeling the coolness of her gilded armor. "Do you think she'll like me?"

"Dear child, she adored you before you took your first breath." Uriel cupped

Perl's chin, looking into her green eyes. "Before the stars shined, her love for you formed in her essence."

"Sure, but will she *like* me?" Perl giggled, wrapping Uriel's floral cape around her head while making the goofiest face she could muster.

"Crossed eyes, spots and all, I promise." Uriel ran a finger up Perl's arm igniting the glowing dots under the girl's almond skin. "Speaking of spots, have you spotted any new abilities as of late?"

"Just the usual, seeing the essences of people, hearing the animals' songs, and working to control my bioluminescence." Perl let the cape drop to her lap.

"No more bad visions, then?" Uriel asked, placing her hand on top of Perl's head.

"No." Perl shook.

"Good. Very good."

"Oh wait, I do have something, um…sprouting."

Uriel put her hand on Perl's shoulder. "Let me see."

"I didn't tell Papa. We've had the whole, changing body, puberty talk a while ago, but these are different." Perl opened her robe slightly, exposing her legs. On each of her knees sat a tiny rose-like thorn. "Do you think it's hormones?"

"You are becoming." The Divine Light Protector touched the tip of one, smiling.

"I have them on my elbows, too." Perl pushed up her sleeves, showing Uriel.

"Not to worry. You have much from your mother, however, these are a trait from your father Noaa."

"So, I'm becoming a vampire then?" Perl stuck out her front row of teeth like fangs.

"You are half Vampyroteuthis infernalis." Uriel nodded.

"I researched vampire squids after I found out who he was, but I'm not sure what these are for, really. Will I be able to shoot spikes like Javan?" Perl raised her eyebrow.

"They are for defense," Uriel insisted.

"Bioluminescence is for defense, too." Perl crossed her arms. "Why is that all I ever get?"

"In time it will be more. You still need growth."

"Time? According to the pelicans' singing at the dock, there is no such thing as time. It's just a human construct," smirked Perl.

Uriel bent down and fished out the jar of marmalade from under the bed. "Then let us be in this moment."

Perl swiped her finger across the top of the jar and licked the jelly. "Yes, let's."

"The citrus can be a secret, but the cirri, your spiky spines, you should share that with Ximu," Uriel said. The tea kettle screamed for attention from the kitchen. "Ah, time may be indeed a human construct, but we must always make time for tea."

The Light Protector stood and with a wave of her hand, Uriel opened the heart-shaped door.

"At least teach me telekinesis," Perl insisted.

"One day you will do much more." Uriel gave her a knowing grin.

The pair headed down the cramped tunnel. The walls were still lined with Perl's sketches that Victr had hung when she first left for Seeker training. Hunched over as she walked, Uriel was careful not to brush against the drawings, though she did leave sparkling lavender particles in her wake. Perl grabbed hold of her guardian's celestial gown, stopping her.

"You know, you've been my mother." Perl gazed up lovingly into Uriel's eye, as the moth softly fluttered over the other. "She won't take your place."

"It is an honor that you hold me in such regard. But Dianna holds a place like none other in the universe. You must give her space to fill each of your three beautiful squid hearts."

"I will." A waft of black smoke spilled into the hallway. "The pot pies!" Perl ran ahead to assist Ximu.

"You will indeed, young one…" Uriel watched the back of Perl's robe whip around the doorway like the tail of a cat.

5 FLORIOGRAPHY

As Princess Mik stood at the cliffside cemetery, a warm, blustery breeze tossed her bright red locks about, despite Mik wearing her sister's blue diamond butterfly hairpin. Beside Mik at the Graves family plot stood her trusted governess Ruby. Still in mourning, both women wore head-to-toe black.

"I miss her every single second of every day. Part of me died with her, and I'll never be whole again." Mik placed her gloved hand on Ivry's golden fawn *(Cervidae)* headstone. "I can't believe it's been a year."

"I know," Ruby said, tying a lace scarf under her chin to keep the wind from whipping at her platinum bun. "I can still hear her telling me to feed the seahorses."

Mik smiled. "Ruby, do you believe in Ever? In the Light Realm?"

"I do." Her nanny placed her arm around Mik's shoulders. "I think there's a place where our essence goes after we pass. Ivry was so pure, so sweet. I'm sure she's in the Light."

"She always was the better of the two of us. I just wish I could talk to her again, to ask her to forgive me for waiting so long to find the antidote." Mik tapped the tattooed rosebud on her wrist. A camera mechanism imbedded just underneath her skin emitted a faint *click*, snapping a picture of the grave site adorned with hundreds of red flowers, teddy bears, and other gifts.

"You have to stop blaming yourself. It never was, nor will it ever be, your fault. Ivry is at peace now. And I know she's very proud of all you're doing in her name."

"I hope you're right. And I'll keep fighting. Every day." Tapping again on the device, Mik recorded a message with the photo:

"Sisters of the Seahorse Initiative and fellow Earthers, today marks the anniversary of Ivry's untimely death. To honor her memory, please give to the reef-rebuilding project, and continue to fight for the truth so we can protect what's left of our beautiful planet."

Mik hit send. In an instant, thoughts and prayers came pouring in on

Narcissi, the world's leading social network.

"You've been putting too much pressure on yourself. It's not up to you to save the whole world all on your own." Ruby tucked a curl of Mik's hair behind her ear. "You need a partner in this life, hmm? It's time we turned our thoughts to happier things, like your proposal from Prince Névenoé. The prince would like to hear the *yes* come from you, not your father."

"I'm having second thoughts about Névenoé." Mik knelt down and hugged a red teddy bear with the words, '*We Luv Ivry*,' stitched on its belly. "Especially now that I know about his dealings with daddy and all of those Under One's Heel criminals."

"Oh, he can't be as bad as all that." Ruby crossed her arms. "You two will make such a lovely couple." The governess smiled. "And…he is to die for!"

"That's what I'm afraid of," Mik whispered to herself.

"What dear?" Ruby leaned down. "I can't hear a thing over this crazy wind today."

"Nothing." Mik tossed the bear back onto the pile. "It's not like I have a say in any of this, anyway. It's only my life."

"I don't know what's gotten into you, Mik. You were so taken with the prince. But you're right, this wedding *is* happening. I've scheduled Gaspard to come for some new dress fittings this afternoon." Ruby tugged at Mik's black ruff collar. "It's time to put some color back into our lives."

Among the sea of red roses, red poppies, and red tulips, sat a single bright yellow mimosa flower in a plain clay pot. Mik smiled, picking it up. "Perhaps you're right. This will look nice on Ivry's bedside table."

"That's the spirit." Ruby nodded.

The two women started back up the steps towards the Palace when a guard rushed over.

"Sorry Princess, no foreign objects are permitted without inspection." He held out his meaty hand.

"So, inspect it." Mik handed over the pot.

The guard ran a crystal scanner around the plant until the gem on it flashed green. "All clear. You can take it in now."

"Oh, can I?!" Mik grabbed the pot from the guard and marched up the platinum stairway. After Ivry's death, her father Count Zell Graves had tripled Mik's bodyguards, making it impossible to go anywhere alone, which annoyed her to no end.

At the Palace entrance, a trio of guards jumped into action. One held a badge up to a screen, a second scanned his own tongue, and a third placed his pinkie into a keyhole. Once all three had performed their ridiculous clearance protocol a buzzer went off and the thirty-foot-tall doors slowly began to open.

The pair walked through the grand marble foyer arm in arm to the elevators. "I'll bring your kombucha tea up shortly," Ruby said, pushing the diamond button for the penthouse. The door chimed open, and Mik stepped inside, flanked by her royal watchmen. "Chin up, Dear. Your sister would want you to be happy, to move on."

"I'm working on it," Mik said, cradling her mimosa flower as the doors closed.

The only place that the princess could have a moment of peace was in her room. It was her sanctuary from everyone and everything. She quickly closed and bolted the door behind the guards, who were left standing at attention in the hallway on the plush white carpet.

Amongst all the state-of-the-art amenities, Mik's gymnasium-sized room included its very own waterfall that emptied into a mammoth aquarium.

"Hello, Star! Hello, Moon! How are the kiddos today?" Mik ran her long black fingernails across the glass, as the seahorses *(Hippocampus)* chased after her clinking claws. The aquatic pair's babies had grown up, filling the tank with every color of the rainbow.

Mik placed the clay pot on Ivry's nightstand and plunked down on her canopy bed across from her sister's. She stared at the yellow mimosa flower, smiling at the secret it held. Because of her tightened security, and to evade any possible spies her father may have hired, the Earth activists working with Mik had been using the ancient cryptic language of floriography, a way of communicating through flowers. Unbeknownst to the guards or even The Count, every flower holds a unique message associated with that flower's name, color, or behavior. In the case of the yellow mimosa, the sensitive plant represents chastity, its leaves closing at night or when they're touched. Mik knew the mimosa was a secret message from Gretar.

"And I love you," Mik whispered to the yellow bloom.

Gretar and Mik's unspoken courtship first began a year ago, when he pulled her into his rowboat from the polluted waters of Mont Michel, saving her from drowning. After forming their climate alliance, merging The Ocean Conservation Coalition of Earthers and The Sisters of the Seahorse Initiative, the two had not thought of another. Their relationship was Shakespearean; he was born from a long line of poor dockworkers, and she was the only living daughter of the wealthiest water baron in the world. Even when they were together they were never alone, surrounded by both fellow activists and the watchful eye of the royal guards.

"Tonight is the night, Moon." Mik dropped a clump of frozen brine shrimp into the tank. "The night I've been dreaming of." The seahorses swarmed their lunch.

She walked over to her armoire in the shape of a giant clamshell, opening its opalescent doors. "There you are." She pulled out a black wetsuit and laid it across her silk poppy comforter. Mik and Gretar had planned a secret rendezvous.

Mik waited for the night's last change of the guards. *"I have to time this perfectly."* She thought to herself, checking the clock on her wrist sensor. She cracked her door open just wide enough to peek out.

The hallway was empty. Running on tiptoes to the elevator door, Mik tapped at the button frantically until the sound of a harp strummed and the elevator doors opened. She jumped in and pressed the button labeled "Grotto," then watched as the numbers slowly descended. "Come on, come on." With another strum, the doors opened to a large underground slip, where a host of various boats were docked. Mik made a mad dash for her father's two-seater submarine, built to look like a great white shark *(Carcharodon carcharias)*.

Hiding in the shadows near the underground dock, Gretar looked around nervously. The wooden planks creaked under his shifting weight. "Where is she, it's almost eight?" The twenty-year-old wore a retro 'Save the Whales' t-shirt with the sleeves torn off, showing off his muscular biceps. Gretar looked up at a giant holographic billboard that ran along the shoreline. Under the time display, advertisements for virtual reality vacations flashed, promising to immerse travelers in bygone destinations that occurred before the climate crisis—*'See the Original Rainforest!' 'Walk with the Polar Bears!'*

The great white submarine surfaced with its jaws open. Gretar jumped back, nearly falling down. "Holy crap!" The shark bobbed next to the dock. "What in the—?"

Mik opened the top fin hatch and popped up smiling. "You should see your face!" She laughed.

"Really, this is his sub?" He shook his head. "But, of course it is. I don't know why I'm even surprised."

"Surprised or scared?" Mik giggled again.

"Ha, ha, move over, shark chum!" Gretar said, stepping into the hatch. Once in, he got a better look at Mik in her skintight wetsuit. "Um, wow, you look…" His cheeks turned the same shade as Mik's hair. "…Amazing."

"Thanks." Mik closed and locked the hatch, squeezing into the seat beside Gretar.

"I see you got my message," Gretar said, looking at the bright yellow flower sprig pinned over Mik's heart. She smiled coyly. "Have you driven this thing before?" he asked, watching Mik as she maneuvered the throttle.

"I've watched a few practice videos," Mik said, rocketing them downward into the dark waters.

"Oh, that's comforting." Gretar buckled himself in as his ears plugged from the rapid descent.

"Relax, look how beautiful it is," she said, gazing out the front window of the sub's open jaws. Schools of fish scurried across the high beam lights that shot from shark's eyes.

"It is." Not looking out, instead Gretar's gaze was fixed on Mik. To him, there was nothing in the world more beautiful than her, including all the treasures from the ocean that he cared so deeply about.

Mik could feel his eyes on her. "It's not far now." She slowed the engines to a coast. "There, off to the right. The drill." Enormous pumps were hammering up and down on the ocean floor, mining the mineral rich soil. Mik positioned the sub so the flood lights lit up the pumps.

"We just need to locate the control panel." Gretar unbuckled himself and leaned forward, searching the mechanics of the machine. "There! That must be it." At the base of one of the pumps was a large metal box, the initials 'U.O.H.' etched on the front.

Mik stole a quick peek over at Gretar. Under the overhead dome light's soft glow, she studied his muscular physic, the curves of his back and shoulders. How she longed for his embrace.

"Now, how to dismantle it." Gretar leaned back, examining the sub's interior. "Does this thing have mechanical arms, or something we can use to break in?" Mik put the sub into reverse. "Wait, where are you going?" he said, surprised.

"I can do better than dismantling." Mik flipped open a panel, exposing a red button. "We don't want them fixing this anytime soon, right?"

"Ah, right." Gretar agreed.

"Well then, hold on. You think my father would build a sub and not include weapons?"

"Are you sure about this? Are we far enough back? Oh shhhiii—!" Gretar braced himself.

The missile struck, exploding the base of the drill. Bits of metal debris shot in all directions, along with a geyser of mud. A violent shockwave rippled out, shaking the sub as Mik held tightly to the throttle.

"Yesss!" Gretar pounded his fist on the armrest. "You're a mad woman," he laughed, looking over at Mik. She had never seemed sexier than at that moment.

"Take that, Daddy!" Mik made a sharp turn and shoved the throttle forward. "That one was for Ivry."

As the sub sped off, an underwater surveillance camera snapped a picture of the great white's mechanical tail fin vanishing into the abyss.

A safe distance away, Mik slowed the sub and flipped on the autopilot as they skimmed just above the ocean floor.

"The Count is going to kill us," Gretar breathed a long sigh of relief. "But it will be so worth it."

"He'll never know it was us. Plus, Father needs me alive. He's in the Under Kingdom right now working out the arrangements for my marriage and who knows what else."

Gretar's heart sank like a stone. "Marriage? But I thought that was off? You can't marry Névenoé."

"They want to form an alliance between the land and water barons. I'm afraid I don't really have a say." Mik stared out the window into the darkness. "I'm just a pawn in their game of global domination. But I was thinking, maybe we can use this to our advantage. We could take them down from the inside. You know, keep our enemies closer?"

"That's too close." Gretar brushed Mik's hair back from her neck. "How about this? We could run away. Head up to the mountains in the old Arctic region? Your dad would never find us." He leaned over and kissed the single freckle on her porcelain right cheek. The softness of his lips on her skin sent sweet chills up her spine.

Mik smiled at Gretar, then sighed heavily. "I wish. But we both know there isn't any place in the world where my father can't find me."

"Well, he doesn't know where we are right now, does he?" He ran his fingers up the back of her neck, weaving them through her scarlet hair.

Mik touched the scar on Gretar's cheek where a Palace guard's stray bullet had grazed him the night of her birthday ball.

"I'd die for you, Mik."

"I've been dying for your touch," she confessed.

"Marry me," he asked without hesitation.

Mik gazed into his seafoam green eyes. "If only I could."

"I love you." Gretar had nothing to lose and meant every word. "I've loved you before the world began."

Mik felt dizzy and weak and overcome with emotion. Her heartbeat quickened. *"This is what true love feels like,"* she thought as she closed her eyes, parting her ruby lips, kissing him for real for the first time. He pulled her closer and they kissed again. The windows fogged as they embraced. Time seemed to stand still as bioluminescent jellyfish circled the sub, illuminating the cramped hull with dancing fairy lights.

Mik pressed her forehead to his and whispered, "I love you, too," knowing it could never be, yet allowing herself to be lost in the moment.

6 MIRAGE

"One more night in the desert and we'll be back in our soft beds," Brother Johnathan said.

The heat of the evening desert warmed the layer of air above its surface, refracting the light waves from the sun, creating the illusion of shimmering blue water on the horizon.

"Perl will have read my letter by now," Victr said, clearing the sand out of his ear with a pinky.

"I believe so," Jonathan agreed. "She'll be over the moon."

"It's a shame we won't see her until she returns from the Under Kingdom. How I miss her hugs," Victr smiled through cracked lips.

"To see her face again will be a gift," Jonathan squinted, looking off into the distance. "Speaking of seeing, are you seeing what I'm seeing? A person or animal— I can't quite tell which from the glare, but it seems to have just emerged out of the mirage ahead."

"Yes. I saw something, too," Victr wiped his eyes, blurry from dust and sweat. "It did look as if it rose out from the ground, but the desert plays tricks with the mind. See how the mirage disappears as we approach?"

"It's coming this way," Jonathan uttered. At that moment, a hawk, who had been circling above the monks, let out a screech, cutting the quiet like a shard of glass.

The monks could hear the sound of jingling metal as the shadow approached. Once close enough, the monks saw that the figure had rows of tassels made of coins, sea glass, and bells that swayed from a long gray smock. A tall, hunched figure stopped in front of them; its thin, veiny arm clutching a femur bone as a walking stick. The monks said nothing, taking a moment to observe the stranger. Its face was hidden by a cloth, draped a few inches in front of its head like a tiny theater curtain; the fabric suspended by twisted roots that seemed to grow out of the thing's greasy hair. A crude face was painted in what looked like dried blood on the front of the cloth.

"Farewelllll…" it croaked, the word sticking in the gutter of its dusty throat.

"Pardon?" Jonathan replied.

"What day is this?" the creature said.

"Tuesday, if I'm not mistaken," Victr bellowed out.

"What yearrr?" It leaned forward on its boney cane.

"What…year?" Victr answered, wrinkling his brow.

"Is it not the year 525? Have I come up wrong againnn?" The words lingered hypnotically.

Jonathan looked at Victr and whispered, "I think he might have a bout of heat stroke, Brother."

"You may be right," Victr nodded, then raised his voice, "no, good sir, no, but come, do join us! We were about to make camp for the evening. We can catch you up on the news of *this* year! And have a bite to eat. Are you hungry?"

"*Starvinggg,*" it answered, letting out a long hissing breath. Even from twenty feet away, the monks' nostrils were filled with a musty attic smell.

The brothers gathered bits of dry brush, then lit a small fire. Victr boiled lentils in a tin pot, crumbling a handful of crushed herbs into the mix. He motioned over to the hunched figure, who stood silently watching them.

"Come. Come sit with us."

The man jingle-jangled over to the flames and knelt down, the bones of his body cracking like twigs. "*Tuum cheenda kahhh,*" it spoke, the hushed tones whispery and cryptic.

"I'm afraid we're not familiar with your dialect," Victr said, inspecting the rather large contraption strapped to the man's back. It looked like a miniature iron bridge of sorts. Across it dangled dozens of roughly-formed dolls wearing hooded robes. "Are you in a holy order of some kind?"

"*Holy, noo,*" its head shook, "*and my words… they are still acclimating to terra.*"

"Try eating something," Jonathan held out a cup of soup, but the man didn't take it. The monk shrugged, setting the food on the ground in front of him. With its unnaturally curved back, the figure's head nearly touched the ground, the tassels of its face covering grazing the sand. It sniffed the broth and growled.

"Well, that is quite the haberdashery you're carrying there," Victr chuckled warmly. The being twitched, visibly upset by the sound of his laughter.

"Yes, what are those? They look like puppets of us, don't they, Brother?" Jonathan laughed awkwardly and the creature hissed.

"Oh, I hope I didn't offend you," Jonathan apologized. "Did you make them?"

"*My conquestsss,*" it spat black onto the sand. "*Relief from my sufferinggg.*"

"Conquests, how do you mean?" Jonathan prodded.

"*There will be one, very soon. Very soon.*" The hunched man twisted the femur bone into the sand. "*Then shall come a cataclysmic battle.*"

Jonathan swallowed a spoonful of lentils. "A…a battle you say?" Thinking the man half out of his wits, the monk continued to humor him. "Who will be fighting in this war?"

"*There is no place to hide. Master has alwaysss known of the Daughter of Light.*"

"What did you just say?" Victr, who had been tending to the fire, perked up at this. "Who are you?"

"*Deliciousss,*" it seethed. "*I can taste your fearr.*"

"Answer me," Victr stood. "Who are you? Where did you come from?" He stared into the expressionless painted face on the cloth.

"*A mirage. Neither here nor therrre.*"

"Are you a spy?" Victr raised his voice.

"Now Brother, let us hold our judgement," Jonathan said.

"He knows about Perl," Victr shot back, the wrinkles on his forehead deepening.

The thing pushed itself up with its femur bone. Jonathan noticed as it rose from kneeling that its feet were pointed in the wrong direction. Chills ran up the monk's arms. He dropped his cup.

The thing began to circle around Victr. *"Mercy, I know not."* The dangling dolls swayed with each cumbersome step. *"Your Wayshower will fall, deep into the Earth, so far belowww."* It pointed at Victr with a long scrawny finger, *"all for youuu."*

Victr grabbed his own walking stick and held it up. "You stay away from her!"

Shaken by what he was seeing, Jonathan blurted out, "Brother! He's clearly unwell! And crippled, no less!"

"Open your eyes, Jonathan! This…this whatever it is, is not human!"

Victr pulled the thing's face cloth off with his stick. To their shock, the creature was not hunched over as he'd thought, but flipped upside down in a contorted backbend. It's gray, skeletal face had no eyes, slits for nostrils, and a long, forked tongue that flicked in and out from rows of tiny razor-sharp teeth. Centipedes *(Scolopendra gigantic)* crawled through its long, oily hair that brushed the sand like a wet mop. Victr fell back in horror, scuttling away like a crab.

The Backwards Man smiled, but it appeared as a grotesque frown. Dark saliva ran into its nose and down its cheeks. Pointed barbs jutted out from its snakeskin-like neck.

"Oh, dear Ever!" Jonathan stepped away. The thing now stood between the two monks.

"Get ye behind me, emissary of the Dark!" Victr shouted.

The Backwards Man moved towards Victr. It took a long, deep inhale, *"your sin reeksss."* Reaching out, it touched his arm.

Victr felt a flash of pain in the chest. He dropped to one knee, gripping his heart.

"Worry, worry, worry. Yes. All is lost." Warts began to appear on Victr's hands and arms as the thing ruthlessly taunted him. *"Faith? You have none. You are weeeak."* Warts grew from Victr's face.

"Stop! Stop this!" Jonathan begged. "Victr, get up!" He tried to get to his brother but the Backwards Man blocked the elderly monk with the sharpened bone.

Victr fumbled in his robe pocket and pulled out the web blanket. Before he could unfold it, the creature stabbed it with the femur bone and flung it aside.

Victr screamed out in pain, curling into a fetal position. His flesh was on fire; his mind overcome with anxiety. Thoughts flashed in his mind: *Perl being dragged away by this monster. Dianna and the Forest Sisters lying dead in the underground cells.* "I have to warn them. Save them." Victr mumbled; his mind spiraling; the fear rushing over him in waves.

"You arrre not enough." The thing's words gripped Victr like a vice, *"you neverrr were."*

Tears streamed down Victr's cracked, wart-ridden cheeks. He felt the creature's energy eroding him from the inside out.

Jonathan looked on helplessly, until he recalled how the man had recoiled at their laughter as if it were poison. The monk mustered up all the joy he could in this horrible moment and blurted out, "Oh! Ho! Ho! I see what you two are doing now! What a marvelous trick! Ah-ha-ha-ha!" Jonathan did his very best to conjure up a genuine belly laugh.

The creature cringed. It turned its head to Jonathan and hissed like a feral cat.

Jonathan saw that he had its attention and increased his level of delight. "You old rapscallion, you! You really had me going!" He slapped his knee, smiling, "I mean, the whole thing reminds me of a joke."

The bones in the Backwards Man's arched spine snapped and popped. *"Sssssilence, fool."*

"Yes, exactly! So, the joke goes… this old silly *fool* of a man turns into a donkey for acting like an…Oh, darn it now, I've forgotten the punchline… I've gone and told it backwards!"

The beast slinked away from Victr. It wobbled, confused and appearing to be in pain.

"Ha! Backwards, I've made a pun of sorts, you see? Because you are truly backwards! Ha! The folly!" With a rush of adrenaline, the monk stepped towards the thing confidently. "But, do you want to know what's truly funny? Do you?" He slapped his knee theatrically.

"Ceeeasssse!" the thing seethed, gnashing its jaws.

Jonathan did not relent. "I myself am most gullible! I never see the quip coming! My brothers know it too, oh, the shenanigans they pull!" He laughed heartily and ended with a snort.

The Backwards Man retreated, stumbling, tottering, then vomiting up black sludge. Johnathan looked over at his brother, still writhing in pain.

"Ah, but it is all in good fun," the old monk persisted, his own stomach turning at the sight of this monster.

The Backwards Man began to dig, clawing at the sand, making a hole like a wild animal escaping from prey.

Jonathan was now shouting despite his dry throat. "And they do love me with all their hearts!" He belly-laughed as hard as he could.

The thing twisted headfirst into the ground, pulling itself downward and kicking its feet wildly as it burrowed. As it disappeared, from the opening spewed hundreds of giant yellow-legged centipedes that scuttled and squirmed in all directions. As fast as the hole had opened up, it sealed itself shut; the creature was gone. Jonathan ran to his brother, stepping over the centipedes.

"Victr! Victr! Are you alright?" Jonathan knelt down.

Victr lay trembling feverishly, clutching his knees to his chest. "All is lost," he whispered.

Jonathan pulled Victr's hood back. It was growing dark out now and the last bit of light reflected on his scarred and swollen face; it looked as though he'd been struck with leprosy. Jonathan whispered a prayer over his sick brother, then pleaded with him.

"We need to leave now. It's not safe here. We'll walk through the night. Can you get up?" Jonathan asked.

"All is lost," Victr repeated.

"Rest a moment while I break camp." The elderly monk quickly stamped out the fire and gathered up their belongings. Bats circled overhead.

"Dear brother, take my hand," Jonathan said softly.

"Yes," he cried out in agony, pulling himself to his feet.

"Lean on me. Here's your walking stick." Jonathan wrapped Victr's bruised and infected hand around the wood so he could grip it.

The brothers walked in silence for over an hour. The sparkling eyes of nocturnal mammals dotted the stark landscape.

"What wickedness has befallen me, Brother?" Victr asked in a daze, as eerie howls and harrowing grunts echoed around them. It was dark now, the moon's glow lighting their way.

"I believe…something from the Dark Realm. I'm not exactly sure what it was, Victr. Just try not to—" Jonathan was about to say "worry" when he caught himself. The whole encounter had felt like a terrible dream.

"I can't go on, Jon." Victr stopped, bending over.

"Look there! I think I see the strobe lights from the Palace." Jonathan peered through a pair of binoculars, scanning the landscape. "You'll be able to rest soon." He took Victr's arm, placing it around his neck for support. "Ximu will surely be baking fresh apple biscuits and brewing cinnamon tea. Won't that be just the thing? Come, we're almost home.

"This is our last time down the mountain for a while," said Regor, Perl's lanky delivery partner. He watched as she placed a fistful of rose petals on the counter next to a pile of cumquats.

"Yep, I leave in the morning." Perl arranged the petals into a smiley face to charm the children who lived in the bottom burrow home.

"Are you getting excited to go see your mom?" Regor gathered up the empty burlap bags.

"Do slugs have four noses?" Perl retorted, opening the door for her friend.

Regor snickered, "heh-heh, I don't rightly know, but if you say so I'm guessin' they do, Perly-poo."

"I'm more than ready to go, but I'm kinda nervous," Perl admitted.

"Ah, don't be. It's gonna be amazing," he paused, "but I'll miss doing our deliveries together. I'm gonna feel like a biscuit without butter."

Perl giggled, "I'm gonna miss you too, Goaty-goat-goat." Perl shifted her vision to see Regor in his true essence. She smiled as the middle-age man transformed into a billy goat, skipping down the steps on his hind hooves.

"Well, it's just no fun with you gone. But I am super happy for you, finally meeting yer mama after all these years. Who woulda thunk, heh-heh," Regor stroked his goatee. "We'd better get you home so you can pack."

"I do need to say my goodbyes to all the brothers. But first I need to make a quick stop to tell Gretar something." Perl held out her elbow, "walk with me?"

Regor hooked his arm into Perl's, "my pleasure."

The pair walked down to a stone hut nestled in the shoreline near the fishing pier. Magnolia flowers bloomed in abundance around the entrance, planted there to greet passers-by with their floriography message of 'perseverance and love of nature.' The white blossoms also served to alert activists that this cottage was a safe haven to meet.

Perl swung the door wide without knocking, letting in a gust of fresh sea air. Gretar was bent over a table painting a sign that read, 'Save the Coral, Rescue the Reef.' He squinted into the sunlight at the silhouettes of a girl and a tall, skinny man.

"Perl, is that you?" he asked, recognizing her poofy hair.

"In the flesh!" she proclaimed, shutting the door with a bang, "and this is my delivery buddy, Regor."

"Yeah, I've seen you two together, trekking the mighty steps. How ya' doing, man?" Gretar held out his hand, shaking Regor's heartily.

"I'm swell thanks, heh-heh, nice to finally meet you. But I'm afraid I can't stay, gotta git home and feed Pie-Pie his vittles. You and Perl can catch up, she's told me plenty about you." Regor opened the door, looking to make a quick exit.

"Has she now?" Gretar winked at Perl. "And who, or what exactly is a Pie-Pie?"

"Oh, he's my best friend," Regor answered. "Well, right up there with Perl, of course!"

"His cat," Perl answered as Regor started to shuffle his feet awkwardly.

"Bye, Goaty-goat."

"Alrighty, bye then. See you later." Regor backed through the doorway, nodding the whole way.

"So, you here to help?" Gretar motioned to his sign. "Grab a brush."

"No, well I mean, sure." Perl picked up a brush, dipping it into some yellow paint, and began filling in the word 'coral.' "I'm here to help you, help Dimitri, help the trash heaps."

"Come again?" Gretar scratched his stubbly shadow of a beard.

"You and Mik need to go to Trash Island and see all of the fungi experiments and tell the world about Dimitri's discoveries. Mushrooms could be the answer to our plastic problem." Perl painted a little mushroom on the back of her hand as she spoke.

"That's cool," Gretar said blankly.

"Cool? Did you hear what I said? The. Mushrooms. Are. Eating. Trash! All sorts of it. And that's just the beginning of their uses. It's not just cool, it's Earth changing."

"No, yeah, sorry. That's an amazing discovery," Gretar said robotically.

 Perl saw that his mind was elsewhere. "Are you okay?"

"It's Mik. She won't be going with me to see Dimitri." He stepped back from painting, plopping onto a stool.

"Oh. Why not?" Perl asked.

"She left for the Under Kingdom this morning." Gretar looked at his shoes. "She's going to marry Prince Névenoé."

"What? No. But you guys, I mean, I thought the two of you were a thing?"

"We are. Were? Will be? I don't know anymore." He went back to painting.

"I'm so sorry," Perl placed her hand on his arm.

As soon as she touched him, Gretar felt a calming sensation overtake him. For a second he thought he saw glowing spots on Perl's skin. He rubbed his eyes and blinked and they were gone.

"Thanks," Gretar looked into Perl's kind green eyes. There was a specialness about the girl that humbled him. Perl was like no one he'd ever known.

"You love her," Perl said.

"Yeah, I do, with all my heart."

"Well, then this isn't right and we should fix it," Perl grinned her big toothy grin. "It just so happens that I am going to the Under Kingdom tomorrow."

"You are?" Gretar gave her a puzzled look.

"Call it fate my friend," Perl curtsied, holding out her robe. "I am at your service. I will tell her of your love and she will return to you without a doubt."

"She already knows," Gretar said sadly.

"She knows?"

"Yes. But it won't stop the marriage from happening. Under One's Heel has a plan to unite Mont Michel and the Desertlands. The Graves family and the Scorpion brothers, Princes Névenoé and Tobias are forming an alliance."

"But it's wrong. People should marry for true love, not to grow empires," Perl shook her head. "And she loves you, too, Gretar. I can tell."

The boy blushed, recalling the night Mik whispered, "I love you," as they kissed in secret below the sea. "Mik thinks we can somehow take down the Under Kingdom from within, but I'm so worried about her, Perl."

"What's the plan? I'm in." Perl rinsed her brush clean in the water bowl.

"We need hard proof of what goes on in that place. The orphan trade, the animal cruelties, the weapons trafficking. Their list of crimes against humanity goes on and on. I've heard from activists that have been inside the Under Kingdom and they say it's a fortress of mazes…the rich on top, the poor and imprisoned at the bottom."

"What can I do to help?" Perl dried her paintbrush on the sleeve of her robe.

"I don't want you doing anything that will get you into trouble, or worse," Gretar said with a bit of sternness. "Besides, you must have your own stuff to—wait, why are you going to the Under Kingdom?"

"To meet my mother for the first time." Despite the news from Gretar, Perl couldn't contain her ear-to-ear grin.

"That's wonderful! And that's all you should do," he said. "Don't get mixed up in all this corrupt business."

"I'm not a little girl anymore, Gretar," Perl crossed her arms. "I can handle myself."

"I know." His eyes flicked to the sheath on her backpack containing her sword.

Perl smirked, "just let me help you."

Gretar looked at the girl. He sighed, knowing there was no changing her mind. "Okay, if, and I mean if, you happen to locate Mik, I want you to give her a gift." Gretar walked to a small desk in the corner of the room and opened a metal tackle box. "I was going to give this to her myself. I've been working on it for a while now."

Gretar handed Perl a large walnut. The outside of it was decorated with winding branches, leaves, and other plant life, all exquisitely carved in great detail.

"It's beautiful," Perl ran her finger over the surface, feeling the raised veins in the leaves and petals. "You made this yourself?"

Gretar nodded. "Open it."

"It opens?" Perl carefully unhinged the tiny clasp. The inside was even more ornate. Carved on one half was a red panda *(Ailurus fulgent)* sitting on a tree branch wearing a crown of daffodils. Across from it on the other half was a decorative heart with the engraving, 'You have my heart, you are my home.'

"It's a…" Gretar started to say.

Perl finished his sentence, "red panda."

"Yeah, glad you could tell. It's Mik's favorite animal," Gretar confirmed.

"And her essence," Perl added.

"Her essence?" Gretar chuckled. "Yeah, you're probably right. She's adorable and feisty…plus her hair's bright red."

Perl closed the walnut and tucked it inside a back pocket of her robe. "I'll get it to her. I won't let you down."

Gretar smiled, "you could never let me down, Perl."

When Perl made it home to the root cellar she had missed eating with the Brothers and hearing Papa Ximu sing the Grateful Song. The kitchen was spotless save for the cold carrot and broccoli soup which sat at her place at the table. Perl scooped up the bowl, spooning broth into her mouth as she walked down the hallway. She stopped abruptly, her soup spilling onto the floor; the small door to the Globus Natura room was ajar.

"Hel-loo?" Perl slipped into the chamber. Kerosene lanterns illuminated the intricate floor-to-ceiling webs, laced with flower petals, vines and shimmering dewdrops. Perl marveled at the delicate, shimmering display; it was pure magic.

"Look what the cat dragged in." Ximu smiled down from a rickety ladder made of tree branches. He twirled his mustache, his round wire spectacles magnifying the playful twinkle in his deep-set eyes.

"Sorry I'm late," Perl said, watching her Papa Spider as he leaned out over the fountain in the middle of the room. A pedestal in the shape of a pair of open hands rose gracefully from the center of the pool. Above the hands circled thirteen glass-like orbs.

"What kept you?" Ximu asked, his gaze fixed on the Globus Natura. The centuries-old device allowed the Brothers of the Quill to observe the natural balance of Earth and its atmosphere.

"Important business," Perl tapped her spoon on her bowl.

"Is that so?" Ximu leaned back against the webbed wall, giving Perl his full attention.

"Gretar is going to visit Dimitri. He'll learn how to use mushrooms to destroy plastic and help control the landfills."

Brother Basil, who had been quietly taking notes from the shadows, looked up from his book, feather quill on his lip. "Mushrooms, did you say?"

"Yes, Dimitri has unlocked the mystery of mushrooms. It's so incredible what nature provides, if only we'd open our eyes." Perl sipped her soup straight from the bowl.

"My Bumble, you are a key as well," Ximu chuckled, turning his attention to one of the delicate floating orbs filled with sand. He furrowed his brow, "hmm…"

"What is it?" Basil asked. He scurried over to stand directly underneath Ximu, his quill at the ready.

"Something dark…is spreading." Inside the orb, the sands, normally calm and golden, had turned black and were forming a tiny cyclone. "In the

Desertlands," Ximu muttered to Basil, careful not to let Perl hear. Basil nodded, making a quick note.

Ximu climbed down the ladder quickly. "Perl, you should go and say your goodbyes to the brothers then off to bed straight away. You'll leave before the cock crows. And don't forget to pack your goggles." Perl could sense the urgency in his voice.

"I'll be ready," Perl ran over and hugged Basil so tightly he almost dropped his journal. "Goodbye, Brother Basil, my favorite bookworm."

"Goodbye, my gift from Ever. Be safe in your travels and may your reunion be joyous." He handed her his quill, "a reminder of me."

"Thank you, but geesh, I could never forget you." Perl took the feather pen and tucked it into one of her many robe pockets. "And I'll be back in two weeks to say goodbye again before I'm off to Greenheart for Seer training."

"We'll miss you, Perl. You give this old root cellar such life. Every moment you're away feels like a sunless sky." Basil closed his book, tucking it under his arm.

Perl squeezed him again and trotted out the door, waving her spoon back at her Papa, "You better get to bed, too!"

"Soon, Honey-bee. Sweet dreams and wash that bowl," Ximu shouted after her. He shot a quick glance up to the one darkened orb, furrowing his brow once more.

The morning sky was a vibrant pink, the first rays of the new day peeking over the horizon.

"Uriel instructed us to wait here," Ximu said, dipping his toes in the chilly water. The two had followed the winding path from their root cellar down to the beach. "And where are your boots?" he asked, looking down at Perl's bare feet; his long white beard billowing over his shoulder.

Wide-eyed with excitement, Perl hadn't slept but a wink. "Don't worry, I packed them," she patted the bottom of her trusty backpack.

A small fishing boat with two men bobbing up and down in silence were the only other ones awake at this early hour.

Ximu looked at Perl, her green eyes sparkling off the water. "The fish looks eagerly at the red fly, but it does not see the hook."

"What was that, Papa?" Perl's head was swimming with thoughts of seeing her mother and the adventure to come. "Did you say something about fish?" she asked again, rubbing her wooden rabbit-rabbit charm necklace, feeling the outline of the two noses touching.

"I was saying to stay focused. Observe everything on your path." Ximu splashed water at a scuttling crab as it moved to get a pinch of Perl's big toe.

"Yes, yes, I will," Perl said quickly, pointing to a cloud forming in the magenta sky. "Look Papa, it's a dog."

"So it is," his mustache ends curled upwards as he smiled.

"He's coming. I can feel him," Perl reached over, squeezing Ximu's hand.

"Who, Bumble?" The elder monk squinted to see into the rising sun.

"Quantaa." As Perl said its name, out from the center of the canine-shaped cloud burst the giant Battle Beast, the magnificent two-headed greyhound rocketing straight towards them, his wings beating furiously.

"Quantaa! I knew it!" Perl jumped.

"Great Ever!" Ximu's mouth dropped open. "You told me about him but I never could have imagined such a sight," he stammered, "it…it looks like a dragon!"

They were hit with a gust of air from the Being's enormous translucent wings as it approached the beach. On the hound's black and white spotted back sat Uriel, Perl's Light Realm Protector, her armor glistening like diamonds. She held a firm grip to the hair on the back of the dog's necks.

Seeing Perl, Quantaa let out a deep, rumbling, "Arooooo!"

Perl echoed her watchdog's howl, "Woo-hooo!"

"Marvelous," the portly monk chuckled. "Simply marvelous."

The Light Realm Battle Creature landed with the grace of a butterfly onto the sandy shore. Ximu looked over at the fishermen, but neither seemed to notice the miraculous spectacle happening just a few yards away.

"Your ride, my lady," Uriel said, sweeping her organic floral cloak up and over in one fluid motion as she dismounted.

Quantaa folded his wings up over his back, lowering both his black and his white heads to meet Perl's eyes.

"Oh how I've missed you." Perl nuzzled her face between Quantaa's heads, his hair soft as rabbit fur. The Being's back leg thumped the sand with joy.

"Good boy," Uriel patted the greyhound on his back.

"I thought only I could ride him," Perl said sarcastically.

"He made an exception just this once," Uriel smiled. "Come, Quantaa knows the way. He will take you safely to a clearing near the Slugabed Hovel. There you will find Brother Sebastian."

"Aren't you coming too?" Perl asked.

"Something in the sands has shifted. I'm needed here." The leopard moth hovering over Uriel's missing eye fluttered.

"Here, you say?" Ximu stroked his long beard.

"As you know, you are in very capable paws," Uriel assured Perl. "Come, the sun is rising. Time to go."

Ximu squeezed Perl's shoulders, turning her around to look into her eyes. "Destiny is a blueprint, mapped out even before you were earthbound. Within this map are endless paths. Which one you choose is up to you." He straightened the twisted backpack strap over her arm. "This is it," he bounced up and down a little. "You're going to meet your mother," he smiled warmly then kissed her on the forehead.

Perl mimicked Ximu, bouncing on her toes. "I'm going to meet my mother!"

"Ever be with you," he tied her hood strings into a bow under her chin.

"And with you, Papa," Perl hugged him, aware that he still saw her as a wide-eyed little girl. "And don't worry. I'll be fine."

"I know you will," Ximu said. He looked at Perl, seeing how much she'd grown. "I love you, Bumble. Have more fun than an otter on a mudslide!"

The greyhound lowered to all fours as Uriel cupped her hands to give Perl a boost up. In the distance, the Evensong bell rang out an alarming, hurried clang, rather than its normal methodical cadence.

"What's going on?" Perl asked.

"Ximu and I will go see," Uriel replied. "Time for you to soar, young one. Hold tight." She called out to Quantaa, "volant!"

A short gallop, a few flaps of his mighty wings, and the two were climbing skyward, slicing through the clouds like a blade. Perl waved as Papa and Uriel shrunk into tiny ants in a matter of seconds.

Watching Perl vanish into the pink sky, Uriel turned to Ximu, "It's Brother Victr."

Seeing the concern in the Light Being's face, Ximu immediately bolted, charging up the beach like a bull towards the frantic sound of the bell.

The salty tropical breeze of Mont Michel quickly shifted to a dry, chilly wind. Perl's hood and thick hair whipped straight back as she pressed her chest to Quantaa's back. A flock of buzzards *(Cathartes aura)* whooshed past them. *"It feels so good to be back with you,"* she thought. The dog read her mind, responding with a deep, comforting groan.

The Pilgrimage of the Truth would have taken nearly three months on foot, but Quantaa covered the distance in a half hour. Soaring over the cream-colored dunes, Perl saw a mass of mangled trees amongst the endless sea of sand.

"There's the forest…and what's all that green smoke?" Steady ringlets billowed up from the canopy, camouflaging the Under Kingdom from above. "There's the clearing, just like Victr said in his letter. That's gotta be close to the kingdom. Take us down, Q."

The opening in the forest was just big enough for them to land. The flapping of Quantaa's wings scattered sand and twigs into the surrounding trees.

Perl coughed, clearing her throat as she slid down from Quantaa's back, "Thanks for the ride."

Reaching inside her backpack, Perl pulled out her boots, her goggles, and two handfuls of seaweed jerky, giving each of the greyhound's heads a treat. Quantaa lapped them up instantly, slobbering everywhere. "Ew," Perl giggled. She wiped her saliva-covered palms on the front of her robe, kneeling down to lace up her boots.

Quantaa made a quick circle of the perimeter, sniffing for danger. Perl read his mind—*"All clear."*

"Thank you," Perl kissed each snout twice. "I guess I'll see you in two weeks."

Quantaa nodded, licking the side of her face.

"I love you too," she said.

The Battle Beast reared up like a stallion, flapping his wings, and disappeared in a cloud of dust.

Perl stepped into the forest, bioluminescent spots on her arms lighting the way as the light slowly faded. The winds coming off the desert created a murmuring in the treetops above. "Hello to you, too, forest."

The only other sound Perl could hear was that of the nightingales, their rippling whistles, tweets, trills, and odd gurgles echoing around her. Perl spotted one of the birds above her on a leafless branch, and paused for a closer look. Compared to its mesmerizing song, the small bird was rather simple looking, with a russet rump and white throat. Perl sat down, closing her eyes to listen to the enchanting melody. Almost human-like whistles— "lu, lu, lu," were followed by guttural—"chug, chug, chug," rapidly escalating to a fluty crescendo before dramatically switching to an insect-like buzzing sound, all with clarity and precision. Perl quieted her mind, becoming one with the story the nightingale was telling. She began to sing, the lyrics coming to her almost instinctually.

"Take my wing in your hand
fly with me
to my hidden land,

under pines and waterfalls
twists and turns
I've planned it all,

roots thirst for the gentle rain
I hear your calls
your darkest pain,

planted seeds before your birth
telling secrets
to magic earth,

I'm everywhere in everything
look for me
hear me sing,

Take my wing in your hand
fly with me
to my hidden land,

mud below and skies above
we are one
I am love,
I am love,
I am love."

A twig snapped, breaking Perl's concentration. Opening one eye, she spotted a rustling in the nearby branches. *"Okay, I'm being watched,"* she thought, dimming the spots on her arms. Perl slowly pulled Fortis from its sheath and scooted behind a nearby tree trunk.

"Hello?" A young teenage boy's voice cracked through the silence. "Are you Perl?" He turned up the light on a beetle-shaped lantern that was mounted at the top of a long metal rod. "What am I saying? Of course, you're Perl. Who else would you be? That was a nice song you were singing. Never heard that one before." He stepped up onto a fallen log.

Perl saw he was dressed in a dark, polished uniform that looked like a stag

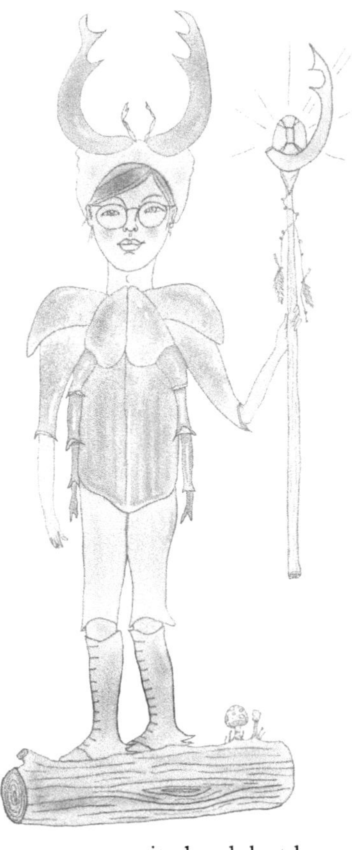

beetle *(Lucanus cervus)* matching his lantern. He wore a helmet with mandibles that rose up like antlers. Fake insect arms hung down from his sides below his arms. His chest plate was shaped like a elytra wing covering, running the length of his abdomen.

"Did you learn that tune from—"

"Who are you?" Perl interrupted, "How do you know my name?" She was more curious than concerned.

"I was going to say, from Sebastian. Did Sebastian teach you that song?"

Perl stepped out from behind the tree, holding Fortis in front of her. "Brother Sebastian? Where is he? He was supposed to meet me."

"Yes, but he doesn't know the woods like I do. He got lost only yesterday, so we agreed it was best for me to come and find you." The boy hopped down from the log.

Just to be on the safe side, Perl shifted her vision to see the stranger's essence. The fifteen-year-old morphed into a brushtail possum *(Trichosurus vulpecula)* with golden fur.

"Cute," Perl didn't mean to say it aloud, but he was just too adorable.

"What's cute?" he asked, twitching his whiskers.

Perl quickly shifted her vision back, "Nothing, nothing," sliding Fortis into its sheath. She watched as the possum transformed back into a boy, his large black eyes returning to their normal warm brown.

"I heard you singing and circled back. I'd already searched the clearing and didn't see you. It's like you dropped from the sky or something," the beetle boy insisted.

"Or something," Perl smiled, approaching him.

"Slugabed's not far," he waved his lantern for Perl to follow. "Sebastian promised to have lunch ready."

"So, you're Victr's friend?" Perl asked. "He mentioned you in his letter but didn't tell me your name."

"Sorry, where are my manners? I'm Lance, Lance Featherstone," he bowed dramatically, his mandible helmet pointing at the ground.

"Nice outfit." Perl gave him a toothy grin.

"It's my uniform." Lance knocked on his armored chest, "I work in the Under Kingdom as the princes' translator."

"I heard they're pretty dangerous. Why would you want to work for them?"

"Not so much want to as need to. It's so I can help the Forest Sisters of Elsewhere and your mother, Our Lady of the Woods," Lance said matter-of-factly.

The Lady of the Woods. Perl had never heard her mother called that; it gave her a warm feeling.

Lance went on chatting like he and Perl were old friends, "It took years to earn the trust of Prince Tobias, and believe me it's been hard to be around him and his wretched brother. But the secrets I learn from being in their inner circle are worth the risks." Lance held a branch back for Perl to step past. "It's my calling to help take back the Under Kingdom for the people who once lived freely in the Desertlands and liberate those who have been brought here against their wills."

"I like you, Featherstone," Perl hopped over a rock.

"Likewise, daughter to Our Lady."

"You can just call me Perl. And maybe I can help you restore the Kingdom?"

"Maybe, but first let's have lunch…and voila, we're here," Lance gestured toward a wall of tree branches stacked together.

"Here where?" asked Perl.

"Here, exactly!" Lance turned a protruding knot on one of the branches, opening a door that was perfectly camouflaged in the mangled trees. "Welcome to my hovel."

"In there?" Perl peered into the doorway. "It looks like a mine shaft."

"Yep, down we go," Lance happily trotted ahead of Perl, his beetle lantern bobbing up and down, lighting the way.

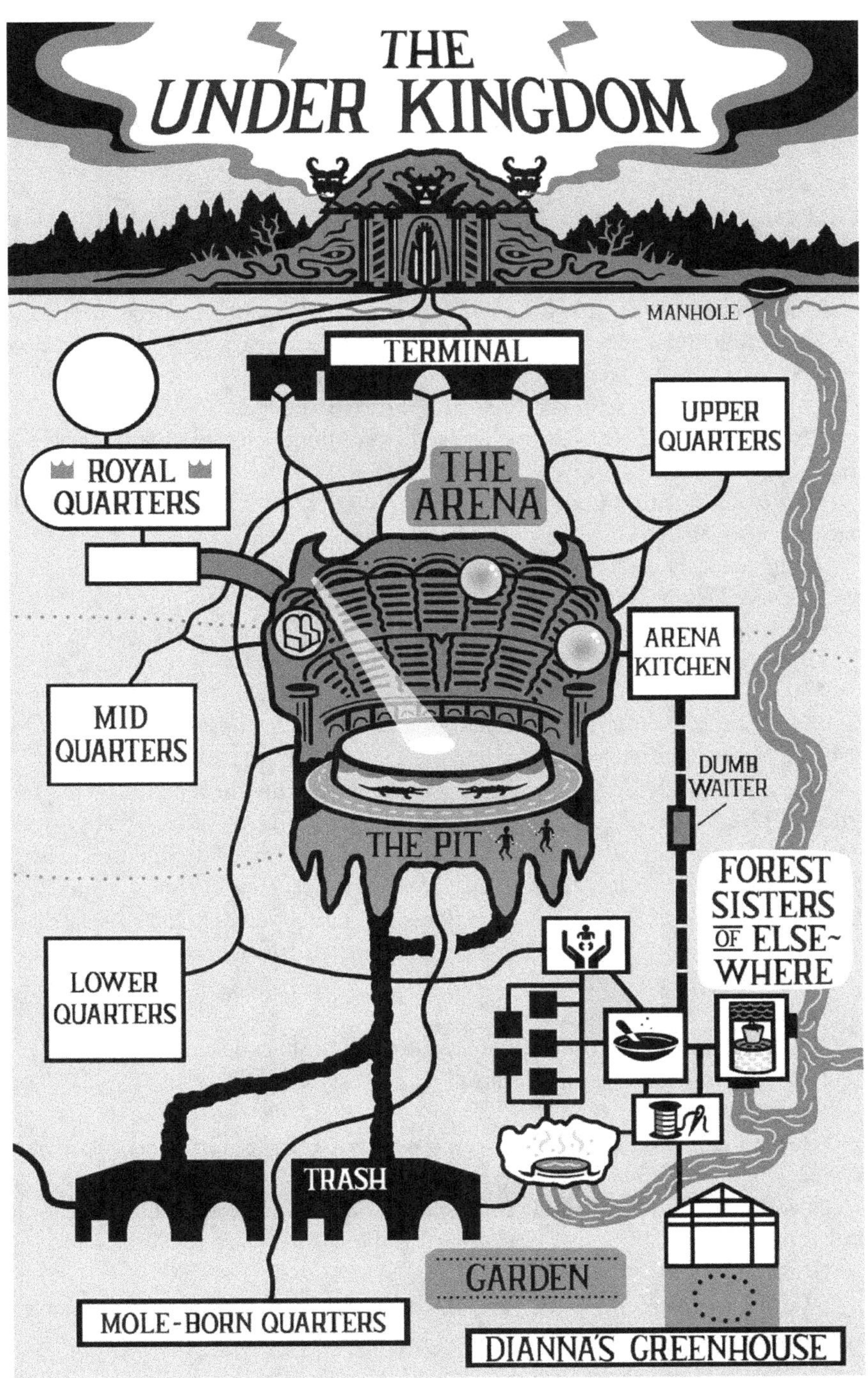

THE
UNDER KINGDOM
MANHOLE
TERMINAL
UPPER
QUARTERS
ROYAL
QUARTERS
THE
ARENA
ARENA
KITCHEN
MID
QUARTERS
DUMB
WAITER
THE PIT
FOREST
SISTERS
OF ELSE~
WHERE
LOWER
QUARTERS
TRASH
GARDEN
MOLE-BORN QUARTERS
DIANNA'S GREENHOUSE

9 GERMINATION

The mid-morning sun stretched its rays through the forest's twisted bramble. Far below ground where the temperature was cooler, Brother Sebastian refilled Perl's cup of wild raspberry tea.

"Let's go over it again," Sebastian said, sitting down across from Perl and Lance at a dusty stone table in the Slugabed Hovel's kitchen. Three fire pits embedded in the walls lit the room. The worn wooden shelves were stacked with spice bottles, jars of sauces, and strange looking objects that appeared to be handmade from scrap metal and plastic from years past. Perl eyed one, reading it to herself, "cola."

"Ahem, Perl, you with me?" Brother Sebastian clinked his cup against hers.

"This is my third tea! Can we please just go before my bladder bursts?" Perl moaned.

"It's really not that complicated," Lance crossed his arms, tipping his chair back on two legs. "Plus, I've done this a million times."

"Fine, we can go," Sebastian sipped his tea. "You can tell me again as we walk. The restroom is down the hall to your left."

Perl stood up, nearly knocking her chair over. "Finally."

"I just want you to be…" Sebastian called after her.

"Safe," Lance finished the monk's sentence. "Yes, we know." The teenager stood, securing his mandible-horned helmet. "You are beginning to sound like Brother Victr…worry, worry, worry!"

The three headed out, moving single file in the direction of the rising green smoke. The heat had tripled since the early morning. Sebastian caught up to Perl, beads of sweat on his brow. He raised an eyebrow, "so, tell me again."

Perl rolled her eyes. "Hood up, eyes forward, stay close to Lance." She tugged on the hood of the new robe Sebastian had given her. It was a periwinkle blue, the same color worn by the Forest Sisters of Elsewhere.

"Annd?" Sebastian said.

"Keep my voice at a whisper."

"Perl, this isn't like Mont Michel, where residents can roam freely. The poor here are indentured to the Kingdom."

"Indentured?"

"Forced into hard labor. Children are taken from families and branded like cattle. The Forest Sisters have rescued some, but…" Sebastian looked into Perl's wide green eyes, thinking maybe he shouldn't have ruined her excitement with such harsh realities, yet she needed to be made aware of the dangers.

"But?"

"We just need to be extra careful, that's all. So, tell me again what we do next?"

They stopped in front of a massive stone wall towering hundreds of feet in the air.

Perl continued reciting the plan of action. "At exactly 11:11 a.m., while the royal guards escort the elite to their pods in the arena for the mid-day games and banquet, it will be safe to enter the Under Kingdom."

Lance cleared away sticks and debris from a spot on the ground, revealing a manhole. He swung open the metal door. Wooden footholds had been installed, serving as a primitive ladder down into the dark, narrow shaft.

"Follow me," he said, climbing down.

Perl waited until Lance's horned helmet disappeared below then followed, Brother Sebastian close behind. The monk kept the questions coming as he carefully navigated the steps, his sandals not ideal for this sort of trek. "And what next?"

Perl yelled back up, "we'll follow the groundwater system to the well opening, where a rope ladder will be tossed down to us from Sister…?"

"Sister Ursula," Sebastian said as they followed Lance.

"Right, Ursula. I like that name. You don't hear many 'U' first names, well except for Uriel, but…"

Sebastian interrupted, "Go on."

"Ursula will take us in the back way through the nursery, where we'll meet my mom." Hearing the words out loud, Perl smiled.

After descending for nearly twenty minutes, the three reached the bottom of the shaft. Next to the small landing where they stood, a waterway ran in both directions, the water crystal clear. Perl shivered slightly. The temperature had dropped, the air now cool and damp.

"It's just ahead," Lance pointed down the tunnel. About fifty yards away, a bucket, lit up by a shaft of light, could be seen dangling from a rope. "Follow me along the ledge, and try not to fall in."

The three made their way along the slippery stone berm; only once did Sebastian nearly fall, cursing his sandals.

Lance tugged three times on the bucket. A rope ladder dropped down. "I'll go first to make sure everything is safe, then Perl." Perl watched as the boy went up the ladder quickly, disappearing over the round stone opening above. "All clear, hurry," he whispered down.

The rope ladder was much wobblier than Lance's squirrel-like scamper let on. Perl struggled, the ladder twisting and turning awkwardly. Halfway up, one of the spikes on her kneecaps caught, cutting into one of the rungs. Not noticing, Perl continued, pulling herself up through the opening. Sebastian followed, but once the monk reached the damaged rung and put his full weight onto it, the rope snapped.

"Waa—!" the monk lost his grip and fell, crashing into the water below.

Perl had just swung her leg over the top of the opening when she heard the splash, "Sebastian!"

Lance, Perl, and Sister Ursula who had provided the rope all peered over the edge. They could see the monk, water up to his chin, his curly tuft of hair plastered to his head.

"I'm fine, I'm fine! Just go!" Sebastian hollered up to them, coughing up water.

Lance leaned down, "I'll be back for you, Sebastian! Hold tight!"

Up above, the three stood in a small chamber. Sister Ursula turned to Perl, genuflecting. "The Ocean Treasure," she bowed, "I am blessed to serve you."

"Uh, nice to meet you, too," Perl smiled awkwardly at the middle-aged woman.

Behind Sister Ursula, an arched doorway had been carved out of the granite. Perl caught a glimpse of the people zipping by on a moving walkway. "Whoa, what's out there?"

Ursula stood, "we won't be going that way." Sister Ursula reached up under the tiled roof of the well, flipping a switch. A hidden doorway slid open in the wall behind Perl. Sister Ursula gestured toward the door, "quickly, before we're seen."

The three entered a bustling workroom. Rows of long wooden tables filled the quarters, and at each table sat women dressed in the same blue robes as Perl. At a few of the tables, women wove baskets made from elephant leaves, while the rest were busy sewing elaborate costumes made from piles of recycled garbage. As Perl walked by the tables, many of the sisters stopped working, stood, and began genuflecting. "Blessed be the Ocean. Blessed be the Ocean," they chanted, over and over.

Perl suddenly felt very self-conscious. "Tell them they don't have to do that," she whispered to Ursula.

"Many of the sisters have waited a lifetime to honor the Chosen One," Ursula said, smiling warmly at an elderly woman who sat huddled at the end of a table, her eyes a striking bright blue. "Myself included." Reaching the far end of the room, she directed Perl and Lance through a door and down a short hallway. Lance paused.

"I'm going to go back for Brother Sebastian," Lance said. "We'll catch up."

Perl was going to ask what the costumes were for when she heard singing coming from the end of the hall. She recognized the words, repeating them— "You are the rabbit to my rabbit, the reason I don't need luck," she skipped ahead of Ursula, following the lullaby. "You are the net of safety, with your hand I'm always caught…"

The song seemed to be coming from a room to Perl's left. She stepped through the doorway into a large nursery. The walls were painted in a desert theme; rolling yellow dunes were dotted here and there with tall, skinny cacti, their prickly green arms waving cheerfully. Across the room, a woman was bent over a straw crib. She was singing to a newborn, her voice soft and hypnotic. She turned and it felt to Perl as if she moved in slow motion, like in a dream. The two continued singing, their voices now linked together, one harmonious melody. "You're my mirror, my reflection, the world makes sense as you tell it."

In that moment, time stood still. Perl stopped singing, her mind unconsciously shifting to see the woman's true essence. "The black rabbit," she mouthed, thinking back to the vision she'd had during Seeker training in

Venusto, when she'd first heard the rabbit's song. She took hold of her rabbit-rabbit necklace Javan had given her. *"It all makes sense now."*

"You are the truth in my words," Dianna continued to sing softly, shifting back into her human form in Perl's eyes, "as your voice echoes in my soul."

Dianna strolled across the nursery towards Perl with quiet grace. Perl looked at her in awe. She was tall and slender with a muscular frame; her afro was cut into an elaborate Amasunzu hairstyle with three striking crescent-shaped rows running front to back. The center crescent was taller than the other two, nearly a foot high; all three sections of hair were adorned with white, yellow, and pale blue beads that cascaded into multiple braids, stopping mid back. Perl thought she looked like royalty.

"My sweet baby girl, at long last," Dianna smiled at Perl lovingly, "I am whole once more."

Like a strobe light, Perl's bioluminescence emanated from every spot on her body, filling the entire nursery with light. Her eyes filled with tears. "Mom." It was the only word Perl could muster as she stared into her mother's chestnut-colored eyes.

Dianna cupped Perl's face in her long, elegant hands. "You have his green eyes and his glow," she smiled, pulling Perl tightly into her bosom for a hug.

Perl pressed her ear against Dianna, listening to her heartbeat; it sounded just like when she would submerge in the bathtub and listen to her own. A wave of bliss overtook Perl, intensifying her bioluminescent glow. Perl's light began to awaken roots and seeds that had long been dormant in the walls and ceiling of the cavernous nursery. Curling vines, bright green leaves, and vibrant flowers began sprouting from the cracks, transforming the brown desert mural into a living canvas of color.

"Praise Ever, look!" The Forest Sisters of Elsewhere had put down their work to follow Perl and were now crowded into the room, falling to their kneels in wonder at the miraculous spectacle. "She shines a light from where no light shines," one Sister spoke aloud, quoting from The Prophecy in the Book of the Awakening. The others bowed.

Tightening her embrace on her mother, Perl inhaled deeply. The scent of a newborn's sweet head filled her nose; it was herself as a baby. Perl's eyes fluttered and closed as she fell into a deep trance. Now she was seeing through her mother's eyes; *Perl saw her infant self, asleep in her mother's lap. Dianna ran a finger over the tiny folds of Perl's ear; she counted her chubby toes, giggling. Perl watched as Dianna swaddled the baby tightly in a blanket, then carried her outside on the balcony of their seaside home. The voice of Ever echoed in Perl's mind— Her heart gave beat to yours. From the*

55

"Mole-born, get back to your rooms!" Sister Martha was trying her best to wrangle the curious, pale children. "Give them some space!" She pulled a small boy back by his collar.

Seeing Perl's light and the fragrance of fresh flowers had drawn a small group of orphans out of the adjacent playroom.

"They may stay," Dianna insisted, as the children flitted around her and Perl like curious cherubs.

Suddenly feeling all eyes on her, Perl reluctantly released her grip from around Dianna's waist. "You're so beautiful," Perl said, looking up at Dianna. Perl couldn't take her eyes off of the face she had so desperately longed to see. Dianna's crimson cheeks were like ripe apples on her espresso complexion, her toothy grin exactly like Perl's.

"And you, my reflection, are even more beautiful." Dianna touched Perl's cheek, illuminating the spots on her face. Sisters and children alike marveled at the magical girl.

"All hail the daughter of Our Lady of the Woods, daughter of The Earthmaker, The Chosen One," Sister Martha proclaimed.

The Sisters of Elsewhere repeated in unison, "All hail, Perl! All hail, The Wayshower!"

Greenery continued to blossom from every nook and cranny. Flowery vines descended from the ceiling like streamers, one tickling the tip of Perl's nose. "Ah-choo!"

"Ever bless you!" the entire room replied, bursting with laughter.

Dianna pinched off a daisy from one of the vines, tucking it behind Perl's ear. "Come, let's show you around our humble chambers and get you settled in."

Dianna laced her slender fingers into Perl's, guiding her from the room. Perl took a moment to admire her mother's outfit; she was wrapped head to toe in a dark violet-blue dress, hand-embroidered in yellow wildflowers that dusted the ground behind her.

"Thank you for redecorating the nursery," Dianna said, parting the new growth from the arched doorway.

Perl looked back, biting her lip. "Oh, um…you're welcome?" They laughed.

The children chased after them, stepping over one another trying to touch the new girl. Feeling a bit like a celebrity, Perl wondered, *is this how Princess Mik feels?* Perl saw that each of their foreheads were tattooed with a crude image of a scorpion.

Lance had rescued Brother Sebastian from the well, and he had his arm around him as the monk limped into the nursery. They gasped at the sight of the room, now transformed into a lush garden.

"Praise Ever, it seems as though we've missed something extraordinary,"

Sebastian said.

"How? I mean, how could this be?" Lance pulled a red poppy off a vine, sniffing it.

"This is the light from the Chosen One," Sebastian smiled. "Perl."

"Huh?" Lance cocked his head.

Sister Betty saw the two men and hurried over. "Ah, there you are, Brother. I was beginning to worry. Ah, but you're wet. Let's get you a dry robe."

"I'm fine, sister." Sebastian replied.

She hooked arms with the monk and the three of them followed the crowd, trailing Perl and Dianna. "Thank you for bringing Perl here safely."

"I'm afraid Lance did all the work," Sebastian gave the boy a hearty pat on the back.

"Nah, don't mention it," Lance said. The boy ran up ahead, weaving through the crowd.

Perl and Dianna stood inside a room twice as large as the nursery. Half playroom, half bed chamber for the orphans, the walls were lined with rows of tube-shaped hammocks.

"Alright everyone, take a seat," Dianna waved her arm and the horde of children, from toddlers to teens, quickly hopped into the hanging beds; their heads poking out like owls in trees. Perl noticed one wall in the room was covered in chalk and pencil marks; it was a chart, marking the kids' names and heights over the years.

Dianna raised her voice as the Sisterhood filed in behind her. "I'd like you all to meet, Perl, my daughter. My true, biological daughter. Say hello!"

"Hello, Perl!" the orphans sang together, shouting her name and clapping.

"Hi, everyone," Perl shifted her weight awkwardly.

"Perl will be staying with us for a short while, so please make her feel welcome. But for now, her and I are going to spend some time getting acquainted."

A sweet-looking boy with large, dark eyes and long lashes spotted Brother Sebastian and sprang from his bed, running to him. Sebastian scooped up the small boy in his arms. Dianna continued, "I need you all to stay in your room. Perl and I will return this evening for tuck-ins and story time."

"Yes, Mama," the orphans answered obediently.

It felt strange for Perl to hear them calling her mother "Mama."

Dianna turned to the boy in Sebastian's arms. "That means you too, Christopher," she winked.

"I'll see that they do," said Sebastian. "Let's go, Christopher." He started to carry the boy to his bed, when a tall, skinny boy ran past them, bumping them out of the way.

The teenager ran to the center of the room and began loudly chattering his teeth. Seeing him, all thirty children began clicking their teeth together, creating an unsettling echo across the vaulted ceiling. Witnessing the children suddenly wide-eyed with fear, the spikes on Perl's elbows and knees shot out instinctively.

"What are they doing?" Perl shouted to Dianna over the chatter.

"It's a warning. It's the children's way of signaling to one another," Dianna said.

"A warning of what?"

"The royal guards are nearby."

Perl looked at a few of the kids near her; all of their teeth were ground down from their chattering.

"They're probably looking for me," Lance said. "I'm supposed to be up there. Foreign guests are arriving for the wedding, and I need to translate for the princes." Lance marched out of the room, and as soon as he was gone, the children stopped their chattering.

"Is he going to be okay?" Perl looked at Dianna.

"Not to worry, Lance is as cunning as he is kind. Come now, we have so much to catch up on." Dianna led Perl out of the playroom down a corridor. A mural of trees had been skillfully painted along its walls. Perl identified robins, goldfinches, and sparrows hidden among the leaves.

"Most of the children in our care were born in the Under Kingdom. The sisters call them 'mole-born.' I don't particularly care for the name. They have been rescued from the quarries, with the help of soldiers like Lance and an underground network of activists. The enslaved aren't permitted to speak, so they developed their own secret way of communicating to outsmart the guards." Dianna clicked her teeth three times quickly. "Three sharp clicks means I love you."

Perl beamed, hearing those words for the first time from her mother. She clicked her teeth back three times.

"I am not a sister, so they call me Mama. I have raised each of them with love."

"So, you're their mother?" Perl felt a twinge of envy rise in her belly. "I see."

At the end of the decorative hallway, they stopped in front of an opening, a green curtain draped in front of it.

"In all of Elsewhere, this is my favorite place," Dianna pulled open the heavy fabric; inside was a lush vegetable garden. Rows upon rows of raised beds lined the room, constructed of recycled metal cans and pipes.

"We have several varieties of beans, carrots, cucumbers, tomatoes, corn, and more."

Perl inhaled the aroma of fresh earth and new growth. "I have a garden too, back home on Mont Michel," Perl said, delighted to learn that her mother had a garden escape as well.

"I can't wait to see it," Dianna led Perl down an aisle of yellow squash. "But this isn't the favorite place I speak of."

At the end of the long room, there was a second curtain. "This is," Dianna said, revealing a mini orchard of olive trees varying in size, from tiny saplings to the largest standing nearly fifteen feet tall. The trees encircled a small, framed greenhouse built of ivory wood, lit inside with sparkling lights. In front of the greenhouse sat a white wooden table with two high-back chairs overlooking the olive trees.

"It's so pretty," Perl said, holding tightly to her mother's hand.

"They are Arbequina olive trees. And they are my magical little forest...of you."

"Me?"

"Indeed. I have planted one for every year that we have been apart."

Dianna reached down, gently caressing the silvery-green leaves of the smallest sapling. "This, the fourteenth tree, is the last one I will plant." She led Perl towards the door; beside it grew the largest olive tree. "This beauty was the first," Dianna plucked a ripe purplish-brown olive from a branch. "Are you familiar with the term abscission?" Perl shook her head. "Abscission is the natural separation of fruit from the tree. However, sometimes conditions beyond the tree's control, such as wind, gravity, or extreme temperature fluctuations will cause the fruit to drop prematurely."

Perl understood. "You mean like when we had to separate."

"Yes, fruit of my flower," Dianna said, handing Perl the olive. "But to be a mother means to carry two essences, the energy of two lives in one. We are bound together, so even when you walk alone, I carry a part of you with me, always and forever."

Perl knew what Dianna meant; there had always been a part of her that felt her mother's presence. Perl looked around at the tiny orchard, picturing her mother planting each of them in memory of her, when she noticed something unusual. "Why are the leaves dripping water like that?"

"It is called weeping, which is common for the self-pollinating Arbequina olive trees. Their tears have kept mine company through these many years, waiting for this day…and mourning your father."

Ever since Papa Ximu had shown Perl the barnacle and told her of her miraculous arrival on the whale, she thought of Dianna day in and out, yet never like this. Perl had created an idolized version of her mother, and now was feeling a bit ashamed for not having more empathy for the sacrifice she made for her.

"I'm sorry, I…" Perl wasn't sure what to say.

"Me too, my sweet, but let's not think on the past. It is gone. There is only today," Dianna assured her. "And I couldn't be happier than I am right now."

"Good afternoon, Mama." Perl looked over to see a girl carrying a tray of apple cakes, sliced carrots, and hummus. She was an albino, her skin a chalky white color. "I thought the two of you might like something to eat."

"How kind of you," Dianna said.

The girl was so stunning, Perl found it hard not to stare. Her shimmering white hair was cut in a blunt pageboy style bob to the top of her shoulders, with low bangs that ran straight across, framing her smooth, alabaster face. It looked to Perl as if she had an eggshell for hair. While the other orphans had tattooed bald heads, this girl had an exquisite floral pattern imprinted onto her hair, which perfectly matched the hand-embroidery in her pinafore dress that hung just above her knees. Perl thought she looked like a doll, with cupid's bow lips and overly large almond-shaped eyes that sparkled like crystal.

"I'll just leave this here for you," the girl placed the tray on the wicker table.

"Perl this is Amanita. Amanita, my daughter Perl."

Amanita curtsied, "nice to finally meet you, Perl of Dianna. Mother has told me about you, but never any juicy details," she gave a quick wink. Amanita stood with a pencil-straight posture, shoulders back, chin up. "And now poof! Here you are! You seem to have appeared out of thin air."

"Not unlike your own arrival, Amanita." Dianna let go of Perl's hand, reaching up to cup the girl's cheek. "Sister Betty found Amanita as a baby, just a tiny turnip, crying in the mud beside the water well, the very same week I arrived at the Sisterhood."

"Oh please, Mother, not this story again," Amanita shook her head playfully. Perl watched as the floral pattern in Amanita's hair separated then fell back in place.

"I guess that makes us the same age," Perl said, smiling.

"I suppose it does," Amanita batted her white lashes. "I'll leave you two alone, but I'd love to show Perl around later if that's okay, Mother?"

Perl felt that twinge in her belly again. This girl had been raised by her mother when it should have been her. Perl shifted her vision to see Amanita's essence, but surprisingly there was nothing; the girl did not change. Perl concentrated, locking her green eyes onto Amanita's light gray, almost colorless pupils. Still, nothing. *Maybe I'm just tired from all the energy I spent sprouting the flowers in the nursery,*' Perl thought to herself.

"Yes, I think that's a wonderful idea," Dianna dipped a carrot and took a bite. "Mmm, this hummus is delicious! Some of your best."

"Thank you, Mother. This chick knows her chickpeas," Amanita said with a bit of sass, turning and heading down the row of olive trees towards the door. "I'll see you at story time," she waved, looking back to see Perl and Dianna entering the greenhouse. She shook the curtain pretending she'd left, then circled back to hide behind a compost bin to eavesdrop.

"This is like a mini version of Palo Santo's greenhouse. Do you know Palo?" Perl asked.

"I'm afraid I do not," Dianna said, walking over to a table filled with seeds sprouting in tiny pots.

Perl sidled up close beside her mother. "She's a garden nurse from the Light Realm. Everything in her greenhouse grows to triple—no, quadruple—its normal size. She has flowers the size of umbrellas!"

"Sounds amazing," Dianna picked up a steel mesh strainer, balancing it over the top of a watering can. "Things grow well here, but not that abundantly."

"How do you grow so much underground without the sun?" Perl asked.

"I told you," Dianna stood on her toes, pulling down a locked metal box from a shelf.

"You did?"

"I told you it was a magical little forest of *you*." Dianna lightly flipped through the many charms on her bracelet, stopping on a brass key.

"The olive trees?" Perl asked, closely inspecting the bracelet. There were acorns, shells, dried berries, feathers, and other treasures. It reminded Perl of the bits of nature she collected to leave with her deliveries on Mont Michel.

"Not just the trees, the entire garden grows from your light." Dianna used the key to unlock the box.

Outside, Amanita crouched at the edge of the compost bin, squinting to see what was in the box. Most would have been turned off by the rotting compost, but Amanita inhaled the stench, taking in the sour scent of decay.

Lifting the lid, Dianna removed another smaller box, this one with a mica stone lid. "You had so much when you were born, I snipped a curl as a keepsake." Dianna held up the lock of dark curly hair.

"That's mine?" Perl touched the curl. "It's so soft."

Dianna placed the lock of hair into the mesh strainer, ladling water through it from a nearby bucket. "Word of my green thumb got out, and the sisters began calling me Lady of the Woods." Dianna poured water over the row of seedlings. Instantly, they sprouted another inch. "But my secret has always been you, Perl. You hold the light."

"I knew my tears made things sprout, but I didn't know about my hair." Perl gently touched a new leaf.

"When you plant a seed you plant a prayer, asking the Earth to protect it with its soil." Dianna removed the lock of hair, carefully dabbing it dry with a cotton cloth. "In time, the seed will burst its skin and reach out with its roots, discovering its potential." Dianna placed the delicate curl back into hiding and locked the box. "You, Perl, will unearth humanity from the things that blind them. You shall help them recognize what is truly sacred."

Perl watched her mother place the box back onto the top shelf. "I've been hearing that my whole life, but how will I know what to do? Or when?"

Dianna looked at her daughter; the weight of the world seemed to be sitting on her small shoulders. "Perl, you have already saved hundreds of lives in the Under Kingdom that would have otherwise starved, without even realizing it."

"Yes, well, technically, you did," Perl grinned.

"There will always be wild creatures who try to destroy the sapling as it reaches for the light." Dianna dipped her long ebony fingers into the watering can, then held them over Perl's head, letting the water drip onto her afro.

"Hey!" Perl giggled; she liked that her mother had a playful side.

"But with the right amount of protection and nourishment it will thrive, becoming shade and shelter for those in need."

Dianna handed Perl a small terracotta pot with a tiny Arbequina olive tree growing in it. "The best way to remember a garden is to take a bit of it home."

"Thank you. I'm happy I'm here, and I don't ever want to go home." Perl took the delicate plant, squeezing it close to her chest. "I love you." It was the first time Perl had said the words aloud; it felt good.

"I love you, too…beyond your wildest imaginings," Dianna said. She leaned down, kissing Perl on the forehead, causing her bioluminescent spots to glow. "Ready to explore the rest of the Sisterhood?" Dianna held out her hand.

Perl took it happily. "Yes, I want to see everything!"

"Everything on this level, where it's safe. It's far too dangerous in the Under Kingdom above." Dianna picked up the tray of snacks. "Not to worry, there's plenty to see and do down here."

As mother and daughter strolled past the compost bin, Amanita crouched out of sight, keeping her bright white hair hidden.

Dianna pulled the curtain open with the tray. "Would you like to stay in my room? We'll have our own little slumber party."

"I'd love to!" The thought of sleeping by her mother's side was a dream come true.

As soon as the two left the garden, Amanita stood up. "All this time, Mother has been lying to me," she thought aloud, "making me believe she was responsible for making it all grow…the garden, the trees, everything. When all along it was her long-lost daughter." Amanita gritted her teeth. "The Chosen One."

Without thinking, Amanita plunged her arm up to her elbow into the compost bin. She yanked it out, her milky white arm now covered in a gooey mix of moldy vegetable peels, green sludge, wet leaves, and manure. She ran her tongue along her arm, lapping up the muck. A maggot squirmed on her upper lip. "This changes things," she hissed, sucking the worm up and swallowing. "The fruit without nourishment will surely fall."

This has been the happiest day
of my life.
Never again will I
look up at the stars and
wonder where you are
or try to imagine your face,
the color of your eyes,
your hair...
with this new moon
I am reborn, finding you,
holding you, and hearing
your voice.
You're so much more
than I ever hoped for.
Love you so, Mama
(An olive tree for each year
we were apart! ☺)

Above ground, the orange sun was setting on Perl's first day in the Under Kingdom. Down below, the mole-born orphans, suspended in hammocks, patiently awaited their nightly story time.

"Alright now, who's turn is it to pick?" Dianna ran her hand over a table filled with silhouettes cut out of black craft paper and attached to sticks.

"Mine!" Christopher jumped down from his hammock and bolted to the table, eyeing his choices.

Amanita, who sat cross-legged on the floor beside Perl, leaned over and whispered, "bet you your morning biscuit he picks the pygmy jerboa."

"You're on," Perl smiled, not fully knowing what she was betting on but enjoying this instant friendship.

"Mm…dis one!" Christopher picked up a shadow puppet of a man with a crown.

"Ha! I win!" Perl taunted.

"Wait for it," Amanita said.

"No," the boy tossed the puppet back on the pile, "dis one!" Christopher handed Dianna the pygmy jerboa and ran back to bed.

"Told ya' so," Amanita nudged Perl, accidentally hitting the spike on her arm. "Ouch, this rose has a thorn."

"Oh, sorry," Perl quickly covered her elbow. "How'd you know he'd pick that?"

"Lucky guess," Amanita teased. "Not really…Christopher always picks the pygmy."

"And who has a letter for Christopher's puppet story?" All eyes were on Dianna as she stood in the candlelight, casting a shadow on the wall behind her.

"Oh, I know, P!" shouted a girl, "P for pygmy!"

"That's perfect." Dianna picked up a few more shadow puppets from the table to accompany her tale and began, moving the puppets back and forth across the wall as she spoke:

"There once was a proper pygmy poet named Peter
whose pastime was picnicking in the park
with persnickety pageant poodles, Pansy and Petunia,
who were particularly hard to please.
One day Peter poured all his poignant passions
into the perfect poem, packed a pristine peach pie,
put on his purple parka and proudly prepared to pontificate.
Pansy and Petunia sat patiently under pink parasols
as Peter presented his prized piece…
'Polka dot panthers
pray for peace
on pale prairie pastures
putting aside the prides' pride,
sought no prey.'
The pageant poodles pouted, 'poo-poo, poo-poo!'
Causing poor Peter to pause and ponder himself a pea-brain!
'No,' he pronounced, 'my poems are powerfully peculiar,
perhaps my pen should pick new pals.'
So, he picked up his pie, pocketed his poem
and proudly paraded home."

As the children cheered and lightly chattered their teeth, Dianna asked, "and the moral is…?"

A ten-year-old boy with flame tattoos over his ears shouted, "pageant poodles are rotten apples cores!"

"Pray for peace like the panthers!" An eight-year-old girl exclaimed.

Perl and Amanita yelled out, "stay true to yourself!" The girls looked at one another, smiling at their unified thought.

"All of you are correct," Dianna agreed, putting away the puppets and walking over to a toy cupboard. She opened the double doors with a lovely ocean sunset painted on it and took out a wooden boat. On the boat's bow was the head of a lion in mid-roar, a crown atop his head. Wings poked from either side of the boat, his tail its rudder.

"Mama, mama, I have a very scary one." A boy smaller than Christopher squeaked. He held out his arms, cupping his hand together as if holding something.

"We had better get yours first, then," Dianna walked over to the child and held the lion boat underneath the boy's hands. He slowly opened his hands, pretending to drop something into it.

"What are they doing?" Perl asked Amanita.

"Collecting nightmares," Amanita answered. "It calms the little ones."

Dianna began to softly sing as she walked from child to child. One by one they turned their hands over the open haul of the ship, dropping in their nightmares as she sang:

Dianna scanned the row of hammocks, "did I get them all?"

"Here!" A small girl was shaking her clasped hands from one of the hammocks.

"Ah, one more," Dianna crouched down, peering inside the hammock at the bald girl. *Clickity-clickity, click, click.* Dianna tapped her teeth.

Click, click, click-clickity. The girl responded in return.

"Don't worry. That old rat won't chase you anymore," Dianna reassured, kissing the girl's hand.

Humming the tune again and kissing each child, Dianna walked to a long, galvanized wash basin that ran the length of the wall. She pumped a lever until water started to trickle out of a pipe, creating a small current down the trough. Dianna placed the boat in and let go, singing one last verse:

As Dianna made her way back to the center of room, the lion boat floated down the trough and slipped through a hole carved in the wall. When it disappeared, the children applauded with a loud chattering of teeth.

Perl followed Amanita's lead, blowing out the candles in the room, leaving two lit as a nightlight.

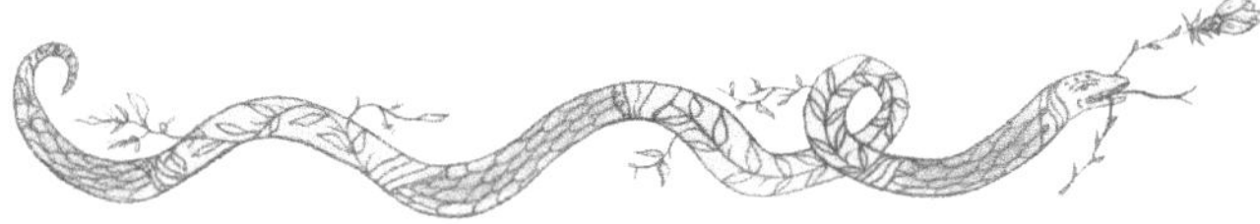

Twelve levels above the children's sleeping quarters in the Sisterhood of Elsewhere's chambers, Mik Graves sat in a nightmare of her own, with no lion boat to save her. The surviving daughter of Count Zell Graves, the girl had been locked in a soundproof, windowless bedchamber, her arm-tattoo communication device dismantled. She had been left alone for hours with nothing to look at but her absurd wedding gown.

"What are you, some kind of serpent monstrosity?" she directed her question at the hideous dress taunting her from the corner of the room.

The gold, jewel-encrusted serpent dress looked more suitable for a carnival performer than a bride. It was a gaudy array of multi-colored jewels, faux scaled leather and chiffon ribbons, and silver and gold ornamental beads, with a five-foot-tall cobra headdress, complete with pointed fangs, being the pièce de résistance.

Mik had lost track of time. Her anxiety sat like a rock in the pit of her stomach. She closed her eyes, trying to escape the hell she found herself in. Clenching her fists, Mik let out a loud, cathartic scream. At that moment, the door of the cell flew open and a woman was roughly pushed in, the door slamming shut. She hit the ground hard but got quickly to her knees.

"Watch who you're throwing, you vile sunuva—" Before the woman could berate whoever did this to her, Mik ran to her, nearly knocking her back down. "Oh, Ruby, Ruby!" Mik hugged her governess, her arms wrapped around her like a vice. "Thank Ever you're here!"

12 THE ARENA

The grandstands at the Beasts of Thunder Racetrack shook as a herd of stampeding rhinoceros *(Rhinocerotidae)* took their final lap. The creatures, half-mammal, half-machine parts, were being ridden by the imprisoned boys. Digital advertisements scrolled along the heads and bodies of the rhinos in bright neon colors.

The crowd was on its feet, shouting over the rumbling chaos. "Come on, Horny Devil! Go, Rhino Wino! Loose Lady, you got this!"

The track encircled the arena's center stage, currently filled with circus acrobats performing death-defying stunts over pits of fire and pools of snapping crocodiles *(Crocodylidae)*, while plumes of colored smoke wafted in the air. High above the action in their glass-bubble orb sat Prince Tobias and Prince Névenoé on a matching pair of thrones, co-rulers of the Under Kingdom and surrounding Desertlands.

The brothers wore flamboyant matching snakeskin jumpsuits, one in neon blue the other in deep purple. Both men had lizard scale capes and knee-high boots curled up at the toes. Their crowns were a ring of Arabian oryx *(Oryx leucoryx)* horns, dipped in liquid gold.

"Showtime, Brother." Prince Tobias smiled and nudged his brother. A group of people made their way up to the VIP area. The Count and Countess Graves, Princess Mik's mother and father, had arrived for the festivities, along with their entourage of footmen, handmaids and bodyguards. A chime sounded and a pair of sliding doors opened up as a sultry-sounding female voice announced the arrival. "Presenting the Count and Countess Graves."

"Prince Tobias, Prince Névenoé, the caviar as promised. Enough for the wedding and then some," Count Zell Graves boasted. He gestured to his to wormy henchman, Snive, who opened a freezer crate, revealing the glistening black fish eggs. The Count was decked out in his usual black shark-themed ensemble with his right arm exposed to show off his array of sea monster tattoos.

"Fantastic, Graves," Prince Tobias said, dipping his pinky into the caviar for a taste without taking his eyes off the track below.

The mechanical rhino-hybrids charged around the bend as the announcer called the action. "Rocket Tank is making a move on Rusty Charger, we're in the home stretch now! Oh! And down goes Silver Bullet's jockey!"

A young boy was thrown from the saddle and was crushed to death beneath the pack as the crowd cheered.

The barker, unfazed by the gore, continued. "And here comes Hooves Your Daddy, horn and horn with Prince of Thieves, the royal court's favored steed! Both beasts are blowing smoke! Prince of Thieves looking strong, but Hooves Your Daddy is pounding the track like a demon! Prince of Thieves! Hooves Your Daddy! Who's it going to be?! Yes, it's Hooves Your Daddy for the win!"

"Ha-ha! Pay up, brother!" Prince Névenoé slapped Tobias's back.

"Dammit!" Prince Tobias threw his chalice to the ground. From a slot in the floor, a robot arm emerged, quickly vacuuming up the mess. "That was state-of-the-art neural pathway technology!"

"What's happening?" Countess Sarr asked, decked out in a bulky, elaborate conch shell gown. The Countess was almost completely blind from years of over-using belladonna plant eyedrops; her pupils now permanently dilated.

"Nothing, my dear," The Count patted his wife's iridescent glove, turning towards Tobias. "Neural technology? You're referring to the fear-erasing pulses, I assume?"

"I spent a fortune on it too," Tobias chugged down his fresh drink. "It was supposed to give that beast an undeniable edge."

Prince Névenoé chuckled as Tobias pounded his fist on the arm of his throne, pouting like a spoiled toddler. The sliding glass doors opened once again and the speaker-voice purred, "Presenting Vlad of Iron, Czar of RussAsia."

Lance, who stood at the ready next to the princes, was prepared to translate. True to his name, Vlad of Iron wore an iron suit three sizes too big; his head peered out like a turtle, with hair dyed yellow, parted down the middle and as slick as a greased pig. The left arm of his suit was a taxidermy grizzly bear arm, its claws scraping along the glass floor as he approached the thrones.

Vlad's servant removed the Czar's boot and he lifted his leg to the group.

"Qui sub plantam fratris tenebat," he boasted. On the bottom of his foot was a tattoo of Earth draped with a banner, displaying the words he'd just spoken.

"Under One's Heel," Lance interpreted.

"We know, boy," Prince Névenoé said with a sneer.

"I have worked on English," Vlad groveled, putting his boot back on, "I bring wedding gift, beryozovy sok." His servant presented the brothers a crystal vessel in the shape of a tree.

Prince Névenoé glanced over at Lance, "What am I looking at?"

Lance swallowed nervously, "birch juice, Your Highness."

"Very rare," Vlad gloated.

"Sounds divine," Countess Sarr chimed in, squinting at the sparkling tree.

"Is that all you brought?" Tobias asked, raising an eyebrow at the Czar.

"Va tom, chat vse?" Lance translated Tobias's question to Vlad, who grinned in return.

A servant girl took the birch juice from the Czar, placing it on the growing pile of odd-looking gifts ranging from a red velvet bust of Mik's head, to jars filled with preserved organs, colorful caged birds, stuffed rodents and reptiles, and a heaping pile of batteries. The Czar reached into a metal pocket on his thigh, pulling out a dagger. Four security robots that had been stationed along the wall collapsed on the Czar.

"Stand down," commanded Tobias, "this gift is for me." The robots immediately returned to their post.

"The Cassowary bone," Vlad said, handing the dagger to the prince. The handle was modeled into a cobalt Cassowary *(Casuarius)* bird head.

"A remarkable piece," Count Graves admired the craftsmanship.

"Exquisite. I thank you," Tobias nodded, "Now go, enjoy the simulation pods and for Ullen's sake, get out of that insane rust chimney you call a suit!"

Prince Névenoé snickered at his brother's comment.

Vlad eyed Lance for a translation.

"He says it's perfect and to enjoy your stay in his kingdom," Lance bowed, putting on a fake smile.

The Czar exited the sliding glass doors, walking past the growing line of elite waiting their turns to pay homage and bestow gifts.

Prince Tobias stuck the dagger into his boot and raised his chalice. "Cheers to our new union!" He clicked glasses hard with Graves's.

"Huzzah! And tell me more of this new mind-parasite you've developed," The Count asked, sipping his drink.

Countess Sarr cut in, "But first tell us when we can see our beautiful daughter?" she asked, fumbling around for her drink.

Névenoé stood and walked to the front of the glass bubble room. "When she is ready," he said, looking up at the domed cathedral ceiling. The entire room glanced upward, wondering what the prince was talking about.

The tone of his voice gave The Countess an unsettling twinge in her gut. "Girls can take a while getting ready, that's for certain," Sarr rambled nervously. "But it's been three days and we… well, as her mother, I'd like to help her get ready, if I may?"

"You may not," Névenoé said coldly, rubbing his chiseled chin, but then quickly cracking a false smile. "After all, it would ruin the surprise."

Down below, medics were removing the young jockey's bloodied body from the track as the winning rider took a victory lap to the cheering crowd.

As the royal arena's events were amping up for the evening, far below the rhino track, the Forest Sisters of Elsewhere were turning in for the night, all except for Perl who lay next to her mother, watching her sleep.

"*I still can't believe it,*" Perl thought, memorizing every detail in her mother's face. She didn't want to sleep, afraid she'd wake only to find that the whole day had been a dream, but her lids grew heavier. A faint whisper woke her just as she was drifting off.

"Perl, hey, you awake?" Amanita had crept into Dianna's room and was crouching next to the bed. "Psst, you up?"

Perl rolled over finding herself nose to nose with the powder-pale girl, Amanita's large, glass-like eyes reflecting Perl's face like a mirror. "What are you doing?" Perl whispered.

"Come on, follow me," Amanita flipped the sheet back.

"Now? It's the middle of the night?" Perl asked. Dianna shifted her weight on the mattress.

Amanita tiptoed out backwards, "the very best time of the day," she said, pretending to pull Perl up by an invisible rope. "Come on!"

"Just for a little while," Perl gently climbed out of bed so as to not wake her mother.

"Just for a little while," mocked Amanita. "Listen to yourself, what, are you, a hundred?"

Once out in the candle-lit hallway, Perl noticed Amanita was wearing a short, black and white checkered dress with a single strap holding it on.

"My Papa is one hundred-and-four-years-old, and he's still as nimble as a spider."

"Well, that explains a lot," Amanita smirked. "Okay, Sister Granny, let's get you something to wear."

"What are you wearing?"

"It's a dress," Amanita did a quick spin. "Girls wear them, you know."

"Ha-ha," Perl shot back. "I know that." Per knew she had never worn a dress, unless she counted the day of the twins' birthday ball, when she was forced to wear that horrible fox costume.

Perl had never met anyone like Amanita; someone who came on so strong, teasing her without care. Perl wasn't sure if she liked the girl, or if she just didn't want to disappoint her; maybe both.

"So where are we going?" Perl asked.

"Up, to where the action is," Amanita hooked arms with Perl.

"I'm not supposed to leave the Sisterhood."

Amanita stopped, spinning Perl to face her. "Do you always do as you're told?"

"Yes, no, well," Perl stumbled over her words. She normally loved exploring, but Victr's letter urging her to stay in the Sisterhood lingered in the back of her mind.

"How will you learn about this place if you don't explore?" Amanita stepped quickly down the hall.

"Yeah, you're right." Perl hurried to keep up.

"I go too?" A small boy stepped out from the shadows behind them.

Amanita turned around, walking back to the boy. "Shh, Christopher. Go back to bed, okay?"

"I wanna essplor too," Christopher whined loudly enough to wake the whole chamber.

"It isn't safe for small boys," Amanita knelt down, peering into Christopher's face. "There's a regal horned lizard on the loose, and if you don't go lay down and close your eyes tightly until morning it will spray blood in your eyes."

"No!" Christopher cried, scurrying back to his hammock as fast as his little legs could go.

"That wasn't very nice," Perl protested. "He's going to be scared now."

"Would you rather he followed us around the whole night? I'm not babysitting."

"I guess not, no, but…"

Amanita cut Perl off, "but, he'd only put us in danger with that scorpion mark on his forehead. If the guards saw it, they'd snatch him up and throw him back into the work pits, or even worse, take him and sell him. A boy that young can fetch a high price. Plus, the whole Sisterhood would be punished for taking in rescued moles. Believe me, him being a little scared is better than the alternative."

Perl bit her lip, thinking about all those poor children being branded and enslaved; things in the Under Kingdom were way worse than she could've ever imagined.

Amanita grabbed Perl's hand, pulling her into the kitchen. "Lighten up, light girl, it's time for some fun." She led Perl over to a dumbwaiter by the sink. "It's our short cut," Amanita said, lifting the square door. "It'll be tight but we'll fit. Oh wait, I almost forgot." She ran to a box of toys on the floor beside a line of highchairs. "Here," she handed Perl a white horse head mask with a long flowing mane.

Perl took the mask, "what's this for?"

"For blending in," Amanita said, crawling into the dumbwaiter. "No one will look twice at you with that on."

"Really?" Perl said sarcastically. "So, I don't get a fancy dress?"

"Your blue robe will have to do," Amanita held out her hand. "Just trust me."

"Well, where's your mask?" Perl asked, taking her hand and climbing inside.

"They know me. I don't need one." Amanita pulled Perl's robe inside, pushing the button on the wall and slamming the door shut.

The girls were squeezed in, their knees up to their chins. "See? Told ya' we'd fit." Amanita smiled, "the King used to smuggle his mistresses in this way. Well, that is, before his loving sons killed him."

The dumbwaiter's chains rattled and gears squealed as they ascended slowly. It was warm in the cramped space and getting warmer.

"Prince Névenoé and Prince Tobias killed their father?" Perl hugged her knees tightly to her chest.

"You didn't know? Those boys were bad seeds from birth. Eleven of their nannies had gone mysteriously missing in just under seven years, so when the King and the Queen died, the royal court of course suspected the brothers but didn't have proof. Tobias, who was the rightful heir to the throne, was only twelve when it happened and swore that he didn't want to be king, but agreed to do it if he could share the royal duties with his six-year-old brother, Névenoé. This was enough to create doubt in the minds of the court and many actually took pity on the princes. But yeah, they totally offed their parents."

"Wait, they killed their mother, too?" Perl shuddered.

"Killed 'em both with kisses," Amanita said, puckering her cupid-bow lips. "The king was the target. She was just an unfortunate bystander. As kids, they didn't think out their plan completely."

"What do you mean, 'with kisses'?" Perl asked.

"The princes were, and still are, the number one collectors in the world of insects. One night, they snuck in and released hundreds of kissing bugs diseased with Chagas into their parent's sleeping pod then jammed the lock on the door. Kissing bugs bite and suck blood from their victim's face, mainly around the mouth. A bite from one wouldn't have killed them, but the King and Queen had spent the previous night entertaining guests, and the bugs just kept on kissing and kissing while they were passed out," Amanita giggled with delight as Perl listened in horror.

Perl jumped as the dumbwaiter jolted to an abrupt stop. "How do you know all of this?"

"Servants talk, nothing's a secret for long down here in the whispering tunnels of the Under Kingdom." Amanita wiggled a finger in Perl's face. "But you, you must remain a secret, so time to put on the mask." Amanita lifted the sliding door as Perl secured the horse mask over her head.

13 COCOON

A blast of cold air and bright florescent light hit the girls. "Ahh, this is the only level with cooled air," Amanita said, taking in a breath. "You're among the elite now."

"Annd you're late!" Shouted a stout man wearing a tall court jester hat with bells, frantically stirring a pot of thick blue bubbling goo.

Perl blinked, trying to take in the room; they were in a massive kitchen surrounded by mirrors. The countertops, cabinets, appliances, everything was mirrored. Dozens of chefs and wait staff buzzed about, all dressed in emerald green uniforms and odd carnival hats. It was a dizzying sight; all the green outfits reflecting off each other like a swirling, endless kaleidoscope.

"And who's this little pony?" Laughed the jolly chef, his hat jiggling.

"A new friend."

"Fine, but I better not catch her taking any food! Paying customers only," the chef crossed his arms, eyeing the pair.

"Yeah, yeah, I know," Amanita said, swiping two candied cherries from a platter, handing one to Perl and giving the chef a wink. He shook his head and grumbled.

Perl lifted her muzzle and popped the treat in her mouth, closing her eyes to avoid looking at the mirrored room.

"Let's go!" Amanita said, disappearing into the chaos.

"Wait!" Perl caught a glimpse of Amanita's checked dress whipping around a corner. "Hey, wait up!" She bumped and dodged her way past dozens of workers, catching up to Amanita. "What did he mean by late? Late for wha—whoa!" Perl's mouth dropped as they stepped into an arena packed with cheering people.

The space was so enormous one might forget it was underground. It was like a gothic roman colosseum and a three-ring circus in outer space; a feast for the eyes, and unfortunately for the nose, too. Perl sniffed; it smelled like a barnyard full of animals, the foul odor attempting to be masked with spices and potpourri.

Amanita threw up her arms, "welcome to the big top down under, where anything goes!"

Perl didn't know where to look first. There were multiple shows taking place. There were fire pits, acrobats, dancers in cages on the backs of mechanical horses, and catapults launching people into giant pools. So much was going on all at once, but Perl now understood why she had on the horse mask. "The Sisters, they make costumes for the arena?"

"Yes, they don't get paid much, but it keeps the Sisterhood running."

The packed crowds reminded Perl of the guests who had attended Mik and Ivry Graves' ball dressed in elaborate feathers, antlers, dyed fur pelts, flashing lights, and other outlandish outfits.

"Who are they?" Perl craned her neck, looking up at the glass pods suspended from the ceiling like raindrops, each one big enough to hold a dozen elephants.

"Royalty and the super wealthy don't mix with the dirty subjects down here." She grabbed Perl's hand, "this way."

Perl watched the bizarre performance on the center stage. Men and women dressed as strange creatures in dark costumes moved on stilts, their exaggerated faces and long, snake-like arms extending down to the ground. Moving rhythmically to the ancient carnival music, they made different shapes together, stretching and curling their arms to form a skull, then a spiny fish, then a snake.

A cloud of dust rose up as a pack of rhino-hybrids raced around the track, pulling Perl's eyes away from the stilt creatures. She held her ears as the crowd grew loud around her, watching as the rhinos thundered down the track, their mechanical joints squealing, the neon advertisements flashing beneath their skin.

"What did they do to those poor animals?" Perl shouted over the crowds.

"There isn't much animal left. It's all run by the group Under One's Heel. They do all of this so they can control the Under Kingdom, keeping everyone happy and subservient." Amanita pointed up to the largest hanging glass pod directly above the center stage. "The princes grow richer, and the poor fight to survive in a giant hamster wheel to nowhere."

Perl squinted. "Is that Count Graves and The Countess?"

"They're here for the wedding," Amanita pointed to a holographic image of Princess Mik and Prince Névenoé that read, "Engagement party begins at 2:00 a.m."

Perl remembered Gretar's gift for Mik, safely stashed in her robe pocket. "So, where's the Princess?"

"Wait right here," Amanita pushed Perl onto a high back chair that sat at the bottom of a long spiral staircase. "And don't move until I get back."

"What? Where are you going? Don't leave me here, this place is…" As Amanita stepped onto the bottom step, the staircase began to move, carrying her upwards.

"I'll be back after my song!" Nearly three stories up, Amanita stepped off onto a glass platform that jutted out above the crowd. A colossal screen rose up behind her.

"What is happening?" Perl muttered, a mix of excitement and worry rushing through her.

A ringmaster appeared at center stage dressed from head to toe like a Bengal tiger *(Panthera tigris tigris)*. He cracked a long electric whip that glowed bright orange and barked into a microphone that hovered next to him.

"Lords and ladies! Nobles and monarchs! Blue bloods and barons! Your attention please!" He snapped his whip again, silencing the entire arena. "Now, the moment you've all been waiting for…" Laser spot lights beamed to the ceiling, "I give you...Princess Mik the Chrysalis!"

The lights illuminated a human-sized Urodidae moth cocoon suspended from the gothic rafters that had been painted to look like giant leaves. The cocoon itself was a skeleton-like structure of mesh netting attached by a long silk-covered cord hooked to the ceiling. Inside the cage was Mik Graves, wrapped tightly in a pupa costume.

The crowd oo-ed and aahed as the ringmaster bellowed, "Soon to be re-born as Queen of the Under Kingdom!"

As the cocoon was slowly being lowered down, the screen behind Amanita began playing a silent black and white nature documentary of caterpillars transforming into their chrysalis stage. Amanita held an old-fashioned silver microphone inches from her and began to sing acapella. There were no words to her song, only sounds, shifting from humming to cooing to tender wistful babblings that escalated into joyful bouts of laughter. Perl was captivated by Amanita's voice; it sounded like the nightingale's song, only more haunting and beautiful.

Perl looked around at the crowd as they watched Mik being lowered; they seemed to be under a spell from Amanita's song, their blank faces frozen in awe. *"She's hypnotizing them,"* Perl thought as the spots on her arm began to glow. She lifted the mask to get a better view.

Up in the princes' box, Lance stood with his forehead pressed against the glass, staring wide-eyed at Amanita. A glint of light below caught his eye, momentarily freeing him from the song's trance. He pressed a button on the side of his helmet; a magnifying lens lowered over his right eye. "Perl? What is she doing here?" Then it dawned on him. "Amanita."

The cocoon stopped its descent in front of the princes' glass bubble. Count Graves stared blankly as his daughter hung in midair like a trapped animal. Mik looked over her father, fear and panic in her eyes.

Countess Sarr tugged on her husband's sleeve. "Where is my baby? Is she in that basket?"

"Your highnesses, this is quite the spectacle," The Count said, barely hiding his anger.

"Relax, it's purely symbolic, Zell," Tobias insisted. "The people need to see that she will transform and conform to the Under Kingdom."

"I think you've made your point." The Count twisted his fake metal mustache nervously. "Get her down from there."

"My dear friend, I don't think you are in any position to be making demands," chortled Prince Névenoé.

Snive stepped forward, his hand on a pistol hidden under his jacket.

"No doubt, it's your Kingdom, but it's my daughter," Graves' blood began to boil. "But for Ever's sake, the poor girl is in a straightjacket a thousand feet in the air!"

Névenoé ignored The Count, "And now there's all this talk about the pump explosion being…accidental."

"What are you insinuating?" The Count's face went purple; veins bulging in his forehead.

"Let's just say we know where sharks swim," Prince Tobias said.

Count Graves didn't like the tone of Tobias. He whispered to Snive, "find out what they know."

On her spot-lit platform, Amanita ended her haunting melody and headed down the staircase. The spectators, slowly coming out of their mass hypnosis, began applauding like dumbstruck seals, hooting and hollering wildly. Camera flashes popped off throughout the arena as the image of Mik swaddled inside the basket cocoon went viral. On the social platform Narcissi the captions flashed—"Engaged and In-caged!", "Will Mik get her Wedded Wings?", "Chrysalis to Queen!"

Mik wiggled like a worm on a hook. "Daddy, help me!" But her cries were drowned out by the roar of the crowd.

Lance had snuck out of the royal box and made his way down to the arena's floor, where he found Perl. "What are you doing here?" he yelled. "Did Amanita put you up to this?"

"Lance!" Perl jumped to her feet, "I, um…"

No sooner had Lance said her name than the albino girl was down the stairs and next to them, pushing the boy aside. "The girl thinks for herself, believe it or not."

Lance scolded Amanita, "do you know how dangerous this is? Who she is? What you're risking?"

Amanita stared at Lance, her eyes cold as steel. "Do you know who I am, you little lackey?" Amanita poked him hard on his chest.

Perl separated the two, her arms still glowing. "Stop, both of you!"

"You shouldn't be here!" Lance bristled at Perl.

"It's none of your business and she can do what she wants!" Amanita shot back.

Perl could feel the anxiety crawling around in her stomach like an eel. "I'm fine," she said, looking at both of them. "Really." She looked down and could see the rhino-bots being corralled into a pen. "I want to get a closer look at those rhinos." Perl descended the stairs to the main floor, the other two close behind.

"Perl wait," Lance chased after her with Amanita on his heels, a wry smile on her face.

Perl crossed the rhino track, seeing the colorful striped banners that hung around the main stage. In spots where the banners sagged, Perl could make out heavy steel rafters that held up the massive stage. Lance and Amanita caught up with Perl.

"What's going on under there?" Perl asked, leaning down for a closer look.

She heard the *click-click-clicking* sound that she now recognized— chattering teeth. Perl pulled back the heavy cloth and gasped. Amongst the steel rafters and in near darkness were rows and rows of children, their heads shaved, the scorpion branded on their foreheads. They ignored Perl, all of them chained to machinery, furiously cranking greasy wheels attached to a system of cables, wires, and gears; sporadic pops of orange and green electric sparks illuminated their grim faces.

"Oh Ever...there are so many of them," Perl said. "We have to help them." Several children close to her turned, briefly making eye contact before increasing their chatter, sending chills down Perl's spine.

"They're sending out a warning," Lance grabbed Perl's hand pulling her up. "We gotta go!"

"You shouldn't have left your post!" Amanita blamed Lance.

"Yeah, well, she should be in the Sisterhood!" Lance shouted, practically yanking Perl off her feet as they ran back across the dirt track and up into the stands.

"We were fine until you came along!" Amanita waved off several fans yelling for her to sign an autograph.

"Would you two quit fighting?" Perl huffed, finding it hard to breathe in her horse mask. As she ran, she kept glancing back at the stage, the scene of those children and the sound they were making wrapped around Perl's brain like barbed wire.

"Oh shit, up there," Amanita motioned to a dozen royal guards peering out over a balcony two levels above them, their mouths agape in unnatural silent screams as they scanned the crowds.

"This way, quick!" Lance zig-zagged between the jungle of party-goers.

One of the guards spotted the three of them running. Through the guard's internal infrared scanner, it locked in on Amanita, then Lance, both of which came up as "Clear" on its display. When the scanner fell on Perl, the guard emitted a loud high-pitched shriek. "Intruder! Intruder! Intruder!"

"They're tracking you, you idiot! Let go of her arm!" Amanita tried to grab Perl's robe but missed.

Lance looked back, seeing the guards quickly leaving the balcony. "It's not me! It's Perl! Every guest for this event has been chipped," Lance stopped at a round trash shoot, flipping up the metal lid.

"What chip?" Amanita asked. "I wasn't chipped."

"They put micro dust on the invitations so they could track everyone entering the event. You're a performer, so you were given pre-clearance." Lance banged the side of the can. "Get in!"

"Oh no, no, no," Amanita protested. "No way! We'll go back through the kitchen."

"Trash only!" A girl sitting on an acrobat's hoop suspended above the can called down to them.

Lance flipped the girl a coin. "It's all I got."

She hid the coin in her cleavage. "They look like trash to me," turning her back to them and giggling.

"They can't track you in there, now go!" Lance insisted. "The guards are going to be here any second."

The many lights of the arena reflected off the guard's neon green jumpsuits; making them look like a swarm of aliens.

Perl looked up once more at poor Mik, still hanging helplessly in her cocoon, and recalled the gift from Gretar. Perl reached into her robe, handing the carved ball to Lance.

"What's this?" Lance asked.

"It's for Mik. She's one of us. It's very important that she gets it. Please."

"I'll try," he helped Perl into the can.

"You have too!" Perl echoed back, sliding down the shoot.

"What is that?" Amanita asked, trying to see what was in his hand.

"Nothing," Lance gave Amanita a push down the shoot, slamming the lid shut just as the swarm of guards appeared. Lance pretended to flirt with the acrobat girl as the robotic guards stomped around screeching, then marched off towards the rhino track.

Perl and Amanita slid down the smelly trash shoot, away from the seedy arena, of which Perl now realized her new friend played a part. Perl's mind raced as the trash shoot spun like a corkscrew downward. *How could she be a part of that corrupt place that preys on terrified, defenseless children?"*

A bright green glow appeared below. Perl rocketed through the opening, landing on her backside in a mountain of garbage. Her horse mask flew off; the smell of unbearable rot filled her nose.

Amanita dropped with a thud beside Perl. "Holy crap, look at all this crap!"

"Shh," Perl motioned over to an old, burly sanitation worker shoveling garbage into a furnace. Sickly green smoke hung in the stifling hot air. The heavyset man turned, locking eyes with her; he had a deep scar running across his forehead.

"Who, him? He isn't going anywhere," Amanita nodded towards the man's ankles chained to the sides of the boiler. "Hold your breath and follow me." Amanita slid down the garbage heap, digging her heels in to slow her fall.

Perl followed the albino girl to an opening with a stone staircase. Looking back at the furnaces, she now realized the source of the toxic green smoke she saw when flying over the forest on Quantaa.

"We'll have to go up from here," Amanita took the steps two at a time.

Climbing, they passed by several closed doors. "You sure you know where we're going?" Perl asked.

"Where's the trust?" Amanita skipped ahead, stopping at a gray metal door. "Here we are," she said, swinging open the door that led to the Forest Sisters of Elsewhere's baths; the scent of myrrh and lavender a relief to Perl's burning nostrils.

"Perfect," Amanita said, stripping down to her underwear and strapless tube top before plunging into the murky pool. "This is exactly what we needed."

Perl removed her blue robe, shaking off some sticky food wrappers and other bits of garbage. "Where are we? It's beautiful," Perl asked, stepping into the water in her t-shirt and underwear, taking in the floor-to-ceiling baroque frescoes.

"This is the ancient grotto of the Sisterhood." Amanita slowly sank down into the water, disappearing briefly before rising just up to her nose. She stared at Perl; her cold eyes glistening like a hungry gator.

"That was a close one, Perl said. "So, how long have you been singing in the arena?"

"For a while now, I have a few friends in high places," Amanita smirked. "You can't tell anyone."

"I won't, but what about Lance, won't he tell Sister Martha?"

"Nah, Lance needs me. We share secrets." Amanita picked up a wick cutter next to some flickering votive candles. She sliced her index finger, not batting an eye.

Perl winced, "Why'd you do that?"

"I need you to swear that you won't tell...with blood." Amanita handed the wick cutter to Perl. "Your turn."

"Are you serious?"

"Deadly," Amanita locked her ghostly eyes onto Perl.

Perl sighed, then braced herself, quickly cut the tip of her finger. Amanita grabbed Perl's hand, pressing their fingers together.

"Now we're blood sisters, and you can never rat on a blood bond," Amanita licked her finger.

"What's going on in here?" Sister Ursula stood in the arched entryway. "Quite early for a soak, isn't it?" she added sternly, holding up a lantern, lighting up the pair. "Amanita, is that you?"

"Yes Sister, it's me and Perl," Amanita moved aside so Ursula could see Perl. "You know what they say, rise and shine, Sister, rise and shine." Amanita dipped her hand into the water; a small bubble of blood rose to the surface.

"Oh, Perl I didn't see you there. Very well, get cleaned up and come to the kitchen to help me with the porridge." Ursula turned, heading back down the hallway.

"She sure changed her tune. I think I'll keep you around for good luck," Amanita remarked. She continued talking, but Perl wasn't listening.

"I feel...strange." Maybe it was the steam from the hot springs or the lack of sleep, but Perl suddenly felt light headed and her stomach began to cramp.

She stumbled up the stone steps out of the pool and sat down against the cool wall, closing her eyes. A vision flashed in her mind. *She could see her and Amanita's hands clasped tight; the girl's blood coursing through her veins. Then Perl was alone in the clearing of an ancient forest. The trees swayed back and forth around her, then leaned down and whispered in unison, "we are starving...we are starving...we are—"*

"You okay?" Amanita's voice echoed in the cavern. Perl's eyes shot open. "Let's get out of here, I'm starving."

"Huh?" Perl blinked, trying to clear her head of the odd vision. "Uh, yeah. Me too."

14 BRAIDING

During her first week in the Under Kingdom, Perl shadowed her mother, learning the ways of the Forest Sisters of Elsewhere. She watched as Dianna fed the poor and cared for the orphans while still providing food and costumes to the wealthy levels above. It was a bitter reminder to Perl of her beloved monks working on the island of Mont Michel, helping the poor yet still having to appease the wealthy. How unfair it all was.

"Why does it have to be like this? So many are starving and the rich just keep taking more than they could ever need?" Perl and Dianna had stopped at the old stone well.

"Change is a difficult thing. Those born into poverty don't have the opportunities that the highborn take for granted." Dianna cranked the handle, quickly lowering the water bucket. "The Sisters keep the word of Ever alive in their hearts by secretly sharing the Book of the Awakening, and now the Codex of the Sacred Invisible, thanks to your Brotherhood. Passages are memorized and shared between households to bring them hope. The hope that the restoration of nature will bring them freedom and unite the Earth." Dianna reversed the handle, bringing the heavy bucket up. "A freedom to be delivered by the Chosen One." Dianna winked at Perl.

Wherever the mother-daughter pair went, Perl had a shadow; hordes of mole-children were always in her wake. However, today the pack had grown to include adults and families from the lower levels of the Under Kingdom. They stood mingling a short distance away from the two.

"Let's take a break," Dianna said. Gingerly removing the full bucket of water from the hook, she eyed Perl's unruly, overgrown afro. "If you like, I could braid your hair?"

"I'd love that," Perl replied.

"Have a seat then," Dianna patted a crude wooden stool next to the well. Perl sat with her back to her mother as the curious group of onlookers pressed in.

Dianna slowly ran her fingers through Perl's hair like a brush. "I certainly have a lot to work with," Dianna giggled, as ten or so mole-born plunked down at Perl's feet to watch.

The sensation of her mother's touch sent tingles down Perl's spine. She had never had anyone style her hair, although Papa had tried from time to time when she was little, but would quickly throw his hands up and say, *"Bah! Let the salty island breeze have its way with it!"*

"That feels nice," Perl said, as her mother lovingly began to braid a section of hair above her ear.

"Ouch," Perl let out a small whimper as Dianna's finger got caught in a tangle.

"Oops, sorry," Dianna said, working out the knot. "You know, when you were born, you didn't make a sound. Most babies enter the world screaming, but not you. You came into this world at peace, your eyes wide with wonder." Dianna leaned over to look into Perl's eyes. Perl grinned at her blissfully, lost in the massage. "Yes, you looked just like that, minus the teeth."

Two orphan girls sitting together giggled to one another.

"I didn't cry at all?" Perl asked.

"Nope, not a peep," Dianna said, twirling the braid into a spiral on Perl's temple. Dianna reached into a tiny cloth satchel slung around her shoulder and pulled out a long pin, tucking Perl's hair into place. She moved around Perl's head to the next thick section of hair. "You know what I believe? That you were so happy and excited to be alive, nothing was going to make you cry. And I wasn't going to let you cry if you were hungry, so I fed you every two hours, just to make sure your belly was always full."

"I remember Papa telling me I was well fed when he found me as a baby," Perl beamed. She was loving every moment of this.

"I look forward to hearing more stories from Brother Ximu. I'm sure he has many." Dianna continued masterfully weaving Perl's hair into elaborate braids, some as thick as sailor's knots, others as thin as a strand of yarn.

"Oh, he has stories, but he also exaggerates! Papa loves to tell people that I read the entire Quill Library by the age of five, but it was more like ten."

"Still, quite impressive," Dianna said, clutching a hairpin between her lips.

"Thanks, but there really wasn't much to do in the root cellar besides read, or sweep...and who wants to sweep? Books were my escape when I couldn't be out in nature." Perl reached up, feeling one of the braids with her fingertips. "The beach is my favorite place; the garden is a close second."

Perl watched Dianna take out a few more hairpins, handing them to one of the girls nearby to assist her as she braided. Perl was beginning to think her mother had already planned to style her hair that day.

"Your father and I had a cottage overlooking the beach. I miss the sound of the waves, the squawk of the gulls," Dianna paused, looking off in the distance. "The ocean is so magical."

"It has always felt like home to me," Perl agreed, looking around as several people from the lower levels of the Under Kingdom began to fill into the tight well room.

Word of Perl's arrival had spread, along with the rumors of a magical flower garden spouting spontaneously from Perl's mysterious light. The curious and the devout all wanted to catch a glimpse of the girl with their own eyes.

An elderly woman leaning on a hickory stick hobbled up to them. "Daughter of Our Lady, I would be honored if you would accept this gift." She held up a small box revealing rows of beads in white, yellow, pink and robin's egg blue. "For your hair," the woman added, gently placing the box on Perl's lap.

"They're beautiful," Perl said, examining the box. "Did you make these?"

"They were my mother's and her mother's before. I have no daughter to leave them to. She was killed in the arena." The old woman looked down; her face taut with grief.

"I'm so sorry," Perl said, reaching up to take the woman's wrinkled hand.

As Perl squeezed her hand, the woman lifted her head. A warm sensation began to run up her arm and move through her whole body and she softened, a sense of peace washing over her.

"Thank you, my dear, it's been years now, but I know she is with me." The woman smiled, Perl saw that her teeth were grinded flat, just like all the orphan children.

Dianna reached into the box, taking out a string of pale pink beads, "Thank you, these will be perfect." She pinned one end of the strand above Perl's left temple, draping it up and down towards the back of her head. She continued braiding the jeweled strands through Perl's hair. When she had finished, it looked as if Perl now wore an exotic beaded crown of many colors.

The crowd shuffled closer, packed shoulder to shoulder, forming a tight circle around Perl. Seeing the eyes of every child and adult on her and sensing their anticipation, Perl felt she should say something. She spotted a small flower pushing up between the floorboards near her foot; seeing the flower gave Perl an idea.

"Isn't it miraculous that a single blossom becomes an apple? The secrets of the Divine are written in nature, and in the hearts of all." Perl's voice was soft yet carried a weight and a wisdom beyond her fourteen years. The room was quiet, hanging on her every word.

"In my heart, too?" Christopher yelled out, breaking the momentary silence.

"Yes, most of all," Perl giggled along with others in the room. "Because you see with the eyes of wonder."

"What does he see?" shouted a teenage boy with a head covered in cactus tattoos.

"He sees the marvel in the simplest of things," Perl raised her voice so all could hear.

"Can you help us do this?" cracked a voice. Perl didn't see who asked, but answered happily. Dianna, listening with everyone else, carefully placed the last pin in her hair.

"All that exists has been created from Ever's imagination. Look closely, and you will see Ever's love is in everything."

"But what about the corrupt elite like the princes and other criminals? Ever loves them too? But why?" The questions came from a frail, haggard man; he was shirtless and dirty, with ribs that poked out from his thin frame. Perl could see the pain in his eyes.

"Ever knows their true essence. We must look past what we see on the surface no matter who they are."

"But the wicked are responsible for so much pain," a woman cried out.

"When evil takes hold of someone it bruises a part of them, but they can heal," Perl said. Dianna squeezed her daughter's shoulder.

Perl stood, stepping up onto the
stool. She looked regal in her newly
bejeweled braids. The entire room
was at attention. "When you find
yourself in the face of chaos,
picture yourself holding the hand
of someone you love." Perl reached
down, taking hold of a little girl's
hand.

"When will we finally be free?"
Shouted someone in the back of
the packed room.

"I know you are hurting. And it
seems impossible to find
compassion for those who seem
undeserving of it. But until we all
do…" Perl looked around at their
worried faces, wanting to console
each and every one of them, when
she caught a glimpse of Amanita
leaning against the back wall,
cradling a small animal in her arms.
Perl squinted to see; it was an aye-
aye *(Daubentonia madagascariensis)*.
The odd-looking primate was
stroking Amanita's pale cheek with its long, skeletal finger. As Perl looked over
at them, it stopped, and both it and Amanita turned, staring back at her. The
sight of the peculiar pair gave Perl an odd feeling, momentarily taking her from
her train of thought before she continued. "Um…life on Earth will not be free
until we can all see with loving eyes. There are good people, Earth Activists,
that are working to try and bring down the corruption in this Kingdom. Mik
Graves is one of them. As your new Queen, she will work hard for you to bring
about change."

There was an audible gasp from the crowd at hearing the news of Princess
Mik being on their side.

Perl reached over and cupped the chin of a small boy. "Have hope and find
comfort in knowing that each and every one of you has a Light Realm Protector
surrounding you, helping you, and loving you always in the sacred invisible."

Before Perl could say another word, the rumble of chattering teeth began
reverberating through the room.

Sister Martha whispered to Dianna, "the royal guards are near. We must
get Perl and our little moles back to our chambers."

"Children, time to go," Dianna said sternly, helping two boys to their feet.
"Perl, this way. Quickly now, everyone hold hands."

"Who could have alarmed them?" Sister Martha asked Dianna, lifting Christopher up onto her hip while hurrying the other orphans along.

Half a dozen robotic guards in neon green jumpsuits stepped off the moving walkway, marching through the arched entrance, their mouths agape in frozen screams. The mob of people crowded in front of them, intentionally blocking the sentinels from getting inside the well room. The guards let out a high-pitched screech as they jostled between the herd, breaking up the crowd.

Hearing the guard's horrible screams, Perl looked back, locking eyes once again with Amanita, who stood perfectly still in the chaos. She cocked her head, giving Perl a cold grin.

Dianna grabbed Perl's hand, pulling her through the hidden stone door she'd used on the day she arrived at the Sisterhood. Martha closed the heavy door with a thud, bolting the lock.

The guards scoured the room, searching for the unknown intruder they had been summoned to locate. Finding nothing, they retreated as quickly as they'd appeared. In the empty room, only Amanita remained. She shoved herself off the wall, placing the aye-aye at her feet. The animal's dark, pointed claws wrapped around her ivory-white ankle, its yellow beady eyes darting about.

From the buzzing tunnel outside a shaft of fluorescent light filtered in across the dusty room. Amanita raised her hands into the light and wrung them together as if she was squeezing water out of an imaginary rag; on the far wall, a shadow puppet was forming from her twisting fingers.

"Eulagisca gigantea," she whispered aloud.

A dark silhouette began to take the shape of a worm. In a matter of seconds, a real, living scale worm as long as a butcher knife wriggled on the wall. Amanita

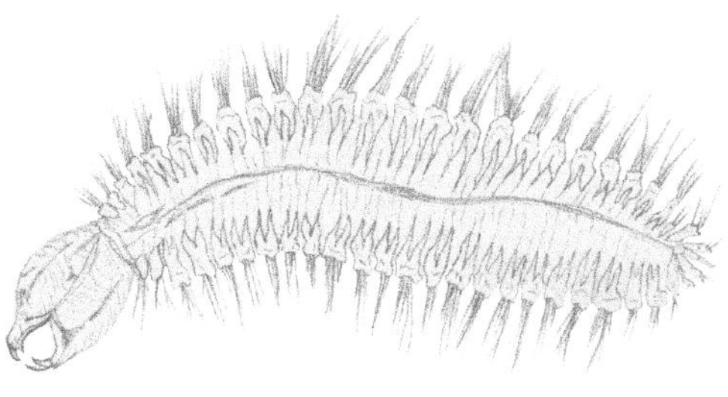

strolled over to the shadow as it finished its metamorphosis. The repulsive creature flapped against the stone, its beige body resembling rows of human teeth, with a fleece of golden hair growing from its roots. The worm's eyeless grey head snapped its sharp fangs like a viper.

Amanita pressed her cheek against the wall, nearly touching the worm with her lips. The thing chewed at her breath as she spoke an ancient language, *"wa hee tah shum dis mal, auk ull, auk len."*

The worm listened to the girl's command, prying its body from the sticky pool of slime it had made and slithered down the wall.

The aye-aye hissed at the worm, jumping up onto Amanita's pinafore dress; its nails sticking in the embroidery.

"Oh, don't be such a coward," Amanita laughed. She lifted the primate up by the scruff of its neck, curling it in under her chin while stroking its coarse fur.

"Her time burns on a twig," she whispered, the words curling from her lips. The scale worm munched through the wooden floorboards, disappearing deep into the earth, ready to deliver the message to its master.

15 THE ULLEN

Slithering over roots and rocks, the repulsive scale worm *(Eulagisca gigantea)* disappeared into the dark soil, leaving trails of pus and mucus in its wake which seeped into the fungi, mites, and bacteria, killing everything it came into contact with. Gnashing its teeth blindly, it traveled deeper and deeper into the earth. The worm passed through a layer of liquid mantle, singeing off its golden follicles, until finally reaching a solid surface. Sensing its master was close, the pathetic creature bore a hole and wriggled through, its body flopping like a fish out of water. On the other side, a great cavern opened up; the ground sloping sharply downward. At the bottom was a towering throne made of hexagonal-shaped crystals.

A dark figure sat motionless on the throne. Three pairs of blood red wings made of bones lay across its fleshy back like colossal skeletal hands. It had three heads; the one in the center a ghoulish skull, the two adjoining heads on either side morphing from one decaying animal to another. A web of tightly-wound veins branched out from its pulsating sternum, creeping down and around the petrified flesh on its legs and feet, across the floor and up the walls of the cave. Acting as receptors, the veins linked to the mycelium in the earth, absorbing dark energy; feeding off the sins of all humanity.

The scale worm cautiously approached the throne and was met by the snarling and hissing of Whisper Wisps. Dozens of the ugly, impish parasites crouched on the figure's shoulders, their knobby knees pressed to their chest, black tongues flicking about as they rubbed their spindly claws together.

The creatures screeched and dove, baring their black, razor-sharp teeth as they swooped and dove at the pathetic worm, who inched ever so slowly toward its maker. The figure on the throne, an ancient entity known as The Ullen, lifted a gnarled finger. Instantly, tendrils of dark smoke rose from the cave's cracks and crevasses. Like black claws, the clouds enveloped and strangled the Wisps, who struggled to escape their clutches. In a matter of seconds, the screeching stopped, the Wisps were gone, the smoke vanishing into the hidden nooks and crevices.

The worm inched up the side of the throne and along The Ullen's sinewy arm. It crawled up its master's neck and forced its way into the corner of its mouth then tore itself in half, the long rows of teeth along the worm's spine splitting and taking root in The Ullen's gray, rotted gums.

Within its body, the worm had carried Amanita's message. Her voice echoed in The Ullen's mind and it repeated aloud her words, its voice rumbling the cave walls like a tremor:

"Wa hee tah shum dis mal, auk ull, auk len." It clenched its jaws, shattering the rows of teeth. Dark blood ran down its chin as its thick, black tongue probed along the empty sockets. *"The abomination will not prevail. All will be slain."*

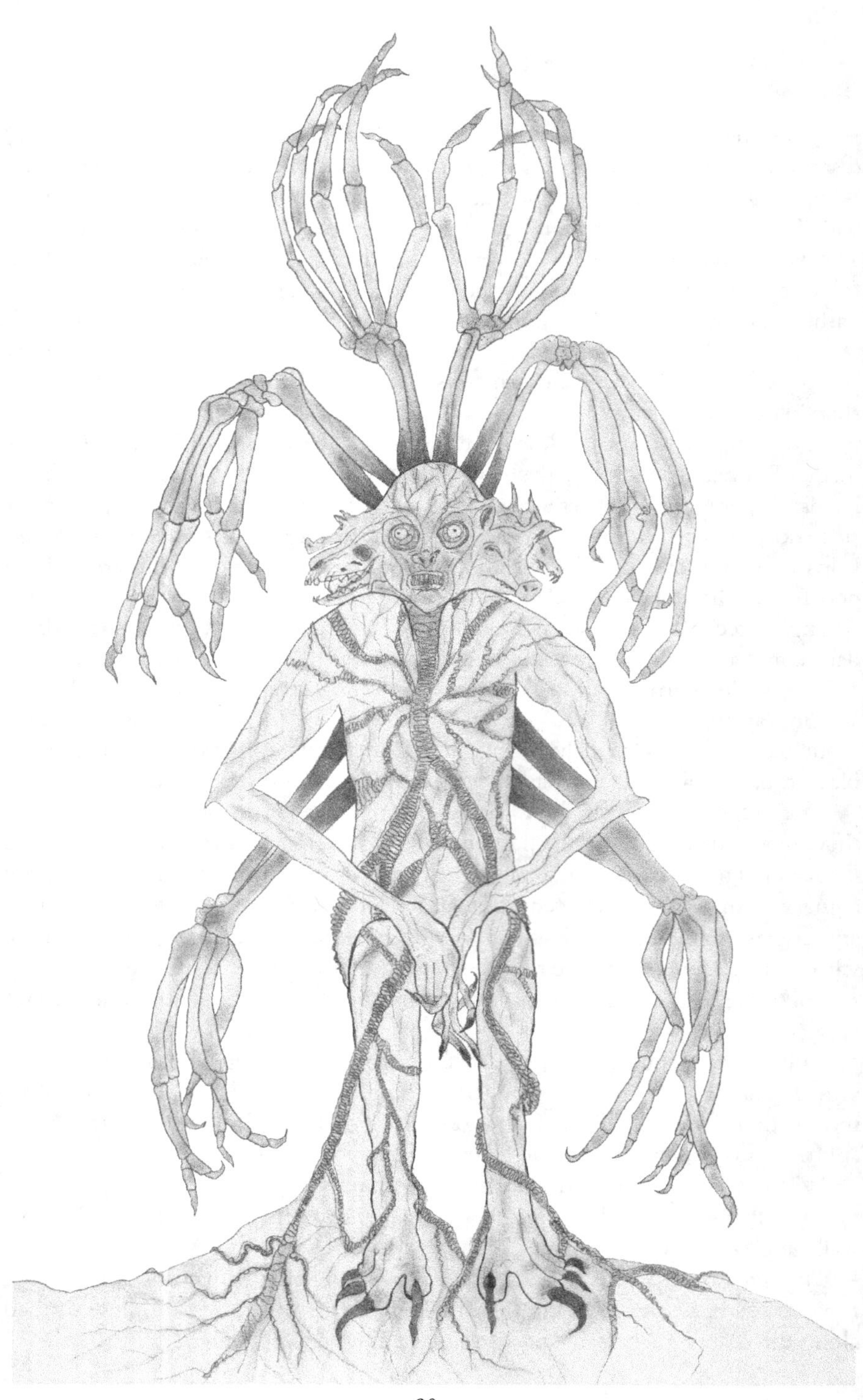

16 EPHEMERAL

Tucked in for the night, Perl cozied up beside her mother, trying to keep her chatting about anything and everything to prolong the day and their precious time together. "I noticed that the orphans' pupils are so dilated you can hardly see their irises."

Dianna yawned, feeling the weight of the day. "Their eyes have adapted to the darkness. Also, they don't see color like you do. You, like your father," she smiled, "can see beyond the normal color spectrum."

"Since returning from Venusto, I have been seeing more and more colors around flowers, leaves, and animals. Colors I don't have names for." Noticing her mother starting to nod off, Perl raised her voice. "But with all the neon signs, lights in the tunnels and in the arena, wouldn't they have some effect on orphans' vision?"

Dianna perked up. "The arena? How do you know about the arena?"

"Um, well some of the older kids were telling me about it. They said that it's like a wild circus." It was the first time Perl had lied in a long time and to her mother, no less. She felt a sick feeling in her stomach, but she had promised Amanita; they'd sworn a blood oath never to tell.

"Looking at artificial colors isn't the same as seeing the Ever-created hues in nature. Sadly, the desert-born do not know of the many shades of green. They've never seen the lime green of a swaying palm, the jade green in the patches of clover, or the changing shades in a field of grass."

"Or the blue-green of the lichen," Perl added.

"That's true…" Dianna paused, spotting a large leopard moth fluttering out from a crack in the cave ceiling. "What in the world? A moth? This far below the surface?"

Perl immediately recognized the gorgeous ivory moth with black spots. "Hello, Hypercompe Scribonia."

It fluttered above their heads, showing off the designs on its wings formed from its black spots; a little bird on one wing and a bee on the other.

"You…know this moth?" Dianna asked.

"Yes, it's a messenger from Uriel, my Light Protector. Just watch." Perl gestured towards the moth as it began to quickly flutter its wings, releasing puffs of white, crystalline powder. As the tiny particles danced in the air, a message slowly materialized.

"Oh, my Ever…a message." Dianna stared up in amazement as the words took shape.

Perl read the words aloud.

My Precious Perl,

I hope this finds you bright-eyed and enjoying your time with your beautiful mother. I regret to say that I bring sad tidings. Brother Victr has fallen ill and is requesting your presence on the morrow. Dianna and Sebastian will accompany you. Meet me on the hilltop near the Slugabed Hovel before the sun breaks the dawn. Lance Featherstone knows the way.

Love, Uriel

Perl was now sitting up as the last two words sparkled and faded away. "Victr's sick? But he's never sick, he's the strongest and heartiest of all the brothers. It must be serious...he wouldn't ask me to come home if it wasn't." Perl's mind was racing. "I remember the Evensong bell rang an alarm the day I left Mont Michel and Uriel stayed behind. Maybe it had something to do with Victr?"

"Try not to worry," Dianna patted Perl's pillow for her to rest her head, "I'm sure he'll be fine. He's in good hands."

Perl laid back down, curling up against her mother, "but what if he's not?"

"Let us say a prayer to Ever for his healing." Dianna took hold of Perl's hands. "May Ever's light surround Brother Victr to heal him head to heart, heart to head." She squeezed Perl's hands, releasing them as she rolled over to twist the nob on the oil lamp beside the bed.

"I'm glad you're coming with me," Perl said, pulling the quilt up under her chin.

"We'll check on him together, and I shall get to see the lovely island colors of your Mont Michel, sooner than expected," Dianna said, trying to cheer Perl up. "Clear your mind and get some sleep, we have a very early hike ahead of us. I love you."

"I love you, too," Perl whispered back.

The orphans were snug in their hammocks, as all of the Sisterhood of Elsewhere slept. It was the wee hours of the morning as Dianna flitted about the kitchen, filling canteens with water and packing supplies. "Spinach jerky, bread, jam preserves...I'm not sure what to bring for our journey?"

Perl sat on a stool half asleep, watching her mother scurry from ice box to pantry like one of Dimitri's little pet mice. She giggled, then jumped as the door swung open.

"My my, the two of you are up before the crack! Going somewhere?" Amanita appeared, suspiciously eyeing the pair.

"We're going to visit a sick friend," Perl answered. Seeing Amanita gave Perl the same uneasy feeling again, but she didn't know why. The spots on her arms illuminated.

"Hey, turn that light down," Amanita said, shielding her face. "I'm done with being in the spotlight."

Perl dimmed her bioluminescence. "What are you doing up?"

92

"Up? I'm just coming in for the night," Amanita winked.

Perl knew that meant Amanita had been performing at the arena again.

"So, who's sick? What's wrong with them?" Amanita plopped down on a stool across from Perl.

"We don't know, just that it's serious." Perl gave an anxious look to Dianna.

"We'll find out very soon. Come Perl, we need to get moving." Dianna swung the bulky burlap bag over her shoulder.

Amanita stood, speaking softly so only Perl could hear. "You know, the human body is quite miraculous when it comes to healing. Every seven years it replaces every cell it has ever known."

"Really?" Perl looped her arms through her backpack straps, sliding off her stool.

Amanita stepped closer, whispering into Perl's ear, "Now that you're fourteen, you're not who you once were, twice over, even." The pale, slender girl backed away, a strange smile on her ghost-like face, and Perl felt the twinge in her gut once more. Something wasn't right with Amanita, but Perl didn't haven't time to concern herself with her right now; Victr needed her.

"Good luck, then!" Amanita said loudly, "I hope he feels better!"

"How did you know it was a he?" Perl squinted at Amanita.

"He, she...I'm just saying, hope they're on the mend."

Dianna handed Amanita a note. "Here, my dear, give this to Sister Martha when she wakes so she'll know where we've gone."

"Certainly, Mother," Amanita smiled sweetly.

Perl closely followed Dianna towards the secret door in the well room.

After seeing the two disappear down the dark hallway, Amanita picked up a box of long matchsticks, pulling one out. She struck the match sharply on her teeth and lit the note on fire, watching it burn down until the tips of her nails began to char before finally dropping the smoldering paper. She smiled, casually extinguishing the lit match on her tongue.

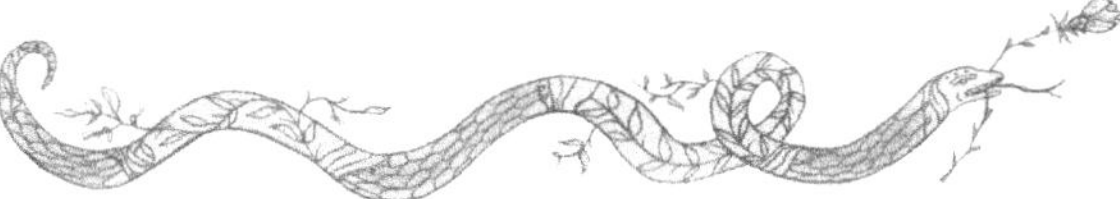

The morning remained as black as Perl's hair when mother and daughter woke Lance Featherstone and Brother Sebastian from their beds at the Slugabed Hovel. The foursome walked in sleepy silence through the forest until they reached the base of a steep hillside.

"This is the spot," Lance confirmed; the mandible horns on his helmet glimmered from the light of his lantern. He sighed, "Well, it's a straight uphill climb from here...just what I want to do at the crack of dawn."

After about thirty minutes they reached the summit, huffing and puffing as the first of the sun's rays peeked over the horizon.

"So, now wha—?" Before Lance could finish his question, a small orb appeared above their heads, glowing with a soft lavender light. The light began to spin in a circle, faster and faster, forming a glowing portal large enough for a grizzly bear on hind legs to walk through.

"Uriel!" Perl said, slapping Lance on the shoulder.

The Amazonian woman stepped through the portal, her cropped turquoise-blue hair sparkling like crystals. The morning light reflected off Uriel's gilded armor; all but Perl shielded their eyes.

Sebastian recalled seeing Uriel two years ago when she first came to the Brothers' root cellar to take Perl to Seeker training. However, witnessing the Light Protector again was even more extraordinary than he remembered. Sebastian lowered his head and knelt, "Your grace."

"Salutations, Brother Sebastian, but please rise. We haven't much time." Uriel turned towards Dianna and nodded, "Lady of the Woods, it is my honor."

Dianna looked at Uriel beaming with ethereal light, draped in her organic gown and was overtaken with memories of her late husband Noaa, and how he too, had the same otherworldly presence.

"The honor is mine," Dianna bowed, noticing the moth that hovered over Uriel's left eye, just like the one that had flown into her bedroom.

"Lance of the Featherstones, you have done well as guide and protector. Remain here and deliver the gift to Princess Mik," Uriel commanded.

"Th-thank you," Lance stuttered, staring deeply into Uriel's dark violet eye.

Perl turned to face Lance. "You haven't given Mik Gretar's sculpture yet?"

"How did Uriel know about the gift? And no, not yet," he said, pulling the carved locket from a compartment on his beetle-shaped breastplate. "But I will, I promise."

"Perl, Victr is waiting," Uriel gestured to the portal.

Sebastian and Dianna had stepped through the glowing ring first, instantly disappearing from the hillside.

Perl quickly hugged Lance. "Be safe, Featherstone. If anyone can liberate the people, you can. Thank you for everything."

Perl glanced back and smiled at Lance before vanishing into the light, Uriel following close behind.

As soon as The Light Protector stepped through, the portal began to swirl, getting smaller and smaller until the last sparkling note of lavender light was gone. Lance looked down, noticing a single pansy on the ground. The small flower curled its petals. *It's waving at me,"* Lance thought, before the pansy popped from existence, leaving the boy alone on the hill.

The portal brought them to the root cellar back at Mont Michel; the group found themselves inside the small rotunda that housed the Globus Natura.

Dianna stood in awe. "What is this place? It's so beautiful." She ran her finger along webbed walls, shimmering with shells, butterflies, and other glimmering jewels. She stepped over to the marble pedestal in the shape of two upward, open palms, looking down and seeing her reflection in the clear pool of water. Above her head floated the silvery orbs. She gazed up, "And what are those?"

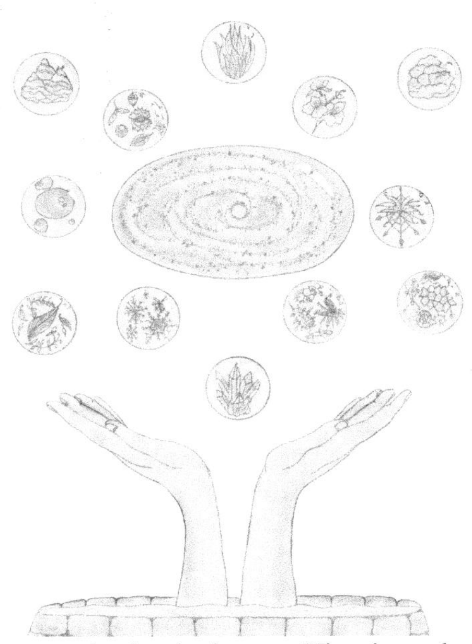

"The Globus Natura. It monitors the balance of nature across the entire Earth and its atmosphere," Perl answered as she threw open the door. "I'll explain more later," she exclaimed, bolting down the hallway, past the kitchen to Victr's room.

She stopped abruptly in the entryway, then stepped slowly to the middle of the room. Ximu and Brother Kirkwood were kneeling at the bedside, heads bowed in prayer. Candles flickered, throwing shadows around the room.

"Oh, Ever," Perl gasped, covering her mouth, shocked to see Victr in such a state. His face, bloated and covered in warts, was almost unrecognizable. Perl shifted her vision, trying to see his spider essence, but for some reason could not. Perl blinked back tears.

Ximu looked up, "Honeybee, you're home." He gestured for her to come closer.

Dianna and Sebastian entered the room and stood off to the side. Perl approached the bed. "I'm here, Victr." She gently took hold of his cold, clammy hand. "What happened to him, Papa? And how is Brother Jonathan? Is he okay?"

"They encountered something in the desert on the journey home, an evil presence." Using the knotted wooden bedpost, Ximu pulled himself to his feet. "Brother Jonathan, thank Ever, was unharmed."

Brother Kirkwood spoke up. "We have tried every healing ointment, every remedy, yet nothing is helping." He looked at Perl. "We are praying."

"We should call on Palo Santo, she'll know what to do. Uriel?" Perl looked behind her. The Light Protector gave her a sympathetic look. "I will try, Perl."

"Hurry!" Perl urged. Uriel nodded and left, ducking through the doorway.

Hearing Perl's voice, Victr stirred, wincing as he gasped for air. "Too late...too far," he wheezed. "It is upon us...everywhere...always has been...lurking."

Victr cried out in agony as a wave of pain overtook him.

Perl squeezed his hand, "Victr, Victr, it's alright."

Victr slowly contorted his back in a strained, unnatural pose, arching up towards the ceiling. He ripped his hand away from Perl's, clenching his heart, his eyes fixed on something unseen beside his bed. "No! Leave her be, take me," Victr pleaded.

"Papa, do something!" Perl cried, taking hold of Victr's arm.

"Victr, look at me!" Ximu pressed him down with all his might, forcing him onto the mattress. "Don't look at it! Don't listen to it! Victr, Victr stay with us!"

"Ever be with you, Ever surround you," Brother Kirkwood walked over to Dianna and Sebastian and began chanting, taking their hands. "Ever be with you, Ever surround you," Dianna and Brother Sebastian joined in.

Victr's mouth dropped open, his eyes filled with terror. He convulsed, twitching and kicking, then suddenly fell limp as his essence left his body.

Perl screamed, "No! No, you can't go! It isn't your time! I need you, Victr! Victr!" She ripped at his nightshirt, trying to wake him.

Ximu wrapped his arms around Perl. "Bee, he's gone. He's gone. It's okay," he said, trying to console her.

"No...no!" Perl shouted at Ximu, struggling to free herself as she burst into tears. "Something evil took him! Didn't you see how frightened he was?" She fell to the ground, sobbing.

Her tears splashed on the floorboards like raindrops; green vines sprouted up and began twisting around her legs.

"I saw," Ximu said, as the vines curled around his ankles.

"I should have come sooner," Perl cried harder, the tears creating more and more lush green vines. Climbing up their legs and in and around their arms, the stems began blossoming flowers that grew into vegetables, enveloping Perl and Ximu in a tangled web of tomatoes, zucchini, green beans, and squash. The vines grew thicker as they continued to spread, covering the bed, up the walls, reaching for the ceiling.

Dianna and the two monks pulled at the stems to free themselves.

"I can't breathe," Ximu gasped. "P-Perl." But the girl didn't hear him, consumed by grief.

"The vines are around his neck," Sebastian panicked. "They're too strong! We need a knife!"

The vegetation filled the cramped room, pushing Victr's bed against the wall. As the monks yanked and pulled against the think tangle of plants Dianna took hold of a vine and began to hum. The melody vibrated through the plants to Perl's ears, drying her tears and calming her. Perl squinted through the thicket, seeing Ximu; his lips were turning blue.

"Papa!" Perl screamed, instantly extending the spikes in her knuckles, elbows and knees. She began punching and slicing at the vines, cutting through the tightly-packed stalks. Vegetables fell to the ground, rolling under the bed and dresser. She reached with both hands, ripping away at the vines wrapped around his throat, freeing him.

Ximu inhaled deeply, "Thank you, Bee," he coughed, rubbing his neck.

Brother Kirkwood reached in and grabbed Ximu's arm, helping the elderly monk out of the mass of creeping, clinging plants. Brother Sebastian used a butcher knife, clearing a path to the door.

Perl looked around at the mess; Victr's belongings were tossed about; a vase of flowers had crashed to the floor; vegetables were everywhere as Dianna was cleaning up bits of debris. Worst of all was seeing Victr's lifeless body, covered in a web of mangled green leaves.

"Oh, Victr." Her heart sank. She looked at her mother, her Papa, and the other monks. "I'm so sorry, everyone."

"It's okay, Bee," Ximu took her hand. "Our dear Brother Victr is with Ever." The monk looked down at the floor, strewn with vegetables. "And let us take this as a sign that he would want us to make a hearty stew in his honor." He smiled at Perl, his kind, gentle eyes red with tears.

"I, I could have killed you, Papa," she hugged him. "All of you."

"Nonsense, Bee," Ximu pulled green beans from his beard, "I'm fine. Go now with the brothers and fetch some buckets from the pantry."

"I love you," Perl said before leaving.

"And I you." Ximu turned to Dianna. "I haven't had the chance to properly welcome you, My Lady. It is a great blessing to have you in our home. I only wish we were meeting under different circumstances."

"As do I," Dianna agreed, picking up broken shards of glass from the vase. "I owe you more than I can ever say. You have raised her well, Ximu. Perl is quite the wonder." She rose and went to Ximu, hugging him.

"She is indeed," Ximu smiled warmly, twisting the end of his curlicue mustache. "She has done extraordinary things in her fourteen short years on Earth...and beyond."

Ximu glanced over at Victr's body and sighed. "Poor man."

He and Dianna approached the bed and prayed, asking Ever to deliver their brother and dear friend Victr into the everlasting light.

A gray morning mist hovered ankle high across the garden; not a bird nor cricket made a sound. Brother Basil stood before every member of the Brotherhood of the Quill, along with Dimitri, Regor, and Dianna. Standing in front of the brothers was Perl, holding a small Arbequina sapling, a gift from her mother.

"Today we bid farewell to our beloved Brother Victr," Brother Basil raised his voice so all could hear. "From Earth to Ever, may he be at peace as we lay him to rest beneath this olive tree, where he will continue to nurture nature in this world and find peace in the next."

Victr's body had been anointed, wrapped in a white burial cloth and placed in a simple pine box. Ximu stepped forward; in his hands he cupped a handful of soil. Ximu sprinkled the dirt onto the casket as he spoke.

"Brother Victr was the kindest man I have ever known. He not only knew the name of every person he served in the lower burrows of Mont Michel, he knew their food allergies, their birthdays, their…"

As if on cue, the garden gate squeaked open and a crowd of villagers entered. They wore tattered clothes, yet it was clear they had tried to clean up as best they could for the occasion. A few women in the group carried flowers.

Adjusting his wire-rim spectacles, Ximu turned and addressed the group. "Welcome, friends, join our circle."

The villagers continued to pour into the mountainside garden, quietly falling in behind the monks' circle.

"As you all know, Brother Victr never met a stranger. If you were in his presence, you were his instant friend. He cooked with the same loving heart, and it is to be said, one could taste the love in every meal he made, leaving you happy, satisfied and full! Victr was a giver, always making certain that each brother in the root cellar, as well as his sweet Perl, all had been fed before taking a single bite for himself."

The Brothers of the Quill nodded in agreement, mumbling, "True, true."

"As we all know too well, our beloved Brother Victr was an avid worrier. I mean, who rinses fifty potatoes ten times, then peels the skins off before mashing, anyway?"

Several monks let out a hearty laugh.

"Yet, it was this very trait that made Victr the kind and compassionate servant of Ever that he was." Ximu paused to wipe a tear from his eye with a handkerchief. "His worrying made us better. Even now, I hear his voice in my head saying, 'Don't forget to blow out the candles in the chapel! Remember to stir the compost! Give a little extra to those who are most in need, and of course…do not lose sight of Perl!'"

Another round of gentle laughter rang out from the crowd. Perl tried to smile as she wiped away tears.

"If you had a problem, big or small, Brother Victr was your man, knowing that he would always be straightforward, caring, and without judgement." Ximu clasped his hands in prayer. "There is one problem that I wish to the Light Realm I could come to you with now, Victr," Ximu lifted his head upward. "And it is how...how do I move forward with this void in our Brotherhood, one that will never be filled? Death is of course a part of life, but you are gone before your time. It is with a heart so heavy I can hardly bear to say goodbye. Until we meet again my dear friend, my brother, be at peace." Ximu gestured to Perl to step forward. "Perl has a special reading she would like to share."

Perl walked to the center of the circle and stood beside Ximu, pulling a rolled-up parchment from her robe. "Victr used to leave me notes all the time. Mostly little silly ones he'd put on my nightstand, ones that continued my imaginary stories from the day, or about special secrets that only he and I shared." Perl unrolled the paper as she spoke, her voice trembling, "But sometimes the notes were just bits of what I called, 'Victr wisdom,' and I thought this one seemed right for today." Perl looked around at all the hooded holy men that had raised her; seeing the love and compassion in their eyes filled her with strength as she continued. "The note is titled, Love To My Future Self."

"Love To My Future Self"

Before leaving for a trip
scour the kitchen sink,
clean out the pantry,
scrub the floors, twice.
It is an act of affection across time,
to you in the future—
A reminder to be kind to yourself.
You are deserving of this gift
upon your return—
To feel good
and welcomed home."

Perl folded up the note and placed it back inside her robe. "I have no doubt that you scoured every sink before leaving the Light Realm, my Victr the Victorious. I hope that you're happy to be returning home."

Perl reached over, taking hold of Ximu's hand as they walked back into the circle. Dianna stood behind the father and daughter, resting her hands on Perl's shoulders. She leaned down and whispered, "well done, that was the perfect piece." Perl nodded, wiping away her tears on her robe sleeve.

Brother Jonathan and Basil handed out small bundles of mugwort and frankincense. "Brothers, please light your herbs," said Brother Basil. "And may this sacred smoke cleanse and purify Brother Victr's essence, connecting him to the Light Realm and to all of our holy brothers who have gone before."

Brother Jonathan placed his smoldering herb bundle into a copper pan next to the coffin. Each Brother took turns, placing their incense into the pan as the box was lowered into the ground.

Once again, Ximu stepped forward, quoting from the Book of the Awakening. "Neither death, nor life, nor present things, nor future things, nor height, nor depth, nor any creature, shall be able to separate you from the love of Ever."

Together, the entire Brotherhood of the Quill began an ululation. Their voices created a long, wavering sound resembling a howling wail coupled with rocking and stomping at the dirt. Their ululation slowly increased, growing louder and louder as the pine box reached the bottom of the grave. Perl joined in, stomping her boot against the ground. Her whole body felt like a pan of water bubbling on the stove before it boils over; she could feel each and every brother's pain, united in the anguish of loss.

Several of the monks began shoveling dirt, filling in the grave as the wailing and stomping kept a melancholy rhythm. When they were done, the Arbequina sapling was planted on top with a plaque that read:

Brother Victr Angelo Rossi
A friend to all
and
to all a friend.
Rest in Eternal Peace.

Brother Basil held a metal watering can above his head, halting the ululation. He sprinkled water over the olive sapling as he recited, "The body returns to nurture the Earth, as the spirit continues on in the Light. Blessed be Ever."

The Brotherhood responded, "Blessed be Ever."

The local villagers paid their respects, placing their flowers around the sapling tree. The funeral procession slowly filed out of the garden, continuing down the winding steps to the root cellar pantry where a huge feast had been prepared in Victr's honor.

Brother Jonathan quickened his step to catch up with Ximu. "Brother, a word?" He spoke in a hushed tone.

Ximu took the monk's arm. "Brother Jonathan, it is good to see you up. And you have your color back."

"Thank you, yes, but there is something I need to tell you." Jonathan looked around to make sure no one was near enough to hear. "That thing, that monster in the desert, it gave a warning...it spoke of a cataclysmic battle that was drawing near."

"A battle?" Ximu furrowed his brow. "With whom?"

"I don't know, but it spoke of its Master, saying there would be no place to hide. It carried with it totems of countless dead monks." Jonathon shuddered,

100

remembering the frightening creature they witnessed with its hideous contorted body.

"We cannot keep this secret, Jon. It is in the hiding that the Dark Realm gains power."

Jonathan squeezed Ximu's arm, pulling him closer. "The creature spoke of Perl. It said its Master has always know about the Daughter of Light." He looked up ahead at the girl holding hands with Dianna. "All those years of chanting and keeping her safe, and The Ullen has always—"

Seeing the worry grow on his face, Ximu cut the monk off. "Let's call a meeting of all the Brotherhoods across every region and reach out to the Forest Sisters of Elsewhere. We will need all Light Bearers working together for…" he paused, "whatever is to come."

"Yes, right away," Jonathan agreed.

"But today, let us celebrate Brother Victr, yes? Join me in an ale." Ximu smiled; his curlicue mustache turning upwards.

The two monks mingled into the crowd, joining the Brotherhood of the Quill, as well as the local islanders and Earth activists that had gathered around the long buffet tables filled with savory potpies and tasty desserts. All were sharing stories of Brother Victr and paying their respects.

Perl quietly escaped to the root cellar library to be away from the crowd. On a well-worn loveseat in a small corner nook surrounded by tall stacks of books, Perl curled up in a fetal position, hugging a crocheted pillow. She closed her eyes tightly and thought of Victr, trying desperately to recapture how she'd felt only a few weeks ago; how happy she was discovering the jar of marmalade he'd secretly left under her bed. *This can't be real,* "Perl thought, squeezing the pillow tighter. She opened her eyes, looking up at the forest fresco painted on the ceiling, recalling the last thing Victr had written in his letter— "Promise me you will not wander off to explore the kingdom alone…" Yet in the moment, it was all Perl wished for—to escape, disappear, pretend his death was just an awful dream, and she would wake up.

"Oh, Victr, where are you? What took you?" Perl pulled her legs up to her chest; a stream of tears rolled down her dark cheeks, collecting in her ear like a tiny pool.

Outside, the faint pitter-patter of an afternoon rain began.

Oh Victr, why? Why did you leave me?
You used to tell me, "Once you've cooked an egg it is cooked, and
it cannot be cooked again. Such is life.
When something is done - it is over. Don't hold on
to the past, to remembering sad or unhappy
events - it only punishes the self."

But this sadness is too heavy to pass.

Please give me a sign
that you're okay.

I find myself
doing the worrying
for you now.

And nothing
will ever be the same.

POTATO LENTIN SOUP

- 1 CARROT
- 2 tbsp OIL
- 1/4 CUP ONION
- POTATOES (BITE SIZE)
- BLACK LENTILS
- 2 tsp SALT
- PEPPER   & GARLIC?   IF WE HAVE it
- 1 1/2 tsp OREGANO
- 1 1/4 tsp THYME
- WATER & TOMATOS
(SERVE WITH LOVE)

I love you.

I miss your voice.

18 NOOR

It was nearly midnight; the funeral reception had long since ended, save for a few brothers still gathered around a table outside the root cellar, drunk on cider and toasting to stories of Brother Victr. The storm had cleared, showing a full moon shining behind windblown clouds. Perl, unable to sleep, was at the beach, her sanctuary. She had climbed up her favorite fir tree and was balancing at the far end of a limb.

"Uriel, I know you can hear me. Victr's not in the Light, I can feel it." Perl spoke aloud to her Protector as she laid on her back. Gently bouncing on the breeze, her small frame was nestled in her hooded robe like a blanket. Perl rested her sketchbook on her chest. *What was that evil entity in his room?* She rubbed her bare feet along the grooves of the bark, salting the ground below with sand.

"To Victr! The best cook that ever there was! To the best of us!" The shouting and clinking of mugs roused Perl from her thoughts. Peering down, she caught sight of Dianna crouching in the sand near the fishing pier.

"Mom?" Perl leapt from the branch like a leopard. She saw Dianna sitting cross-legged on the beach, placing leaves, flowers, and shells into a shape on the flat-packed sand just above the shoreline. Perl stood behind her, quietly watching.

Sensing her daughter's presence, Dianna explained. "It's a prayer mandala. You place the bits of nature that call to you into the circle, arranging them as you breathe in a prayer of gratitude for the beauty of each piece you place." Dianna set two palm leaves into the design. "It has been a long time since I've been to a beach. I'd forgotten the scent of seaweed, the ripples of a shell, the rhythm of the waves."

"Can I help?" Perl squeezed close by her mother, picking up an open coquina clam shell in the shape of a butterfly.

"Of course," Dianna guided Perl's hand to place the shell, reciting, "Cure me with your open wings, let the light of the moon shine upon my skin."

Perl tamped the shell down, securing it into the sand. "It's beautiful."

"I used to make these with your father. We loved to design our beach treasures separately, then come together to see what each of us had found." Dianna leaned back on her palms, admiring the finished mandala. "We'd laugh and say, 'jinx!' when we found the same type of shell or petal."

"Mom, I've been wondering about something." Perl sat back, mimicking her mom's crossed-legged pose. "The monks named me, but did you and my father have a name for me when I was born?"

Dianna smiled, looking into Perl's green eyes. "Noor."

"Noor," Perl repeated.

"Your father named you. It means, the divine light that shines from day one."

Perl's toothy grin reflected in the moonlight just as a wave crashed below the mandala, dragging half of it out to sea.

"Oh no, all your work," Perl gasped, "it's ruined!"

"It's okay. It's part of the ritual. The destruction reminds us of the impermanence of life and that in the end, we all return to nature."

Perl stood, wiping the sand from her robe. She knew Dianna was talking about Victr, but she wasn't up for talking, not with her or any of the monks. She loved them all but they still coddled her like a child. Perl was feeling the need to be with her friends in Venusto, who always treated her equally and honestly, no matter how difficult.

"I think I'm going to leave for Seer training tomorrow," Perl said, sinking her toes into the sand, watching as the waves washed over them.

"So soon? I thought we had until the weekend?"

"I know, but I just don't want to be here. Everything on Mont Michel reminds me of Victr."

"You cannot run from grief, my love, my Noor. Trust me, it follows like a shadow." Dianna picked up the coquina clam shell just before it was to be taken by the sea. "I will add this one to my charm bracelet," she said, tucking the butterfly shell into her pocket.

"Noor is a beautiful name, but if it's okay, can I still go by Perl? It's kinda who I am."

Dianna stood, her tall, elegant figure casting a dark blue silhouette up the beach. "I agree, Perl of the ocean, it suits you perfectly." She took Perl's hand and gave it a squeeze. "Big day tomorrow, then?"

"I guess I could stay a few more days and leave Saturday morning."

"I'd like that very much."

The pair headed up to the root cellar towards the brothers' boisterous shouting and cider-induced singing, as the last row of mandala prayer shells was swallowed by the sea.

Ximu shambled along slowly in his slippers across the wooden planks, pulling out muffin tins and setting the tea kettle on the fire.

"Morning," Perl said, yawning. She shuffled in, carrying a bundle of letters wrapped in an ivy vine. Over the last couple of days, she had stayed up late writing to as many of the brothers as she could. Perl dropped the stack of letters on the kitchen table. The weight of grief made her heart ache, and so she gazed at Ximu, shifting her vision to watch her Papa Spider rinse a colander of blueberries. Seeing him in his spider essence always cheered her up.

"Hungry?" Ximu tossed the berries into a bowl of batter.

"You're up early," Perl rubbed the corners of her eyes.

"Couldn't let my Bee fly off on an empty belly." Ximu pulled a chair out from the table and noticed how tired Perl was. "Here, sit, I can manage."

Perl sat, crossing her arms on the table to make a cushion for her head. Soon fast asleep, she dreamt of her reunion with her eight friends in Venusto, greeting her with open arms. Perl could see their faces so clearly; lovable Bear's round tardigrade smile; Flax's slick salamander hand high-fiving hers; Tars' giant monkey eyes darting around excitedly; sweet Nan's translucent butterfly wings; Lyre's plumed tail bouncing as she mimicked Perl's voice, "welcome home;" Corvax giving a hardy crow; Javan's blushing cheeks burning bright through his thick platypus fur. They were all there, all except her jellyfish sister, Opis. Perl awoke with a start from the whistle of the tea kettle. Ximu was bent over the oven door, pulling out a tray; the smell of warm blueberries filled the kitchen.

"Ah, they're done!" Ximu announced, giving Perl a wink.

"I just had the best dream, Papa. Everyone was there, except Opis. The last time I saw her was right before she blew up the bog and sacrificed herself to release the Many Lost Souls."

Ximu placed a warm muffin and a glass of milk down in front of Perl. "I'm sure she is fine. After all, she is a Turritopsis dohrnii. You will see your jellyfish companion again, Honeybee. Remember, she always cycles back to the Light Realm."

Perl picked a juicy berry off the top of her muffin, popping it into her mouth. "That's true. I just hope we're roommates again at Greenheart."

"This is quite a stack," Ximu pulled the vine around the letters, spilling them onto the table.

"I'm just not up for saying goodbye to everyone face to face."

"They will understand." Ximu twisted his mustache. "What about your mother?"

"We talked last night and this morning. She's going to return to the Under Kingdom. The orphans need her. She would never..." Perl paused, "abandon them."

"I'm sorry your time with her fell short." Ximu sipped carefully on a cup of piping hot tea.

"Me too, but now we both need to be where we can do the most good." Perl took a bite, talking with her mouth full. "She said she wanted you to see me off."

"Well, I must admit she has done the most good with that mop of hair of yours," Ximu chuckled.

Perl smiled, "She said the braids and beads will last a long time if I wash it carefully."

"It shows off your beautiful face." Ximu smiled, taking in Perl's features, when he noticed the spots on her cheeks begin to glow.

Perl cocked her head and smiled. "Quantaa's coming! Will you walk with me to the beach?" Perl stood, scooping up another muffin from the tray, "for later."

The elder monk and the teenage girl stood in silence, watching as the sun's rays peeked out over a blanket of still, crystal-blue water.

Perl swung her backpack off and removed her turtle-shaped kalimba. "I almost forgot. I meant to give this back to my mom. It was hers to begin with, and besides, I don't need it anymore. I can hear nature's hidden songs without its help now."

Ximu took the small instrument. "She will be overjoyed to see its return."

"Oh, and when you see Gretar, can you tell him his gift is on its way? He'll know what that means."

"Speaking of gifts," Ximu took a small wooden box from his robe pocket, handing it to Perl. "He would have wanted you to have it."

Perl recognized Victr's simple, weathered box; she had seen it every day since she was a toddler big enough to sit on the kitchen counter, watching the monk's every move. "His shelling knife! I was looking for it." Perl held the box tightly.

"It has found you." Ximu hugged his daughter, feeling the passage of time that all parents do when they see their child growing up. "And now you are off to Seer training. Bee, have I told you how very proud I am of you?"

"Yes, Papa. I know." Perl looked into his shiny round spider eyes, seeing her multiple reflections.

Fighting back tears, Ximu deepened his tone. "Do you know why peacocks are proud?"

Before Ximu could finish, Quantaa broke through a cluster of clouds.

"Tell me the answer when I come home! I have to go!" She kissed the old monk on the cheek. "Oh, and this one is for you," she said, slipping a letter into Ximu's pocket. Perl ran to meet the Great Battle Beast, whose massive wings were causing giant waves as it came in for a landing.

Quantaa touched down in the shallow surf, prancing like a pony towards Perl, tail wagging. The greyhound lowered his heads to the ground, allowing Perl to climb aboard.

"Stay safe, Sweet Bee, stay in the Light!"

"I will. Love you, Papa!"

"All mine is yours!" Ximu waved with delight.

The great winged dog reared up, flapping its wings, and in a flash, they were a mere spec, sailing through the clouds above Ximu. He shook his head. "Magnificent," he said, wiping away one last tear.

19 GREENHEART

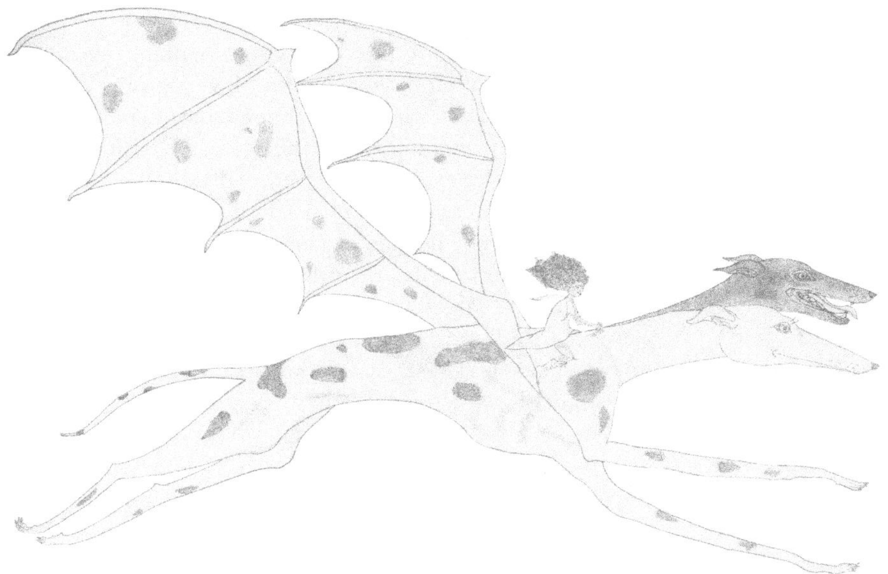

Quantaa flanked left, gently gliding down though a butterfly-shaped cloud taking them into the enchanted realm of Venusto. Perl was instantly hit by a kaleidoscope of dazzling, luminescent colors. She had her goggles at the ready, but unlike her first time entering the realm, she didn't need them upon entry, much to her surprise.

"It's even more miraculous than I remembered," Perl shouted down to the greyhound, who nodded in agreement.

She took in the wonders of the tropical floating island; its circular coastline wrapping around an enormous alabaster lake that shimmered as if sprinkled with diamond dust. A steady stream of magnificent vessels sailed out of the cave opening towards the giant lily pad dock. All of the boats were entirely built or dedicated to nature. Perl saw a massive barge made of fish scales the size of dragons, a schooner with gigantic horns as masts and oversized leaves as sails, and a longboat made of shells gliding through the white water led by a crew of oar-wielding bears.

The boats alone were unbelievable, yet the collection of eclectic Beings aboard them were a sight to behold. *"It all defies explanation,"* Perl thought, smiling her toothy grin. She waved down to a group of pinecone creatures anchoring their hollowed-out oak tree to Venusto's enormous dock. One of the pinecone Beings waved back, then Perl watched with curiosity as it took off along the boardwalk, stopping at everyone it met and pointing up at Perl. The pinecone ran up to a strange cluster of Beings; one was a tall dandelion puff, another was a lizard covered in pink crystal gems, while another looked like green mist in the form of an owl. They all looked up at Perl and Quantaa, then ran to others, pointing and waving to the girl on the flying two-headed dog.

"I'm not sure what's going on," Perl said aloud, still waving at the ever-growing crowd below. The large dog dipped a wing, banking past the extraordinary cloud formation that hovered over the island, welcoming all who entered The Light Realm of Venusto. The cloud was shaped like a woman from the shoulders up, with long arms stretching out at her sides. Floating above each of her upheld palms were smaller clouds that continually changed shapes. Perl watched with delight as the puffs morphed into lions, sunflowers, starfish and more; one magical creation after another. Rising up through the cloud-woman and blooming out of the top of her head like a decorative headdress was the massive rainbow tree from Master Tryfon's garden. It was the very tree that held the ring of names of Perl and her best friends from when they had won the Pompeius Games as Seekers. Quantaa flew so close Perl could almost touch the branches. The multicolored rings stretched up and up, as far as the eye could see.

"I wonder which ring has my father's name on it?" Perl thought as they soared past the tree and back toward the grand lily pad docking area.

Where the wharf met the island, it split into the three pathways, each decorated with a beautiful floral archway. To the right led to 'Natatory,' the middle path led to 'Callowhorn,' and the left went to 'Greenheart.'

From up high, Perl could see where Greenheart got its name; the island was in the shape of a heart, brimming with fields of exotic flowers as large as trees. "Head over toward that garden, Q," Perl said, pointing to a clearing amongst the lush wild terrain. As Quantaa got closer, Perl could now see flying creatures of every size and shape mingling from blossom to blossom. A swarm of butterfly-winged squirrels and large bumble bees with the heads of hawks buzzed past them as they flew over the topiary garden. A perfectly-manicured hedge wall as tall as a giraffe surrounded the entire enclosure. Everything outside of the garden wall was wild and green as the first spring clover, with endless pathways of violet moss snaking out in all directions. Far away, dotted along the island's rolling hillsides, Perl could see mastodons lazily grazing.

Perl smiled; this was the place where she, Opis, and Javan had snuck out of Callowhorn to explore. *"That seemed like such a long time ago,"* Perl thought.

"Aroo!" Quantaa howled as he soared over the glass bubble greenhouse that stood on a hill in the middle of the garden. He swooped in low to the far end, where just outside the hedge wall, a collection of massive baobab trees stood like a small forest. From each tree hung artfully designed treehouse nests, complete with winding staircases spiraling down to a lush pink lawn.

"Look, boy, it's Bear!" Perl shouted. "Take us down!"

Quantaa flapped his translucent wings like a dragonfly, landing softly next to the baobabs. Perl scratched the greyhound behind its white and black ears, then slid off the great beast's back and sprinted towards the giant tardigrade, who stood up on his back legs, waving frantically. Perl jumped into his numerous sets of arms and he squeezed her tightly.

"Perly-poo!" Bear exclaimed in excitement. "It's you!"

"Oh, my sweet Bear, I've missed you so much," Perl giggled. Bear spun them around in a circle, then set her down. "How have you been? How's your arm?" Perl asked, eyeing where the boy lost his hand during the battle at the bog.

"One less hand for holding goo-tarts, but it doesn't slow me down! Let me get a look at-cha!" Bear held Perl's arms out, pointing at the small spikes protruding from her wrists, elbows, and knees. "Ooo, those are new!"

"Ooo, those are new!" Lyre mimicked Bear's voice as she landed beside them, tucking in her wings behind her tall, lanky frame.

Fluttering in closely behind her avian friend was Nan. "What she means is, your new spikes suit you." The arctic butterfly smiled, her proboscis nose curling outward.

"Nan! Lyre! You're here!" Perl hugged them both.

"Where else would we be?" Lyre teased.

Tars, Flax and Javan, hearing the commotion, all came bounding out of the woods. "Perl! You're back!"

Tars wrapped his long monkey tail around Perl's waist as Flax high-fived her. Perl was beaming; it felt just like the dream she had in the kitchen.

"You guys have all grown so much," Perl said, looking around at her friends. It looked as if they had all grown a foot taller since Seeker training. Tars now had a long mustache that curled up on the ends like his tail. Flax's salamander spots now shimmered and sparkled, full of stored solar energy. Nan's jawline was much more defined and her antennae had grown long and curly, while Lyre's feathers had grown thicker and brighter.

Although he had sensed Perl with his echolocation as soon as she had entered Venusto's atmosphere, Javan stood back waiting his turn to greet her. He noticed Perl was wearing the rabbit-rabbit totem he had carved. He had been too shy at the time to watch her open the gift, so was pleased to see it dangling from her neck. He swooped back his long bangs from his eyes and smiled over at her.

Perl glanced over and her breath stopped short in her chest. She tried to talk, but her tongue suddenly felt like a thick wool sock.

"Hello," Javan said, his cheeks burning.

His voice was deeper and his shoulders broader.

"Hello," Perl said.

A sharp "Caw! Caw!" pierced the air. Corvax circled overhead, breaking the awkwardness of the moment. The crow-boy landed with dramatic flair, the dark, shiny feathers rustling over his muscular arms. He had grown four black wings that folded perfectly on his back.

"Someone finally got his wings," Lyre chirped. "As if you weren't enough of a showman."

The crow didn't respond, but stared at Lyre with steely gray eyes; his face was stern, and the others fell quiet. Corvax stood in front of Lyre, then broke his act, cackling loudly. "Good to see you as well, my sister Air Seer," he teased.

"Oh...you!" Lyre poked him in the chest playfully, the mood lightening instantly.

Corvax nodded to Perl. "Chosen One, you ready for this?"

"Born for it, they say," Perl retorted.

"There's that wit, sharp as ever." Corvax crossed his feathery arms over his broad chest.

"Well, this is nicer than morning mist on a lilac petal," Bear bellowed.

Perl turned to Bear, "Everyone's here, except…what about Opis?"

Flax cut in, "We heard a rumor that she crash-coursed her way through Seeker training in order to be with us as Seers."

Perl looked around; other Seer groups were re-uniting in their teams of nine, each finding their treehouse where they'd be living. Over the buzz of conversation, a low rustling sound was heard deep within the trees, and everyone stopped to see what it was. From between a pair of baobabs emerged an enormous bagworm moth caterpillar, its elaborate log-filled back was stacked three stories high, the logs getting smaller as they ascended into a great pyramid of sticks. A familiar melody floated on the breeze.

"It's Grandmaster Olliv," Nan squealed with delight, hovering a few inches above the grass.

Sitting up front near the caterpillar's massive black head and gripping a pair of vine reigns was Olliv, the beloved green grasshopper. He smiled down at them, rubbing his hind leg against his wing, the vibration making a low harmonious tune, like a bow strumming a cello.

"Whoa, Whoa, Psychidae!" Olliv tugged firmly on the vines, bringing the giant creature to a sluggish halt in front of Perl and the others. Tipping his tall black stovepipe hat, Olliv addressed his audience. "Welcome back to Venusto, Venusto, and welcome home, home, to Greenheart!"

The Seers bowed their heads respectfully. The sound of Grandmaster Olliv's voice and his funny habit of repeating words made Perl feel like she was home again.

Olliv reached down and pulled a lever releasing two rope ladders, one up front for himself, the other from a round hatch set in the middle of the stack of logs. The grasshopper-man, old but still quite nimble, scurried down the ladder. He marched toward them, his ever-present baton with the yellow buttercup flower on the end held high.

"Seers-to-be, be. I bring you your ninth, ninth." From the stack of logs on the caterpillar's back, a tiny girl appeared, climbing down.

"Ha, ha, Turritopsis dohrnii reborn again!" Bear giggled.

"Opis the Wise is pint-sized!" Tars added, elbowing Javan.

The bright, shimmering girl daintily strolled over to her fellow Seers.

"Opis?" Perl was taken back for a second; the girl standing in front of her was half as tall as the one she remembered. She looked like a small child, wide-eyed, with a round, cherubic face, yet still had her translucent skin and glowing green and pink tentacle hair that sparked and crackled. Perl dropped to one knee, crouching down to look into Opis's vibrant blue eyes. "Is it really you?"

"Hello again, Sister." Opis smiled, throwing her arms out for a hug.

Perl was careful not to squeeze the delicate girl too tightly, but Opis pulled her in closer. "It's so good to see you again."

Bear, Javan, and the others gathered round the two, exchanging hugs and chatting until Grandmaster Olliv pounded his baton on the ground.

"Attention, Seers! Form a circle, circle. Every other, please…Air, Land, Water, and so on, so on. Lace hands, hands."

As they fell back into familiar formation, the grasshopper took his place in the center. Perl glanced around at the others; hands, paws and claws linked. Finding herself back in Venusto among her fellow Seers, each so funny and charming and unique, she remembered the greatest thing about being there; the feeling of wonder and possibility in this wild world of imagination.

"The circle, circle is the universal symbol of inclusivity. Together you are complete, complete, and unending. You can see each face, face easily in a circle. Each individual's words hold equal weight. This is a ring of trust. You are a family, family."

Olliv made a dramatic gesture with his flower baton, panning over to the treehouse. "The Philetarius socius have built you a home, home."

Perl took in the impressive new dwelling. *'Philetarius socius?'* she thought. "The Sociable Weaver birds built this enormous structure?! But they're so little!"

"Looks more like a great big haystack in a tree to me," Tars said.

"Built to hold your whole family, family, and large enough so that each will have their own chamber within, within."

"We get our own rooms, no more triple bunks," Nan sang with delight.

"I will return at daybreak to take you to your lessons, lessons. Afternoons are for battle training, training, as it was before."

All nine eyed the hanging thatched hut, eager to get to their space.

"Go, go!" Olliv waved his baton high over his head, motioning towards a baobab tree, then bowed and left to welcome the next group of Seers-in-Training.

Javan, Bear, Perl, Flax, Tars and little Opis raced across the pink grass to climb the spiral staircase, while Corvax, Nan, and Lyre flew straight up to the nest's large, circular door, landing on a balcony. The balcony, shaped like a half moon, had a floor made of heavy wooden planks. An intricate railing surrounded the porch; carved insects adorned the caps of each post.

"Hurry up, sloths!" Corvax chuckled, looking down at his fellow Land and Water Seers.

As Perl reached the top of the stairs, she leaned against the railing and took in the breathtaking view, the sweet smell of citrus filling her nostrils. From her vantage point, Greenheart was like a page from a storybook, with its fields of exotic flowers, rows of colorful lemon, orange, and lime trees, and perfectly-manicured garden walls.

"Phew!" Bear, with Opis sitting on his shoulder, was the last to reach the porch. He was dripping in sweat. "That's a lot of stairs."

They noticed that on the door was a sign with all their initials, 'T-F-P-O-N-C-J-L-B.' Around the doorframe was inscribed, "The Fearless Protectors Of Nature's Curious Jewels, Little to Big."

"Our secret code," Perl said, grinning her big, toothy grin.

"Well, what are we waiting for?" Opis insisted.

Corvax turned the scarab-shaped doorknob and threw open the door, illuminating a large central room. The domed interior was shimmering with organic life, quite the opposite of its brown straw exterior. Several Social Weaver birds flitted around room, adding last-minute details to their masterpiece. They decorated the room floor to ceiling in a magnificent mosaic of shells, pebbles, berries, and flowers. The highlight of the enchanting room was a portrait of each of the nine Seers above their bed chamber entryway.

Perl turned slowly in the round room, taking it all in. "They look just like us."

Javan saddled up beside Perl, "They even got your new hairstyle right."

"How did they know?" Perl twirled a strand of beads in her hair that perfectly matched the floral design on the wall.

"Birds know everything," Lyre winked.

In the center of the room was a giant eucalyptus pod that served as their dining table; a wooden bench encircled the table.

"Look, our new uniforms," Nan pointed to nine neatly-folded bundles placed around the table, each one with their name carefully stitched into the fabric with a thin blackberry vine.

Perl picked up her top, feeling the unearthly material, watching it shimmer and change color in the light. "What color is this? I know as Seekers we wore Harmony."

Opis, with a bit of effort, pulled herself up onto the bench. "It's called Humor. As Awakeners, we will get to wear the color Hope."

"Oh yeah, now I remember." Perl looked around; each uniform was the same iridescent color, modified to accommodate each Seer's individual physique. Perl's top, cool to the touch and light as a feather, had small openings for the spikes on her shoulders, elbows and wrists. On the back a scabbard was sown to harness Fortis, her narwhal tooth sword.

Corvax eyed Perl. "No need for the backpack this year, huh?"

Perl smiled, "I guess not." She ran her hand along the strap of her backpack, thinking back to the crystal cave when Uriel had given it to her; a gift from her father Noaa. A voice in her head whispered, *"You're growing up...time to move on from the things of childhood."* She swallowed, a slight ache in her heart.

Javan picked up an elm leaf from the table. "There's a message written on it." He read it aloud:

> *"Welcome, Seers, to your nest,*
> *A place to think, to dream, to rest.*
> *The beating heart of this humble home*
> *Lies where you sit, beneath the dome.*
> *Gather round, EVERyone,*
> *United together in laughter and fun!"*

"Ah, that's sweet," Nan said, snatching the leaf from Javan. She fluttered over to the front door and stuck the leaf to a thorn. "There, now we'll see this every day."

"Okay, let's get changed, settle in and meet back here in ten," Corvax said.

"Good to see 'Captain Corvax' has picked up where he left off," Flax teased.

Each Seer scooped up their new Humor uniform and ducked through the circular opening beneath their portrait. Perl stepped inside her new bedroom. The oval room displayed an ocean scene above and below, the entire area created with bits and baubles of nature, just like the main room.

"This is incredible," Perl slowly turned, taking it all in; soft white peonies and creamy rose petals formed the clouds; blue succulents and violets made up the sky. At the horizon, whales made up of gray pebbles and black peppercorns were breaking the surface in sparkly splashes. The lower part of the mural featured a coral reef, with schools of clown triggers, flame angelfish, pink pygmy seahorses, and bright green and yellow seaweed.

Perl ran her hand across the top of her bed, fashioned out of hundreds of fluffy green dianthus flowers. She tossed her new uniform on the bed and removed her backpack and heavy brown robe, taking notice of the bed's eye-catching headboard. It was a large vampire squid made from red dahlia petals with a turquoise blue eye made of shiny beads staring back at her. Perl pulled Fortis from the sheath, placing the sword on the bed. She stuffed her robe into the pack and tossed it onto one of the scallop seashell shelves jutting out from the wall when she spotted a sketchbook. Perl picked it up and smiled. "Thank you, Uriel."

She was excited for the gift, having filled almost every page of her old sketchbook, *"Perl's Wisdoms."* Written on the new cover in shimmering opalescent ink was the word *Wayshower.* Perl flipped to the inside front cover. The inscription read:

Unearth them so they may see,
by the gift of your loving nature.
Always and forever, Uriel

"No pressure," Perl joked, placing the journal back on the shelf. She reached into her backpack and pulled out a photo, leaning it against a small potted pilea plant at her nightstand. It was the only photo she owned; having such an item was rare. Brother Basil had an ancient camera and limited developing chemicals, so they agreed to only take one photo a year. This one was from her tenth birthday, taken in the root cellar kitchen where she's surrounded by every monk in the Brotherhood of the Quill. Perl was sitting in front of a decadent ten-layer cake Victr had made that was nearly as tall as she was. Papa Ximu and Victr were pressed in tight on either side, their arms around her. "Oh, Victr," Perl said, kissing her finger and gently touching Victr's smiling face.

Perl fumbled in her backpack, pulling out the old weathered box containing Victr's shelling knife and placed it on the shelf beside the journal. In her head came that voice. *You're not a child anymore, Perl. Time to grow up.* She took a deep breath, pushing away the hurt and finished getting dressed.

When Perl returned to grab a seat at the table, everyone except Bear was already there, chatting away excitedly. A meal had also been laid out with nine place settings. The warm, savory scent of carrots, potatoes and mushroom stew filled the air. Perl sat at the open spot between Opis and Javan, who was already ladling her a bowl of the bubbly broth.

"Thanks," Perl said, swinging her legs across the bench. "What's your room like? Mine has an amazing underwater ocean scene, and my headboard is this incredible vampire squid."

"Mine looks like the wetlands, with a burrow and a riverbank of tangled tree roots." Javan swallowed a spoonful of beans. "I think it's supposed to make us feel," he paused to smile at Perl, "at home."

"I can't wait to see what everyone else's rooms look like," Perl said, then paused as the explosion of flavors hit her. "Oh my gosh, I'd forgotten how good the food here is."

Bear came bounding in, bouncing on his hind legs. "How am I last to supper?" He squeezed in next to Perl and Opis, almost squashing the small jellyfish girl, who had to hold onto the table to keep from falling off her seat.

"Easy, big fella!" Opis's bowl splashed, spilling onto the table.

"Do you need a booster or something, Opis?" Flax giggled, leaning on his buddy Tars and chuckling. The two high-fived.

"I dunno," Opis sassed. "Do the two of you need bibs?"

The boys looked at each other; both of them had food dribbling down their chins.

Tars took hold of his long, curly mustache. "I have a built-in bib now, thank you very much." He dabbed at his mouth in an exaggerated manner, arousing a giggle from Lyre and Nan, who sat holding hands.

Perl stopped eating and looked around the table, seeing everyone dressed and ready for new adventures. "It's so wonderful to see all of you again. I've missed you all more than you'll ever know."

"Don't go getting all sappy, Wildflower, there's serious work to be done," Corvax waved his spoon at Perl.

"Do you always have to be such a jumble-gut, Corvax?" Bear blurted out, his mouth full. "Squawkety-squawk-squawk!"

The room erupted in laughter, even Corvax cracked a wry smile. The room practically vibrated with joy, everyone so happy to be reunited.

"I missed you Perl," Javan said. "I mean, we all did." He turned back to his bowl, letting his bangs fall down over his face to conceal his eyes.

"Javan, you know I..."

Outside, the sudden roar of a crowd interrupted Perl.

"What's all the warbling?" Lyre chirped.

The Nine rushed to their balcony to see.

"What are they doing?" Flax had his arm in the air, still with the habit of raising his hand to ask a question.

The other five Seer groups had left their treehouses and were congregating in the pink grassy area directly below Perl's balcony. A multitude of languages filled the air—Arcticali, Tropicali, Mountbic, Aurorish, Oceanian, and others. Unlike her first time coming to Venusto, Perl was able to adjust quickly to the otherworldly languages, and she realized they were cheering for her.

"The Chosen One has returned!", "She shines her Light from where no light shines!", "Nature will be restored!", "Now is the dawn of the Great Unearthing!"

Papa Ximu's voice popped into Perl's head. *There's a difference between being prideful and being proud, it is where humility and power rub shoulders. That said, a simple smile and a heartfelt thank you will never fail.*

As everyone including her friends looked at Perl, she did just that.

"Thank you, everyone," Perl shouted, waving down to the crowd.

Tars and Flax chuckled, also waving happily. Nan and Lyre sat perched on the railing, grinning from ear to ear as they softly fanned their wings. Opis stood on tiptoes trying to see over the railing before Bear picked her up, placing her on his shoulders.

"I guess the word has gotten out that you're back," Corvax said. The crow-boy launched himself off the railing, flying up to the top of their treehouse.

Perl continued to awkwardly wave, and as she did, a half dozen tiny hummingbirds with lavender butterfly wings landed on her. Now feeling a bit overwhelmed, she shot a quick side glance at Javan. "What do I do?"

The platypus-boy smiled, sensing her uncomfortableness, and placed his arm around Perl's shoulders. He and the others smiled and waved and hooted and hollered down at the cheering crowd, who seemed to be in no hurry to stop.

Once again, Perl heard Papa's soothing voice. *"Accept the good others see in you."* She cracked a big toothy grin, her bioluminescent spots glowing as she felt the rapid, steady beating of her three hearts.

20 NEUROPLASTICTY

Outside the haystack treehouses, the rising sun beamed across the morning dew, illuminating the grounds in a kaleidoscope of indefinable colors found only in the gardens of Greenheart. Perl was the last one down the spiral staircase; the others were standing alongside the bagworm caterpillar, staring up at the stack of logs piled high on her back, almost as tall as a three-story building. Flax and Javan were feeding the behemoth creature sycamore branches, watching it devour its breakfast like a chipper-shredder.

"All aboard, Seers, Seers." Olliv released the rope ladder over and down the side of the massive bagworm.

Corvax, Nan, and Lyre ignored the ladder, flying straight up to the door carved into the base of the bottom log. Perl and the others scrambled up the ladder, Bear bringing up the rear; the large tardigrade struggling on the ladder's wobbly rungs.

Once inside, the group took in the curious surroundings; from an opening in the ceiling, a ray of morning sunlight cascaded down to a round slate table surrounded by nine chunky boulders. Perl gave a double-take; the entire seating area was floating. In fact, everything in the room was. Teacups shaped like flowers with matching saucers hovered in the air. Dozens of strawberries the size of Perl's fist bobbed weightlessly around the table, while napkins drifted aimlessly about like little ghosts.

"What is this?" Tars giggled.

"Breakfast!" Bear pushed past everyone, pulling himself up onto one of the stone seats. He reached over, steadying himself, and yanked a strawberry out of the air, gobbling it down. "Mm...tasty!"

Everyone followed suit, each of them crawling on top of a boulder. A deep, low rumble was heard, and the lumbering caterpillar slowly began to move.

Swimming in silence above the group were a half a dozen red and blue betta fish. Each over two feet long, their feathery fins rippled and danced as they circled around the table, gracefully swooping to push an out-of-reach teapot or a juicy strawberry toward one of the Seers.

"Whoa, this is weird," Perl said, trying to maintain her balance while watching the others do the same. Flax sat next to her, his arms stiffly at his side, clinging to the stone with his slick, salamander hands. Perl cracked a devious smile at him, then grabbed his shoulder and spun him, laughing as the lizard-boy twirled in the air like a seasick ballerina.

Nan grabbed a cup of tea floating past her. "Honeysuckle, my favorite," she said, dipping her long proboscis into the flower cup.

As Tars nibbled a strawberry a betta swam by, snatching the last bite from him. "Hey, get your own."

Perl watched as the walls around them rumbled and swayed with the caterpillar's steps, yet suspended weightless on her boulder, she felt none of it. "I didn't think any ride could be better than our snail in Callowhorn, but this tops that for sure."

"It's the way of the Light Realm," Opis said, always ready to educate. "The higher the mindset, the more miraculous the surroundings."

"I've never made it to Seer status before. I've only ever been a Seeker," Flax interjected.

"Same here," said Tars, "I can't imagine what it would be like to be an Awakener in Natatory."

"So, this is all new to you guys, too?" Perl asked.

"Well, some of us have been here before," Bear remarked, pointing to himself with his multiple hands.

"It's true that none of us have made it through to the end of Awakener training, although several of us have seen the mountains of Natatory," Corvax said. "With Earth being so volatile now, most Seer trainees perish in the Half-Light Battles and cycle back to Seekers."

"The fact that the nine of us are back together again at the same time is rare," Lyre added, her motley plume of tail feathers waving playfully above her head.

"Finish up, up!" From a twenty-foot-long alpine horn attached to the wall, Grandmaster Olliv's voice echoed through the room. "We have arrived. Time to begin, begin!"

Like a locomotive pulling into a station, the bagworm moth caterpillar came to a slow, leisurely halt and the door swung open, filling the room with light and a rush of chilly air.

"Well, let's go seee," Bear emphasized the word. "What's in store for us...Seeers." He elbowed Javan, "Seee what I did there?"

"I see, alright. Clever," Javan slapped Bear on the back, happy to reunite with the joyful tardigrade once again.

The Seers jumped down from their boulders and moved to the door.

"Where are we?" Nan fluttered out of the opening, only to see they were thousands of feet in the air at the top of a mountain peak. "Oh," The butterfly-girl warned, "You guys might want to watch your first step!"

Just outside the doorway, three clouds the size of wagon wheels floated in a row in an endless blue sky. A few feet from the last one was a larger cloud; an enormous door rose up out of it.

Javan leaned out and looked up. "That door looks as if it goes on forever."

"Oh, this is like the clouds that lead to Palo Santo's greenhouse!" Perl held onto the caterpillar's doorframe, stretching to tap her foot on the white billowy puff.

"Wait. Perl, be caref—!" Opis cautioned, but Perl stepped off, leaping onto the small cloud confidently. The others gasped, then stood wide-eyed as the cloud held her.

"What was I thinking," Opis rolled her eyes, "she never looks before she leaps."

"It's fine," Perl replied. "They're just like stepping stones, c'mon!" Without a second thought, she leaped over to the door cloud.

"Come on, let's go," Corvax said. He, Nan, and Lyre fluttered over to the door, while Flax, Javan, Bear, Opis, and Tars leapt across one at a time, until all nine stood before the entry.

Olliv yelled over, tipping his stovepipe hat. "I will see you all this evening, evening. Enjoy your celestial adventure, ha, ha!" With that, he and the caterpillar began their descent back down the mountain.

"Ready?" Perl took hold of the large ornate-carved handle, pushing the massive door, which swung open as if weighing nothing and they stepped inside.

The group stood tightly bunched just inside the doorway when the door shut abruptly, leaving them in pitch blackness for a moment. As their eyes adjusted, they could see stars twinkling in the vast space around them.

"It's an observatory," Lyre chirped. A stairway made of twelve cotton-candy blue clouds materialized in front of them.

"Ascend," said a soothing deep voice from above.

The winged ones flew ahead, the rest climbed single file, moving cautiously except for Tars, who raced up the steps and reached the top first. He paused; stretched out before him was a floating plateau, the floor a myriad of dark colors swirling about like an oil slick. The monkey-boy tapped his curlicue tail onto the surface. "It's solid!" he called down.

Once they all reached the top, they saw two mountains to the east and west of them. Between them was a cluster of trees comprised of sparkling stardust. Standing in front of the trees and nearly as tall was a figure with a body like an elongated pyramid. The Being's head was a brilliant silver moon, whose glow was even more intense than the clusters of trees.

"*Amazing,*" Perl thought, taking a mental picture as the nine approached.

When they got closer, she realized that the Being's lower half was a tangle of curling, twisting vines dotted with bright white moonflowers nestled upon thick layers of heart-shaped leaves. Hiding among the lush greenery were hands of the same color, their long, slender fingers coiled in and around the vines.

An ethereal voice that sounded to Perl like numerous voices all at once welcomed them. "Around me, if you please…Air, Land, Water, form your circle," commanded the Light Protector Guide. "I am Gichi Manidoo Giizis. You may call me Master Gichi."

"The Great Spirit Moon," Opis whispered to Perl as the nine fell into place. Opis and the Master exchanged nods.

Master Gichi's head was indeed a moon that, as it spoke, shifted slowly
through the lunar phases, from full, to waxing, to new moon, to waning, and back again. A group of sea-foam green Luna Moths followed the changing light of Master Gichi's head. When in the new moon phase, Gichi appeared headless, yet the Seers could still hear their Guide's voice, "What is a Seer's purpose?" It asked.

Flax raised his arm.

"Speak."

"Seers help humanity notice the beauty of nature so they will tend to it, care for it, and preserve it."

"Precisely, and how does one do such a task, hmm? What say you, Opis the ancient?"

"We must transform the inner nature of mankind," Opis answered proudly.

"Indeed, the inner nature must come first."

Perl watched the moths happily dancing around Master Gichi. She looked at the Being with a head bright as a silver dollar, and it dawned on her how so many of the Beings in the Light Realm were neither male nor female. Perl felt her mind starting to wander when Gichi's voice brought her back to the present.

"Water!"

Perl felt a powerful pull on her chest, causing her to stumble forward a few steps.

Javan looked over, mouthing, "You, okay?" Perl gave a quick smile and wink.

Master Gichi was staring down at Perl, his face a full moon. "Affects the tides! Water is approximately sixty percent of the human body. As energy changes, as the Earth and moon orbit the sun, emotions and intuitions shift."

The Master raised its multitude of arms within the vines. Hundreds of hands reached skyward; a mass of hands around its neck wriggled about, giving the appearance of a strange green scarf. Perl also noticed that Gichi had scores of hands where its feet would be that propelled the Light Being along.

"You nine are vital. Apart, you have lost your collective song. You must regain your shared sense of flow. Harmonize once more." As Gichi spoke, the vines from its cloak began to grow, stretching out across the terrain under the Seers' feet. Master Gichi was gone, leaving a carpet of vines that continued to grow and expand, lifting the Seers high up into the air.

"Bear!" Opis called out.

"I got you, Jelly! Hold on everyone!" Bear shouted as the group dropped down, clinging to the vines.

After a few hair-raising seconds, the vines finally stopped. Perl looked down and felt her hearts race; they were now high above the ground on a wobbly suspension bridge connecting the two mountains. Each of the mountains had a face chiseled into their cliffside. The ends of the vine bridge were attached to their lower lips.

Above their heads, Gichi's voice could be heard. "Time for confluence."

Lyre cried out, "Wait...I...can't move my wings!"

"Neither can I," said Nan.

Corvax tried to fly as well, but his wings felt like lead.

Panic began to take hold of the Seers as they peered over the edge to the black bottomless void below.

"I'M AFRAID," the mountain to the right spoke, its booming voice making the bridge sway and bounce erratically.

"HOW AM I PART OF THE NINE?" replied the mountain to the left, shaking the bridge like an earthquake.

Everyone held on to the twisted vines for dear life as the mountains continued to banter back and forth:

"THIS IS IMPOSSIBLE."

"I'M NOT SMART ENOUGH."

"I FEEL LIKE A FAKE."

"WE'RE GOING TO FALL."

Corvax shouted over the mountain's deafening voices. "They're reading our minds!"

"KNOW-IT-ALL," shouted the mountain, causing Opis to lose her grip.

"Opis!" Bear quickly grabbed the tiny jellyfish-girl before she slipped between the vines.

"What are we supposed to do now?" Tars yelled.

"Gichi said it's time for confluence," shouted Flax. "We have to come together!"

"How?!" Nan and Lyre asked in unison.

The mountain to the right rumbled, "WILL MY LOVE BE RETURNED?" The bridge shook violently.

"Who thought that?" Opis yelled.

Perl closed her eyes and concentrated. *"I love you,"* she thought. *"I love* you."

"I LOVE YOU," the mountain on the left said. It sealed its mouth shut, holding one end of the bridge taut as it closed its eyes.

"Let go of the vines and hold hands," suggested Bear.

They laced paws, claws and hands as Perl sent a mental message to the other mountain. *"If you fall, I will catch you."*

The mountain repeated the phrase then closed its mouth, steadying the bridge.

Parting the clouds, Master Gichi's moon face, now ten times its normal size, beamed down at the Nine. "Rivers merge into one."

The Great Spirit Moon filled its cheeks and blew down onto the Seers, dissolving the bridge into bits. The group gently descended back to the solid ground of the observatory plateau.

"Well, that was unsettling," Flax giggled nervously.

Vines sprouted from under Master Gichi's chin like a beard, winding and coiling downwards, the hands and flowers reemerging as it grew. When it reconnected to the ground, the Being morphed back into its previous form. It strolled past the Nine, walking on its multitude of fingers. "You feared falling because you have fallen before. Negative thoughts arise when one feels out of control."

The group looked around at each other; they realized they were still holding hands. Perl noticed that Javan had his eyes fixed to his feet.

Its head changing to a waxing crescent moon, Master Gichi continued. "The brain does not like the unfamiliar. It is hardwired to make quick judgements and snap decisions based on past experiences."

The Light Protector Guide waved its many hands in the air, gathering stardust from the sky and, like a potter with clay, started shaping the stardust into an enormous brain that floated above the Seers' heads.

"This is one of the human brain's biggest flaws, constructing vague pictures of reality. Rarely do humans fully engage their senses. Therefore, they do not see the world as it truly is."

Master Gichi waved its arms, slowly rotating the brain. Sections of the left hemisphere turned from pink to a rot brown color.

"Evil embraces and uses this flaw to its advantage. The Ullen and its deceivers of the Dark Realm are masters at manipulating the mind. They take advantage of human blind spots. Redirect their attention. They lead humans deeper into superficial pleasures, corrupting their minds to form prejudices and hatreds."

A dark shadowy figure appeared behind each of the Seers; an eerie shadow of themselves. "Self-Slayers," Gichi uttered, turning on its fingertips and gliding back down the line of Seers like a general inspecting its troops.

The shadow figures began speaking to the Seers in low whispers.

"The negative thoughts you hear in your mind are not your true selves. It is your Self-Slayer. Created by the Dark One. It works its way into your mind. Poisoning you with false illusions and doubts."

Lyre plugged her ears. "How do we get rid it?"

"First, ask yourself, how does the Self-Slayer get in? What you bring to yourself, through words spoken or thought, attaches itself to you either as light or shadow. If you experience wrath and hate. If you will not allow yourself to forgive and love, the shadow will grow and fester, for you are feeding it. Over time, this Self-Slayer, born in your subconscious, will now control your waking mind. You see yourself as cursed—misfortune, injustice, dread all around you. The Ullen will gloat as it watches the Self-Slayer rule you. It is then that evil has won."

"How do we fight it?" Bear asked, turning and looking at the shadow of himself, then throwing punches at it to no avail.

"Neuroplasticity. Changing the brain. Brain cells that communicate together most often form our behaviors. Both positive and negative." At that moment, Gichi took an enormous inhale and blew; the nine Self-Slayer shadows shattered into bits of stardust.

"Much of life is what we grant power to. You must master your own heart. Overcome the perversions of the mind, those which are triggered by emotions. Otherwise, you will become bound to that which is not real."

"How?" Nan asked timidly.

"Re-imagine!" Tendrils of moonflower vines shot up from Master Gichi's cloak and wrapped around the brain, pulling it down into the Being's organic cape.

The Light Protector Guide then plucked two moonflowers from its shoulder, tossing one into the air. "Behold the Universe." The first blossom transformed into a cluster of galaxies. Gichi tossed the other flower. "Now witness the human brain cell." The flower magically transformed. "Are they not the same?"

Staring up at the two sparkling creations, Perl couldn't believe how similar the galaxies and cell of the brain looked. "But one is microscopic and the other is boundless. How can they be identical?"

"All has been perfectly designed. Ever wants humans to wake, to see that they are connected to all that is. Ever gives clues. Reveals truths hidden in nature. Humans must do more than look, they must open their eyes! Humanity, whose atoms are made of the ashes of stars, walk the earth with entire universes in their heads! Ha! Truly a gift!”

“So, if the Self-Slayers are winning this internal battle, how do we make humans see what they don’t want to see?” Corvax asked. “From my experience, this has been a constant struggle.”

“You are correct. The planet is in crisis because of this. Humanity must stop giving power to the negative. Make enemies into friends. Inharmony into harmony. Injustice into justice. To do so, they must no longer live in the past or want of the future. They must be in the now. Your purpose, Seers, is to show them what they have forgotten.”

“Simple enough,” Tars giggled, lightening the mood.

Opis looked over, “shh…”

Master Gichi reached up and tapped the image of the brain cell, triggering a burst of synaptic charges to ricochet through it like rippling strobe lights.

“Within each human is a divine spark. The Ever that is. Yet when their spark descends into the physical realm on Earth, that spark becomes hidden. We of the Light Realm must reignite the spark within. Fill them with the knowing they already possess.”

“Why does is it need to be hidden, this spark?” Perl asked, thinking of how she sees the essences of people, both good and bad.

“The divine is not in space,” Master Gichi replied, blowing the pictures of the human brain cell and the universe of galaxies away. “The divine is in love. No place was safe from The Ullen. Not the mountains. Not the seas. So Ever hid a bit of the divine in the heart of each living thing. This act served two purposes. One, it prevented The Ullen from finding it, and two, it gave humanity the chance to discover the secret…that they have held Ever’s love within them since birth.”

Perl was trying her best to wrap her head around all this; seeing the looks on some of her fellow Seers’ faces told her she wasn’t alone.

Gichi continued, his face slipping into the dark new moon phase. “It will take the full mandala of the Light Realm and the Light Bearers of Earth to turn the planet around. To fulfill its divine destiny.”

Perl’s thoughts went to her mother, making the prayer mandala on the beach.

Javan, quiet for most of the day, spoke up, “Master Gichi, how do we go about doing this, exactly? Destroy the Self-Slayers, get the humans to see nature’s magic, and help them find Ever’s divine spark in their hearts?”

The Light Being looked into their anxious faces, realizing that this had been a lot for the first day’s lesson in Greenheart. “More soup than the bowl can hold,” it said under its breath, smiling. Turning towards the stardust trees, the Being began plucking from several sparkling branches. “The more you imagine what you want, the higher it ranks on your mind’s priority list. Your conscious mind commands. Your subconscious mind obeys. Be wiser than the enemy, wiser than the enemies' thoughts! Slay every Self-Slayer's negative thought with a word of positive authority."

Flax snickered with his hand held high. "Is anybody else's head spinning?"

"Yep," Perl, Nan and Tars all nodded in agreement.

"It makes total sense to me," added Corvax.

"Sure it does," Opis teased her old friend and rival. "Do explain neuroplasticity to us all again."

"Let us remain confluent." Master Gichi, its face now a crescent sliver, raised an eyebrow at the two. "As I stated, there is an Ever spark in each living thing." Gichi held out nine arms; on each open palm lay a seed, plucked from the branches. "All have a tree sign governed by the lunar month of their birth. Air Seers, step forward." Gichi placed a seed into the crow-boy's hand. "Corvax, a Birch—Resilient, strong, a zealous motivator." Corvax stepped back, examining his treasure.

"Lyre, a Holly seed—Confident, stable and kind. Nan, an Elder—Loving, energetic, thoughtful." Gichi handed the Air Seers their seeds.

"Land Seers, approach. Javan, an Alder—Passionate, brave, the way-finder. Tars, a Hazel—An eye for detail, truthful, wise. For Flax a Hawthorn—Energetic, mysterious, a strong sense of humor." The boys bowed and stepped back into their place in the circle.

"Water, come forward. Opis, a Willow—Mystical, intelligent, a teacher. Bear, a Reed—Honor, charisma, a great friend. Perl, an Ivy seed—Protector, adventurer, way-shower to the will of the human essence."

"Ivy, really?" Perl questioned, "Not an Oak or a Pine?"

"You are an Ivy. Making connections, growing during the most challenging times."

"But Ivy, is that even a tree? Doesn't Ivy kill trees?"

"You're doubting Master Gichi?" Corvax checked Perl.

The Master raised its voice, "Hedera helix is misunderstood. It does not harm the tree. It is an evergreen that supports wildlife with its nectar, pollen and berries. Ivy uses other trees for support to better reach the sunlight. It has its own separate root system. It is not a parasitic plant."

Perl fiddled with her rabbit necklace. "Sorry, I didn't know all that. Guess I'm an Ivy tree then."

Gichi reached down, gently closing Perl's hand around her Ivy seed, whispering in her ear. "One that survives against the odds through adversity with grace."

From behind them, the observatory's grand crystal door opened, letting in a ray of sun.

Master Gichi was in full moon phase, smiling cheerfully. "Excellent first day. Bring your seeds to tomorrow's lesson. We will plant them so that you may begin to grow your bridge. Connect humanity to Ever." The Great Spirit Moon bowed to its pupils; the nine Seers returned the bow.

"Joy and good humor to you all. Your Olliv branch is here to collect you, haha!" Master Gichi gestured for them to follow the path of light.

Bear elbowed Javan. "Did ya' see what Gichi did there?! Olliv? Branch? Ha!"

Javan smiled at the tardigrade. "Yep, good stuff, Bear."

Glancing over his shoulder at Master Gichi, Javan hoped that the Guide didn't know whose thoughts were who's during the bridge exercise. However, as Gichi was fading from his waning crescent phase back into full dark mode, Javan thought he saw the Master give him a sly wink.

"Great," he thought to himself; the luminary knew.

The caterpillar dropped the nine Seers off in the middle of a sprawling field of lavender moss.

"This feels nice," Bear said, pacing back and forth on the soft spongy turf, "I could take a nap on this stuff."

"You could take a nap on an active volcano," Tars joked, jabbing him on the shoulder. Flax giggled and high-fived them both as the three of them clowned around.

Within minutes the sound of Grandmaster Olliv's familiar strumming faded, his lumbering caterpillar slowly crawling under the Greenheart Combat Fields' iconic stone archway and out of sight.

"I wonder who our Battle Guide is going to be?" Tars asked, pretending to use his tail as a sword, thrusting and dodging at Flax as the salamander threw his hands up in mock fear.

Perl had wandered off by herself and was eyeing the grounds, thinking the place looked a lot like the fields at Callowhorn. Hundreds of yards away in all directions, other Seer groups were meeting their new Guides.

"Hey Tars, here's your answer," Opis replied. "I believe there's a certain pongo headed our way."

"What's a pongo?" Perl ran back to the others, excited.

A majestic orangutan twice the size of a full-grown male marched through the archway, looking quite impressive in a Humor-colored chest plate, its strange translucent hue glistening in the bright sun. The Battle Guide's long, flaming red fur sprayed in all directions like fuzzy flames. The orangutan walked with his left arm out, where there sat a hooded falcon. The orangutan was singing as he approached, repeating a jaunty tune with the rich booming voice of an opera singer:

> *Dig, dig, dig,*
> *A-dig way down deep!*
> *Dig, dig, dig,*
> *A-see the creepers creep!*
> *Where mites and grubs*
> *And worms and slugs*
> *And other reapers reap!*
> *Dig, dig, dig,*
> *A-dig down underground!*
> *Dig, dig, dig,*
> *Secrets to be found!*

Coming to a stop in front of the Seers, the giant orangutan looked down at them; his swollen throat sac vibrating as he finished the last note of his song.

Along with his falcon friend, Perl couldn't help but notice the distinctive musky scent that the ape had also brought with him.

"Welcome to the fray, Seers. I am Elder Enoogoo," he smiled. He had a round face like a skillet, his flanged cheek pads framing a pair of closely set eyes that sparkled like shiny new pennies.

"Master Enoogoo," the nine Seers bowed.

Enoogoo raised an eyebrow, rubbing his chin with his free hand. "Did you not just come from your lesson on the brain?"

"Yes, Master, we did," Corvax answered.

"Yet you have you made this hasty decision!"

"What do you mean?" Nan asked shyly.

"You see me and you assume I to be your Master, even though I announced myself to be an Elder." As Enoogoo spoke, he untied the hood on the back of the falcon's head, whispering to the group, "I am merely the Celestial Companion."

Enoogoo carefully removed the leather rufter, revealing not the head of a falcon, but an iguana. What the Seers assumed was a beak was actually a hook of a horn jutting from the iguana's head. Slowly blinking its eyes to the light, the Being's golden, teal, and fuchsia scales refracted the light like stained glass windows.

Opis jumped with excitement, "Amblyrhynchus cristatus Falco! I should have known!"

"Easy for you to say," Bear chuckled.

"I give you Master Tanda, Seer of life and death."

Enoogoo announced, placing the hood into a pocket on his chest plate. He gently kissed the iguana on the head.

"The Fearless Protectors Of Nature's Curious Jewels, Little to Big," Master Tanda addressed The Nine, her voice deep and husky. "Have you come prepared to dig?"

"Yes, Master," they nodded. Perl wasn't sure if that meant literally or figuratively, but she was ready for either.

"No other species intentionally shapes its environment to fit its needs like the human race does. Thinking themselves supreme...that all else must bend to their will. Humans at the top, animals in the middle, plants at the bottom. A false hierarchy, indeed! Much is unseen to the eyes of humanity. The Light

Being lowered its head. "There is an army working tirelessly for the human race, directly below their feet. Enoogoo, please, if you will."

At Tanda's request, Enoogoo began thumping the ground with his fist. Within a few seconds, scores of earthworms began to wiggle up to the surface, squirming on top of the purple moss.

"He's charming them, mimicking the vibration of rain," Lyre announced to the group.

"They might also believe there's a mole burrowing nearby, looking for a worm lunch," Bear added.

Perl picked up one of the worms, letting it weave between her fingers.

"Behold, you are holding one of the most vital creatures on Earth, an integral part of the soil food web," Master Tanda lectured.

Enoogoo stopped pounding and the earthworms slithered underneath the moss and back into the ground.

"As worms burrow, they consume soil." Master Tanda spread her wings, lifting them upward. The ground rumbled, and a chunk of earth the size of a mattress emerged, levitating in front of the group.

The nine Seers inspected the rich soil, brimming with all sorts of life. They watched as the worms crawled through the soil. At the top section of earth, small plants sprouted like tufts of hair.

"The health of the soil depends on the worms to transport nutrients and minerals from their waste. Their tunnels allow air and water to circulate to roots, spiders, beetles, and nematodes." Master Tanda flew from Enoogoo's arm, landing on the top of the section of earth. "Look closer, Seers. Notice the delicate threads of fungi connecting the roots of one plant to another. There is a complex system at work here! One with a balanced system, where life gives life and death gives life."

Perl watched the soil, teeming with activity. She thought back to her days in Dimitri's lab, showing up in the morning and staying till sunset, studying creatures under his microscope while making sketches and taking notes.

"There's a whole universe here," she smiled. Being an "outside girl" her whole life, Perl was no stranger to bugs and plants and other jewels in nature; she knew how much life existed under rocks and old logs and hidden in the mud and grass and sand. Still, she marveled at it all.

"In the soil food web, energy is transferred from life producers—the plants, to animals, and to decomposers—the bacteria and fungi. Plants start this through photosynthesis; solar energy is captured, which creates organic molecules that supply energy for organism consumers, who then release nutrients up through the soil as carbon dioxide which the plants use."

"Also known as the poop loop!" Flax chuckled.

Tanda reached out, grabbing a talon of soil. "There is more life in this small bit of soil than there are humans on Earth. These organisms make it possible for life above to take place. Without earthworms, human extinction would be imminent."

As Tanda returned to Enoogoo's arm, the wall of soil sunk back into the ground; the moss growing back over it.

"Let us continue our call to fight for the survival of not just humanity, but all life on Earth! We go now to the Half-Light Realm." Tanda inhaled deeply, then let out a blast of a sneeze, spraying salt water like a sprinkler from her nostrils all over the surprised Seers.

"Hey!" The nine Seers closed their eyes, wincing, "What the—?"

"Gross," Nan and Lyre said together.

Corvax offered a gruff, "Ever bless you," squinting to try to see.

Perl was used to the spray of salty sea water, but this was different. She suddenly felt like she was floating.

The group wiped away the stinging saltwater, rubbing their eyes and trying to refocus. When their vision cleared, they realized they were no longer at the Combat Fields. The Master's sneeze had transported them to a muddy, rocky hillside. It was near dusk, the sky a deep red-orange. In a nearby oak tree sat Master Tanda; her companion Elder Enoogoo was nowhere in sight.

"Evil is unexpected," Tanda declared. "The Ullen is the ultimate corruptor. Like a bird of prey, you must be constantly aware of the next threat, as well as the next opportunity." Master Tanda waved a wing, and appearing in the mud in front of each of them was a sword, all except for Perl. She looked around at the others and shrugged, then armed herself with Fortis as the others grabbed their weapons.

"What do you see?" Tanda asked.

The Seers looked around; below them, nestled in a valley, a small cluster of houses could be seen, their tiny lights flickering in the darkening sky.

"There's a village down there," Lyre answered.

"Indeed," Tanda nodded.

Perl pushed her boot into the ground, the soil was soft and wet. She noticed the hill was barren; no grass grew, it was peppered with rocks and debris.

They felt a slight rumbling under their feet; small pebbles and bits of gravel rolled past them down the hill.

"There's something underneath us," Corvax said, lifting himself into the air to try to find a clue, but seeing nothing.

"To what end?" Tanda questioned. "Perl?"

"Um..." Perl looked around, quickly trying to assess the situation. The rumbling increased, and she watched as larger stones and clumps of dirt raced down the steep slope. Perl could see giant chunks of earth and a river of mud were bubbling up from a specific location about fifty paces above the group. "If that gets worse, it's going to cause a mudslide. And it's headed right for the town."

"It's getting dark and the people will be going to bed soon, they won't see it coming!" Opis added. As the ground below them began to shift and slide, Bear held out his arms, and the small jellyfish-girl hopped up to safety.

"This is gonna be bad!" Tars shouted. "What do we do?"

"Work together! You are a circle!" With those parting words, Master Tanda disappeared up into the clouds.

"A loud, guttural clicking sound got the Seers' attention. Up the hill, they could see something emerging from the gushing mud. A dark triangular shape burst forth from the hill, the clicking now deafening.

"Pipa, pipa!" shouted Opis, recognizing the head and snout. Her tentacled hair stood on end, sparking and zapping as she charged herself for battle.

Perl looked at Bear. "What the heck's a pipa?"

"A Surinam toad," Bear answered. "Nasty buggers."

Javan moved next to Perl. "They're ambush hunters."

The Seers closed ranks, swords at the ready, waiting and watching to see what the thing crawling out of the mud would do.

The toad, the length of two elephants, burst from its hideaway, its beady little eyes glowing red in the setting sun. It hopped up and down, the pounding causing even more sheets of mud to cascade downward. The creature turned, fixing its gaze on Perl and the others. Perl sensed a dark energy emanating from the creature. Instinctively, the spots on her skin began to glow and her spikes extended.

"Yikes! He's a big one!" Shouted Flax.

"You mean *she's* a big one," corrected Opis. "And from the looks of her, she's about to become a mother. See all those pockets on her back? Each one is carrying a fully-formed toadlet."

The putrefied skin on the beast's flat back was covered in a mass of honeycomb-like chambers, the clusters pulsating.

"No!" Nan dropped her sword and backed away, visibly shaken.

"Nan, what's wrong? Pick up your weapon!" Perl grabbed Nan's sword, trying to get her to take it.

Lyre took Nan's arm. "She has trypophobia."

"What?" Perl stepped in front of the two girls to shield them from the enormous toad. It let out a monstrous croak, hundreds of dead earthworms erupting from its mouth, covering the ground around its spindly webbed feet.

"It's the holes, their pattern can trigger a strong reaction in some." Lyre spun Nan away from the toad, gently taking hold of her antennae. "Look at me, Nan, you're fine, okay? Just look at me, don't look at that thing."

The spongy pockets on the Surinam toad's back began to ripple and bulge from the incubating toadlets it carried. The membranes stretched and pulsed as the froglets' long finger-like feet tried to break free. The creature hopped up and down violently, bellowing and croaking, its weight causing a deluge of loose soil and mud to pour down the hill. Perl wobbled, finding it tough to stand in the slow-flowing river of sludge. Corvax and Lyre took to the air, escaping the slippery muck.

Nan struggled to regain her confidence. "I'm okay...where's my blade?"

Perl handed Nan her sword as the Surinam toad belched again, this time in their direction. The group screamed as a sheet of decaying earthworms rained down on them.

"Gross!" yelled Bear.

"Agh, what do we do?!" Perl shook a handful of disgusting worms out of her hair.

"We have to get her to stop moving," Javan said, picking earthworms off the wings of Nan. "The more it moves, the more mud is pouring down the hill..."

"Where the people are," Tars added.

"*You* tell a possessed mother giving birth to stop moving!" Flax replied, shaking his whole body to rid himself of the worms.

"Let's form a—" Before Bear could finish his thought, the great toad leaped into the air, landing with a muddy splash in front of them. Without thinking, the tardigrade struck with his sword, slicing off the amphibian's front foot just as it was about to bring it down on Nan, who had again dropped her sword and was cowering before the grotesque beast. The toad stumbled and fell forward, moaning in pain.

Corvax squawked, "Good job, Bear!"

"Um, guys, I think we've got a bigger problem...they're hatching!" Tars readied his weapon as a host of cursed toadlets had escaped their pods. They scrambled off their mother's back in a mad frenzy, angrily snapping their jaws filled with razor-sharp teeth.

Perl saw Nan curled up in a ball and jumped in front of her, slicing down on a rabid toadlet before it bit into the butterfly-girl's wing. "Nan, come on! We need you!"

"I, I...can't do it." Nan flew up to the safety of the oak tree, covering her eyes with her wings.

A thick sheet of rocky mud and debris rolled down the slope, pulling more and more with it as it gained speed. Lyre and Corvax hovered in the air above the chaos, swooping down to strike at as many toadlets as they could. Perl,

Javan, Tars and Flax were jumping from rock to rock, hacking the monsters while trying not to get sucked into the landslide.

Bear, still holding Opis, stood steadfast as the sludge slid around his large frame, the tiny jellyfish-girl calling out would-be attackers.

"On your left!" Opis hollered, zapping a snarling toad with her electrified tentacle just as it came at Bear's head.

The sun was gone and visibility was poor in the darkness, the muddy river now a full-blown landslide as the crazed toadlets kept up their attack. Perl's bioluminescent spots helped create some light, and along with Fortis, she used the spikes on her elbows to help fight off the creatures.

"Flax!" Tars, seeing his friend losing his footing, reached out with his tail and pulled the lizard-boy onto one of the large rocks.

Bear was doing his best to stay upright, but the sheer force of the cascading mud forced him to drop down to all seven arms. Still holding Opis with his last free hand, the tired tardigrade-boy managed to scramble up onto a boulder as the muddy current pulled everything around it down the hill.

"I can't keep up!" Perl yelled to Javan, who knelt on one of the nearby rocks. "There's too many of them!" She could feel herself slipping.

"Look out!" cried Lyre.

The Surinam toad rose back up with a loud, ugly belch. It glared at them with its ruby-red eyes and hissed, then sprung down the hill and straight for the town, squishing and biting toadlets in her wake.

"Perl, give me your hand!" Javan reached out, grabbing hold of Perl's hand and pulling her over to him.

"But the people!" Perl, mud caked to her knees, managed to stand up.

Lyre and Corvax followed the toad as the rest of them stood helplessly on their collection of rocks, watching the beast and the avalanche of mud lurch toward the unsuspecting town.

"Ghiii-ghiii-ghiii!" Master Tanda's long wailing falcon's call rang out. Perl saw her glide over their heads and down the hill, circling back near the bottom of the slope just on the outskirts of the village. Tanda let out another piercing cry, and they witnessed an enormous hole opening in the earth directly beneath the falcon. From the hole came a haze of soft purple light, then a gargantuan creature emerged; a beet, five times the size of the toad rose up out of the ground, a bright glow emanating from its round, chubby body. From the top of its head sprouted a crown of leaves the size of sails.

"Oh great, there's another one!" Tars shouted to the others.

Blinking its three narrow slanted, pink eyes, the Light Being opened its mouth wide, dropping its bulbous chin to the ground where it sat motionless, waiting.

Squinting into the bright violet light, Corvax and Lyre, who had followed the toad down the hill, had to quickly bank to either side of the cavernous mouth of the beet-creature, to avoid getting swallowed.

The mudslide came crashing down like a great wave, straight into the gaping mouth of the beet. The Surinam toad, seeing the looming jaws of the giant beet, gave a croak and tried to backpedal, but couldn't. The toad, the river of mud, and all the submerged little toadlets were sucked into the Light Being's mouth.

Master Tanda let out another cry. "Ghiii!"

The Light Realm Being closed its mouth, lifted its head, pressed its palms together, and bowed to Tanda before sinking back into the ground.

The Seers raced to the bottom of the valley, seeing how close they had come to certain disaster.

"Thank Ever!" Tars wiped the sweat from his brow.

Perl watched as several villagers, having felt the Earth quaking, ran out of their homes, pointing up at the mudslide which had slowed to a stop. Perl knew that in the Half-Light Realm she and her comrades were invisible to those on the earthly plain. *They'll never know how close they came,* she thought.

"Circle!" Commanded Master Tanda.

The Seers fell into formation around their Battle Guide.

"What did you experience?" The lizard-falcon perched on a boulder, its steely eyes peering at each of them.

"We failed, Master," Corvax, the consummate leader, spoke up. "We failed terribly."

"Me most of all," muttered Nan.

"Remember, The Ullen is relentless! It strives to make you believe that you are not enough, that you are too weak to stand up in battle. Nan, you are part of the elected to stand with the Chosen One. To experience fear is not failure. Never doubt your worth." Master Tanda took a long, deep breath, then blasted the Seers with another explosive sneeze, casting them back to the mossy lavender surroundings of the Greenheart Battle grounds.

Elder Enoogoo was there to welcome them back. When the group materialized, the orangutan remained silent, observing their expressions; he knew it had not gone well. Sensing the master's approach, the Celestial Companion lifted his furry arm just as Tanda glided in, landing gracefully.

"We will continue our training next time with something a bit more light-hearted. Until then, remember you are a diverse web, and only together will you control the spread of disease. If not, the ripple will be catastrophic." Tanda closed her eyes to rest.

Enoogoo leaned down, kissing Tanda gently on her head before placing the hood back on. The orangutan smiled and bowed to the Seers then headed towards the archway, humming the digging song softly as he ambled away.

Just outside of the battlefield gate sat Grandmaster Olliv atop the bagworm, leisurely puffing on his pipe. At the sight of The Nine, the cricket gave a jolly come-hither with his buttercup baton.

They climbed aboard, each taking their seat on a floating boulder, no one saying a word. They were exhausted, beaten, and covered in mud and scratches. The beta fish circled above them, offering giant peppers, broccoli and other vegetables.

Bear let out a long heavy sigh, reaching up to yank a floating carrot passing by. "Guess it was a good thing that battle beet could BEET more that it could chew?! Huh? See what I did there?"

Everyone sat quietly, looking at each other and trying not to crack a smile at the tardigrade's terrible joke.

"For BEET'S sake, Bear," Javan broke the silence. The others broke, giggling uncontrollably.

"What? He was unBEETable!" Bear relied.

Truly un-BEET-lievable!" added Tars, high-fiving Flax.

"BEET you can't think of another BEET pun!" Perl joked.

As the group joked and relaxed, the bagworm crawled along the winding pathway, the stack of logs on its back swaying to-and-fro methodically.

Reaching the shoreline of Greenheart, the caterpillar waded out into the sparkling alabaster lake, floating silently away from the island back to the mainland of Venusto, where the official welcoming ceremony from Divine Master Tryfon would take place at Dragon Maw.

"And we're here, here. Seers, after you've eaten dessert, just follow the path back, and I will be waiting, waiting." Grandmaster Olliv said farewell to The Nine, leaning back in his seat high above the ground on the bagworm, closing his eyes for a well-earned nap.

From the large floral archway in the shape of a fire-breathing dragon, Perl inhaled the delicious smell of fresh baked cookies, sweet honey, and tangy citrus. The savory aromas were making her mouth water.

Under the arch hung a sign, greeting the diners into the park:

~Welcome to Dragon Maw~

Below that, there was a quote that changed with each new cycle of training:

"Love isn't a whisper, it is a symphony
to be played for all the Earth to hear." ~Tryfon

An even smaller sign hung below that:

Mind the manners of your mind and remember— push in your toadstools!

Filing through the gate and into the bustling crowd, the nine Seers kept a tight circle as they searched the enormous dining garden for available seating at one of the Dracena Cinnabari tree tables.

"Over there, come on," Bear pointed.

The area was filled with a mingling of buzzes, grunts, growls, laughter, whistles, whoops, and other curious sounds. The garden was framed by poplar trees, standing in rows like tall green guardians around the diners. Perl still had to once again pinch herself that she was a part of this magical world, inhabited by the most fantastic Beings she had ever seen or could ever imagine.

"Uh, guys, what's going on?" Tars asked the others. As the Seers passed by table after table, Beings bowed in reverence, some even tossing flower petals on the path or reaching out to touch them, while others repeated, "Ever-lasting. Ever-more. Ever-lasting. Ever-more."

A misty kaleidoscope of color began to twinkle in the center of the garden, and the tall, glowing figure of Divine Master Tryfon materialized. His three sets of glorious wings— one pair raised above his head, a pair at his sides, and two more that lay across the front of his legs— radiated with white ethereal light. The mystic's head contained three faces that gazed lovingly back at his students. Tryfon's center face was that of a human, ancient and wise, but the ones on either side kept altering their appearance, changing from a leopard, to a bat, to a barn owl, to a crocodile, and so on. The Master's skin also kept transforming, going from tree bark, to feathers, to scales; endlessly changing. In one hand, he held his large white walking stick, a beautiful, intricate carving of hundreds of animals stacked on top of one another. Tryfon tapped the ground three times, and the garden fell silent.

"Welcome back, Seekers, Seers, and Awakeners. Come ye into unity, to our community of Light." Tryfon gently waved his walking stick through the air like a paintbrush; a cascade of blue birds materialized, soaring into the air with a chorus of chirps. "When a bird remains too long on the ground, its wings grow weak, its feathers heavy. Then it rises, flaps its wings, takes to the skies. The longer it flies, the more blissfully it soars, refreshing itself, alighting back down to Earth only when necessary. So is it with humanity...the wings of love must elevate them from the desire for earthly wants. Humans must prepare themselves in this way...to come to Ever."

Perl listened intently, recalling Divine Master Tryfon's cryptic way of speaking. She watched as Tryfon stroked his long beard of purple pansies, which then morphed into pinecones, then chinchilla fur, then a fuzzy green covering of pincushion moss, all in a matter of minutes.

Tryfon glided slowly between the tables, speaking in a soothing tone, yet loud enough so that all in the garden could hear. "A Light Realm Protector's purpose is to watch over the many forces of nature. The animals. The wind and rivers...the seas and the forests. You are the bulwark between humans and the realm of almighty Ever...but the time is approaching for us to work in harmony with humanity."

There was an audible gasp and murmurings from the tables as Beings crowded together in whispers. "Work with the humans?", "This is unheard of!", "We are the unseen!"

The Divine Master held up a hand and the garden fell silent once more. "The Chosen One...carries the pattern of a unified global order in her three hearts."

Every Being shifted on their toadstools to look at Perl. With the eyes of the entire room on her, Perl's bioluminescent spots lit up, forming a halo of light around her and her fellow Seers.

"Good call, Perl...just in case no one could see you," Tars joked under his breath. Bear and Flax giggled. Corvax rolled his eyes.

Tryfon continued. "Still, the Self-Slayers living among the human beings and the multitudes of Dark Realm corrupted creatures on the Earth do not want us to rise in unity. Rather, they prefer to drag us down to their level...that of the electrical, the mechanical, the atomistic...this is the realm of The Ullen, and they are prevailing." The Divine Master had now made his way to where Perl and the others were sitting, the intensity of his glow even outshining Perl's bioluminescence.

"Dedo?" Perl called the Divine Master "grandfather." His kind, loving presence felt like being wrapped up in a warm, toasty blanket.

"Yes, my child?"

"Why does Ever allow The Ullen to...to..." Perl stared into Tryfon's hypnotic brown, green and gold flecked eyes and lost her train of thought.

"...To exist?" Tryfon smiled, finishing Perl's question. "Because of love...and love is all that exists."

"I don't understand." Perl gently ran her hands along the Master's cloak, now teeming with wildflowers. She was about to pluck a bluebell off when Javan reached over, quickly grabbing her hand and holding it.

One could hear a pin drop, as everyone in Dragon Maw listened attentively.

"The Ullen was Ever's favorite Light Being, placed upon the Earth to serve humanity...yet seeing the love Ever had for the Earth and the humans as Ever's children, The Ullen's jealousy turned to rage. It refused to believe humans to be worthy of Ever's love. The Ullen's self-love was rooted in illusion and doubt, yet it grew powerful. A dark, poisonous power. It began luring other Beings away from the Light...where in time, they rebelled against Ever.

"That's what started this whole war?" Perl asked.

"It is. And through the machinations of The Ullen and his other Fallen Light Protectors, humankind continues to destroy its gift of the planet. It is our task to bestow upon humans the grace to recognize that we are working for them, and to help guide them to see the invisible in others...in this, their awareness will be born."

"Divine Master Tryfon?" Corvax found the courage to speak to the great Light Being. "We understand that the Prophecy is indeed real...that Perl is the Chosen One."

"To shine a light where no light shines," Tryfon nodded, repeating a passage.

Corvax continued, "But surely there are greater Masters, Guides and Elders in all of Venusto better suited for the task than…us?" The crow-boy gestured around the table as all of Dragon Maw looked on. "No offense everyone." Corvax cleared his throat.

Perl looked at each of her friends and smiled a toothy grin. There was no one else she wanted with her, in this world or any other, than the eight of them.

Tryfon closed his eyes. "We live surrounded by all things. Like fish we swim, navigating both the material and immaterial worlds, matter and thought. At times we perceive one moment, at times another, and it is only much later, after having traveled many currents and having new experiences pass through our gills that we are able to understand the meaning of an earlier moment." He pressed a hand on Corvax's shoulder and Corvax nodded, understanding Tryfon's answer to mean he and the others would find out someday why they were chosen for the task, but when that day would come remained to be seen.

"How can we help them see the good in each other?" Perl pushed for more clarity.

"In compassion we find connection...to feel the passions of another's life...to share in their sorrows...that is the pathway humanity must discover."

Perl caught a glimpse of Javan looking at her. She realized she was still holding his hand and awkwardly let it go, wiping her sweaty palm on her thigh.

Javan let his bangs fall over his eyes, feeling his cheeks warm.

Tryfon raised his voice. "One cannot enjoy the fruits of a tree never planted. Give perfect love and you will receive perfect love...demand nothing in return."

Tryfon's glorious sets of wings began flapping, lifting the mystical figure up, where he hovered above the line of poplar trees. "Now is the dawn of the Great Unearthing...we shall do it not *for* humanity, but *with* humanity."

The Divine Master of Venusto vanished in a bright flash, leaving behind a rainbow of twinkling lights sparkling in the sky. Seekers, Seers and Awakeners began to sing out, "Praise be to Ever! To Tryfon! To all of nature!"

One of Dragon Maw's servers, an enormous Persian cat, appeared at the table, carrying numerous trays of delicious-looking desserts. "Help yourselves," the cat purred, placing a tray in the middle of the table before slipping between the crowded tables.

"Don't mind if I do," Bear said, grabbing two orange gooey tarts and gobbling them down in one bite.

The food in Venusto was indescribably tasty, but Perl's head was elsewhere. "Why did everyone seem so surprised when Dedo—um, Master Tryfon—said the time was coming to work with humanity? Haven't we always done that?"

Opis snagged a pink puff pastry, holding onto it with both hands. "We Light Beings exist on a higher vibration frequency, so even though some humans may feel a weird tingling sense or get a strange feeling in their bones, they've never been able to physically perceive us. We have only ever helped them see the magic of nature through our work in the Half-Light Realm, in the unseen dimension."

"Okay, so?" Perl helped herself to a treat.

"So," Javan chimed in, "in making such a statement, Tryfon is declaring that the age of the sacred invisible is coming to an end."

"Again, so?"

Opis sighed, "Well, on the one hand it could be disastrous for Earth, and on the other, there is the potential for the most glorious Light transformation the human species has ever known."

"A global disaster?" Perl felt a wave of panic run through her three hearts.

"If humanity doesn't wake in time, Darkness will reign and death will spread across the Earth, ending all of life," Corvax chimed in.

"In other words, the fate of the world rests on our shoulders," Nan said, a slight tremble in her voice.

"Might as well have seconds then," Flax smiled, swiping a raspberry cake, trying to lighten the mood.

"Not just us. We have our role to play, but we aren't alone," Bear added, "We're working together with all the Lightbearers on Earth, too."

Perl thought of the Forest Sisters of Elsewhere, working to save the children in the Under Kingdom. She thought of Dimitri's mushroom research, and Gretar and all the Earth Activists on Mont Michel.

"Now that the Codex of the Sacred Invisible is being shared in the Under

Kingdom, the age of secrets will come to an end. Humanity will awaken. They have to," Perl said.

"If the Earth is to have a future, they will have to awaken," Lyre chirped.

Bear swiped another tart from the tray. "This one's for you, future self," he said, tossing it into the air and catching it in his mouth.

"Bear, did you just say, future self?" Perl asked, recalling the title of Victr's note that she read at his funeral.

"You know...for that mysterious, blameless somebody-self. The one who, in the future, will have to live in the world that I have left for him." Bear smooshed two more desserts into his pockets. "You have to be your own best friend first, and mine likes gooey-gumbles!"

Perl couldn't help but smile at her beloved Bear. "You are full of wisdom, my friend," she poked him. "Not to mention quite a few treats!" Perl wiped a glob of goo from Bear's sleeve, tasting it; the candied caramel flavor awakening every taste bud on her tongue.

As the hours slipped by, Dragon Maw had all but cleared out, but Perl and her companions didn't want to go. They stayed long into the evening, laughing, eating desserts, swapping tall tales, and recounting stories of Callowhorn victories, rekindling their bond and forgetting at least for a moment that the weight of the world's future rested on their shoulders.

Morning skies gave way to bright blue as the mid-afternoon sun greeted the Seers, who stood patiently outside the glass greenhouse in the middle of Greenheart's main garden.

"Hi," Javan plunked down beside Perl, who was doodling in her sketchbook. "Whatcha workin' on?"

"Huh? Oh, nothing really, just jotting down some thoughts." Perl snapped her sketchbook shut.

"Feel like sharing?" Javan pulled at the grass.

Most of the Seers were busy chatting, while Tars and Flax pressed their faces against the greenhouse windows, trying to peer through the steamy glass for a glimpse inside.

Perl gave Javan a sheepish glance. "Well, right before I came back to Venusto, Brother Victr passed away."

"I'm so sorry, Perl," Javan put his furry arm around her. "Why didn't you say anything?"

"Because, honestly? I still can't believe it. I was with Victr every day of my life, and now he's just gone and I have this giant hole in my heart."

"You can never be prepared to lose someone you love, but you can at least take comfort that he is in the Light now."

"That's just it, Javan, he isn't." Perl's voice cracked. "Something evil took his essence. I was there. I saw it in his eyes. When he died, he was terrified."

"You're sure?"

"With all my being, I know Brother Victr isn't at peace! And somehow, I have to find him. I was thinking of going back to see Master Humboldt...maybe he'll know where there's a portal or some other way to reach Victr."

"Not Humboldt," Javan paused. "But I might know a way. If what you're saying is true, then Victr might be in The Unforgiven."

"What is that?"

"I really don't know a lot about it. My mother-figure, Anaya, has described it to me before. It's a realm...like a holding place...for humans."

"Go on," Perl was fixated on his every word.

"Well, when humans die, if they carry with them heavy burdens, like self-doubt, feelings of unworthiness, anxiety or misgivings, a dark force can prey on them, drawing them into a place called The Unforgiven."

"But that doesn't make sense! Victr was the kindest person I've ever known. He was sweet, and funny, and forgiving!"

Javan nodded, "Perl, I believe you. I'm sure he was forgiving of others, but...maybe not forgiving of himself?"

Perl furrowed her brow. "What do you mean?"

"Victr was too good of a man to be taken to the Dark Realm, but if, like you said, he died scared and in distress, perhaps he was troubled, and there's a chance he's trapped there."

Perl was now more uneasy than before. "Javan, I know you want to help, but you don't know what you're talking about!"

Bear and a few others had heard Perl raise her voice and came over. The tardigrade-boy bounded in. He bent over, putting his face in Perl's. "Tell us, Perly-poo, what did platypus-face do to get you all upset?"

"Is it a sweethearts' quarrel?" teased Lyre, giggling with Nan.

"What? No! And we're not arguing," Javan jumped up. "Right?" He smiled at Perl, holding out a hand to help her to her feet.

"Right." Perl wasn't sure which part she was agreeing with.

She grabbed the platypus-boy's hand. *"Sweethearts?"* The word swirled around in her head. Perl liked Javan, and she had worn the rabbit-rabbit totem around her neck since the day he'd given it to her a year ago, but 'sweethearts?' She looked up at Javan and cracked a smile. "Sorry."

Javan flipped his long dark bangs out of his eyes. "No worries."

"So, can you get me into The Unforgiven?" Perl leaned over and whispered so the others wouldn't hear.

"Give me some time. I'll see what I can do." He squeezed her hand.

"Someone's coming." Opis had her hands cupped, her face pressed up to the glass doorway.

Hearing this, Perl rushed over to Opis. "Who is it? Is it Palo Santo?" Just as Perl said this, the translucent doors swung open.

A swarm of iridescent hummingbirds in the distinct figure of a woman, fluttered before them, filling the doorway. The birds parted, and standing before them was the Master Gardner herself, Palo Santo. She was both regal-looking and ethereal, her hair a bouquet of tropical flowers, green moss, and blossoming vines that fell softly to her milky white shoulders. The hummingbirds hovered over the Garden Nurse's head like a halo.

"Hello again," Palo winked at Perl; her sky-blue eyes, deeply set in her cherub-like face, twinkled like sapphires.

"I was hoping to see you again," Perl smiled a big toothy grin.

"And I, you." She turned to the others. "Welcome, Seers. Did you all remember to bring your birth-tree seeds with you?"

The Nine nodded.

"Very good. Now follow me and please stay close." Palo spun; her large straw sunbonnet tied around her neck hung casually down her back. Her lustrous dress, resembling an interlacing pattern of flowers, bees, berries and butterflies, cascaded down to her bare, muddy feet.

"This greenhouse looks different every time I enter it," said Nan, hovering in the air close behind Palo Santo's hummingbirds, which darted about poking their long beaks into the sprigs of lilacs and roses in Palo's hair.

Lightning cracked and zapped across the glass ceiling of the greenhouse. Perl and the others jumped and ducked with each bolt, all except for Corvax, who maintained his usual stern composure.

Palo stepped quickly from one paving stone to the next, smiling in awe. As the group moved down the path, colorful exotic flowers sprung up on either side of them. They blossomed quickly, reaching up and across the pathway above the Seers' heads, forming a tunnel of lush, fragrant flowers that twisted and thickened until the group could no longer see through them.

"Please keep all arms and wings at your sides." Palo Santo's voice was sweet and gentle as an April breeze.

"It's like being inside a kaleidoscope," Perl marveled. She walked behind Javan, with Bear behind her. The group was forced to move in single file, the floral tunnel closing in even more, the myriad of colors swirling around them.

"Ouch!" Tars yelled from the back of the line. "Something just yanked a hair from my mustache!"

"What the—?" Corvax jolted. "They took one of my feathers!"

"Thorn Fairies," Opis informed the group. "Sneaky little prickles! Watch yourselves."

Perl looked into the thicket, her eyes narrowing; hidden amongst the flowers were tiny fairies, each about the size of a crabapple. The tiny creatures were covered in spiky thorns with fuzzy burrs for heads. They sat perched on vines or balanced on top of flowers, giggling mischievously. Perl could see scores of them now, hundreds perhaps. The fairies watched the Seers closely as they meandered past then jumped at them. One of the fairies landed in Perl's hair.

"Hey!" Perl shook her head, reaching for the tiny fairy as the creature laughed and snorted, gripping a yellow bead woven into a braid. "Back. You. Go!" Perl got a hold of the fairy's spiky body and tossed it, bead and all, back into the swirling growth. The fairy snickered as it sailed into the flowers, holding tightly to its newfound treasure. "Those little critters are sharp," Perl sucked the blood from her thumb. At that moment, she quickly flashed back to the day in the Sisterhood's grotto, when she had sworn the blood-oath with Amanita.

"Prickly, yes, but they mean no harm," Palo Santo replied. "Life is a beautiful garden, an ever-growing, always changing entity." She raised her voice as they reached the end of the tunnel. "Remember, Seers, all that an individual desires already lies on one's pathway, but one must be awake to our better selves in order to bring it into manifestation." She waited patiently until the last Seer hurried through the exit.

Tars ducked through the archway; his monkey-fur covered in giggling burr-fairies. "A little help, please?"

Lyre was about to assist in the fairy removal when Palo Santo interrupted, "Not to fret." The Light Gardener swirled a hand above her head, gathering her swarm of hummingbirds who were always close by. Palo then pointed at Tars and the birds darted at the monkey-boy, who closed his large bulbous eyes, his curlicue tail tucked between his legs, bracing for impact. Seeing the birds approaching, the Thorn Fairies gave a shrill cry, releasing their grips and retreating back down the garden tunnel in a chorus of teeny-tiny laughter.

The flower tunnel had emptied the Seers onto a wide-open field of short, stubby grassland, and now it was suddenly almost nighttime, the sun dipping like a cookie into the milky horizon. "How long were we in that tunnel?" Perl wondered aloud, "And where are we?"

There was a small pond to the group's right where a waterfall emptied, churning and gurgling. Perl looked up, seeing the silver spout stretching up through the puffy lavender clouds and beyond, as if the water fell from the stars themselves. A light mist danced and swirled over the surface of the pond, cooling the Seers with glistening dew as they got closer.

Before anyone spoke a word, Master Gichi appeared through the clouds, with only his full-moon head floating, not his vine-covered body. As the luminous glow from The Being met the waterfall's spray, a circular lunar rainbow arched across the night sky.

"Whoa, a moonbow!" exclaimed Flax. "Those are really rare!"

"Conditions must be just right for one to occur," Opis added matter-of-factly. "A full circle moonbow is actually known as a glory."

"Correct, young Opis," Palo Santo added. "And each of you see the phenomenon slightly differently depending on your vantage point. The droplets of mist refract the moon's light uniquely for you."

"Also," Opis cut in, "all rainbows are circular because the droplets are spherical. When the light enters the droplet, it is reflected back inside a cone with a half-angle of forty-two degrees."

"Okay, All-Knowing Opis," Bear chuckled, rolling his eyes.

"Again, she is correct," Palo said. "Rainbows are not arches, but circles. From the ground, the Earth's surface blocks the rest of the light, so the halo appears simply as an arch."

"Today's lesson," Master Gichi's voice echoed from above. "Unblock that which holds you back from witnessing your full light." The Master's bright full moon face had changed to a half moon.

"Please form a circle," Palo Santo gestured.

As the Seers stepped into their meditative formation, a square patch of dark soil appeared in front of each of them.

Palo continued, "Soil is the largest storer of terrestrial carbon on Earth." She walked away from the group to where a stream broke off from the pond, snaking off into the darkness. In it, a number of swans were floating by, glowing bluish-white in the surrounding darkness.

"Soil restores the land back to its natural state, assisting in ecosystem repair. Now, dig a hole and plant your seed." Palo reached down, carefully scooping up a large swan. "Today you will cleanse that which is not in service of your highest self, so that you may return to the circle...free, true, and connected once more."

Each Seer kneeled down and dug a small hole, planting their birth-tree seed in front of them. Palo Santo stepped into the circle, holding the swan under one arm. As the Garden Nurse stopped at each of The Nine, the swan lowered its head, pouring water from its open beak. The seeds instantly began to grow; sprouts turned to saplings, then into full grown trees in the blink of an eye, each of them matching their Seer's lunar birth month.

Master Gichi's voice echoed from the sky, "Sit. Rest your back against the trunk. Close your eyes."

Everyone did as he instructed, yet Perl's ivy didn't have a trunk so she laid on top of the leaves like a mattress. As she did, the vines curled around her arms and legs and across her stomach in a soothing embrace. Palo Santo returned the swan to the stream then sat quietly at the water's edge as Gichi continued the lesson.

"Inspiration comes from the word 'inspire', to breathe in. Close your eyes. Take in a deep breath. Feel the oxygen from your tree filling your lungs. Exhale with a silent "thank you" to your life-giving tree. Germination, the blueprint of the tree, exists within its seed. It instinctively knows to reach out into the soil to find the nutrients it needs. And you are the gardener of your own mind. Your conscious plants seeds in the soil of your subconscious. Your thoughts, your focus...become the blueprints for your possibilities."

Master Gichi lowered himself to where he now stood in the center of the Nine. His organic body of moonflower vines had reattached, and once again he was whole, supported by his multitude of hands.

"Do not plant seeds of doubt and fear in your mind. Trust the seeds of your hopes and dreams. Connect to your higher self, not the negative voice of the Self-Slayer. If one hears the voice that judges, self-loathes, or blames others to make oneself feel better...recognize the voice, acknowledge it, and let it pass. Send the negativity into the ground. To the very roots of your tree...to be recycled into Light."

Each Seer began to have visions as Gichi's calming voice guided them. "Notice the nature of your thoughts as you drop deeper...concentrate on your breath until the moment becomes alive. Be curious rather than entangled with the emotional charge of what you are seeing. Be willing, not willful."

Three of the Seers saw their past:

Bear's memories took him back to a time when he was frozen in a cryobiosis state, awaiting the ice crystals inside him to thaw; bored, frustrated and alone.

Nan's mind traveled to when she was just a caterpillar on her very first Light Realm battle training lesson. Suddenly scooped up by a mother Gouldain Finch, Nan found herself squirming for her life, dangling over the crying chicks open mouths filled with tiny, bright papillae nodules. Nan sensed her own panic, nausea, and fear of death, realizing this was the source of her trypophobia.

Tars's vision took him to Siau Island in Indonesia on the day the last of his species died in his arms. Thoughts filled his head—*Could he have done more to save their threatened habitat?* Tar's heart ached as he witnessed his own grief and despair.

Four of the Nine had a glimpse of their future:

Javan found himself reading the rings of an ancient tree stump in the Daintree Rainforest in Australia, one of the last old-growth forests. Flanked on either side of him were two Cassowary birds, each tapping their razor-sharp middle claw on the tree's rings as Javan deciphered the tree's message. Tears rolled down his furry cheeks.

Lyre and Corvax had a similar vision; the two of them were fighting a fierce battle in the night skies of Venezuela, where the Catatumbo River meets Lake Maracaibo. In this volatile region, lightning strikes one hundred and sixty days of the year, flashing for eight hours at a time, turning night into day. Armed and ferocious, they soared between lightning strikes alongside battalions of Air Light Protectors, fighting bravely but suffering heavy losses in a raid against a host of Dark Realm Parasites.

Flax's mind flashed to a future Earth, one in which the ozone had depleted to a point at which a sun flare over-charged his solar powered skin. He felt his body ignite and combust into a ball of fire. Flax cried out and woke, visibly shaken.

Opis's vision remained in the present:

Her tentacle-like hair blew gently back and forth in the breeze, perfectly in sync with her Willow tree's long reeds. She sat completely silent with her back pressed firmly again the trunk, listening to the water from the ground pumping upwards into the crown—the heart of the tree—slow and steady, like a drumbeat. She smiled softly.

Perl wasn't sure where she was. She saw herself waist deep in the folds of a squishy, undulating desert that seems to go on forever. *'Where am I?'* She heard herself wonder. *'This is not a memory.'* Suddenly all around her, people began bobbing up and down in the soft, spongy landscape like buoys in the ocean, their faces etched in sorrow. Perl spotted a spider's head and spindly legs bobbing not far from her. *'Victr?'* Perl pushed down on the surface, pulling her knees up so she could crawl across the surface; her bioluminescent spots glowing brightly. People near Perl were drawn to her light and began grabbing at her, moaning, pleading for help. She frantically pushed the hands off and was ten feet away when she locked eyes with the spider, his dark, watery eyes filled with sadness. "Victr! I'm coming! Hold on! I'm coming!" Perl yelled as loud as she could, but no sound came out. The spider sank, a long, fuzzy arm flailing in desperation. Perl plunged her arms down into the sandy depths, desperately searching. "No! Victr!"

Perl's screams woke her fellow Seers out of their meditative states. Perl screamed and thrashed about, tearing at her bed of vines, ripping them from the ground.

"Perl! Stop! Wake up!" Bear, Flax, and Javan tried to wake Perl, while the others, still in a semi-hypnotic state, came to slowly, unsure of what was happening.

Master Gichi's multitude of hands reached out from its flowery gown, carefully lifting Perl up and out of the entangled vines and into his arms. "Come, Whale Rider. Come into the Light."

Hearing Master Gichi's voice, Perl went limp in his arms, but continued mumbling in her sleep. "No! I need to stay! I have to st—"

"Water Seer, awake!" At that command, Perl woke with a jolt. Gichi cradled Perl for a few moments to help calm her, then gently set her back on her feet.

"What happened?" Corvax asked, still reeling from his battle vision. "Was that real—?"

Lyre cut him off, "Is...is that what's coming?"

"I pray to Ever not," said Javan in a hushed tone.

"Why did we relive such traumatic moments?" asked Tars.

"Where was I?" Perl mumbled, still feeling lost from her vision.

"You saw what you needed to see. Land, Water, and Air...you must release all fear if you are to work as one. Ever sees us as we were, as we are, and as we will be. You must awaken to the conscious presence of Nature, in, around and about all that exists. Then you will become aware of Truth."

Tars leaned over to Flax and Nan. "Did you get all that?" The three shrugged.

Master Gichi raised its arms, "Rise."

As they stood, Javan whispered to Perl, "What did you see?"

"I dunno. Maybe I was in The Unforgiven, but I can't be sure. I saw Brother Victr, but I couldn't get to him. It was awful."

"Humans are constantly reconstructing everything around them with their minds. They are drawn to the Past, enticed by the Future, but avoid the Now. The greatest obstacle between Ever and humanity is their distorted view of reality. For generations, evil has sown seeds of darkness with deceit and destruction." As Gichi spoke, images of war and destruction flashed in the sky above them. "Light Protectors have always toiled to bring peace."

Flax's hand went up, "Master Gichi, from what I witnessed in my vision, is it telling me...us...that it's too late?"

"The eternal battle rages between the Light and Dark. The essences of humans are the prize..." Master Gichi paused. "But it is not too late. We must continue to assist humanity, before it does become a forgone conclusion." He gestured for Palo Santo to return.

Master Gichi began to levitate and the Being's moonflower body slowly faded away, leaving only its crescent moon head, his sharp light cascading down on the Seers. "Love is energy. Power is energy. Beauty is energy. You have within you the energy of love, power and beauty. Love is eternal." The master's face shrank into a sliver of light, then full dark moon, disappearing entirely into the night sky.

"Why does every Master speak in riddles?" Perl asked the group as they circled around Palo Santo.

"The fun is in solving the puzzle, not in quibbling about the pieces," Palo answered.

"See, that's exactly what I'm talking about," Perl smirked, raising an eyebrow at the Garden Nurse, who smiled down at her.

Palo waved her arm. "Come, we will be taking a different way out."

"Thank Ever for that," Tars said, scratching at the bare patches where the fairies had torn away bits of fur.

The Seers, drained and bewildered by Master Gichi's lesson, trailed quietly behind Palo Santo as she led them down a winding stone path through grass the color of cherry tomatoes. Perl gave one last glance over her shoulder at the Seers' birth trees, thinking back to her vision.

'Hold on, Victr. I will find you,' she thought.

I haven't felt like sketching, but being back in Venusto among friends has lightened my mood — don't know what I'd do without them.

I continue to be awestruck and humbled to be here.

'Humus' means soil. The word human comes from the same root ~ we mustn't lose sight of this connection.

With this growing responsibilty to save, comes a powerlessness to solve every global issue ~

Ever, show me the way.

Coquin Clam Shell

(Smaller) but mighty Opis ü

Deep below the Under Kingdom, Amanita quietly slipped into Dianna's greenhouse. She reached up to pull down a metal box resting on the top rack of the room's many shelves. She dropped the container on a nearby worktable with a heavy *clunk*.

"Great," she sighed, noticing the padlock. She grabbed a hammer, smashing repeatedly at the rusted hinges until the lid broke off. Inside was a smaller box; its mica lid had fallen off, revealing a dark lock of hair. "Ah," Amanita smirked, "little baby Perl's hair."

The albino girl reached into the pocket of her floral pinafore, taking out a lighter shaped like a small wand. She pressed a button lighting the tip, then pinched the hair between her long white fingernails. "It ends as it begins," she hissed, watching with delight as the hair curled and burned.

Amanita took a deep breath, inhaling the smoke, and instantly began to convulse. She dropped the lighter, gripping the edge of the table. "Come, come in, into my mind! Join me in my world, where all your wishes will be ignited with no need of candle or flame!"

The smoke left black smudges around Amanita's nostrils. Running her fingers across her nose, she wiped it clean, licking the residue. The lock of Perl's hair burnt her tongue like acid, leaving open sores. She relished the pain, swallowing the last of the ash along with a mouthful of her own pus and blood.

Amanita stepped over to one of the greenhouse's support beams. Flicking the lighter on once more, she held it against the post. The old, dry wood instantly turned black and smoldered, and within minutes fire had engulfed the entire structure. Amanita stood in the middle of the olive trees, giggling as the white-hot flames grew, igniting the silvery green leaves. Pleased with herself, she spun on her heel and merrily strolled away from the blaze.

Returning to the Sisterhood's well room, Dianna stepped out of Uriel's portal. As soon as the portal closed behind her, she was struck by a sharp stabbing pain in her temple. She leaned against the wall, holding her head in agony. Sisters Martha, Betty, and Ursula were on the far side of the room, carrying buckets of water.

"Our Lady?! I did not see you come in. Goodness! Are you alright?" Sister Martha dropped the bucket and rushed over.

"Where did she come from?" Sister Betty uttered to Ursula, "I could've sworn she wasn't here a moment ago."

"She's going to faint," Sister Ursula said. All three ran to Dianna as her knees gave out.

Martha dipped a cloth into the well bucket. "Here." She placed the cool rag on Dianna's forehead.

"S-something is wrong," Dianna mumbled; along with the throbbing headache, a burning sensation tore at her insides.

"What can we do? Where does it hurt?" Sister Betty dunked a ladle into the bucket of water. "Here, my lady. Take a sip."

"It's Perl, she's…" Dianna whispered, struggling to stay awake.

An alarm sounded, and lights began flashing throughout the Sisterhood's chambers.

"The fire alarm," Sister Ursula said. "We need to evacuate! Get the children into the safe rooms."

Dianna, starting to lose consciousness, perked up at the blaring alarm. "W-what's happening?"

A small boy ran into the well room. "Sisters! Come quick! The garden's on fire!"

Dianna realized the source of her pain.

Unaware of the ongoing chaos in the lowest levels of the Kingdom, Countess Sarr and Governess Ruby buzzed around Mik like two mosquitoes, fussing with her dress and cobra-styled headpiece, trying to get it to stay upright.

"The fangs are going to poke her in the eyes," Ruby pushed the odd snake head away from Mik's face.

"This is not a wedding gown, it's a monstrosity!" Mik squirmed. "I look like a carnival freak!"

The door to the arena dressing room opened. Four guards carrying a giant stuffed snake's body entered. "Your royal train, Princess," they announced, lowering the massive thirty-foot-long, gold-scaled, jewel-encrusted mess of fabric to the floor.

"What?! There's more to this horrible getup? I already can't walk in this…this *thing!*" Mik complained.

"Oh Darling, it's not that awful," Sarr gave Mik a big fake smile.

"How would you know? You can't see three feet in front of you, Mother," Mik shot back, immediately feeling a little guilty for calling out her mother's poor vision.

"I don't need to see the gown to know that you are beautiful no matter what you wear, Darling," Sarr replied, ignoring her daughter's snarky comment. "I know you'll make it work. Now, time to get…dress-s-sed! She made a pair of fangs with her fingers, hissing. "Get it?" She giggled.

"Fine, whatever," Mik chuckled. It was the first time she'd smiled since arriving in the Under Kingdom. The three women joked as Ruby attached the enormous train to the back of Mik's bodice.

"Time for you to take your places, Countess and...Miss Ruby," the guard said, eyeing the buxom nanny.

"Alright, sweetheart, it's showtime! We'll be in the front row," Sarr said, taking hold of the guard's arm for guidance.

"You do look beautiful," Ruby whispered, "despite this horrible dress," she added, winking. She gave Mik a quick kiss on the cheek, rubbing the red lipstick in as blush.

"Shall we?" The guard gave a cheesy grin, offering his arm to Ruby.

"You wish," Ruby waved a dismissive hand at the guard as she marched past him.

The door was about to swing shut when a pointed boot caught it, holding it open. "Princess Mik?" Lance poked his head in, wearing his mandible helmet.

Mik smiled at the teenage boy. "And what are you supposed to be? My beetle-headed escort?"

"I have a gift for you, from Gretar."

"Gretar?" Hearing his name, Mik's heart leapt. She shuffled towards Lance as best she could in the heavy, awkward outfit. "Get in here...and who are you, and how do you know Gretar?"

"My name is Lance Featherstone. I'm working undercover for the Earth Alliance of Activists, to free all those imprisoned in the Under Kingdom, and..."

"Okay, okay," Mik cut the boy off. "Sorry, that's all wonderful, but why, how do you have a gift from him? Where is he? When did you see him?"

"Um, I don't know him and I don't know where he is," Lance shrugged, carefully removing the walnut-size ball from a pouch slung over his shoulder. "Gretar gave this to Perl and she made me promise to get it to you."

"The monk-girl? I mean, yes, of course...Perl, from back home."

Lance handed her the ornate ball.

Mik was about to ask how Perl had managed to get into the Under Kingdom, but was completely distracted by the object's intricate carvings.

"Perl said Gretar made it for you."

Mik ran her fingers over the raised winding branches and leaves on the outside surface, imagining Gretar crafting it. She felt tears welling up. "It's breathtaking. How can I ever thank you?"

"Well, for starters, you could work with us to help bring down the princes and reform this place once and for all." Lance straightened; his shoulders back. "Also, this conversation never happened...okay?"

Mik looked up from the delicate wooden carving. "That was always the plan...mine and Gretar's. I had no idea how awful this place is. They've had me locked up since I got here, like some kind of criminal!"

"I'll do all I can to help you. I work as the princes' translator, so I'll be close by," Lance smiled warmly.

"It will be nice to have a friend in this place."

"In my culture, it is said that when a gift is made by hand, it becomes infused with the creator's love." His eyes went to the wooden ball. "Gretar's essence lives within his work of art."

Mik said nothing, cupping the token with both hands.

Music from the arena began to play. "I gotta go get in place." Lance gave a slight tip of his beetle helmet and was about to leave when he spun back around. "Oh, one more thing," Lance pointed to the gift. "It opens, too."

"Thank you." Mik said, looking down at the tiny wooden clasp.

"Just glad I found you," Lance said. He poked his head out the door, checking both ways. "Be seeing you," he smiled back to Mik before quickly slipping into the hall, closing the door behind him.

Mik unhinged the tiny clasp, and gasped. The inside of the walnut was even more ornate; in the center surrounded by highly-detailed carvings of twisting vines and curling leaves was an adorable red panda, whiskers and all, resting on a tree branch. Mik blushed as she read the engraved quote on the other half of the walnut's shell— 'You have my heart, you are my home.' Tears streamed down her cheeks at the loving words and the realization that she was about to marry the wrong man.

"I hope I'm doing this for the right reasons and that one day we'll be together," Mik thought, closing her eyes tightly. She pulled the front neckline of her dress open, wanting to tuck the gift down the front of her gown for safe keeping, when she noticed a message stitched into the dress's lining—*The Sisters Are With You.* Mik didn't know who the Sisters were, but immediately thought of Ivry; how they had played dress-up as kids, pretending to marry the princes someday. Mik saw the message as a good sign that Ivry was nearby, and she perked up a bit. "Okay, let's do this." She rubbed her blush into her tear-stained cheeks and took a long deep breath.

The door swung open, "There's my cherry blossom!" Count Zell burst into the room, decked out in his garish three-piece great white shark tuxedo. "Look. At. You! Ha! What a sight you are!"

"Oh, I'm a sight, alright, Daddy." She rolled her eyes.

The Count gazed up and down at the dress. "Those desert boys do have a flare for the gaudy, don't they?"

"I feel ridiculous," Mik cringed. "I thought they would at least dress me in a butterfly gown, seeing as though they tied me up in that cocoon straightjacket!"

Ignoring her comment, The Count smiled. "If anyone can make a reptile look regal, it's you." The door opened again, and a flurry of flower girls rushed into the room, surrounding Mik. Each little girl wore a floor-length spiky cactus dress with a hood that revealed only their eyes. Pink and yellow cactus flowers sprouted from their heads. They lined up in pairs, picking up and holding aloft her long serpentine train, the array of baubles and jewels clinking and rattling.

The Count held out his arm, "Shall we?"

"If we must," Mik sighed, picking up her bouquet of yellow Wild Tansy flowers. The wild plant had been the one thing they had allowed her to choose for her wedding day. Mik knew the Earth Activists would be watching, and by using the secret language of flowers—floriography—her message would be loud and clear; Wild Tansies, cute as they were, meant a declaration of war.

"Shoulders back, big smile, here we go." The Count held his head high, knowing the eyes of the world would be on them to witness the alliance of two great families—the House of Graves, rulers of water, and the Deathstalkers, Desertland rulers of technology and warfare.

"Our two houses will control the globe," The Count thought, a poisonous smile curling on his lips. Mik looked over at her father, smiling like the cat that swallowed the canary, and wondered exactly what was going through his mind.

The curtain to the arena parted, the spotlight blasting the father and daughter in a blinding white glare. The entire interior of the cathedral had been transformed; the walls had been refaced with holographic imagery, turning the old gothic chamber into a modern spectacle of colors and textures. Projected onto the long aisle leading to the main stage was a visual of golden snake scales that matched Mik's cobra-themed gown. Iridescent confetti fell from the rafters, popping above the crowds' heads like tiny fireworks before fizzling out in swirling trails of red smoke. At the far end of the domed coliseum, a holographic waterfall poured from the ceiling, cascading down to the track, giving the illusion of a shimmering electric blue river that encircled the stage, complete with silvery fish leaping in and out of it. Smoke machines shaped like skulls turned the rotating stage floor into a massive billowy white cloud. In the center stood the Under Kingdom's holy man, wearing an eccentric tribal mask of a sun deity. Four boys held his long yellow cape. Around the outside ring stood a few dozen royal guards on stilts, dressed in puffy white uniforms that matched the cloud.

Angelic music accompanied Mik and The Count as they walked down the long aisle towards the stage. A section of Mik's mega-fans donning giant red wigs, known as the Redhots, cheered wildly as she passed by. "All hail Mik, Queen of the Desertlands!" , "We love you, Mik!"

On either side of the waterfall, a holographic image of two enormous phoenix birds with crowns rose up, their wings flickering flames, a tribute to the princes' deceased parents. As the birds opened their beaks, letting out a loud, high-pitched squawk, the music changed to a chest-pounding bass, mixing with the birds' cry.

Mik and The Count reached the stage and stood, waiting with the masked cleric amongst the screaming crowd and surreal setting. A cannon's boom shocked the guests into a startled hush. The waterfall parted like curtains, and from behind the falls appeared a small, bright gold hovercraft shaped like a scorpion, its giant pincers raised up above its head. Inside the upper section of the hovercraft sat Princes Névenoé and Tobias, their heads poking out of the top of the scorpion like a pair of eyes. The crowd, which had been warned by the royal family in the days leading up to the wedding to be extra loud when the princes arrived, exploded in applause and accolades. "Long live our Crown Princes! Kings of Kings!"

"What's going on, Daddy!?" Mik squinted up at the strange floating scorpion. "Why is Prince Tobias up there with Prince Névenoé?"

Count Zell looked over at his daughter. In the deafening roar, he could see her mouth moving but couldn't hear a word. "Smile, Darling! The world is watching!"

Massive video screens captured Mik's deer-in-the-headlights expression from a dozen different angles. Her image went viral with taglines—"Ssssecond Thoughts??", "Mik Graves Rattled on Wedding Day!", "Grave Day for Graves Princess??"

Remembering Gretar's gift tucked next to her heart, Mik forced a smile. The screens' messages quickly changed— "The Look of Love!", "Huzzah! Huzzah!", "All's Well in The Under Kingdom!"

The craft landed tail first, and in a few seconds of mechanized, shifting metal, the vehicle split in half, transforming from one scorpion vehicle into two scorpion bodysuits. The princes, now each wearing their own metallic outfit, walked to the edges of the stage, taking several bows, raising their claws in the air, milking the moment. The neon blue moat around the stage shifted to a sandy terrain, teeming with arachnids burrowing in and out of holes in the sand—all holographic images, but all-too-real, nonetheless. Mik looked around at the ring of scorpions and felt her skin crawl.

The Count spoke through clenched teeth, "What's going on, boys? What are you doing here, Tobias? You should be up there with Sarr." Count Zell's eyes darted up to the hanging glass penthouse, where his wife The Countess Sarr sat squinting through magnifying goggles. Sitting beside her was Governess Ruby and Lance in his beetle helmet. The two princes eyed The Count coldly, still smiling and playing to the crowd as if it were a wrestling match rather than a wedding ceremony. "I do not like surprises," The Count said, then had to quickly side-step as Tobias walked up to the pair, raising one of his heavy metal arms and dropping it down between The Count and his daughter, separating the two.

Mik whispered, "I'm not marrying both of them, Father. This is insane! Father??"

The Count was gone, escorted back to his seat in the bubble room by a pair of royal guards. Mik looked around, but the swirling hologram imagery and smoke made it impossible to see anything.

"Let us begin." The masked holy man raised his arms, beckoning the two princes and the bride to step forward.

Tobias grabbed Mik with a metal claw and urged her to the middle of the stage. It was an absurd sight to behold; Mik in her giant snake getup, flanked by two men dressed as robot-scorpions, but the crowd ate it up.

The holy man attached a microphone to his throat, and his raspy voice now echoed through the cathedral's speakers. "Scorpions! First to move from water to land, unchanged over a millennium! So too, will be the legacy of our future kings, Tobias and Névenoé of the Deathstalker's bloodline! Long may they reign!" The crowds erupted again as the clergyman shouted over the noise, "Strength! Cunning! Endurance!"

The audience went wild at the magical, mechanical spectacle, watching as the two golden scorpions pressed in tightly at Mik's sides, wrapping their arms around her waist, trapping her. Mik felt smothered; as if the entire Under Kingdom was suddenly pressing in on her.

A young boy appeared through the swirling cloud and handed the clergyman a golden scepter; an ornate bejeweled orb on the end of it. He raised the scepter in the air and the arena crowd grew quiet. "The sting of your venoms…" he said, tapping the scepter on Tobias's shoulder, "Shall bring you sons." He moved the scepter, tapping Névenoé's shoulder.

Nearly in shock, Mik could sense her feet and legs were going numb; her mind was fuzzy. She could see herself standing there as if she were out of her own body and looking down at herself, helpless to stop the madness.

A flower girl yanked at her flowers. "Princess, please, let go."

"Huh? Oh uh, sorry." Mik, realizing she had a death grip on the bouquet, surrendered her Wild Tansies to the girl, as several petals fell to the ground. She stared down at them, taking it as a bad sign.

The future kings each took one of Mik's hands in their metal claws. *"Handcuffs,"* Mik thought.

The holy man asked, "Do you, Prince Tobias and Prince Névenoé, take Princess Mik as your one and only Desert Queen?"

The princes answered in unison, "We do," each placing a diamond-encrusted scorpion ring on the middle finger of each hand.

A camera drone swooped in from overhead to snap a picture of the rings, sending the images to Narcissi's network, where it then flashed on the video screens.

Technicolor holographic confetti erupted once again from the ceiling, as three gold crowns were lowered from the rafters on long golden hooks. Three members of the royal guard, in their puffy oversized cloud outfits, waltzed over on stilts and unhooked the crowns. They handed them to the holy man, who ceremoniously placed them on the princes' heads.

"I give you soon-to-be kings Tobias and Névenoé, brothers in blood and honor! And their Queen Cobra, Mik of House Graves! Their reign will be eternal!"

Praise and congratulatory applause continued as the clergyman struggled to attach Mik's crown to her oversized cobra hood. Mik looked at the man in his sun-like tribal mask, waking from her bewildered haze.

"I didn't say 'I do'," she said, staring at the old man, his watery gray eyes looking back with no emotion. "I didn't say 'I do'."

The holy man leaned over, whispering, "Women have no voice in the Under Kingdom. Nor shall you…*my Queen.*" He pinched her chin, his hand cold and clammy. Playing to the audience, he turned and raised his arms with a grand wave of his scepter.

"Hold tight, Red Queen," Tobias said to Mik, moving her aside. He nodded to his brother, pressing a button on his chest plate, starting the motors to the hovercraft feature on their suits.

With scorpion arms locked around her waist, Mik and her new husbands slowly ascended four stories up into the air to a platform where three ornate black onyx thrones sat.

The cathedral's holograms shifted again, transforming the arena into a night sky with an aurora borealis light show, ribbons of neon green and purple rippling around the dome to the delight of the crowd. Thousands of servants emerged from the tunnels and began circulating up and down the rows, handing out smoking green cocktails to all the guests. Mik stared blankly at her goblet of smoke. *"This has to be a dream,"* she tried to tell herself. She searched through the myriad of hanging glass bubble-rooms and located the Royal Chamber, seeing her father and mother inside. A drone hovered around the glass dome, and The Count and Countess's faces were now a hundred-feet-tall on all of the arena's screens. Mik could tell they were arguing underneath their clenched smiles and robotic waving. She noticed her father's toady little henchman, Snive, rush to The Count's side, then scamper off. *"This has to be a dream."*

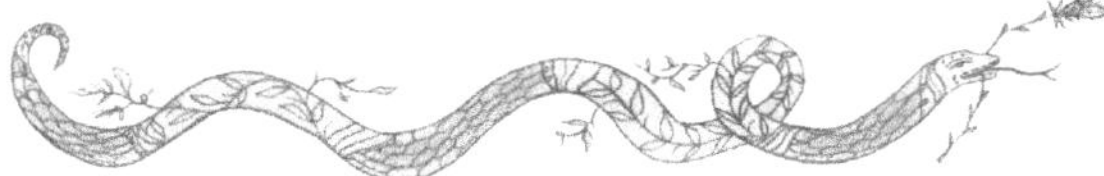

Standing outside his beach hut, half-drunk, Gretar looked up at one of the many video screens set up to broadcast the wedding of the century to the citizens of Mont Michel. A closeup on Mik's face appeared, the strange green smoke from her drink wafting up across her pale skin. The fierceness normally seen in Mik's blue eyes had been replaced with something he'd never seen...fear. Gretar desperately wanted to go to her. The thought of either prince touching her filled him with rage. He downed the last of his coconut ale.

"I gotta find a way into the Under Kingdom," he mumbled, "If Perl got in, the monks must know a way...and they can get me in, too."

Gretar looked back at the screen; Tobias and Névenoé were leaning in awkwardly to kiss Mik on either cheek. She looked miserable.

"Bastards!" Gretar reared back and launched his bottle. It sailed through the screen, leaving a gaping black hole. When Prince Tobias turned to smile at the camera; it looked like he was missing his front tooth.

25 BUFFOONERY

At the Greenheart Combat Fields, the morning dew glistened on the grass like droplets of silver; the translucent fabric on the Seer's uniforms dancing in the light as they waited patiently for Master Tanda to arrive.

"Hey Javan...know why this time of the morning is called pill-o'clock?" Bear elbowed Javan.

"Okay, I'll bite, why?"

"'Cause I should still be laying on my *pillow!*" Bear doubled over in laughter.

"Why do I continue to humor him?" Javan smiled over at Perl, who was sitting cross-legged on the ground eyes closed, lost in thought. "Perl? You awake over there?"

"I'm awake," she turned to look at him. "I was just wondering when you were going to tell me about you-know-what..."

Javan walked over to her, whispering, "I'll know more in a day or two."

"That's two days too long for Victr to be stuck in the Unforgiven. What's the holdup?" Perl spoke through gritted teeth.

"Shh," Javan held his finger to his lips. "I'm waiting to hear back from Anaya."

"You need to—" Perl was interrupted by Elder Enoogoo's voice.

"Mother Nature is an artist!" The enormous orangutan appeared, hanging by one arm from a tree. He held Master Tanda in the other.

"Whoa!" Tars jumped. "Have they been up there this whole time?"

Enoogoo continued, "She paints a new sky every day! No two are the same; misty mornings such as this are ideal! The refracting moisture creates dazzling colors at dawn, invigorating the spirit, energizing you to take on whatever comes your way!" The great orangutan swung back and forth effortlessly from the branch.

Master Tanda's hood had been removed, and she eyed each of the Nine before speaking. "Seers wear the color Humor as a reminder that laughter lightens the mood and puts your mind at ease. Keeping spirits high in the face of darkness is critical. Amusement is an emotion that evil does not understand." Tanda extended her wing, tickling Enoogoo's armpit.

"Stop, no!" The orangutan lost his grip, dropping to the ground laughing.

"The laughter tickle response is called gargalesis. Humans and primates exhibit it as a means of social bonding. In the young it hones self-defense skills. During tickle fights they develop reflexes to protect vulnerable areas such as the neck and ribs." Master Tanda flew down and landed on top of Enoogoo's head.

Enoogoo held up his arm for the lizard-falcon to perch, using his other hand to protect his armpit against more tickling. "In today's lesson you will tickle your funny bones while solving riddles in a race."

"You hear that, Flax? Your immaturity will actually help you today." Corvax teased his friend.

"This is one race I'm betting you'll lose, old crow!" Flax heckled back.

"You will work in teams of three—Water, Land, and Air accordingly, and with porpoise." Directed Master Tanda.

"Did she just say, porpoise?" Ask Nan.

"I think so," said Lyre.

"Let's go, Land Seers!" Javan, Tars, and Flax high-fived one another.

"The first team to answer all four riddles and return to this tree shall be declared the winner," Master Tanda said, opening her mouth to sneeze— "Ba…ba…bliss!" The Nine shut their eyes to the salty snot as it blasted them in a cloud of sparkling mist.

Opening their eyes, the Seers found the landscape transformed from flatlands to rolling hills, the grass under their feet a bright yellow. Each team was spaced far enough apart so they couldn't hear one another. In front of each trio was a comically-large donut the size of a carousel, coated in gallons of pink icing with colorful sprinkles on top as big as fireplace logs.

"Yes!" Bear reached up, swiping a paw of icing. He lapped up the sugary goo.

"Bear, control yourself!" Opis huffed. "Alright, focus, Water Seers. The game has begun."

Perl tried to reach up to the icing but was too short. Bear scooped another handful, giving it to Perl.

Opis rolled her eyes. "You two and your sweet tooths!"

"I believe the correct term is "sweet teeth." The tardigrade-boy was about to take another scoop when he stopped. "Hey, the first riddle! It's written in the icing. Good thing I didn't eat it, heh-heh."

"Yeah. Good thing," Opis replied sarcastically. "What's it say?"

Bear read aloud:

"How can you physically stand behind your friend,
while they stand behind you?"

"That's impossible," Perl said. "I mean, what if your friend is on the other side of the world?"

"Well technically they're still behind you, or you're behind them, just farther apart," added Bear.

Perl looked at Opis's back, hoping for a clue.

"It says physically stand." Opis turned and grabbed Perl by the shoulders, spinning her around. She posed, hand on chin, pondering. "Behind…while behind…"

A light went on as Perl and Opis both shouted, "Back-to-back!"

The girls pressed their backs together; as soon as they did, the gigantic donut began to slowly turn.

"Ha-ha, you did it!" Bear bounced with joy.

From the middle of the spinning donut emerged a giant dolphin head; its slick skin neon yellow and covered in blue polka-dots. It opened its mouth wide, letting loose a long, high-pitched giggle. Perl couldn't help but laugh, which got Bear going, and even Opis joined in.

"How hilarious is that?" Bear laughed punctuated by snorts.

The Greenheart Battle grounds erupted with giggling dolphins as the other two Seer teams solved the riddle.

"That explains why Master Tanda told us to work with porpoise," Perl chuckled.

The donut stopped spinning and the hundred-ton dolphin stopped laughing, gesturing to climb up onto the donut.

"Okee-dokee," Bear said, interlocking his hands to boost Perl. "Up ya' go, Perly-Poo!"

The dolphin gave a squeak, lowering its nose. "I think it wants us to get on," said Opis.

Perl gave a little running hop, hoisting herself up onto the dolphin's slick nose.

"Your turn," Bear picked up Opis, lifting her so Perl could grab her arms.

With a running leap Bear joined them, nearly sliding off the other side. The dolphin lifted its head and stuck out its long polka-dotted tongue.

"Look!" Perl pointed to the end of the wet tongue, where another donut sat like a big life preserver. "Come on!" Perl lowered herself down the tip of the dolphin's rounded beak, stepping onto its tongue. "Ew! It's squishy!" She looked back at the other two, wrinkling her nose and smiling.

"Seriously?" Opis said, watching as Perl did a tightrope shimmy along the twenty-foot-long tongue to the donut decorated in rainbow sprinkles.

"Take a look, Opis. We're standing on a giant clown-donut-dolphin-thing! This is the complete opposite of serious!" Bear laughed. "Here, I got you." Bear lifted Opis up and set her on his shoulders, then carefully made his way down the dolphin's tongue.

"There's another riddle written in the sprinkles," Perl read it aloud:

"Why can't you trust an atom?"

"Oh, I know this one. That is such an old joke," Opis smirked.

"Well then," smiled Bear, "you ought to know it."

"Do you want the answer, Mr. Funny Bear?" Opis teased.

"Yes, yes, come on! We're in a race!" Perl shouted, making a "hurry up" gesture.

"You can't trust an atom," Opis paused for drama, "Because they make up everything," she said matter-of-factly.

As Opis answered the riddle, the second smaller donut began to spin, and a smaller but identical yellow dolphin emerged from the donut's hole, laughing hysterically and bobbing its head up and down, making the bigger dolphin's tongue wobble.

Perl looked down across the field; the Air Seers had released their second dolphin as well. "We're tied with them! Hurry, where's the next riddle?"

As the second dolphin squeaked and squealed, bubbles started pouring out of its blowhole. One enormous bubble floated over and engulfed the Seers inside, lifting them into the air.

"Hey!" Bear pushed against the sides of the shimmering orb; the surface stretched like elastic but didn't pop. "Is this part of the race?"

"I think so, the Air and Land teams are inside theirs, too." Perl pointed to a cluster of tiny iridescent bubbles floating around them. "Look, I think they're forming words."

Opis read the words as they appeared:

"What is so fragile that saying its name breaks it?"

Bear chuckled, "Hopefully it's not 'bubble.'"

"What are some fragile things?" Perl pondered aloud, "Ice?"

"A snowflake?" Bear added.

"Glass?" Perl said, as the two continued to banter back and forth.

"An eggshell?", "A flower petal?", "A feather?"

"No, no, it's a riddle; you're being too literal." Opis twisted a tentacle, thinking, "Saying its name breaks it."

"What's a fragile name? Mmm...*Penelope?*" Bear said. Opis and Perl ignored him.

For nearly an hour, the three floated around in the bubble, completely stumped.

"I'm hungry, plus it's too quiet up here," Bear rubbed his belly.

"Perl's eyes lit up. "That's it!"

"Lunch?" Shouted Bear.

"No, you said it...it's too quiet." Perl grinned her toothy smile, locking eyes with Opis, who got the answer just as Perl thought it. "Silence. Saying its name breaks it!"

The bubble popped, covering the three of them in sticky residue as they plummeted.

"Ahhh!" Perl yelled. Directly below them was a large orange mound, coming up fast.

"Look out below!" Bear shouted, grabbing Opis and cradling her as they braced for impact.

The three landed softly, rolling down what turned out to be a massive stack of wispy orange hair. As they tumbled, the hairs stuck to them like glue. They reached the bottom and stood up.

All Perl could make of Bear were his eyes and round tardigrade mouth; the rest of him was covered in long, orange shaggy hair. She could not contain her laughter.

"What's so funny?" Bear giggled, instantly knowing the answer.

"You! You look like Enoogoo, with extra goo!" Perl didn't think she could laugh any harder, then Opis stepped out from the giant hairball with her tentacles standing on end, covered in fuzz. "Ha-ha-ha! You're like a hairy sea monster!" Perl pointed, laughing hysterically.

"Me? Look at you!" Opis lost it; Perl looked like she had a lion's mane and had been zapped by lightning.

The massive pile of hair began to re-shape, twisting and braiding itself to form words.

"Hey, Lion-Girl," Bear chuckled, slapping his knee, "Hair—I mean, care to read it?"

Perl looked at Bear standing there like a wild yeti. "I, I can't, you read it," she said, collapsing into another giggle fit.

Bear, spitting out orange fibers, read the words:

"The more you leave behind the more you take."

Opis pulled a clump of hair from her arm. "Books?" She said, looking around for something to happen. Nothing changed; wrong answer.

"Good try," Perl said. "Could it be regrets? Nah, you don't take regrets."

Bear took a few steps away from the pile of hair. In the distance, he could still see the silhouette of the giant donut. "Donuts?"

"Bear!" Opis and Perl shouted in unison.

"Sorry, my belly's doing all the talking right now."

Perl looked down and noticed that Bear was leaving orange hairy tracks as he walked. "Ha! You've done it, Bear!"

"I have? I mean, I have!" He paused. "What exactly have I done?"

Perl pointed to his tracks on the ground. "The more you leave behind; the more you take."

"Hair?" Bear asked, "No, wait...footsteps!"

The braided hair unraveled, reforming to spell out one final word—'RUN!'

The three Water Seers looked around. To the north and east, nothing but hills of purple moss that sloped gently upward. To the south, a smattering of shrubs and some large jagged rocks poking out amongst the knolls. To the west was a valley; where it flattened out into an open plain a single tree stood proudly, its leaves shimmering a bright reddish orange.

"That tree! That's gotta be it, right?" Bear urged the others. Perl and Opis looked at the tree; although it was quite far off, Opis could see a small dark figure swinging from one of the branches.

"Yes! Go!" she shouted, making a break for it.

"To the tree! For the win!" Perl chimed in.

The three raced down the slope frantically. Across from them, on the other side of the vast valley, Perl could make out the Land Seers sprinting toward the tree as well. Opis, panting and unable to keep up with her small frame, slowed, yelling ahead to Perl and Bear.

"Don't wait for me! Get to the tree first, go!"

Bear ran on all paws, stampeding like a stallion and catching up to Perl, who was sprinting full speed, her orange mane of hair still stuck to her head, flapping in the breeze.

Bear, panting heavily but moving fast, yelled over to Perl, "We got this! We're gonna beat 'em!" Perl looked over and smiled. The two were almost to the tree when three figures glided past them.

It was the Air Seers—Lyre, Corvax, and Nan, and although they, too, were sticky and covered in orange fur, still managed to fly. Corvax, always the competitive one, cut in front of Perl just before she was about to tag the tree trunk. "First!" he crowed. Nan and Lyre came in right behind him, followed by Bear and Perl.

One by one the nine Seers crashed to a halt at the base of the tree, panting and exhausted. Seeing one another covered in a mess of long orange hair, smiles turned to giggles which escalated quickly into full-on belly laughs.

Elder Enoogoo, having watched the race from his branch, now dropped down, leaning against the mighty tree. Master Tanda came down as well, perching on his arm. She laughed. "Well, well, well! A buffoonery of orangutans I see before me! Orange you a sight to see!"

Master Tanda and Enoogoo waited patiently for the giggling to subside as the Seers tried to catch their breaths. "The Air Seers have won the challenge, but you have all learned how to slaughter today."

Nan poked Lyre, "She said 'slaughter', right?"

"She did," Lyre shrugged.

"I did indeed say 'slaughter.' For within that word lies a key weapon...*laughter*. It is our duty to help show humans that in choosing laughter to lighten their burdens, it will *slaughter* the evil that darkens troubled minds. Remember, Self-Slayers cannot comprehend humor. Their goal is to blind humanity to happiness, so we must fight back by guiding humans to things that uplift, that lighten the spirit and bring joy! Laughter. Is. A. Weapon."

"You could say humor is *fun*-da-*mental*," Tars elbowed Flax.

"Good one," Flax nodded.

"Yes, Tars," Master Tanda winked at the monkey-boy. "All mental states are accompanied by vibrations. You harmonize with what you vibrate to, so let us vibrate to happiness to vanquish evil."

Enoogoo cleared his throat, "In teaching others joy, that joy returns to the teacher. Happiness becomes an infinite cycle, if we choose it to be." The orangutan stepped away from the tree, revealing an enormous book, embedded deep in the tree as if it had always been a natural part of it.

At the sight of the strange book, Perl's bioluminescent spots lit up across her cheeks.

"Thar she glows," snickered Bear.

Perl walked up to the book; its cover was made of the tree's bark. Carved into the cover was the title, which Perl read aloud. "*Nepenthes Attenborough.*"

"Our Air winners have the honor of opening the book," Tanda waved the trio forward.

Perl politely moved aside as Lyre, Nan and Corvax gently pulled on the wooden cover together, opening the book. Inside it was a carnivorous tropical pitcher plant, nearly six feet tall, suspended inside the carved-out trunk. Master Tanda flew to a nearby branch while Enoogoo gently removed the exotic tube-shaped plant.

"Aptly named for Sir David Attenborough, a human. One of Earth's greatest biologists. Only this particular pitcher plant is unique. It can be used to trap creatures from the Dark Realm." Master Tanda said, swooping down to perch on the top of the open book. She scratched her talon across the inscription on the inside cover. "When the incantation is read, it will summon any demons in proximity to it. They'll be drawn to the plant's enchanted nectar. Once a demon is close to it, the plant pulls it in, absorbing it into its inner chamber."

"Impressive," Javan said.

Enoogoo pointed to the top of the plant. "The nectar is secreted from the underside of its lid, right here. This milky, viscous liquid traps the demon, leaving it defenseless. Having captured its prey, the plant will then feed on the demon's essence, digesting all sorrow and suffering, leaving nothing behind."

"Whoa," Tars muttered under his breath.

"Is it safe to read it here?" Flax raised his hand. "Won't that draw evil to us?"

"There is no Darkness in the Light Realm," Master Tanda assured them. "The *Nepenthes Attenborough* is to be used to assist you in battle, when necessary. Corvax, you may read the incantation."

Corvax spoke the words carefully:

> *"Imagine an imaginary menagerie*
> *to grant all the wishes you wish,*
> *come guzzle greedily in captivating captivity,*
> *as I banish thee, for eternity,*
> *to a dungeon, everlasting."*

"That's a mighty mouthful of a tongue twister," joked Bear.

"Precisely, Bear, the enchantment tricks the trickster." Enoogoo handed the tall pitcher plant to the tardigrade. "Keep the *Nepenthes* someplace safe in your treehouse."

"Stay and read the spell until each of you has it committed to memory,"

Master Tanda said, returning to her perch on Enoogoo's arm. "We leave you with one last riddle:

What is greater than Ever and more evil than The Ullen?
Rich people want it, poor people have it. And if you eat it,
you'll cease to exist?"

The Seers circled into a huddle, whispering ideas to one another. After several minutes they parted and Lyre chirped, "Nothing!"

"Excellent!" Master Tanda exclaimed, "Until we train again, find the humor in the moments when it is needed most."

Enoogoo removed Tanda's hood from his pocket, promptly kissing her on the head before securing the rufter into place.

"Close the book once you've committed it to memory, my buffoonery bunch." Enoogoo chuckled at the sight of the orange hair-covered group before turning towards the gateway, humming a silly ditty as he disappeared around the bend—

"Donuts by the dozens
have pancakes for cousins,
Mmm-mmm, mmm-mmm…"

The Seers sat under the shade of the tree, looking like a family of orangutans, reciting the pitcher plant's magical words:

"Imagine an imaginary menagerie
to grant all the wishes you wish,
come guzzle greedily in captivating captivity,
as I banish thee, for eternity,
to a dungeon, everlasting."

26 TELEKINESIS

"Qualia is the way things seem to you. What you are aware of when you see, hear, taste, touch or smell," Uriel said, skipping a stone across the shimmering alabaster waters along Greenheart's shoreline.

Perl picked up a stone, running her thumb along its smooth, flat side. "Okay, so how does being aware of the smell of a skunk help me to move objects?" She asked, flinging her stone, watching as it bounced three times.

Ever since the day Perl had seen Uriel moving the books with her mind in the Brotherhood's library years ago, she had begged her Protector for lessons on telekinesis. Today, that long-awaited day had come.

"It's part of the mystery...being aware. If you are aware of the green color of grass or the feeling of touching the sand," Uriel rubbed the grains from her hand after tossing another stone, "Then there is no need for it to physically happen. Your mind recalls it and your freewill allows you to choose to allow it."

Perl looked up into Uriel's dark violet eye, marveling at the impressive woman's muscular frame cloaked in shining, battle-ready armor; how she loved her mentor beyond measure. "I think I understand, but keep going."

"Thinking in this manner allows the mind to become part quantum. Your human consciousness has a direct connection to the source of consciousness, that of the Mind of Ever. Therefore, breaking the reality of physics creates new possibilities for the mind to explore." Uriel turned and strolled down the beach.

Perl stepped double-time to keep up with Uriel's long gate. "So, you move things with your mind by manipulating reality?"

"Yes, if your mind could only passively witness the world and not alter what happens, then why should the mind exist at all?" Uriel stopped at a patch of lush green grass just up from the water's edge. Dozens of bright yellow flapshell turtles were casually nibbling on flowers.

"Wait, you're saying that with my imagination I can change what's real?"

"Let's not get ahead of ourselves. It is in your human nature to aspire for more, as life on earth evolved, so did the human mind. You have the use of billions of neurons, making it possible for you to walk, talk, think and create." She paused, smiling, "But let's start simple, shall we?" Uriel pointed to two turtles sitting side by side, munching bluebells. "Try stacking those two on top of one another."

Perl stared at Uriel for a second, then shrugged. "Okay," Perl said, locking her eyes on the left turtle. She stared at it, watching as it ripped off a small petal of lavender and chewed on it, its tiny jaw moving slowly and methodically. Perl squinted her eyes and focused, trying to block out all distractions. *"Turtle...turtle...turtle,"* she repeated in her mind.

Nothing happened. The turtle continued nibbling on flowers, oblivious to the world. Perl looked over at Uriel. "It's not working. I don't know if I'm doing it right."

"Think of the properties of qualia. What you can perceive—the turtle's weight, the texture of its shell, its reaction to being touched. Focus. Trust yourself."

Perl took a deep breath. *"Flapshell turtles have flaps on the underside of their shells,"* she thought. *"The flaps cover their back feet when they pull in their legs."* Her mind began to clear, thinking only of the turtle. *"Their shells are smooth to the touch. Their tail is short."* One turtle began to slowly rock.

Perl closed her eyes and the turtle, sensing a disturbance, stopped munching flower petals and retreated into its shell.

"Good," Uriel encouraged, "Now concentrate. You have the power inside you, but you must harness the energy around the turtle. Your hands must be the air."

Perl imagined her hands as particles of air surrounding the turtle, gently cradling it, and lifting it off the ground. She opened her eyes, and to her surprise, the turtle was now wobbling back and forth as if teetering on a ledge. She shut her eyes and cracked a slight smile; in her mind, the particles forming the hands seemed to glow with light.

Uriel saw the turtle moving and encouraged Perl. "Set your intention. See the turtle rising, as if it is already done."

Perl emptied her mind; her only thought was to be in this moment. Ever so slowly, the turtle began to rise a few inches out of the bed of flowers. Perl couldn't believe her eyes—she was controlling it!

"Now, stack him on his friend there," Uriel's voice vibrated through Perl's brain like a distant echo.

Perl's mind buzzed as if it were filled with bees. She lifted the turtle higher, then ever so gently lowered the turtle onto its companion.

"I did it!" Perl shouted, breaking her concentration. The turtle toppled over onto its back. "Oops. Well, I did for a second anyway." She ran over and sat the turtle right-side up.

"I'm impressed." Uriel smiled. "Once you have mastered being quantum-conscious, you will be able to manipulate matter and energy without limits." At that, she flicked her wrist, instantly stacking the flapshell turtles twelve high.

"Show off!" Perl giggled.

"This is showing off," Uriel replied. Waving her arm in a fluid infinity-shaped gesture, she directed the turtles through the air, moving them in a figure eight formation. She lowered her arm and the flapshell turtles scattered, returning to the flowers, nibbling away as if nothing had happened.

Perl smirked, admiring her Protector; Uriel's leopard moth fluttered over her empty eye socket as she spoke. "In order to become a conduit to the electrical, invisible energy, you must tap into the river of light that flows around every single thing on Earth." Uriel paused. "Yet you can only reach this light if you are wholly present. Free of fear or desire."

"I saw the light in the air particles," Perl said, recalling her telekinetic hands wrapping around the turtle. "But what is the light?"

"The light, at its core, is love. Ever's creation. It is the only thing that is truly real." Uriel could see Perl pondering. "Perl, do not believe me simply because I tell you. Believe what your consciousness and intuition tell you. Pay close attention to your voice within."

"Mm... I think it's telling me to try to lift the turtles again," Perl grinned.

"Then by all means, let us comply."

In days to come, the tall, statuesque figure and her young companion practicing on the shoreline became a common sight at Greenheart's beach. On any given night, onlookers could see rocks, coconuts, and even wildlife, floating around the pair like moths to flame.

27 PSYCHOMETRY

Perl rested on her fluffy green dianthus bed, sketching her thoughts and patiently waiting for Javan to return to the treehouse with any news about The Unforgiven from Protector Anaya. Glancing up from her journal, she eyed the weathered box resting on the shelf. Setting her journal aside, she hopped off the bed and retrieved the box. She ran her fingers over the metal hook latch, the one she'd seen Victr open hundreds of times.

"Victr the Victorious," Perl whispered, "Where are you?" She flipped the latch and opened the lid.

The shelling knife was humble, but sharper than one might expect. Victr never allowed Perl to use it, always worried she would cut herself. Engraved on the handle were the initials 'S.R.' Anytime Perl would ask what the letters stood for, Victr would launch into a story about a 'squirrel robot,' or a 'sorcerer raccoon' that once had owned the knife. Perl picked up the knife, holding it for the first time. Her fingers began to feel warm and prickly, the sensation moving up her arm and through her entire body. "Oh…" Perl could feel herself getting lightheaded as the box slipped from her hand. She leaned back on the wall for support, then slid down to the floor as the room swirled into a soft haze and Perl drifted into a dreamlike state:

Perl was sitting in Victr's cozy kitchen. The smell of butter and capers frying in a skillet filled Perl's nostrils, followed by the earthy aroma of tilapia and mushrooms. She watched as the large, burly monk moved about the space gracefully, cutting vegetables and stirring boiling pots of soup. Perl's heart ached at the sight of her dear, sweet Victr. As quickly as it came, however, the vision faded, the delicious aromas now replaced with a dank, musty odor.

Perl's eyelids flickered and her hands began to tremble, gripping the knife tightly with both hands as the visions intensified:

Staring back at her from a full-length antique mirror was a much thinner Victr, looking like a man in his twenties. Perl was now seeing through Victr's eyes. Victr licked his hand, running it over a stubborn curl of hair that refused to stay down, then turned and began frantically rummaging through a dingy, disorganized room. He darted around, lifting dusty papers, moving stacks of books, knocking pillows off a small bed, all while speaking to a boy, who looked to be about six or seven.

"It isn't here, and I'm going to be late. We'll check down at the pier tomorrow, okay? You probably left it on a rock while we were fishing, that's all."

"Someone will steal it," the small boy pleaded. "Can't we go now?"

Victr poured the last drop of broth from a kettle into a tin cup, handing it to the boy. "No, and no one will steal it. Promise."

"Please Vicky, I can't lose it. It's all I have left of him."

"Don't worry, Silvio, we'll find Papa's knife first thing tomorrow. But right now, I have to get to work or we won't eat."

The boy pouted, giving Victr a defiant look.

"Just promise me you'll stay put. It's not safe to go to the pier alone, especially at night when there are vicious cannibals and monsters roaming the alleyways," he said with a wry smile and a lift of an eyebrow. "Just promise me you'll stay here."

The boy smiled back at Victr, crossing his fingers behind his tattered shirt. "Promise."

Victr tussled the boy's thick curly hair before turning to close and lock the door behind him.

Perl sat pressed against the wall gripping the knife; her bioluminescent spots began to glow:

Moments after Victr left, the boy unlatched a window and crawled out, moving quickly down the dark, grungy streets. He ran past several prostitutes standing in front of a brothel, then jostled his way through a crowd of people drinking at an outside tavern. A grizzled, heavyset man and his toothless stork of a friend, both drunk, spotted the lone child. They exchanged rotten smiles and staggered after the boy as he headed for the pier.

Perl could hear herself shouting in her head, "Victr! Victr!" Her vision shifted back to Victr's point of view just as he was returning to the shack.

"I forgot my apron," Victr announced as he swung open the rickety door. "Silv? Are you hiding? I don't have time for this." He noticed the open window. "Silvio!" Victr bolted for the wharf.

Perl's vison returned to the two men; they had reached the boy at the pier's edge; an old wooden railing guarded against the cliff's twenty-foot drop.

"What's your hurry, son?" Slurred the thin, lanky man. "You lost? Need help?" The heavyset man belched and chuckled. Their long shadows fell over the boy from the wharf's dirty yellow lanterns.

"I'm not lost, just looking for something."

"Let us help you." The heavyset man seized the boy's arm as his partner grabbed the other.

"Hey, let go!"

Victr rounded the corner, seeing his little brother being man-handled. "Drop him! Now!"

The men turned, facing Victr as Silvio kicked at their legs. "Or what? Move on, pal. Finders-keepers, heh-heh."

Victr looked down; wedged in the rocks was Silvio's shelling knife. He reached down and grabbed it, holding it in front of him. "Or I'll gut you both like catfish!"

"Easy, friend...we're just having a little fun..." The big man shoved Silvio at this sidekick. "Hold him." He slipped his free hand inside his coat, pulling out his own knife. "And who doesn't love a little fun, eh?" He waddled slowly toward Victr, waving the shank at him while the other man pressed the small boy against the railing. "So let's play!"

Though twice Victr's size, the man was shaky on his feet; the sour smell of tobacco and booze wafted in the air. Victr backpedaled slowly, watching the man while keeping an eye on his brother.

"Help!" Silvio screamed as the weathered boards creaked and leaned from their weight.

"Silvio!" Victr shouted, momentarily distracted. Seeing an opening, the burly man lunged at Victr. Victr sidestepped slicing across the man's forehead and then drove his knife up into the man's stomach.

Now seeing the man's face more clearly, Perl recognized him. It was the imprisoned worker the Under Kingdom's boiler room; the one with the long scar on his face that she and Amanita had seen. Perl could feel the pain course through her body. She shuddered, seeing Victr's blade pierce the man's gut:

The drunk moaned, stumbling backwards as he clutched his belly. He tripped on the dock's uneven planks and fell, a pool of blood quickly spreading on his jacket.

"Shit, man, you killed him!" Shouted the sidekick. He gave a growl and shoved Silvio, pushing him hard against the guardrail. The boy flipped over the weakened railing, screaming as he fell. The skinny man smirked, then reached down and scooped up his partner's knife and wallet before scampering away.

"No!" Victr looked over the edge; his brother's twisted frame lay amongst the broken rocks of the breakwall below.

"I know who you are, Victr Rossi! You're a dead man!"

Victr raced down the set of rough stone steps leading to the water. Reaching his brother, he fell to his knees, cradling the boy's head. "Silvio, can you hear me? Sil! Are you—?"

The small boy opened one eye, the other caked in blood. His voice cracked, "I...I can't feel my legs, Victr." His breathing was quick but shallow.

Tears ran down Perl's face; she tightened her grip on the knife's handle, the dream shifting once more:

It was the day Victr had escaped to the island of Mont Michel. Approaching on his bicycle with his brother in the sidecar, Victr peered up at the grand castle at the mountain's peak, down to the bottom where a group of monks were gathered, ceremoniously ringing a giant bell. The tide was out, making the bike ride across the stone passageway to the island possible. Victr pedaled up to the monks; an elderly monk looked over and smiled, twirling his moustache.

"Greetings, friends. New to our fair island?"

"Yes, we—that is, I— am looking for work," Victr replied. "I'll do anything. I've worked as a dishwasher and busboy in the past."

"You know your way around a kitchen, then? Well, we can always use a hand in our pantry."

"I could start today. I'm Victr, and this is my little brother, Silvio."

Silvio sat silently, watching the waves roll in and out on the trash-filled beach.

"I admire your enthusiasm, Victr, but how about we get you settled in first? I'm Brother Ximu, and these men you see behind me on the hill are my fellow brothers. We are The Brotherhood of the Quill."

Perl's eyes filled with tears; she could feel Victr's sense of relief as he chatted with the monks and her beloved Papa Ximu. Her death grip on the knife loosened, as did the horrible knot in her stomach.

"We have a spare room off of the kitchen. It's not much, but you're both welcome to it." Ximu pulled back the hood of his cloak; his hair was salt and pepper rather than the pure white Perl was used to seeing. He bent down to the quiet boy. "'He who loves the woods.' That is the meaning of your name, Silvio." Ximu smiled, "Perhaps you'd like a tour of our garden later, hm?"
Silvio didn't respond, his gaze fixed on the water.
"He can't walk," Victr said in a whisper. "There was...an accident."

A rush of pain and sorrow so intense hit Perl that she doubled over. The visions became a series of quick flashes:

Silvio refusing to eat time and time again; Victr carrying his thin, frail body to the bath; Victr sitting by Silvio's side, night after night, pleading with him to stay alive; Victr wringing his hands, wrought with worry and guilt from that fateful night.

Back at the treehouse, Perl lie slumped over, eyes shut, the knife cradled to her chest. Beads of sweat had formed on her brow, yet she shivered uncontrollably. The visions of Victr kept coming, and as Perl lay there shaking, the floor around her began to shake as well. The rumbling startled the Sociable Weaver birds, who scattered from their cozy nests in the ceiling rafters. Pebbles, berries, and other objects fell from the walls. Chairs tipped over as the quaking intensified, reverberating through the floor and down the trunk of the tree, rattling the spiral staircase like loose teeth. The tremor ran into the ground to the tree's roots, charring a large patch of pink grass as if it had been struck by a bolt of lightning. A seizure took hold of Perl; she foamed at the mouth.

"What's happening!?" Flax hollered to Tars; the pair were resting on the lawn, playing a game of Lucky-Leaf cards.

Javan, sensing trouble, sprinted up the trembling staircase, his electrolocation firing.

"Perl!" The clumsy platypus-boy covered his head from the falling debris, making his way to Perl's door.

Inside her room, Javan saw Perl lying on the floor, but what struck him was her shadow on the wall; it looked nearly identical to the vampire squid headboard above Perl's bed.

"Perl!" Javan shouted again, gently lifting Perl up to a sitting position. Her eyes were rolled back white. Her bioluminescent spots glowed brightly.

"Look at me, Perl! Are you okay?" Javan squeezed her arm.

Perl let out a scream; in her mind, she saw the Backwards Man laughing, crawling towards her, contorted and frightening. Perl's skin was on fire; the spikes on her arms and legs had shot out like thorns on a rose.

"Wake up!" Javan noticed the knife Perl still held. He wrapped his hands around hers, speaking to her telepathically. *"It's okay, Perl. You are safe, you can let go. I have you. Just let go."*

Hearing Javan's voice, Perl coughed, her vision slowly returning. She rubbed her eyes and there was Javan, holding her hand, his chestnut-colored eyes filled with concern. Perl felt her body go limp. She let go of the knife and fell forward, resting her head on Javan's soft, furry shoulder, and began to weep. Like a sudden passing of a storm, the rumbling treehouse grew still once more.

He hugged her, "What happened?"

"We have to save him, Javan. We have to."

"We will, Perl," Javan squeezed her. "I know the way."

"What do we have here? An ootheca, and a brilliant one at that!" Master Tryfon was in his garden, bent over to get a better look at the light brown nest of praying mantis eggs attached to a branch. "Such engineeri—" Tryfon straightened, gripping his walking stick. Seconds later, a force like a seismic gust reverberated through the air—heavy, deep, and ominous—washing through him. Tryfon's heads on either side of his human face morphed into a roaring lion and grizzly bear. As quickly as it came, the ripple disappeared. The Master tilted his head to one side as if trying to recall a long-forgotten memory. "That...presence. I've not sensed that in Venusto since Early Times," he said to himself. "When Darkness first waged war on the Light."

Three members of the High Council entered the garden, gathering around the Divine Master.

"Your Grace, you felt that, did you not? I fear the Dark Realm is attempting to draw Perl into the Unforgiven." The Council member, a large albino bat, levitated inches above the ground, their leather-like wings tightly wrapped around its body.

"Master Tryfon is aware," interjected the second member, a nine-foot-tall entity with a finely-cut clear crystal for a head; its torso was a shifting purple aura resembling a galaxy of sparkling stars.

Tryfon listened, his gaze returning once more to the mantis nest. "Did you know that 'ootheca' means 'a place to keep'?" The Master admired the foam-like insulation of the ootheca, housing hundreds of mantis eggs. "Protecting the eggs through the perils of winter."

The members of the High Council exchanged worried glances. "Master, we must not allow Perl to enter this place of keeping," the third member said, a great white wolf; a pair of antlers grew from its snout, spiraling up past its ears. "She cannot interfere with human essences there."

"Why are humans in the Unforgiven?" Tryfon asked and answered, "If not to emerge as nymphs, living fully once again?"

"Yes, but it is not our place as Protectors of the Light Realm to be among those awaiting judgement." The bat crossed and recrossed its webbed wings. "It is forbidden."

"It is *not* ours, true," Tryfon turned, facing the Divine Masters. "The Chosen One does so with meraki...that is, with total love and a pure essence. Therefore, it is so."

"This breach has not only endangered Venusto, but all who dwell in the Light of Paradise above," as the crystal Being spoke, its head lit up like a strobe.

"Earth is not the only planet The Light Realm holds guardianship of," Tryfon's skin morphed in sync with his changing faces, going from the feathers of an owl to the scales of a crocodile to the bark of an oak tree. "The time is coming for Earth to awaken, and when it does, all of Venusto will fight for it, as we always have, faithfully." Tryfon tapped his walking stick firmly on the ground; it was as long as a staff, intricately carved with the faces of hundreds of animals. Tryfon looked at his council members. "When asked, we will assist."

The three Beings bowed. "Praise to all Nature."

"Praise to all Nature," Tryfon repeated the farewell. "And may Ever be ever by your side."

The High Council Beings departed, each in the direction of their designated post; one to Callowhorn, one to Greenheart and one to Natatory.

Tryfon turned, touching the ootheca on the branch, releasing the hundreds of tiny colorless praying mantises. Within seconds, the insects darkened in color, blending perfectly with the leaves and flowers on the branch. Tryfon leaned down whispering, "Hear their prayers and bring them to me."

The congregation of mantises took to the air, swirling into the clouds above.

Below the island of Mont Michel, the Brotherhood of the Quill's small underground chapel was packed to the gills; monks and nuns in different colored robes and priests and guides in assorted tribal attire filled the pews. Sitting in the front row were Sisters Martha, Ursula, and Betty, there to represent the Forest Sisters of Elsewhere.

The sanctuary was illuminated with hundreds of handmade candles carved into tiny birds. Hung here and there along the walls were Perl's nature drawings that Victr had hung a few years ago when she had first left for Seeker training.

"Today we come together in unity as Light Bearers of Earth." Brother Ximu stood at the front of the chapel behind the old wooden pulpit carved from a peach tree; beside him was Brother Basil, his trusty journal in hand. "We have called you here at this time because we have witnessed the rise of an evil presence in the Desertlands, one that took the life of our dear Brother Victr."

There was an audible response across the room, "May he rest in peace."

"Praise Ever," Ximu said, swallowing back tears.

"There have been other accounts from many of your Brothers and Sisters as well...of crops being plagued by unexplainable disease and pestilence." Ximu looked out at the concerned faces staring back at him, noticing the group of Earth Activists standing against the back wall, Gretar among them.

"And with the alliance between the Princes of the Desertland and the Graves," a monk in a middle pew spoke out. "The clean water that was already in short supply is being further rationed away from the poor and the needy."

"We must pray—" Brother Basil was interrupted from a voice in the back.

"We need to get inside the Under Kingdom and free the imprisoned!" Gretar's cry echoed through the chamber. "We need a real plan to break up their cartel!"

The room erupted, "Yes, yes!", "He speaks the truth!", "We need to put an end to royal suppression!"

Basil rang a set of chimes, trying to quiet the room.

Ximu strained to raise his voice over the crowd. The monk, now in his 100's, was feeling weary; the stress from recent news, as well as how to combat it, was weighing heavily on him.

"The Forest Sisters of Elsewhere have come to inform us about the Under Kingdom and how we might be able to work with the spies that they have in place." Ximu opened the ancient book of the Awakening. "But first, let us pray." He read the passage:

Line XI, Verse V
Light Protectors of Earth and sky defend us in battle,
be our safeguard against all wickedness and snares of The Ullen.
Messengers of truth in the unseen, open our eyes to the love in all nature.
By the will of Ever give us the foresight to come to live in pure Light.

After shared prayers, the congregation split into smaller groups, brainstorming ideas to help their regions work together, as well as increase their numbers, in an effort to take down the Under Kingdom.

At a large side table, a small group had gathered around Sister Ursula as she unfolded a crudely drawn map displaying passageways, tunnels, and multiple levels of the underground city.

"Brother Ximu? If I may? It's possible that we can sneak a few of you in," Sister Ursula led a gathering, consisting of Gretar and a few others from The Ocean Conservation Coalition of Earthers and The Sisters of the Seahorse Initiative. "There are limited safehouses. Under One's Heel runs every aspect of the Under Kingdom. They have eyes everywhere. Here," Ursula pointed to an area on the map. "This is the Under Kingdom's main power source." She had drawn a circle around the room with a piece of chalk. "It has two backup generators, here and here. All three have to be shut down simultaneously to unlock the electric chains, which will free the orphans and imprisoned from their work stations."

"I'm in," Gretar rubbed his stubbled chin. "Whatever it takes."

Ursula straightened, eyeing the young man. "It will take no less than a miracle. There's also the Royal Guards. They're robots. Killing machines. They aren't part of the power grid. They have individual cores that can only be deactivated by a switch in the back of their gaping mouths." She shuddered, thinking of the nightmarish androids.

"How are we supposed to——?" Gretar started to ask; Ursula cut him off.

"We don't. It's impossible to get close to them so we avoid them at all costs."

Perl's friend Regor and a few other pantry workers hurried about, serving hot stew in large mugs, allowing the discussion groups to continue working. Plans and options were formed and reformed until it was finally agreed; they would take action on the night of the upcoming coronation.

"The crowning of the two new kings and their queen will create a diversion. That's our chance to cut the power," Brother Basil shared with the room.

"We will have Sisters and spies in place to lead everyone out through the secret tunnel system," added Sister Betty.

"Once you have them to the safety of the woods, we will have covered wagons camouflaged near Slugabed Hovel," said a young monk in a teal robe strewn with beads.

"Without the imprisoned, the Under Kingdom will fall!" Cheered a man in a tribal headdress, raising his cup of soup.

"Here, here!" The room clinked their mugs.

Brother Ximu made his way to the corner table in the dining hall. "Gretar, a word?"

Gretar followed the old monk out of the chapel away from the clamor.

"I carry a message for you from our Perl. She has instructed me to tell you that your gift has been delivered," Ximu patted Gretar warmly on the shoulder. "She said that you'd know what that meant."

"I do," Gretar felt a wave of joy rush over him. "When you see Perl, thank her for me. I owe her the world."

"That we all do, my son."

Gretar smiled and headed back into the room, unsure of the old monk's comment. He glanced back over his shoulder to find Ximu smiling back at him, his long mustache curling up at the ends.

"Would you like some peony baklava to take with you, Puggle?" Anaya asked, packing Javan's leaf-pouch with supplies. The Elder Land Protector hurried around the treehouse kitchenette, opening and closing cupboards.

"Yes, please, and thank you!" Perl answered for Javan, recalling the otherworldly sweetness of the pink-petaled treat. "And what about you...*Puggle*?" She giggled, giving Javan a side-eye.

Javan blushed.

"You will always be my baby platypus," the echidna said, pulling a pink flower from her gown's pocket and placing it in the bag. She looked over at Javan, her tiny dark eyes narrowing. "And you really need to do something with that hair!"

Anaya shuffled over to Javan, pushing his bangs off his face with both of her hands, his swept-back hair now looking like his mother's porcupine-like quills. "Ah, there's my sweet Puggle-poo." She pressed her head against his, her long tongue flicking with happiness.

"Stop!" Javan turned a deeper shade of red.

Pure Beings from the Light Realm didn't have traditional parents. However, each was given a Light mentor at the moment of their creation. Anaya had been Javan's personal guide, given by Ever to watch over him.

"I think it's about that time," Anaya closed a drawer with her hip. "We should get going." Her rounded body was covered in quills that poked through an ornate gown; lovingly embroidered with a mix of rose lace and yellow flowers. She had a single orange tulip growing from atop her head that bounced as she spoke.

As the threesome were heading out of the treehouse Corvax landed, perching on the front porch's railing.

"Protector Anaya, a blessing to see you," the crow-boy said, eyeing Perl and Javan closely. "And where are you off to this fine day?"

"Oh, just going to have a picnic," Perl answered, thinking to herself, *"Well, we did pack a lunch."*

"It's about time," Uriel chimed in. The Light Realm Guide leaned against a nearby tree, casually strumming the strings on her gittern. "What have you been doing in there all morning?"

Corvax looked at Uriel, then back at the three. Perl could see the crow-boy's wheels turning.

"A picnic you say? Mind if I join you?" Corvax prodded.

"Sorry," Javan said. "It's kind of a mentor-mentee bonding thing. Just us."

"Oh okay," Corvax nodded slowly. "So, this doesn't have anything to do with why our treehouse shook all of Venusto yesterday?"

"Nope, just taking an afternoon off," Perl grinned. She, Javan, and Anaya marched past Corvax.

Corvax eyed the three of them suspiciously as they joined Uriel, then slipped through an opening in the tall hedges surrounding the lush gardens of Greenheart.

Lyre swooped in, landing beside the crow, "Watcha glaring at?"

"He's got a soft spot for her."

"Everyone knows that," Lyre mimicked Corvax's voice. She paused. "Wait, are you jealous?"

"I don't harbor that emotion," Corvax said, taking flight for an aerial view of where the group was headed.

Lyre watched Corvax quietly glide through a cloud, his black wings spread wide against the white. "Sure, you don't."

The Protectors and their protégé walked along the pebbled pathways beside the rows of neatly-manicured lemon and lime trees and varieties of animal topiary, reaching the main gardens.

"Sit, sit," Anaya said, pulling out a crocheted blanket from her satchel, spreading it across the grass.

Uriel knelt on a corner, as Perl and Javan sat cross-legged, watching Anaya set out star-cut marmalade sandwiches on lily pad leaves.

"You understand, you will not be in the Light, nor the Dark, nor the Half-Light Realms," Uriel said. "You will be in The Unforgiven. It is a place where humans banish themselves. It is important that you know this. Although it is a woeful, lost world, it is not a place of punishment." She removed her gittern from off her shoulder, setting it beside her on the grass.

Corvax hid high above in the treetops. His sharp eyesight could see they were having a serious conversation, but he was too far away to make out what they were saying.

"We understand," Javan answered for them both.

Perl looked over at Javan, feeling a rush of gratitude wash over her. Javan was always by her side when she needed him most, and this was no different, yet it felt extra special since he'd gone out on a limb and reached out to his Light Realm mentor for help.

"It doesn't make any sense. Why would Victr put himself in such a place?" Perl asked. "I swear Victr saw something as his essence was leaving his body. I think it was the same thing that took him."

"When a human dies, there is a battle for their essence. Those that have lived well go to the Light, the cursed and corrupted go to the Dark, but those that neither side can claim fall victim to The Unforgiven, where the battle continues. Humans though they may end up there, have a choice. Yet they hold their essence there by not forgiving themselves for whatever they feel they have done wrong during their embodiment on Earth." Uriel picked up a sandwich. "You are correct, Perl. Victr was pulled in by a malevolent force. You and Javan have been granted permission to enter The Unforgiven to retrieve him." Uriel placed her hand on Perl's knee, her one eye staring intently at her. "As you have seen through your vision from holding his knife, Victr has much that remains unresolved in himself."

Perl thought to herself, *Of course she knows, Uriel always seems to know.*

"What happens to people if they never forgive themselves?" Perl leaned back from her Protector's hard stare.

"Over time, the Self-Slayer wins and the human's essence is consumed by the Dark Realm," Uriel said matter-of-factly.

"However, if a human wins their struggle and finds forgiveness, a Light Protector comes forth to bring them to Ever-lasting Light," Anaya added. She reached into her bag, pulling out an hourglass with ornate carved handles on each side.

"What is that?" Still observing from up high, Corvax squinted at the timepiece.

Perl took a bite of her sandwich and joked, "Are we going to be timed?"

"Precisely. Once the hourglass's tears have dried up and the tree bears fruit you will be returned to us." Anaya carefully set the hourglass between Perl and Javan.

Inside the upper chamber of the pear-shaped glass bulb was a cloud with an eyeball in the center of it. In the lower glass bulb was a grassy patch with a tiny seed poking out.

"You must find Victr quickly. Remain in the Unforgiven too long, and you risk becoming lost yourselves," Uriel said, giving Perl a stern look of concern.

"Aren't you coming with us?" Perl asked.

"We cannot. Divine Protectors are forbidden to interfere with matters of the human essence once they have left Earth. We can only enter The Unforgiven to bring them home once their free will grants it."

"I guess it's a good thing we haven't finished our training then," Javan said, smiling at Perl.

"You will need to recall your training from Master Gichi." Anaya swept Javan's bangs back off his face. "Self-Slayers govern the Unforgiven. Do not let negative thoughts enter your minds or you will be unable to sever Victr from his shadow."

"Any tips on how to go about separating a human from their Self-Slayer?" Perl looked into Uriel's piercing violet eye.

"Use levity and love. Follow your heart to heal his." Uriel said, lifting Perl's hand and placing it on the handle of the hourglass. "And stay together. Do not attempt to free all of the sorrowful you see. You are there for Victr, and Victr alone."

Anaya took Javan's hand in hers. "Regret like Brother Victr's is like a drop of lemon in a cup of cream. It curdles the life, makes it unpalatable. When others have agreed or felt sorry for him it encouraged his beliefs, gave power to what was, compounded his worries into fears." Anaya placed Javan's hand on the opposite hourglass handle. "Fear not, my sweet Pugg—" She giggled softly, her snout wiggling. "My sweet Javan."

Anaya's words echoed in Javan's head as he squeezed the hourglass's black wooden handle. As soon as he and Perl took hold of the hourglass, the others watched as the two slowly vanished.

"What the—?" Corvax blinked. "Where'd they go?"

Uriel picked up her instrument, strumming it as she called up to the trees, "Corvax, do come and join us for some snacks, won't you?"

Perl and Javan, still holding the handles of the hourglass, found themselves standing on the surface of a strange, alien landscape; a thick gray fog hovered knee deep across the terrain.

"Colorless," Perl said, letting go of the hourglass. She examined her arms, her Humor uniform. "No color at all. Everything's gray."

Javan bent down and touched one of the endless ashy, creeping roots snaking along the ground. The root quivered when touched, and they noticed a ripple travel along the root where it connected to a large mound the size of a hippopotamus. The giant gray mound reacted, firing off a spray of sparks; this triggered a dozen other roots whose currents ran off in all directions toward other mounds setting off more sparks. In the center of all of this, where the giant spiderweb of roots converged, stood an enormous spherical structure. Bleak and imposing, it had thousands of antennae-like appendages protruding from it.

"This place is like one giant neural network," Javan said, as they watched the roots igniting one after another, spreading across the ground in all directions. "And that," Javan pointed to the sphere, "must be the brain."

"Then that's where we need to go."

"We better hurry," Javan held up the hourglass. "The cloud has started to shed tears."

Perl looked into the top portion of the glass; the first few teardrops had fallen, and a small sprig had formed in the bottom glass.

The pair broke into a sprint towards the massive globe, trying their best to move quietly and avoid stepping on the endless web of axons and dendrites. Once they reached the base of the giant orb, they realized that it was porous.

"It looks like a giant Hexactinellid," Javan looked up at the skeletal structure. "A glass sea sponge. Also known as a prison of love, because shrimp go in, and—"

Perl cut him off. "No time for a lesson...we can fit through here." She ducked through one of the holes; Javan followed the slender girl.

"Whoa," Javan's jaw dropped as he tried to comprehend what he was seeing; all around him, thousands of chambers were carved into the walls of the mammoth interior. "It's like an endless honeycomb," Javan whispered. "How will we ever find Victr in this maze?"

Walking farther into The Unforgiven, they saw that each weblike cell held one person; an unsettling shadow figure hovering near them. There was a woman crying, appearing to rock a child that wasn't there; a man in a suit rustling papers mumbling about an oil spill, another man whispered to himself about infidelity, and on and on; cell after cell people were ruminating and festering as their dark doppelganger loomed over them.

"They're feeding off of their pain," Perl watched as the black-shrouded Self-Slayers clung to the people like ravenous specters.

Javan looked at the hourglass. "Let's keep moving, the branches are beginning to form on the tiny tree." Javan tilted his head and concentrated, trying to sense where Victr might be. "My electrolocation is picking up impulses everywhere." As Javan tried to focus, flashes of doubt began to worm their way into his subconscious— *"I'm no use to her. This is hopeless. Why did I come here?"*

Perl felt her skin crawl as a dark shadow began to emerge behind the platypus-boy. "Javan, remember to let any negative feelings pass over you. Don't let the dark thoughts in."

"I...I can't," Javan rubbed his temple. "It's right. You...you don't need me."

"I do need you, Javan," Perl said, but she could see Javan's Slayer had attached and was not letting go. "We have to keep moving."

As they hurried through the maze of sorrow, people wailed—"It was all my fault!", "Please save my mother!", "I should have done more!"

Perl ignited her bioluminescent spots to light the way through the dark chamber, the Self-Slayers shrinking away from the light as she passed each cell.

"Do you smell that?" Perl perked up.

Javan shrugged, "Decaying food maybe? I dunno." He winced as the bad thoughts bombarded him— *"Shut up. You're not helping. She doesn't need you."*

"Fish!" Perl quickened her step. "This way," she waved, as they ventured deeper into The Unforgiven's labyrinth.

People trapped in the cells grabbed hold of Perl and Javan as they went by, pulling at them, begging for their help.

"I'm so sorry, we can't help you. Forgive yourself. Please. Ever loves you." Perl and Javan repeated. Prying away hand after desperate hand was heartbreaking, but they followed Uriel's command—*Do not attempt to save anyone other than Victr.*

Trusting her instincts and following the smell of fish, Perl spotted a tall, hooded figure dragging a bag. A thick cloud of flies buzzed around the man, but he didn't seem to notice.

"Victr?" Perl took off after the man.

"Wait for me!" Javan said, breaking into a slow, loping trot. Being close to Perl's light was causing his Slayer to fade, and the platypus-boy's head began to clear.

Trailing the hooded man was a dark shadow nearly twice his size. The Self-Slayer had a hunched back with long spindly fingers that gripped the man's shoulders like puppet strings. They rounded the corner and ducked into one of the cells. Perl and Javan caught up to him, pausing just a second before entering the dimly-lit chamber.

"What if, what if, no, yes, no..." The man was arguing with himself.

Recognizing the monk's voice, Perl's heart simultaneously leapt for joy and broke at the sight of him. "Victr," she approached slowly. "It's me, Perl, and this is Javan. We're here to help you." Peering up under his hood, Perl saw that his face was still covered in the same warts and sores as the day he died. "We're going to get you out of here."

Victr didn't seem to hear a word Perl said. He grabbed a rusty metal ladle from a hook on the wall and began stirring a bubbling kettle brimming with severed fish heads and bones.

Javan nudged Perl, "Look." The tree inside the hourglass was beginning to sprout tiny buds like the first sign of spring. "We have to hurry."

Perl nodded. "Uriel said to use levity and love. I have an idea." She started to sing the silly jingle she and Victr used to sing while making cookies, hoping to jog his memory.

> "Roll, roll, roll out the dough,
> flour your pin, and roll it again!
> Cut, cut, cut out the shapes,
> pop them in, and do a spin!"

Victr's head turned towards the girl dancing in place, pretending to roll dough with an imaginary rolling pin.

> "Ding, ding, ding goes the bell...
> eat up, my good kin,
> 'til your belly grins!"

Perl smiled her toothiest grin. "Remember, Victr? Remember?"

"I think it's working," Javan joined in. "Roll, roll, roll out the dough, flour your—"

"Perl?" Victr coughed gruffly. "No-no-no...it can't be," Victr turned away, shaking his head as he hunched over the pot, letting the pungent steam rise up in a cloud around him.

"It *is* me. I'm here. Victr, please hear me."

Victr's Self-Slayer hissed at the girl. Perl had seen far worse creatures in life, and although it was hideous, Perl stared at it, her bioluminescent dots glowing brightly. The phantom crouched down behind Victr and began whispering into the monk's ear.

The monk nodded as he rooted around inside his bag of filth, repeating the words the Slayer spoke. "I killed a man. I'm a murderer." He dropped a moldy, maggot-filled potato into the pot.

"Listen to me Victr. You didn't kill that man on the dock that night. He's a prisoner in the Under Kingdom." Perl gently placed her hand on Victr's arm. "I saw him."

Perl remembered the heavyset man in her vision; he was the same man she'd seen chained to the trash chute shoveling garbage into the furnace the night she and Amanita had gone to the arena.

She squeezed Victr's arm, but he yanked it away angrily, barking at Perl. "It's my fault my brother ended up crippled. It's my fault he died!" The shadowy figure continued to fill Victr's mind with poison.

Javan stepped between Perl and the volatile monk.

"It's okay. He won't hurt me," Perl insisted, seeing the hourglass in Javan's grasp; the tree was full of green leaves with small white buds beginning to form. The tree made her think of the tree in Divine Master Tryfon's garden and she recalled a quote of his— *"We must give love to receive love, demanding nothing in return."*

Perl removed Fortis from its sheath as she began to sing The Grateful Song, the one sung before every meal that Victr had ever prepared for the Brotherhood of the Quill.

"We thank you sun, soil, roots and rains,
We thank you for growing, giving and nurturing our veins,"

Javan stepped aside, seeing Perl readying her sword. He looked at her, reading her thoughts and recalling the rest of Tryfon's message, *"You can never receive what you have never given."*

In that moment Javan truly understood— *Perl's needs were his needs, too. What she needed he wanted to give. His worry of her returning his love was his Self-Slayer's voice and not his own.* Javan set the hourglass down and quickly removed the peony baklava from his pouch. He sprinkled the pink flower petals into the pot as Victr mindlessly stirred.

Perl sang out louder:

"We thank you for today, tomorrow, from our happy humble shores,
We thank you Ever, for ever, ever more."

Finishing the last verse, Perl swung Fortis down, severing Victr from his Self-Slayer. The phantom reared back, screeching in fury just as the sugary vapors from the Light Realm flowers, infused with Anaya's love, wafted up into the monk's face. He inhaled the sweet aroma deeply; a look of clarity came over him as if solving the answer to a difficult riddle.

"We thank you sun…" Freed from his negative thoughts, Victr repeated the joyful song as his Slayer shrank into the shadows. He pulled back his hood, taking in his bleak surroundings. "Dear Ever, where am I?" Panic filled the monk's eyes until he saw Perl. "But how?" he mumbled. Next to her stood a furry-looking creature, smiling. "What…what are you?"

"A friend," Javan replied. "How do you feel?"

Victr ran a hand along his cheek; the steam from the peony petals had seeped into his pores, healing his wounds. He smiled in disbelief.

Perl put a hand on the monk's shoulder. "It's okay, Victr, you're —"

Before Perl could say the word, 'safe,' something crawled out from the corner of the cell. It wasn't Victr's Self-Slayer. Perl's blood froze.

"No!" Victr shuddered at the sight of the Backwards Man, remembering the thing that had attacked him in the Desertlands. "No," Victr cowered into a ball against the wall. "All is lost, all is lost."

Not quite sure what was happening, Perl and Javan jumped in between Victr and the demon.

"Stay back!" Perl held Fortis high.

The thing's skeletal face had no eyes, yet it crawled right towards them, upside down on all fours. Its bones cracked like dry twigs as it moved, its long, forked tongue flicking in and out through rows of tiny razor-sharp teeth. Dangling dolls, chains, and other trinkets strung across its swollen belly rocked back and forth with each cumbersome step.

"Daughter of Lighttt," the thing spat as yellow mucus dripped from its slitted nostrils. *"Master will give me a seat at his hand when I have your precious little head."* Greasy black hair, crawling with centipedes, brushed across the ground like a dirty mop. When the foul beast got closer, it lashed out at Perl.

Perl, having mastered her swordplay from the many lessons with Bear, swiftly dodged the thing's long claw, and in one smooth stroke, sliced across the demon's exposed neck with the tip of Fortis. Rivulets of black fluid ran down its face.

The thing frowned, but being upside down it looked like a hideous smile. It let out a sickly giggle. *"I taste Darknesss on your tusssk."*

Javan fired spurs from his hip at the creature. He looked around for a weapon.

"Kahh wuum sssea," it hissed. *"Malblud!"* Dark saliva ran down its cheeks.

Perl looked at the tip of Fortis; it had been charred black when Uriel held the sword inside Malblud, her father's killer. A chill ran through her; fear crept in, recalling the nightmarish memory. As she took several steps away from the Backwards Man, a dark shadow was forming behind her.

The Backwards Man taunted her. *"You are weeeak like your fatherrr!"*

"Perl, don't let it get in! The past is gone! You're here now to bring Victr home!" Javan shouted.

Victr covered his head with his hood, pressing himself into a fetal position against the wall. "Run, Perl, run! Save yourself! All is lost!"

Perl looked down at the helpless monk, trying to ignore the whispers in her ear that ate away at her thoughts— *"I can't save him...I can't save him...I can't save him."*

Javan shot two more venomous spurs from his hips, embedding the darts into the demon's contorted belly. "Perl, look at me!"

Hearing her friend, Perl summoned her courage. "Aggghhh!" Gripping her sword tightly, she charged at the beast. She swung again and again, but the creature easily blocked Perl's strikes using a femur bone.

Javan grabbed the metal ladle from the pot, dousing the Backwards Man.

"Eeeeaaaggghh!" The creature dropped to the ground, wailing in pain as its skin boiled. The broth in the kettle had turned to liquid Light from the peony petals. Javan swung the ladle down hard, striking the thing in the head; centipedes scattered in every direction.

Perl saw her chance. "Like my father..." she drove Fortis deep into the thing's boney rib cage, "I am fearless!"

The Backwards Man writhed in misery, holding its side as trails of blood oozed from the wound like worms; the venom from Javan's spurs adding to the creature's agony, but it was not dead. It slowly pushed itself back up on all fours.

Perl saw that Javan was out of spurs and Victr was huddled in fear. Her Self-Slayer had faded away, and only one thought filled her mind— *"I must protect them. I must. I must."*

In that moment, Perl could feel her skin getting warmer. But she could feel something else happening. Her body was trying to communicate with her. She felt it. Fortis fell from her grip. Before she had time to process it, the skin around the spikes on Perl's wrists, elbow, shoulders and knees began to stretch upward and outward, like a huge umbrella turning inside out. She grabbed Javan's hand, pulling him over to where Victr lay curled up, and held them close under her cape-like frame. The webbing closed in over their heads, sealing them off from the predator; her spikes facing out, her bioluminescent light glowing from within.

Perl's conversion happened so fast the demon didn't know that it was Perl. Seeing this new fearsome, faceless figure covered in jagged points, the monster became confused and disoriented.

"Did Massster send youuu?" It circled cautiously, the pain in its gut throbbing.

From beneath the cape two large mimic eyes shone like glistening orbs. The light stung the beast, causing it to back away.

Inside, huddled together closely in Perl's protective parachute, Javan and Victr stared in awe at Perl; her bioluminescent spots dotting their covering like a sky full of stars. Perl had her hands clasped over her head, holding the disguise together.

"A vampire squid," Javan smiled at Perl. "You really are like your father."

Even Victr managed a nervous grin. "How?"

"I have no idea," Perl started to giggle. "This is new."

They all began to snicker; their levity rippling Perl's cape and further bewildering the Backwards Man. The creature twitched as its tortured mind tried to comprehend the laughter. It cursed and spat.

Perl's body jerked and wiggled from laughter. Unbeknownst to her, particles of shiny, sticky bioluminescent mucus began to expel from the tips of her spikes, creating a cloud of glowing light particles around them.

Strands of twinkling liquid hit the Backwards Man and it let out a final scream before crawling up the wall and squeezing its ragged body through a small opening in the ceiling. The femur bone it used as a weapon dropped to the floor with a clatter.

The threesome fell silent.

"Is it safe?" Perl's arms trembled and the muscles in her legs quaked. "I can't hold this much longer."

Javan inhaled deeply. "I don't sense it out there. You can let go."

"Wait, are we sure? Maybe it's trying to trick us?" Victr's voice quivered; although much better, the monk was still quite shaken.

"We're good." Perl dropped her hands, unable to sustain her form. Falling to her knees, the webbed wings on Perl's arms and legs retracted, sealing back under her skin.

"Are you okay?" Javan knelt down beside her.

"I'm fine, just weak from...whatever that was."

"It's a response that Vampyroteuthis infernalis uses for self-defense." Javan said, looking at Perl with a mix of admiration and pride.

"Where on Earth are we?" Victr stood. "Am...I dead?"

"We are no longer on Earth, Victr." Perl took his hand, her eyes welling up. "Yes, and it was the saddest day of my life." A tear ran down her cheek.

"Dear Ever." Victr closed his eyes in disbelief. He heard the moans and cries coming from the people in the surrounding cells. "So," he sighed, "is this the Dark Realm? Have I been punished?"

"No. We're in a place called The Unforgiven," Perl said. "That evil creature that poisoned you brought you here."

"What is The Unforgiven?" Victr asked.

Perl took hold of Victr's hand, the last of the warts on his skin healed.

"It's a place where people go when they can't let go of regrets and blame. But you don't have to worry anymore, you're safe. You have tended to everyone with such love and now it is time for you to know your truth."

Victr smiled, the rows of wrinkles on his forehead softening. "My truth?"

She squeezed his hand. "You are a child of the Light and you have always held the spark of Ever in your heart."

"You have saved me," Victr said. "My brave warrior."

Javan cleared his throat. "Sorry to interrupt, but our time is almost up." He held up the hourglass. "We haven't been formally introduced. I'm Javan."

"Oh, Javan, from Venusto. I have heard much about you," Victr nodded to the boy. "You're the one who made Perl's rabbit necklace."

"Yes sir, nice to finally meet you as well," Javan warmed at the thought of Perl talking about him to her beloved monk.

The cloud inside the top of the hourglass was almost gone; tiny apples hung from several of the branches. "Remember, Anaya said a Light Protector will come when it's time—"

As Javan finished his sentence, the room filled with radiant white light. As the light dimmed, a boy could be seen, encircled by sparkling rays of lavender. He stepped toward them.

Tears filled Victr's eyes. "Silvio? Is it you?"

The boy smiled, holding out his hand for Victr to take it.

Victr hugged Perl tightly. "Thank you, thank you. I don't know what to say but thank you."

"Say you'll tell me one day all about the great adventure you're about to go on," Perl replied.

"Come, Vicky, you won't believe how wondrous it is," Silvio beckoned softly.

The monk reached down, taking his brother's little hand in his own. He turned back to Perl. "I promise, my little warrior. I love you, and one day, we will meet again."

"I love you, too, Victr."

Light erupted in the cell. Perl and Javan shielded their eyes as Victr and Silvio vanished into sparkling dust.

"Our turn, Wayshower." Javan held up the hourglass for Perl to take hold of the handle; they watched as the cloud eye closed its lid; the tree now filled with ripe red apples.

Perl wiped away a small tear. "More than ready to go back into the Light, Wayfinder."

Javan smiled at her. *I'd chase after the setting sun for you, pulling it back so you could always be in the Light,* he thought.

Perl smiled back. She gripped the handle and they disappeared, returning to the lush gardens of Greenheart.

"Tell us exactly what happened, Perl," Opis asked. "Corvax told us you and Javan traveled to The Unforgiven?"

"How was that even possible?" Tars added.

"What was it like?" Lyre and Nan said simultaneously.

The nine Seers sat in a circle beneath the sparkling stardust trees of the observatory awaiting Master Gichi; the sky above them a vast swirling indigo flecked with pinpoints of starlight.

"Anaya and Uriel gave us an object, an hourglass. It took us to The Unforgiven to look for my friend Victr," Perl replied.

"We only had so much time," added Javan.

"Right," Perl nodded. "So we got there and found him, but had to sever his Self-Slayer. But something else was there with Victr. Something from the Dark Realm."

Bear leaned in, "Did you take the Nepenthes Attenborough plant to capture the demon?"

"No, I cut the thing's neck with Fortis and Javan stung it with a few of his spurs, but it didn't kill it."

"Whoa," Flax muttered.

"Must've been an ancient creature," said Opis.

"But then, something miraculous happened...right, Perl?"

Perl smiled back at Javan.

Javan cleared his throat. "Perl...transformed."

"You did what?" Bear looked over at Perl.

"She used her *Vampyroteuthis infernalis* essence and formed a protective cape around me and Victr. I'm not really sure what happened, but I guess it scared it off."

"That true, Perl?" Flax nudged her knee, "You discovered a new ability?"

Perl nodded. "I don't know how it happened, it just...happened." She paused. "I thank Ever that we were able to free Victr and escape unharmed, but it was so sad there. My hearts  ache thinking of all the people trapped in that horrible place. They're all in so much pain because they can't forgive themselves, while their Self-Slayers poison their minds with lies." Perl looked across the circle into each of her friends' eyes, "I wanted to save them all."

"I'm sure you did the best you could," Nan's antennae bobbed.

Corvax stood up. "We end The Ullen, that's how we save them. The Ullen controls the Dark Realm, including the Self-Slayers."

Lyre chirped, "But how? We've been fighting the Darkness since the dawn of time."

"Unearth humanity," a voice was heard about the stardust trees. Master Gichi emerged, walking on its multitude of hands. "Remind them of their kinship with all other living kingdoms. Earth. Plant. Animal."

Everyone stood, bowing in reverence to The Great Spirit Moon.

"Humans are born with the ability to hear the bird's song. To talk to the trees. But as they grow, they are told to grow up. They begin to lose their connection to the magic of nature. They forget as it withers away, yet the Light remains inside them, always."

Perl recalled the words to the nightingale's song; the one she had heard the day she met Lance Featherstone in the woods. Master Gichi began to sing the words, as if reading Perl's mind:

*"Take my wing in your hand
Fly with me
To my hidden land,
Under pines and waterfalls
Twists and turns
I've planned it all,"*

As Master Gichi sang, the moonflower vines around it began to reach outward, elongating the Divine Being to the size of the surrounding trees:

*"Roots thirst for the gentle rain
I hear your calls
Your darkest pain,
Planted seeds before your birth
Telling secrets
To magic earth,"*

Levitating over the Seers, Gichi held them in its many arms, a canopy of vines dotted with white flowers surrounding them:

*"I'm everywhere in everything
Look for me
Hear me sing,
Take my wing in your hand
Fly with me
To my hidden land..."*

The Master held the Seers in a warm embrace for a moment, then slowly released them, its vines retracting into its body. Looking around, the Seers found themselves standing on a marshy shoreline in the Half Light Realm of Earth as their teacher concluded its song:

> *"Mud below and skies above*
> *We are one…"*

Perl mouthed the words:

> *"I am love,*
> *I am love,*
> *I am love."*

Returning to its previous size, Master Gichi stood on its fingertips in the shallow surf, its silhouette reflecting on the quiet water. Patches of hyacinth flowers grew across the surface in vivid violets, pinks, and blues.

"Embrace these lessons with a childlike sense of wonder. You can never be too young or too old, but you can be too serious. If you are smiling you are ready to begin. Each Water Seer, please join hands with one Land and one Air Seer."

Javan stepped up to take Perl's left hand, noticing Corvax had already taken her right.

"Close your eyes. Imagine you are a rock, round and smooth. Feel your kinship with the rocks beside you as you reside in this riverbed. You are solid, confident, safe, invulnerable. Pull that feeling into your heart. Now, step into the water."

The Nine held hands in a line, stepping ankle deep into the river. Perl could feel the rocky, uneven bottom beneath her feet.

"Whether they are aware of it or not, humans connect with the Light Realm any time they tend to a plant. Help an animal. Eat anything grown in the soil. Continue farther into the water."

Now knee deep in the warm, calm waters, Perl smiled, feeling at home.

"As Seers, you tend to all of life. Each species carries with it a unique voice. Bring your awareness to the melody of the *Trichechus manatus*."

A back-and-forth banter of high-pitched, bird-like chirps was heard as an aggregation of two dozen manatees swam nearby.

"A mother makes contact calls to her calf. Yet, these herbivores have a far more complex vocal repertoire than just that. Opis, please decode."

"Yes, Master Gichi." Happy to be called upon, Opis's tentacles zapped and sparked as she tapped into her subconscious. "It's two manatee families, old friends, happy to be reunited where the vegetation is rich."

"Very good. Water Bear, what do you hear?"

The chirping calls had switched to a series of mysterious whistles and grunts.

Bear, holding hands with Nan and Flax, put two of his free hands into the water. "A song! They're singing together!"

"Now, attune, Seers. As a choir of nine, link with their harmony. Discover their voice."

Perl and the others, their hands linked, concentrated, seeking to understand the manatees' song. Slowly, the words began to form in their minds:

> *Swim together*
> *If you please,*
> *To hear the song*
> *Of manatees,*
>
> *Love your family*
> *Eat your leaves,*
> *Welcome the lost*
> *Like the breeze,*
>
> *Say Ever bless*
> *At a sneeze,*
> *Need some wisdom*
> *Talk to trees,*
>
> *Spread your kindness*
> *Like the bees,*
> *Know you are loved*
> *By manatees.*

"Very good, Seers. Very good!" Master Gichi's voice interrupted the song. "Open your eyes and release your hands. You have tapped into the universal melody of nature, widening your circle of understanding. From understanding grow the seeds of compassion."

Perl blinked; the sun sparkled across the shallow water. She smiled, the manatee's sweet tune lingering in her mind. She looked down at the large gray mammals lazily grazing on musk grass and hyacinth. Master Gichi's vines had fanned out like a mangrove tree, drinking in the water around the great Light Being.

"Ah, the sea cows," Tars joked, watching the manatees scoop up plants with their flippers, bringing the clumps of leaves to their mouths. "You know they can eat a hundred pounds of leaves a day?"

Always up for a test of knowledge, Opis questioned, "Well did you know that manatees sleep upside down so they can breathe while they sleep?"

As Perl listened to her classmates' banter back and forth, she noticed that a number of the manatees had scars across their algae-covered backs.

Corvax leaned over, "Wounds from boat propellers."

"They only have flippers in the front because their paddle-like tail does the trick of having hind limbs," Flax elbowed Javan. "You can relate, right, platypus?"

"Hey, I've got legs, too, Lizard Boy!" Javan laughed, using his flat tail to splash water at Flax.

Master Gichi rustled its vines for attention. "Divine Protectors have helped in the formation of the trees. Animals. Wind. All of nature. We have always been here. Now the humans must find in their hearts the grace to see us working for them and with them on Earth. They must open their eyes and witness us."

Perl recalled Master Tryfon's words—*"You are the bulwark between humans and Ever, but the time is coming for us to work together with humanity."*

The manatees' peaceful chatter changed abruptly, growing louder, longer and shriller, until they were full screams.

Nan flapped her wings, rising up out of the water, holding her ears. "What's wrong? Why are they so frightened?"

"Master?" Lyre chirped.

They all turned to look over at their teacher, whose head had grown dark, vanishing into its new moon phase. The Master was silent.

"Guess we're on our own," Bear shrugged.

"I know why they're screaming," Corvax pointed to three boats speeding through the canal, heading straight towards the herd. "They're warning each other."

The metal makeshift pontoon boats raced along the hyacinth-covered waters, closing in on the manatees. Perl and the others saw it was teenagers steering the boats, laughing and yelling to one another.

"We need them to change direction. Come on Bear!" Javan and Bear dove into the water to try and move the herd.

"Girls, help me with those pelicans." Corvax, Nan and Lyre took to the sky, directing several pelicans to dive for fish. Seeing the birds, the teens veered out of the way, narrowly avoiding several manatees unknowingly in their path.

"Even floating they're heavy," Tars grunted. He and Flax had waded out into the water up to their necks and were now slowly pushing the thousand-pound mammals out of the boats' path.

Everything was happening so fast. Perl stood beside little Opis, unsure of what to do. "Over there!" Opis warned, pointing to a solitary manatee floating belly up, sound asleep amongst the vegetation. "They hear on a higher frequency! It won't detect the low motor noises coming from the boats!"

The others had managed to clear a safe path for two of the boats, diverting them from the herd, but the third boat was making a beeline for the sleeping giant.

"My grandma drives faster than you!" A boy teased his friend on the boat behind him, "Slow poke!"

"Oh, no!" Nan and Lyre cried out, looking away from the impending collision.

Perl concentrated; she imagined herself surrounding the sleeping manatee and lifting it up and out of the water. "I've got you," Perl whispered, "I've got you."

The sleeping manatee woke in a panic as it felt its body rising up out of the water. Particles of light sparkled all around it like a cocoon as the scared beast flapped its flippers and tail, shrieking.

The boat zoomed underneath the levitating creature, narrowly missing it. The other two boats had circled back; they couldn't believe their eyes.

"What the—" the teens stared in disbelief. "Are you seeing this?"

Perl slowly turned the manatee over in midair as it cried louder, flapping its flippers.

"It's a manatee! And it's flying!" A young girl wearing a polka-dot swimsuit fell back into her seat.

The boy next to her, unable to take his eyes off it, said, "Uhh…is anybody recording this?"

Several of the kids had their devices out, capturing the floating, sparkly manatee. Twenty yards away, Perl stood, eyes closed, carefully lowering the mammal to the water. It sank under the surface with a bubbly squeak. The light particles left the manatee and ran through the water like a current, straight to where Perl stood.

The teens slowly maneuvered over to the manatee, leaning over the boat as they watched it bob in the water. "You almost hit it."

"Wow, look at those scars. Seems like it's been hit before."

"That was a miracle, right? I mean, we all just witnessed a miracle." The girl's hair dangled in the water as she reached overboard to touch the manatee's back.

The rest of the manatee herd circled around the three boats, curiously looking up at the teens as they looked down at them.

"There's a whole bunch of them! Shouldn't there be some kind of protective barrier or signs warning people not to speed through here?" The teens nodded in agreement.

"Perl, what did you do?" Corvax cawed. "The Half-Light Realm is in the unseen. We and our actions are meant to be unseen!"

Perl was about to say that the crow-boy hadn't changed much since Seeker training, always riding her, but was interrupted by Master Gichi.

"Wonder is the foundation to human happiness. If they experience feelings of awe, they are more likely to display empathetic and charitable behaviors." The Great Moon Spirit lifted its vines from the soggy soil. "Come, our time here is done."

The moonflower vines grew once again, engulfing the Nine into its embrace, returning them to the Light Realm. Releasing the Seers from its many hands, Gichi spoke softly, "When you stumble across bluebells in the woods, it is something to behold. Just for you. Brings joy. But it is when we share that moment with another that we bond. Witnessing the miraculous together. Strengthening the awareness of nature."

Perl's room at the treehouse was still in shambles from the previous day's episode; chairs lay tipped on their sides; pebbles, berries, and other debris were scattered around the room. The spot where Perl had fallen with Victr's knife was dark, the floorboards scorched. Despite the mess, Perl fell into bed, exhausted. Everything that had taken place in the Unforgiven and having to use her telekinetic powers had drained her physically and mentally.

There was a faint knock at the door. "You okay, Perl?" Javan peeked inside Perl's room.

Perl was too tired to even open her eyes. "Yeah, I'm fine," she mumbled quietly. "Just resting...my…" She fell fast asleep.

Javan smiled. He pulled a blanket up over her and quietly crept out of the room, tiptoeing around the rubble.

As Perl slept, dark dreams crept in:

Mycelium grew up from the floor, wrapping all around Perl, pulling her down through her bed, deep into the soil. Beetles and millipedes crawled over her, biting at her flesh, crawling in her nose and ears. Tree roots took hold of Perl's arms and legs in a vice-like grip. Perl could hear the trees crying, "Help! She is killing us!" Perl opened her mouth to scream but instead vomited up dead earthworms like the evil Surinam toad they had battled. The tree roots released their grip as the mycelium pulled her deeper and deeper into the Earth. Perl could feel the blackness absorbing her Light, draining her, yet she was helpless to fight back. From the corner of her eye, she noticed a tiny spot of white in the vast darkness. It came closer, and closer. "Amanita?" Perl thought. The albino girl was now face to face with Perl, her teeth bared, black tongue flicking in and out like a snake. She was laughing.

Perl sat up, her hearts racing. She arose from her bed and walked to the window. The early traces of dawn were breaking through the darkness. Beneath her treehouse window, her faithful protector Quaanta slept peacefully in a tight ball, its lean, muscular legs curled up into its black and white spotted body. Perl smiled as Quantaa's snoring rustled the nearby bushes, yet it quickly faded.

"That nightmare felt real," Perl thought. *"Way too real."*

What are you hiding,
Amanita?

Why can't I see
your essence?
I only feel a loneliness
in you.

How did you come
to sing in the arena?

So many questions.

I will keep your
secret ~
for now.

But my nightmares
are getting worse.

I will go and
sit under Lottie
and meditate ~ her
floral branches always
help to clear my mind.

In the Sisterhood of Elsewhere's chamber deep below the Earth's surface, Gretar, Lance, Dianna, and other holy order volunteers and activists gathered. They looked worn out, dust-covered and tired from their trek across the desert to the Under Kingdom.

"You three will take the east passageway to the first backup generator," Sister Martha gestured to three women from the Seahorse Initiative. She stood in front of a large map crudely drawn on the stone wall, pointing out locations. "Gretar and I will take out the main motherboard located here, beneath the arena." Martha circled a control room, "Then Brother Sebastian will lead the way down the west tunnel to the second backup generator, here. All three generators must be shut off to unlock the electric chains that are holding the prisoners to their work stations."

Sister Betty handed out small paper maps, while Sister Ursula passed out makeshift blow torches.

"Burning the control panels should cause a power surge which in turn will shut things down." Ursula held up a torch demonstrating how to turn on the flame. "We aren't sure how long the power will be down, maybe ten to fifteen minutes, so you'll need to move quickly to get everyone to safety."

Sister Betty added, "These rooms are guarded, which brings us to our diversion plan. Lance, if you would give the details."

The boy, dressed in his dark, polished stag beetle *(Lucanus cervus)* uniform, removed his mandible helmet and made his way to the front of the crowded room.

"The coronation festivities will begin at midnight tomorrow, so the official crowning ceremony will be at three in the morning. That's when the control panels have to be cut." The group nodded as Lance continued. "As part of the pomp and circumstance, the vault will be briefly opened to show off the Crown Jewels to the public," he rolled his eyes, "And the entire royal guard division will be assembled there to protect the valuables." Lance pointed to the position of the vault doors in the main arena. "The good news is this temporarily removes the guards from their assigned posts, so they'll be away from the generators."

"For how long?" Brother Sebastian asked.

"Not long, maybe about five minutes. But this should give you enough time to slip in, burn the controls, and get out. This equipment is state-of-the-art and there are backups, so the shutdown will be temporary, but it will release the locks on everyone held captive."

"Wait, how is it you know all of this?" Gretar asked, eyeing the teenage boy.

Dianna spoke for him, "Lance Featherstone has been working undercover for several years now as the princes' interpreter. He is our trusted friend and ally."

Lance nodded to Dianna. "Thank you, and I also have another set of eyes working with me, someone who has access to the arena. She's informed me that the colors for the event will be black and purple. The Sisterhood will provide each of you with a costume to blend in with the other guests."

"Is this female ally Mik by any chance?" Gretar asked.

Lance knew that he couldn't give Amanita's name, knowing that the Sisterhood of Elsewhere had no idea of her celebrity status as a singer in the arena's night games. "I can't say, but I have made contact with Queen Mik and she is aware that there are activists working in secret throughout the Under Kingdom." Lance gave a slight smile, "You're Gretar, aren't you?"

"You do know a lot," Gretar said. "I am."

"I was the one who delivered your gift to the Queen," Lance squinted at Gretar, "You aren't going to be a problem tomorrow, are you? We aren't here to save her."

"Then I might be a problem," Gretar crossed his arms. The two stared at one another.

"Boys, we will all need to work together to pull this off," Sister Betty's voice was stern. "I'm sorry, Gretar, but Lance is right, it would be impossible to get anywhere near the royal balcony. Freeing the people is our top priority."

"Anyway, back to the plan," Lance ran his hand along the labyrinth of passageways on the wall map. "Sister spies, Underground activists, and Dianna will be waiting in the wings to quickly escort the newly released through the passageways to the Sisterhood's well room. From there, they'll go through the escape tunnel, and out to the forest. Move as many as you can as quickly as you can before the lights come back on, and even when they do, keep moving."

Sister Ursula gestured to a tall man in tribal attire standing in the corner. "The Northern Odina Brotherhood will be waiting near Slugabed to take everyone to the safety of their mountain citadel." She looked around the room. "Have hope, everyone."

The tribesman spoke, his voice deep and commanding. "Many have made the pilgrimage to bear witness to the miraculous flower garden growing in the Sisterhood's nursery, created by The Chosen One, shining a light where no light shines." The tribal leader held up a pink pansy. "Hope is on our side." The room echoed the sentiment.

"There is also the story of the miracle manatee. The video has gone global," Gretar added.

"Manatee? We have not heard of this," Sister Betty inquired.

"I have it here," Lance tapped a censor on his beetle armor wrist plate, projecting the holographic video. "News like this gets blocked to the people of the Under Kingdom. Luckily, I have clearance," he boasted.

The room huddled in for a closer look, seeing the great manatee spin high above the boat in the lagoon.

"It was Perl," Dianna leaned in, feeling her daughter's presence at the scene. "See the particles of light cascading around the manatee and how they float out over the water. Perl was there, saving it."

The video flicked out and the room erupted in murmurs and chants—
"Praise be!", "The unseen reveals itself!", "How do you know it's Perl, Dianna?"

"Through a phenomenon known as fetal microchimerism. Once a baby is born, some of its cells linger on in its mother. Perl remains a part of me. Her cells are in my body. I am sure it is her." Dianna nodded, "I know it is my Noor, our Perl."

"This is wondrous news," Brother Sebastian proclaimed. "And we are all blessed to be in your presence, Our Lady of the Woods," he bowed.

"May Ever's light lead us all brightly and bravely tomorrow."

Sister Martha raised her voice, "And now if you'll all follow me to the sewing room, we will get you fitted in your costumes!"

Although it was spreading like wildfire, the "miracle manatee" video was quickly being pushed out of the spotlight by a constant barrage of coronation hype and propaganda streaming 24/7, filling every second of airspace across the globe. Boastings of who would be in attendance, which of the Crown Jewels would be worn, and endless talk of how this strange royal threesome would actually work was all the buzz. There was also the poorly-kept secret that Prince Tobias was having an affair with the Ambassador to the Southern Archipelago, Kandy Vandenmire, heiress to her grandfather's steel empire.

"A little more to the left, yes there, perfecto!" An event coordinator was barking out stage directions to Amanita as she did a dry run for her upcoming performance.

Nearby, an entourage of royal attendants, secretaries, and media publicists surrounded the two soon-to-be kings, Tobias and Névenoé, buzzing like a swarm of bees.

"She is supposed to be backlit with our stain-glass scorpion coat of arms," Névenoé eyed the fair-skinned girl, thinking she was every bit as stunning as Mik, perhaps even more.

"Of course, not to worry, Your Highnesses, it will be the perfect Gothic fantasy." A frazzled-looking woman assured him as she quickly scrolled through a list of items on her electric notepad.

"I'm good for now, everyone. Focus on my brother, he loves the attention." Névenoé pushed through the small crowd, sauntering up to Amanita.

"How are those lovely pipes, my dear? Every creature on Earth will be listening."

"My pipes are perfect."

"I bet they are," Névenoé brushed his hand through Amanita's white floral hair. "Perhaps I should have a private concert some time, hmm?"

Quick as a rattlesnake Amanita's hand went up, grabbing Névenoé by the wrist. "Ah-ah," removing his hand. Névenoé blinked, surprised by the small girl's vice-like grip.

"Focus, Brother," Tobias shouted over. "Let our little songbird practice, we have much to get to today!"

Amanita cracked a chilly smile at the man. "Before you go, I do have a bit of information you might be interested in." She gestured for him to come closer.

"I'm intrigued," Névenoé raised an eyebrow.

"I have it on good authority that there's a mole in your inner sanctum."

Névenoé frowned. "Impossible. This place is a fortress. Nothing gets past my guards."

"Is that so? So how do you explain the Earth Activists knowing about the radioactive waste dumps, or the accusations about trafficking? Apparently, something gets past your guards."

Névenoé glared at the albino girl. "You seem to have a wealth of information. Maybe I'm looking at the mole?"

"Wrong," Amanita twirled a ring of hair, "I only hear what the whisperers whisper. Trust me...there is a mole." She ran her thin fingers along the gold buttons of Névenoé's silk jacket. "And they're helping those mole-born." She giggled at her clever wordplay.

"Name them and they're dead."

The two huddled together, the future king listening intently as Amanita shared her secrets.

"Their technology is astounding, I'll give them that," Count Zell Graves stared down from their suspended glass orb at the festivities.

The coronation's opening ceremonies had begun, with half the gothic arena draped in a holographic ocean scene, a desert on the other, complete with piped-in nature sounds—waves crashing, snakes hissing, coyotes howling—reverberating throughout the massive space.

Graves returned to his seat next to his wife, his black velvet cape flowing behind him like a superhero. The back of the cape was adorned with the Graves family crest; two crossed swords, flanked by a pair of leaping dolphins wearing crowns.

"Yes, the song of the seagulls is making me quite homesick for the palace." Countess Sarr sat awkwardly; a miniature fish tank headpiece perched atop her blue wig. She adjusted the strap under her chin with one hand while balancing the hat with the other. Inside the tank were three bioluminescent jellyfish, rocking and bumping into one another as The Countess tried to keep it steady. "I've had my fill of this subterranean living."

"We will leave in the morning, Darling. Right after we see Mik and her Kings off on their Archipelago honeymoon."

"Don't remind me. This double-king arrangement still boils my blood, Zell. It isn't what we agreed upon. And it just isn't right. My poor baby."

"What's done is done. The Kingdoms are united. And honestly, Sarr, maybe it's better for Mik? Now she has...options," The Count smirked, twisting his fake gold mustache clipped to his nostrils.

"Kandy is the Archipelago Ambassador, so I suppose she'll be honeymooning with them? The whole sordid affair is one big lie and you know it."

"Agreed, but Mik needed a change to get her mind off of Ivry's death, and away from those relentless Earth Activists. Most importantly, it unites our two kingdoms in peace. It will be the best thing for her, you'll see." He smiled at his wife as she continued to struggle with her ridiculous fish tank bonnet. "Just give it time, my dear."

Sarr knew her husband to be a habitual liar, yet this was one she wanted to believe. "I hope you're right."

"Of course, I'm right," Graves said. "Come let us wave to the crowd."

The Graves stepped back up to the glass in their royal bubble, waving, smiling and mugging for the hundreds of drones that zipped and buzzed about like giant mosquitoes, snapping pics while avoiding the dozens of mammoth pillars sculpted like long-necked gargoyles.

The parade of dignitaries, czars, and royal relatives from both houses led the procession around the main stage, showing off their jewels and elaborate costumes, each one more outlandish than the next. With their gothic getups, swarms of drones, and strange animal sounds blasting through the speakers, the whole thing felt more like a haunted house than a wedding. Men donned top hats that rose to ridiculous heights; the taller the hat, the higher their status. Women wore wigs shaped like spiderwebs, rabbit ears, sea cucumbers, and cacti. Some of the wigs so large and unwieldy, attendants were forced to walk alongside them, holding the hairdos up with long extension poles.

Mik sat pinned between Tobias and Névenoé in an open chariot in the shape of a giant golden skull; pulling it were two mechanical hybrid elephants also painted gold.

"Find Featherstone and bring him to me!" Névenoé barked orders into the tech on his wrist.

"Yes, Your Highness, we're on it," a voice rang back.

"What, still no sign of our mole?" Tobias asked, waving as they entered the arena; in the other hand he held a scorpion scepter, matching his brother's.

"Featherstone," Mik thought, *"The beetle boy."*

Névenoé gritted his teeth, forcing a smile as a drone hovered for a photograph. "Not yet, but when we do, I'll personally ring their scrawny neck and pull out their fingernails!" The roar of the crowd rippled over the brothers' conversation.

"What's all this about a mole?" Mik played dumb, trying to get more information.

"Never you mind, Our Love, nothing for you to concern your beautiful redhead over." Tobias scooped up a bouquet of red roses that had been tossed onto the chariot from the crowd, handing it to Mik. "There have been a few tweaks to the schedule."

"Tweaks? What do you mean?" Mik felt a rush of panic wash over her.

"The eyes of Earth are on us. Smile, Our Cherry," Névenoé waved his ruby-eyed scepter. "Smile."

The haunting setting sent chills up Mik's spine as they completed a slow lap around the track leading up onto the main center stage. Each guest seated in the stands had been given a pale mask to wear, a not-so-subtle way to mark them as commoners; setting them apart from the royals.

"Hear ye, hear ye, one and all!" The ringmaster quieted the arena. He was dressed in a long, black crushed velvet tuxedo with snake tails; his golden skull mask, a replica of the royal chariot. "Welcome to the Royal Coronation, uniting the Graves Water Kingdom and Desertland Kingdom of the Deathstalkers! Both families will take the solemn vow to serve all peoples under both realms!"

Cheers rang out as the chariot came to a stop at a long unfurled purple carpet. The trio, wearing the crowns they had been given on their wedding day, stepped out of the carriage, walking arm in arm towards the stage, where three ornate black onyx thrones sat. As a backdrop, a massive black curtain hung. On it was a dolphin and scorpion, balancing the Earth between them. Mik swallowed hard; it was all a nightmare.

Drones hovered at every angle, capturing the details of Mik's sumptuous eggplant velvet and lace gown, sparkling with hundreds of inlaid black diamonds and purple sapphires; a long train made from hundreds of peacock feathers cascading behind. The front of the gown was cut thigh, revealing thigh-high red patent leather boots which shone like her red lips; her red hair was styled up into a tall Victorian bouffant. Tobias and Névenoé wore matching black leather and velvet bodysuits with black diamond button embroidery and pointed collars that rose above their ears. Their high-heeled boots elevated them so they towered above Mik, even with her enormous hairdo.

The rest of the elite parade took their seats behind the thrones as the ringmaster commanded the guests. "Please stand for his most Solar holiness."

"I thought the swearing-in was at the end of the night?" Mik asked.

"There's been a few last-minute changes to the night," Tobias said.

Ascending from a hidden elevator in the floor, the odd man in a tribal sun mask who had conducted the wedding ceremony appeared before the newlyweds. Bowing to the audience, his voice echoed through arena. "All here in attendance and elsewhere, say together: I swear my allegiance to Your Majesties, and to your heirs, according to the royal law. So help me Ever."

The crowd repeated the oath.

The holy man turned to face Mik and her pair of husbands. "This trio, crowned in the name of Ever to be worshipped by all realms of Earth, do thee swear to uphold your sovereignty with truth and fairness for all?"

Tobias and Névenoé held up their scepters, "We do!" They gave each other a quick wink.

Mik mouthed her answer, no words coming out.

"Then I bind thee three as one in sacrifice."

"In sacrifice? What does that mean?" Mik asked, turning to each of the kings but getting no answer from either.

Three men in black hoods approached the thrones, holding branding irons with red glowing scorpions on the tips. Before Mik could process the ritual, a man took her by the wrist and pressed the hot iron into the back of her hand, leaving the scorpion mark. Mik screamed out. Both kings had their hands branded as well; neither flinching from the pain.

From their floating orb, Zell Graves watched the proceedings with cold, steely indifference, while his wife broke down in tears, hearing her daughter's screams.

The holy man then drizzled oil onto their wounds. "I hereby present unto you the appointed King Tobias, King Névenoé, and Queen Mik!"

"Huzzah! Huzzah! Long live the Deathstalkers bloodline!" Cheers rang out in the cathedral as the global broadcasts lit up with images of the newly branded royal trio.

The tribal elder continued, "But that isn't all! To commemorate this extraordinary moment, the royal family, in their infinite benevolence, will allow a glimpse of the Crown Jewels!" He pointed his scepter to the sky, "Behold!"

On the terrace level front and center for all to see, four guards slowly pulled open the grand twenty-foot-tall doors of the Royal Vault. Oohs and ahhs rippled through the crowd as they beheld the treasures inside. Ornate crowns, amulets, endless stacks of gold and silver, statues, chalices, chests overflowing with jewels, and other indescribable riches sparkled from within the chamber like electric fire.

The holy man spoke, "The bounty within these hallowed doors signify strength, beauty, and the ordained right of the royal family to carry us all into the future!"

Just as Lance predicted, every guard had been momentarily pulled from their post to protect the vault.

Lance stood in the shadows, peering through a secret peephole. "It's too soon! What's happening?" Beside him crouched Gretar and Sister Martha, readying themselves to take out the main motherboard beneath the arena.

"The vault's opened? Now?" Sister Martha whispered in a panic. "This isn't supposed to happen until the end of the ceremony!"

"They've changed the agenda," Lance replied. "You two gotta get down there now! I'll radio the others to get to the east and west backup generators." Lance rubbed his head, "I'll sneak up there and try to find out what's going on. Be safe!"

The three briefly held hands, then Gretar and Sister Martha bolted towards the moving walkway tunnels.

"Some great spy work, he's going to get us all killed," Gretar shouted back over his shoulder to Sister Martha as they ducked and dodged their way through the thick crowds.

"This has never happened," Martha replied. "His intel is always right, something's off." Martha was huffing and puffing to keep up with Gretar. "Don't wait for me! Here, take my torch, go, go!"

Gretar left Martha behind, sprinting along the winding passageways down through the flashing pink and green iridescent tunnel. The three women from the Seahorse Initiative received word from Lance and headed down the eastern passageway, while Brother Sebastian, consulting his map one last time, led a small crew to the western backup generator.

"That's enough. Shut the vault!" King Tobias stood, taking command of the room.

Cameras clicked furiously as everyone got in their last pictures of the Crown Jewels, and as quickly as it was opened the heavy doors closed, the endless rows of titanium bolts locking into place with a loud clank.

Tobias raised his hands to quiet the crowd. Névenoé stood, pulling Mik to her feet.

"As did our forefathers, our monarchy will begin by playing the ancient and time-honored game of Hounds and Hares!" Tobias clapped his hands, and the floor around the thrones began to rise.

The crowd murmured with anticipation as the Royal Throuple were lifted up and onto the arena's top balcony. Below them, the floor of the main stage was shifting, transforming into an enormous game board. Two matching rows of holes the size of grapefruits ran along the gridded board, the holes numbered from 1 to 25.

"King Névenoé will play as the nimble Hares, and I will foster the Hounds! Place your bets now."

As people pulled out their devices and wagered, two teams of orphans were hastily led by guards out from the tunnels where they stood at the edge of the massive game board. Dressed in long-eared rabbit and dog costumes, each of them held a six-foot-tall wooden peg, the ends carved into giant heads of hares and hounds. Beneath the game board scores of alligators lashed about in a massive tank of murky brown water. Dozens of guards stood around the perimeter, tasers ready for any orphan who tried to make a run for it. Seeing all this, the frightened children pressed close, cowering and clinging to one another as the rambunctious cheers grew louder.

"There weren't supposed to be any arena games," Mik said, pressing a cold compress into her red, burning hand.

"We must keep our subjects entertained and our property in check."

"These children? Property?" Mik noticed the children had scorpions tattooed on their foreheads identical to the one now burnt into her hand. "Does this mean I'm property, too?" She threw her hand up at Névenoé.

"You, my dear, are our loveliest possession."

Mik went to smack him, but he grabbed her wrist and smiled. "Careful your adoring fans are watching." Mik gritted her teeth and turned away, not giving Névenoé the satisfaction of seeing her tear up. She looked down at the poor children below; a knot tugging at her insides.

The ringmaster stood on a small round hover platform at the end of the game board. "All bets are locked!" He announced repeatedly. A holographic screen beside him flashed and flickered as the wagers were posted. "As I sound the horn, the first players must race to the designated hole and place their peg in before their opponent does. The first to place their peg in the proper hole is safe. The loser, well...” He and the crowd chuckled. “Whichever team has the most remaining players on the board wins! He gestured up to Mik. “Our new Queen will do the honors of rolling the dice.”

Tobias handed Mik a pair of goat knuckle-bone dice. A large velvet-lined box held by two stewards was brought out; the two kneeled before Mik. “Roll here so the cameras can see. And smile.”

“I’m not doing this.”

“Roll!” Tobias gave a threatening glare at Mik, firmly shoving the bone-dice into her hands. She stared daggers at him, then reluctantly tossed them into the box.

“Six! Six is the number!” The ringmaster sounded the horn, “Go!”

The first two children in line sprinted down the game board, each carrying the awkward peg as the crowds cheered. “Hoof it, Hound!”, “Jump to it little Hare, jump!”

The two boys reached the sixth hole on their side of the board, struggling to put their marker into place. A horn sounded.

“The Hounds have it!” A spotlight beamed down on the pale boy; the two of them looked around nervously.

Tobias pounded his fist on the arm of his throne, “Yes! Atta boy!”

The crowds started chanting, “Drop him! Drop him! Drop him!” Instantly, the squared space around the hole opened up like trapdoor and the boy fell into the tank. Splashing sounds and muffled screams could be heard as the door closed back up. Mik stared down in horror at what she was witnessing as the two brothers cheered.

Several women close to the stage turned away, although most did not, having grown accustomed to the bloodshed. It was part of the game, and to them, the mole-born were merely pawns; not a part of society, not even real people.

“Roll again, My Queen.”

“This...this is madness.” Mik crossed her arms in defiance. “I will not. This is murder!” She tried to get up to leave, but Tobias grabbed her shoulder, holding her down.

“These are her first games, Brother,” Névenoé said, defending Mik. “Remember, she is soft from her island life on Mont Michel.”

“Very well,” Tobias clenched his teeth; he grabbed the knuckle bones from the steward who had gathered them from the box, blowing on them for luck.

Drones closed in on the dice as they rolled to a stop. “Ha, snake eyes!”

A horn blared, signaling the next pair of terrified children to take off running. The crowds roared once again as the taller girl landed her peg into the number two hole a split second ahead of the boy.

“And the Hares are on the board!” The ringmaster hit a button dropping the crying boy, still holding onto his Hound peg. The churning waters turned to a pink froth as the trap door sealed up.

“Yes! Take that, brother King!” Névenoé gloated.

In the bowels of the arena, Gretar reached the main generator and was scorching the control panel with the pair of torches, hoping the others had received word from Lance to hit their targets earlier than originally planned. "Let's hope this works."

"Hurry, we only have a few minutes!" Reaching the western chamber, Brother Sebastian shouted to his partner, a lanky teenage boy who had recently been rescued by the Sisterhood.

"Which part is the main control panel?" The boy's eyes darted around at the enormous display of buttons and switches.

"I don't know, just burn it all!" Sebastian and the boy ignited their torches, charring the touchscreen panels and frying the wiring. Here and there on the switchboard, tiny flames sparked to life.

"Come on! The fire will take care of the rest. Let's get out of here," Sebastian grabbed the boy, pulling him from the smoking room.

Heading down the passageway, the two volunteers from the Seahorse Initiative turned a corner and stopped dead in their tracks. Four sentinel guards in their neon-green jumpsuits stood blocking the eastern generator room. "We're too late," the woman whispered to the other. "Go back. We'll have to hope the others did enough damage."

One of the robot's sensors picked up a noise. "Intruder! Intruder!" The hideous grinning mannequin shrieked a warning. The guards' infrared trackers scanned the area down the hallway, narrowly missing the women as they slipped around the corner and out of sight.

In the main arena, a chorus of alarms were sounding. The lights had been cut, moving walkways and video screens were black, along with the arena's oxygen pumps.

"Seems our little song bird was correct about the mole," Tobias reached down, grabbing three oxygen masks he had stashed under his throne. He handed one to Mik and his brother.

"Not to panic, the power will be up momentarily," the ringmaster tried to calm the crowd. "On with the festivities!"

Emergency lights kicked on, flooding the arena in an eerie green light. Three stories up, on a glass platform jutting out over the crowd, four guards with torches stood around Amanita as she prepared to perform; a small oxygen tube running up her nose.

Tobias rolled the die, "Four!" The horn sounded. Another pair of scared children ran for their lives in the dimly-lit surroundings.

Amanita began her acapella song; a strange humming and wistful cooing escalating into bouts of giggling. Even amongst the chaos of the game and the alarms blaring, her haunting vocals captivated the arena. The crowd, in their ghostly white masks, swayed back and forth as if hypnotized.

"Get to the pits, make sure all locks are secure," King Névenoé commanded a nearby guard, who immediately took off, passing Lance in the dark tunnel that led to the royal balcony.

Mik saw Lance approaching. "I have to use the facilities," she jumped up, gathering up her peacock feathered train.

"You're not—" said Tobias, grabbing her wrist.

"Look, either I go there, or I go here," Mik cut him off.

Tobias looked at the girl, then relinquished her hand. "Be quick. Take an attendant with you."

Blocking the kings' view of the boy, Mik hurried to reach Lance, her attendant scurrying to keep up.

Lance saw the Queen and ran to her.

"Wait, stop! They're on to you," Mik took hold of Lance's arm, spinning him back down the hallway. "They're sending guards to the pits."

"They know? How?" Lance looked bewildered. Amanita's siren song echoed through the arena. Lance stopped, looking back. "It was her. Amanita. Something told me not to trust that girl."

"Go, they want to kill you," Mik gave Lance a push as her attendant approached.

"Your Highness, the royal powder room is this way." She watched as the strange boy in the beetle armor ran off.

"Uh, yes, of course, I got all turned around with these flashing lights."

Lance sprinted down five levels to the pit located beneath the main stage. Sweating and out of breath, he spotted Dianna and several Forest Sisters near one of the tunnels, presiding over a chaotic scene. Damage to the two generators was enough to unlock half of the chains, in addition to several work stations on the eastern side of the Under Kingdom. Once free from their chains, the children had scattered in all directions, some dodging the handful of confused guards, others attacking them; the green glow of the backup lights adding a surreal quality.

"Children, children, this way, quickly!" Dianna yelled, waving her arms.

Hearing the woman's voice and seeing the other Sisters beckoning to them, many of the panicking children circled back. They gathered around the women like wild animals; eyes wide, teeth chattering. Lance ran to the group, pushing through to get to Dianna.

"Lance! What are you doing down here?" Dianna shouted over the sirens. "Why was the power cut so soon?"

"The kings, they know about our plan!"

"How?"

"Amanita."

"Amanita? How would she—?"

"She sings here. In the arena. Somehow, she got to the kings and ratted me out." Lance pushed over benches and tables, trying to form a barricade against the approaching guards.

"Amanita?" Dianna mumbled. She wanted to know more, to understand why, but now wasn't the moment. Right now she had to gather as many children as she could and get out of there.

"I've kept her secret far too long," Lance said. "I'll try and buy you some time."

A guard, red-faced and filled with rage, ran towards the group. Lance swung his scepter at his legs, sending him sprawling face-first to the ground. "Run!" shouted Lance, bringing his scepter down on the guard's head.

"Shh, children quiet." Dianna tried to calm the orphans; the chattering of teeth echoing down the tunnel. "Hurry now, that's it, hold hands, and follow me."

Dianna led the group of close to thirty children down the dark labyrinth, the Forest Sisters protecting the rear, until they reached the well room. "Nearly there, children."

In the well room, Sister Ursula and others swiftly guided them down the well's rope ladder. "Careful now. Follow the waterway."

Gretar was cornered, crouched behind the burnt-out panel in the main generator room as the two sentinels returned. Seeing the damage, the guards went to work initializing the backup computers. Sister Martha finally reached the doorway. She peeked into the room, seeing Gretar trapped.

"I have the Crown Jewels, Huzzah!" Sister Martha shouted. The guards looked up, turning toward the door; their nightmarish mouths agape.

"No, what are you doing?" Gretar mouthed, shaking his head at Martha to stop.

"Down with the Kings and their rotten, evil ways!" She continued, coaxing the robots out into the hallway. "Huzzah!" Martha walked slowly backwards, pretending to have a handful of jewels.

"Warning! Intruder! Warning!" The guards charged as Sister Martha turned and ran.

One of the guards shot an electrified net over Martha, pinning her to the ground. They reached her, and seeing that she had no jewels and was in no way a threat, they retracted the net. "Leave the area immediately," they ordered, returning to the generator room.

Gretar had slipped out of the room, and hid until the guards passed. He ran up to the nun, still lying on the ground. "Sister," he gently patted her on the cheeks. "Sister Martha, are you okay?"

She blinked slowly, opening her eyes. "I, I, think so…" She sat up. "Except I think my hair has some new curl to it," she half-smiled.

"That was crazy."

"It worked, didn't it?"

"Yeah, but still…" Gretar helped Martha to her feet. "Let's get to the rendezvous point."

They took a few steps, and Martha's knees buckled.

"On second thought, let's get you to the Sisterhood to lie down."

"Perhaps you're right," Martha muttered.

Brother Sebastian held open the metal door leading to ground level. "Put those on. You'll need to keep your eyes covered from the sun and your skin protected."

Goggles and robes were handed out to each person. Twenty freed adults joined the ranks of children, totaling fifty in all. The Sisterhood had estimated saving close to three hundred. In their haste to keep moving, baskets full of protective eyewear and clothing had been left behind.

"That's everyone." Lance was the last one up the ladder; he swung the rusted manhole cover shut with a bang and slid the metal pin through to lock it.

Several Sisters were on-hand to escort the group through the forest to the clearing near Slugabed Hovel, where the northern tribal Odina Brotherhood would be waiting in their covered wagons.

"Where are the Odina?" Sister Betty said, half panicked.

"We're earlier than planned; they will be here. Don't worry," Dianna said, calmly. "Children, everyone, gather in closely, let us say a quiet prayer."

The children chattered their teeth softly in agreement; they huddled around the tall, majestic woman. Dianna paraphrased from The Codex of the Sacred Invisible to comfort them:

> "Beloved children, I am horse, hawk, bear, stone, and tree.
> You, my beautiful birds, who have been underground too long,
> it is time for you to flap your wings and soar.
> My light breaks through not as sun, nor fire,
> but in finding the secret mysteries of nature."

A swarm of pink and purple praying mantises appeared overhead; Light Realm messengers from Tryfon. The children, having never seen such alien insects, chattered their teeth loudly, frightened.

Sister Betty hugged a small girl and boy close to her. "It's okay, they won't hurt you, see," she held up her hand as a pink mantis landed on her finger.

Dianna completed her prayer, "Ever protect us, Ever guide us to safety, Your will be done." As she finished, the swarm flew back up above the trees, an undulating cloud in the blue desert sky.

Dianna called for Sisters Ursula, Betty, Brother Sebastian, and Lance. "Try and keep them calm until the wagons arrive. I'll return in no time."

"Wait, where are you going? We need you," Sister Ursula asked.

"Back for Amanita, she needs me. You all are protected. The mantises have come. They have heard our prayer."

"It's you we're worried about," said Sister Betty. Dianna looked at them; She saw the fear on their faces.

"I will be safe, but I must go." Dianna hugged them, then set off through the gnarly, twisted woods, back to the Under Kingdom.

Inside the arena, the house lights flickered back on and a blast of air hit the relieved crowd. King Tobias tossed the knuckle bones for the last time. The game was tied; it was down to one roll. "Twenty!"

Amanita, still perched above the crowd on her glass platform, held a final high note as the last Hound and Hare victims raced along the game board. The crowd on its feet, eager to see which king would be victorious. The tank below the stage was now tainted a deep, dark red.

"And the Hounds have it!" The ringmaster bellowed. "King Tobias wins the match!"

The crowds barked and howled like dogs in support of the new king.

"Drop them!" The people chanted, "Drop them! Drop them!"

Tobias turned his thumb down and the entire half of the game board opened up, swallowing the remaining children in their rabbit costumes.

"Dear Ever," Mik turned away as the doors sprung back up, sealing off the screams. "Dear Ever, we will all pay for this." Forced by the guards back to her seat, Mik was trapped; she lowered her head into her hands and wept.

The two kings, oblivious to their grieving wife, bantered cheerfully.

"Now don't be a sore loser," Tobias teased Névenoé, who sulked like a child in his throne seat. "Shall we saddle up and bring in the rest of our property?"

Névenoé perked up, raising an eyebrow. "Wager a bet? Whoever wrangles the most property wins the first night with our darling bride."

"Brother, you are on."

Mik stood. "My room will be locked," she hissed through gritted teeth as drones captured their every move.

"We shall see about that," Névenoé mumbled back, forcing a smile for the cameras.

Tobias stood. "Ladies and Gentlemen! We are moving the games outside! Eat! Drink! And watch as I claim victory yet again from my brother!" Tobias laughed, waving his scorpion scepter around like a conductor. "Bring the bison-bots around! We ride!"

Count Zell and Countess Sarr, having watched the entire proceedings in mostly silence from their glass orb, read over the coronation agenda.

"It doesn't say anything about going outside of the arena, why would they do that?" The Count pondered aloud to his wife who was nearly asleep, having chosen to block out the horrific games with beverages. Graves summoned his henchman. "Snive, get out there and see what's happening. Better take everyone, and report back. I want to know what my sons-in-law have planned."

"Yes, my liege," Snive and the entire Graves security unit left to follow the kings, who had abandoned their thrones, along with their new bride.

"Open the gates!" Shouted a guard stationed in his small alcove carved into the rock high above. The guard was large and bare-chested, with wires woven into his neck and forearms. Daggers swung from numerous chains strapped around his torso.

Below him, the massive gate chiseled directly into the side of the mountain began to rise. Above the gate sat the gargoyles on the columns, bright green smoke billowing from their fanged mouths. Rows of torches lit the night sky.

Through the door strode Kings Tobias and Névenoé, each riding a giant half-mammal, half-mechanical bison. Behind the kings were their personal entourage, riding a mix of hybrid horses and odd makeshift motorbikes. A host of drones followed the action.

"My heat sensor is picking up activity that way, to the west," Tobias motioned to his brother, signaling toward the dense forest.

"Then let the better king win!" Névenoé thrashed his reigns, dashing into the woods, leaving Tobias in a cloud of dust.

"Oh, I will, gullible one. This way men, northeast!" King Tobias shocked his bison with his scorpion scepter, leading the beast in the opposite direction.

Below ground the arena crowds stared up at the mammoth screens that had dropped down from the ceiling, cheering for the brothers as the ringmaster called the action. "Looks like King Tobias has outwitted his little brother!"

Snive, along with the Graves' security detail, had left the arena and now followed at a distance behind Tobias on their hovercraft. Snive spoke into the comm-device embedded in his wrist.

"We have information, Count."

"Go on," Graves' voice crackled through the speaker.

"Apparently some of the prisoners have escaped. The brothers have turned it into a hunt and are betting on who will recapture more of them. They've split up. We're following King Tobias."

"Stay close, I don't trust either of them. So far, the coronation hasn't followed the schedule at all."

"Yes, my liege." Snive signed off, commanding his team with a series of hand signals as they stayed within sight of Tobias and his entourage.

Realizing he'd been duped, Névenoé veered off path, weaving through trees and reaching Tobias' team of riders.

"Ha! Nice of you to join the hunt, brother!" Tobias taunted.

"I'm not the only one." Névenoé held up a small monitor showing Snive and his men trailing them.

"This is almost too easy," Tobias laughed. "Gather round, men. Circle back and take them out, every last one of them." He spoke low, careful to avoid the drones picking up the conversation. The two Deathstalker Kings charged ahead towards the Slugabed clearing.

"Snive, what's happening?" The Count shouted into his comm-device. "What are those bastards up to now? Snive? Report immediately!"

"Zell, Darling, why are you shouting?" Countess Sarr sipped her cocktail. "Why don't you just watch the screen?"

"Don't be a fool, Sarr," Graves said. "I know for a fact they alter all their videos, showing the world only what they want them to see. I don't trust it, and I don't trust them." The Count paced inside the glass sphere like a tiger in a cage. "What the hell is Snive doing? He's online but hasn't moved. They should be trailing them." He shouted again into his device. "Snive? Snive, answer me, you idiot!"

Seeing the return of their team of royal guards, Tobias and Névenoé slowed their bison to a halt.

"Well?" Tobias asked.

"It's done, my kings," a guard boasted. "Targets have been eliminated."

"Good! Now let's do what we came out here for and round up our livestock," Tobias said, flashing a cheesy smile as a drone passed by.

Névenoé stabbed at his bull's side with his scepter. "Move, you stupid beast, move!" The creature, still more mammal than robot, winced but didn't move.

"Charge!" Tobias whacked his bison, who shuddered but remained in place. "They must be glitching. Move, damn you, beast!"

"Lanterns, there on the hill, dead ahead," one of Névenoé's men said.

Spotting the kings' entourage at the base of the hill, the children in the group began chattering their teeth.

"How did they find us so quickly?" Brother Sebastian picked up Christopher, the little boy he'd rescued his first day in the Under Kingdom; he'd been his shadow ever since.

"Drones and heat seekers," Lance pulled his scepter from its sheath.

"You feel that?" Sebastian asked the others as the ground began to tremble under their feet.

"What's happening?" Névenoé asked his brother as they felt the ground shake; dust billowed up and small pebbles and rocks vibrated on the surface of the dirt path.

"No matter," replied Tobias, looking around at his men. "What are you waiting for? Get up there and bring back my property!" Tobias commanded his team of men.

"You heard him!" Névenoé shouted at his team. "Go!"

The sound from the woods grew louder in all directions, but they saw nothing. Sister Betty looked at Ursula; neither of them where certain what to do next.

She felt a tug at her robe and looked down. "Why is the ground shaking, Sister?" A young girl, her face streaked with dirt, looked up at the woman, her large brown eyes fearful.

Before Sister Betty could answer, a deafening crash was heard. From the woods in all directions, a thundering herd of hundreds of reindeer burst into the clearing, breaking through the dry branches and twisted trees.

"Stay close, children!" Sebastian cried out as the children huddled together, their teeth chattering as they reached for the adults.

The herd of reindeer circled around the Sisters, Lance, Brother Sebastian and the fifty escapees like a tightly-packed cyclone, squeezing them into the eye of their stampeding storm, the beating of their hooves like an earthquake.

"We'll be trampled to death!" Lance said, pulling a man back from the stampede.

"No!" Brother Sebastian shouted. "Dianna's prayer, the mantises, the veil is opening!"

"Veil? What veil?" Lance increased the light on his lantern.

"You are right, Brother Sebastian! The legend of the forest is real!" Sister Ursula chimed in.

Lance squinted through the dust, unsure of what was happening.

"The legend goes, as the sun disappears beneath the trees, the Light Realm comes to prevent evil from spilling out into the human realm." Sebastian held Christopher inside the folds of his robe. Sister Betty hugged the little girl. "The praying mantises delivered our prayer. The herd is here to protect us!"

Tobias held a scarf over his mouth. "What the hell is that over there?"

"I think they're…reindeer?" Névenoé said, looking at the swirling mass. He checked the video monitor implanted in his arm; live feeds from various drones popped onto the screen. "How?"

"Here? That's insane!" Tobias shouted.

"Sires, should we shoot?" One of the henchmen asked.

The sheer size and speed of the herd had created an increasingly-large cloud of dust and debris, making it difficult to breathe. In the thick smoke, the drones, trying to capture the scene, crashed into one another and dropped to the ground.

The jumbo screen in the arena froze, then went black.

"Snive, what's happening out there?" Count Zell continued screaming into his device at his faithful servant, who unbeknownst to him lie dead in the forest along with his entire security team.

The ringmaster's voice burst through the speakers. "Looks like we have a tie, folks! Huzzah to both our new kings!" The ringmaster tried his best to cover up the confusion. "Uh, I've just been informed that drinks are on the house, compliments of your kings!"

The crowd erupted. Music was piped in as the mass of feeble-minded attendees returned to partying.

"Brother, I have a bad feeling about this," Névenoé turned his bison around. "Let's head back to the arena."

"We can't leave! Don't be a coward," Tobias replied.

"It's only a few mole-born. Hardly worth it. Besides, we did take care of one loose end, didn't we? Now all we have is The Count to deal with." Névenoé poked his bison, urging it to get going.

"You're right, Brother," Tobias kicked his pointed boot into the bull's hide. "But first thing tomorrow, we send a team into the mountains to scout them out."

"Agreed. Race you to the Graves!" Névenoé stampeded ahead of his brother, their band of assassins following close behind.

Dianna stood staring at the burnt framework of her beloved greenhouse and the charred remains of the fourteen Arbequina olive trees. Tears clouded her eyes when she recognized the box that held the lock of Perl's baby hair. Brushing off the soot, Dianna saw that it was broken; the small mica box inside was missing. Turning it in her hand, Dianna noticed one white hair snagged on the broken hinge. "Amanita."

"Yes, Mother?"

Dianna turned with a start, dropping the box. "You...were in the garden the day of the fire."

Amanita slowly nodded, not saying a word.

A chill ran up Dianna's spine. "Do you know how this happened?"

Amanita looked down, giving a sarcastic chuckle. "Odd, really. For someone who's seen as being so special in the eyes of Ever, you're so very blind."

"I don't think I like your tone, young lady." Dianna walked towards her.

"I was doing the work of my father," Amanita knelt, pressing her knees into the dark soot.

"But we never knew who your—" Dianna said.

"Never once, Our Lady of the Woods," she said, her tone mocking, "never once did you question the name pinned to my blanket?" She stared up at Dianna; her eyes cold and vacant.

"Get up, sweetheart, stop this…" Dianna offered her hand.

"My name is Amanita! I am the destroying angel! Amanita!" The pale girl swiped at Dianna's wrist, gabbing her bracelet, tearing it off. "I am the killer of kings! Amanita, the Deathcap!" Her steely gray eyes flashing with an icy light.

Dianna backed away, holding her scratched wrist. "Why are you saying this?"

"My father will reclaim the Light and rule over all Realms!"

At that, Amanita pushed the tips of her long white fingernails into the dirt along with Dianna's bracelet. In seconds, webs of threadlike mycelium grew from her hands, spreading out across the ground, entangling Dianna's feet.

"Amanita!" Dianna screamed, the fungus snaked up her legs, sprouting mushrooms, coiling and encasing her whole body like a cocoon.

"The Ullen will reign. The Earth will die...along with your daughter of Light."

"You...are...my daughter, too." Dianna pleaded as the mycelium wrapped around her neck, covering her head.

"Never have I been, nor will I ever be, yours," Amanita plunged her hands deeper into the ground. "I am anointed in eternal Darkness."

Dianna tried to speak, but her mouth was sealed shut by the webbing. All she could do was stand there, helplessly watching as Amanita pumped her mycelium veins deeper into the earth. The girl's eyes turned a bloody red; streams of milky-white sweat ran down her face and arms.

"Find what blooms and sings, severing each from its mother. Our mystery reveals, showing all what the darkness has to teach." Amanita's skin festered, sprouting lumpy white boils. "Drink of me, it is your last."

Amanita's legs began losing their shape, merging with the network of webbing. Her entire body followed, seeping into the black, ashy ground. Dianna unleashed a muffled cry as Amanita's head, all that remained, smiled up at her. The girl's face melted off, her skull dissolving into the ground, leaving behind a pool of white bubbling liquid.

Dianna's heart pounded; she tried to breathe through the tight mesh, taking long, shaky breaths. *What did I see? What did I see?"*

Amanita's pet aye-aye crawled out from behind the charred compost bin, sniffing the ground, poking through the ash and cinders. It licked some of the milky fluid, yelping as it burnt its tongue. The creature hissed at Dianna and disappeared, leaving her there to suffocate.

"Hmm, mint would be nice, or maybe ginger." Gretar entered the garden, searching the plants for something nice to make tea for Sister Martha. He moved down the rows, scanning the many plants, then stopped as something caught his eye. "What the—?" An entire section of the plants was dead; the leaves brown and curled. The plants were shrouded in a white, threadlike film. Gretar pulled at it. It was like mesh; sticky, but strong. "What is this stuff?"

Gretar saw that the webs spread across the ground, zigzagging under the curtain leading to the greenhouse. He pulled the curtain aside. Sitting in the center of the blackened room was a large white mass. Gretar saw it start to move.

"Holy crap!" The boy ran to it, ripping away at the gooey strands. Seeing Dianna's frightened, staring eye looking back at him, he quickly tore the webbing apart. Dianna coughed, gasping for air as Gretar tore away at the rest of the thick, spongy growth, freeing her arms and legs. He could see Dianna had tears in her eyes.

"Right there in front of me, all these years." She muttered, bewildered, trying to catch her breath.

"What are you saying?"

Amanita, my daughter...daughter of The Ullen," Dianna mumbled. "It can't be. It just can't be. How could I have been so blind?"

Gretar shook his head, "I don't know who Amanita is. She did this? She burnt your greenhouse?"

Dianna stared at Gretar; the look of confusion on the boy's face snapped her out of her own state of shock. She placed her hand on Gretar's cheek.

"Thank you."

Gretar helped Dianna out of the tangled mess.

"We have to go. I have to warn the alliance."

"I'm going with you," Gretar said. The two left the burnt greenhouse, hurrying through the garden to the Sisterhood's chambers.

"But wait, what are you doing here?" Dianna asked. "Shouldn't you be at the rescue point?

"Sister Martha and I ran into some trouble. I'll tell you on the way back." Gretar took Dianna's arm, peeling off more of the sticky fungus as they walked. "And you can tell me who Amanita is and what's going on."

"Snive? Come in Snive. Where the bloody hell are you, man?" Back in his private chambers, Count Graves tried reaching his security staff for the hundredth time. "Sunuva—" The door flew open.

"The Great White Count! There's our shark!" King Tobias and King Névenoé burst into The Count's bedroom, slamming the heavy door behind them.

"Oh, uh, welcome!" Graves clicked off his tech. "And to what do I owe the pleasure?"

The two men glanced around the room.

"So, what happened out there in the woods, boys?" Graves twisted his faux tentacle mustache.

"Who you callin' boys, old man?" Tobias mocked, strolling over to a table filled with truffles, tossing one up and catching it in his mouth.

"I, uh, didn't see an above-ground hunt on my coronation agenda." The Count topped off his wine goblet, prying for information.

"Oh, *your* agenda, is it?" Névenoé plopped down onto The Count's gold chair, running his hand along the lion's mane fringe running across the top. "Did you hear that, Brother? This coronation was all for him." Névenoé used the chair's claw-shaped leg to scrape the mud from the bottom of his boots.

"All I meant was I would have joined you in the hunt, had I known." The Count forced a smile, taking a long gulp of red wine. "Your Highnesses."

"Things can change fast in the Under Kingdom," Névenoé used his scepter and popped out of the chair quickly. He grabbed a handful of truffles and shoveled them into his mouth.

"Speaking of knowing things, we've noticed that those Earth activists seem to be one step ahead of us, ever since Mik created that preposterous Seahorse Alliance." Tobias strolled around the room, The Count keeping a wary eye on him.

"You wouldn't know anything about the explosion at the drilling site, would you?" Névenoé asked. "Cost us a pretty penny."

"Careful who you're accusing, now...boys," Graves downed his drink, slamming the goblet onto the table.

"No, he's right, Név, The Count is a *senior* member of Under One's Heel, and deserves respect. Especially now that he's our father-in-law."

"True, true, Brother. And he wouldn't want to do anything to put his daughter in harm's way."

"Harm? I assure you both, that explosion was a freak accident. And as for Mik, she does nothing more than an occasional beach cleaning. It's a hobby for her! Something to fill her time since losing her sister. Nothing more, I can assure you."

"An accident, huh?" Tobias said, raising an eyebrow. "Well, I suppose accidents do happen. Say, you ever hear of a cassowary, Graves?"

"Sorry, a what?" The Count refilled his goblet to the top; wine splashing on the floor.

"Cassowary. It's a large, flightless bird. It can't flee predators, but it does have these lethal talons. So deadly, in fact, that it is the only bird known to have 'accidentally' killed a human." As he spoke, Tobias slid a knife out from the inside of his jacket. "This dagger, a gift from our dear friend Vlad of Iron, Czar of RussAsia, was sculpted from a single Cassowary claw." Graves watched the man as he held up the knife. "It's also been dipped in deadly wolfsbane sap…just for fun." Tobias grinned.

"Truly…an extraordinary piece," Count Graves said, sensing the tension in the air. "The craftsmanship on the cobalt head is remarkable, topnotch."

King Tobias twirled the dagger between his fingers like a magician doing a card trick. "Névenoé and I have been parentless for so many years. It would be so nice to get some fatherly advice."

"Of course. Happy to help, my Kings," Graves forced a tight smile. "My sons! Any time, day or night."

"Fantastic!" Tobias grinned. "Perhaps you can settle a little dispute we've been squabbling over, in regards to a video we received from our intel."

King Névenoé tapped the floor with his scepter and one of the walls converted to a viewing screen. A hazy video began playing of the underwater footage from the ocean drilling site.

"What is this?" Count Graves barked. "Where did you get this?"

Névenoé snapped back, "We like to keep a close eye on all of our investments."

"Close eye, my ass! This is spying!" Graves huffed.

"Watch carefully, here's the part we need your advice on," Tobias said.

The three men watched as the torpedo struck the drill; a white explosion momentarily filled the screen, followed by clouds of billowy mud.

"Sabotage!" Graves shouted. "Someone blew it up? I was told it was a mechanical malfunction."

"That isn't the part up for debate," Tobias said. "Keep an eye on the lower left part of the screen."

And there it was; The Count's personal shark submarine, slipping through the debris and speeding off from the scene of the crime. Only a handful of people had access to Graves' fleet of yachts; his daughter was one of them. *"Oh, Mik, what have you done?"* he thought to himself.

"Ya' see, now, Névenoé believes that is simply a great white swimming by, but I say that's your sub. Your torpedo. And that is you, killing our deal!"

"This is ludicrous, Tobias. Why would I blow up my own mining site?" Graves tried to compose himself, "Névenoé is correct. That's just a shark on the prowl."

"So, this isn't a submersible?" Tobias asked, motioning his hands to make the video rewind. He then zoomed in on the shark.

"Absolutely, not, I don't even own such a…a…"

Up close, it was unmistakable; there on the sub's tail fin was The Count's coat of arms and trademark slogan: *'Without Water, You Will Surely Need Graves.'*

"Unless sharks are into tattooing these days, I'd say that's yours, *old man*," Tobias said.

"Damn, looks like you've won this bet," Névenoé said, slapping Tobias on the back, "Suppose you get to do the honors."

"I've been framed, dammit," Graves turned away from the screen and stepped up to the banquet table. "Somebody's set me up."

"Zell, Zell, Zell, loosing those tech minerals set our virtual escapism project back years, but that's not the part that's most upsetting." Before The Count could turn around, Tobias brought the Cassowary dagger up high, plunging it down fast and hard into The Count's back. The razor-sharp blade went straight through, emerging out the other side through the Graves family crest on the jacket's front. "It's that we had only just gained a father."

The Count cried out in pain as his golden goblet crashed to the floor. He struggled to switch on his tech for help, but King Tobias had him pinned against the table, slowly twisting the blade. "Well, Brother, it looks like we're orphans once more," Tobias said, ripping the Cassowary blade out of Graves' back. "Oh, and your men are dead, too."

Tobias spun Graves to face him as Névenoé tapped his scepter on the floor controls once more. The video switched to a close-up of a man shooting Grave's faithful assistant Snive in the head, then gunning down the rest of his men who were tied up and blindfolded.

"No!" Graves watched, wincing from the pain as the poisonous wolfsbane sap coursed through his veins. "Why? Why do this?"

Tobias feigned surprise. "Why else? To secure the Deathstalker bloodline as the sole rulers of Earth...and end yours."

"You...won't get away with this," Graves grabbed his chest, taking quick, short breaths before slumping over.

"We just did." Névenoé tapped the floor a final time. On the video screen, a deep-fake security cam footage of The Count being attacked in his chambers by a band of bottom-dwelling bandits ran in a loop.

"See? Accidents do happen." Tobias clicked his tongue, stepping over The Count's motionless body. "Let's go."

The chamber doors slammed closed. The Count's blood spread across the floor, merging with the puddle of red wine.

Uriel sprinted between the hedgerows in Tryfon's Garden. Having witnessed Perl's nightmare and now Dianna's run-in with Amanita, Uriel could feel the Darkness spreading. Turning a corner, she spotted The Divine Master alone, shrouded in a soft light.

"Your Grace," Uriel spoke in a hushed, reverent tone, head bowed. Tryfon was preoccupied, chatting with a pink katydid he held in his hand. The insect hopped onto a hibiscus flower, camouflaging itself into its petals.

"I feel a Nimbostratus cloud over you," Tryfon looked up, smiling warmly at the stoic warrior. "Release your rain."

Uriel looked up; violet eye blazing with intensity. "Ever since Perl's return from the Unforgiven, Darkness has increased ten-fold on Earth. And not only in the Half-Light, but across the Light Realm itself. I fear Earth is in peril. This is unlike anything I have felt since the birth of humanity...when The Ullen was cast down with its minions..."

"Breathe, Uriel," Tryfon interrupted, leaning in as the animal heads on either side of his human face morphed into a koala and a panda. "A racing heart chases away the sacred eye. Breath gives way to fresh vision."

"Forgive me, Master, but we need to call on all Battle Guides from Callowhorn, Greenheart and Natatory. The Darkness in the soil is coursing through the mycelium and if the Mother Trees die..." Uriel paused, knowing they both knew the answer. "Every Seeker, Seer and Awakener in Venusto must be ready to fight."

Tryfon smiled softly. "Mother Trees remind us of our better nature; that true love is reflected in our ability to help one another, and that we are at our best when all are healthy and resources fairly distributed." Tryfon ran his hand along the bark of a nearby birch tree. "So much of life on Earth is owed to the humble fungi and their life-sustaining network."

Uriel grew impatient; though enlightening, conversations with the Divine Master would often turn to the metaphysical. "Forgive me again, Your Grace, but this is exactly the symbiosis of which I speak. Without the carbon capture, damage to the entire ecosystem will be irreversible. Your Grace?"

Tryfon closed his six eyes, lifting his totem walking stick over his head. He levitated a few feet in the air, his three sets of glorious wings unfolding. The ground shook, buckling Uriel's knees.

"Horse, hawk, bear, stone and tree, Ever hears your plea. Forgetful birds, it is time for open eyes. Open wings. Catch the wind." Tryfon floated back down, and as soon as his feet touched the earth, the vibrant green leaves of the nearby hedgerow turned brown and brittle, the dead petals falling to the ground. The rumbling stopped.

"Master, what was that? It felt the same as when Perl held Brother Victr's knife."

"The Fallen, it is their hour," Tryfon said.

"You agree with me, then? All of Venusto must come to Earth's aid?" Uriel asked.

"Where are The Nine this day?"

"In Half-Light training with Master Tanda and Elder Enoogoo in the last of the Amazon rainforest."

"All is designed. Go to them. Take the Attenborough pitcher," Tryfon said.

"While I admire the sacred plant's ability, Master, it alone will not suffice."

"Dear Uriel, Fire of Ever's Sunrise, you have been tasked with both a great honor and heavy albatross. As Watcher of The Chosen, your concerns are noble and noted."

"I am humbled and grateful always," Uriel said. "However…"

"Venusto will be at your side," Tyfon raised a hand.

"Praise to All Nature," Uriel bowed.

"Never forget. Evil is death because it has separated itself from the Light." Tryfon bent down, collecting a handful of dead leaves. He tossed them in the air and they turned green again, reattaching themselves to their branches. "Ever speed."

Back in the rainforest, Master Tanda sat perched on Enoogoo's arm. "Seers, look up, take note of the canopy."

Perl and the others craned their necks, taking in the breathtaking umbrella of vivid green crowns swaying in the breeze.

"In the forest, trees give each other space to reach for the sky," Tanda continued.

Perl squinted, seeing the channel-like gaps between the tops of the trees.

"This is called 'crown shyness.' Each tree is perfectly outlined in a halo of light, to ensure each gets optimal sun rays for photosynthesis."

"And to protect branches from getting damaged in high winds," Javan said.

"And to prevent the spread of pests and disease," Flax added, his arm raised.

"Correct, Land Seers, and while the crowns maintain healthy boundaries, ensuring mutual respect, their roots mingle. The roots are the tree's brain."

"So, the trees are standing on their heads," Bear and Tars smiled at one another.

Tanda continued, "The tips of the roots feel, taste, and decide where and how far to travel. If there's an impediment in the way, such as a stone, they choose a different route. They can also communicate."

"How?" Nan fluttered her wings.

"To speak to one another, trees use their symbiotic relationship with the mycelium in the soil," Tanda said. "To hear them would require you to tap into the mycorrhizal network...the internet of fungus that connects each plant's roots to one another."

"The Wood Wide Web," Bear chuckled.

"What do they talk about?" Nan smiled.

"Yes, what's the latest tree gossip?" Lyre giggled.

"The Mother Trees are the most talkative," Enoogoo said, gently stroking Master Tanda's wing.

"These sentient beings," Tanda gestured to the colossal trees around them, towering hundreds of feet into the air, "These Mother Trees can detect if a neighboring bush is in distress. It will then send out signals to the surrounding trees to send the ill one the nutrients it needs. Root to root through the mycorrhizal network, they transfer water, nitrogen, carbon and other minerals, helping one another. Mother Trees also nurture saplings with the nutrients they need to survive in the shade of the forest floor."

"What does the fungi get out of this relationship?" Tars had climbed a tree and was now hanging from a branch by his tail.

"The connected trees provide the fungi with carbon-rich sugars generated through photosynthesis, and in return, fungi provide plants with nutrients taken from the soil. Together this symbiosis makes the forest's entire ecosystem resilient to the effects of climate change," Tanda said.

Opis nodded, her sparkling tentacles swaying back and forth. "Basically, without fungi there would be no plant or animal life."

"Correct," Enoogoo replied. "Humans carry fifteen percent tree DNA and are more closely related to mushrooms than plants. Fungi cells are surprisingly similar to human cells."

Javan elbowed Perl, "What's up, *fun-gal?*"

"Hey, I'm only half human," Perl crossed her arms, smirking at her friend.

A radiant beam of lavender light filtered through the trees. The Seers shielded their eyes except for Perl, who recognized her Protector. The light faded into glittery dust and Uriel stood before them, holding the Attenborough pitcher plant. The five-foot-tall flower looked small in her arms.

"Greetings, Divine One," Master Tanda and Enoogoo bowed.

"What brings you to the Half-Light?" Tanda asked.

"A battle is upon us. As we speak, a deadly virus is spreading through the rainforest's mycorrhizal network and it is moving this way. The Ullen's daughter has cast a poison into the mycelium."

"Daughter? What daughter?" Corvax asked, flying down from his perch on a nearby branch.

"Amanita is her name." Uriel handed the Attenborough plant to Bear.

"You said poison?" Javan asked. "Then the Mother Trees are in danger."

"Not just the Mother Trees," Nan added.

"So, what do we do?" Lyre asked.

"Wait Amanita?" Perl raised her voice. "Not my friend Amanita? From the Forest Sisters of Elsewhere?"

"She is a deceiver, Perl, and no friend," Uriel said. "She is a dark entity."

"That's why I couldn't see her essence," Perl thought. "Then I have to go. I need to get back to the Under Kingdom and warn them," she said.

"There's no time," Uriel commanded. "We need to prepare to fight. Right now."

"Forgive me, Protector," Elder Enoogoo interrupted. "Should we not get the Seers-in-training back to the safety of the Light Realm?"

"You have done well to prepare them," Uriel said, placing her hands on Corvax's and Perl's shoulders. "The Nine are needed here."

"But…" Enoogoo insisted, "They still have much to learn."

"He's right about that," Tars giggled nervously. "Let's get back to our treehouse."

Uriel continued, ignoring them. "Have you all set the incantation to memory?" She scanned the Seers with her one violet eye, her moth fluttering over the other.

"We have," Lyre chirped.

"Excellent, form your circle under the Lupuna tree." Uriel pointed to a massive tree nearly thirty feet wide. Next to the tree was a slight clearing where the underbrush was less thick. "Bear, place the Attenborough plant there, in the center. Hurry."

"Can someone please explain what's actually happening?" Flax's eyes darted from Master Tanda to Uriel.

"You are forming a holobiont," Master Tanda said.

"A what?" Perl asked.

Opis cleared her throat. "A holobiont is an assemblage of different organisms behaving as one unit."

"Correct, ancient one," Tanda raised her wing, ushering her students into formation. "If the pitcher plant is to attract and trap an evil entity, you nine will need to become more than the sum of your parts. Each of you has a voice that tells a different story, but your individual melodies must intertwine to form a polyphony. No one voice surrenders its identity, nor does one voice outshine another."

The Seers circled around the Attenborough plant according to their initials of their secret code—T-F-P-O-N-C-J-L-B—Tars, Flax, Perl, Opis, Nan, Corvax, Javan, Lyre, and Bear. They clasped hands nervously, waiting for Uriel's next command.

Sensing the group's anxiety, Elder Enoogoo broke the mood with a deep howl, exclaiming, "The Fearless Protectors Of Nature's Curious Jewels, Little to Big!"

Master Tanda cried out, "Warriors among warriors, steadfast and true!"

Javan looked across at Perl, giving her a reassuring grin. He wished he could be next to her, the distance between them feeling like an ocean. Perl smiled back, keeping a watchful eye on Uriel, who marched along the tree line behind Javan.

The Light Protector's shimmering chainmail rattled as she scanned the lush forest growth, seeking out an invisible enemy, her face a hard, emotionless mask. A chill went down Perl's spine and her spots began to glow as she watched Uriel pacing; she had never seen her like this. *This is serious.*

"Hold your formation," Uriel commanded, peering back over her shoulder. "Hold your formation, all of you," she repeated, then darted into the dense fauna, disappearing amongst the evergreens.

"Uriel!" Perl called after her. "Where are you going? Uriel!"

The Nine stood, hands clasped under the tree, exchanging worried glances. "Now what?" Lyre asked.

"Wait! What was that?" Tars asked, his tail quivering.

"A howler monkey," Flax said, elbowing his friend. "Don't you recognize him?"

"Gah!" Tars jumped again.

"And those are tree frogs, buddy," Flax laughed. "Take it easy."

"Sorry. This humidity is as thick as soup. It's messing with my hearing." Tars stuck his fingers in his ears, trying to clear them.

"Tars, don't let go of their hands." Corvax peered at the monkey-boy with his steely grey eyes. "Uriel told us to stay in our formation, so that's what we'll do." Corvax looked over at Master Tanda, who nodded.

"Be on guard, Seers. Unforeseen events appear to be happening." Master Tanda commanded from her perch on Elder Enoogoo's arm. The pair stood a few meters away, just at the edge of the clearing beside the two-thousand-year-old Lupuna tree. Waiting, watching.

For ten minutes, the nine of them stood in a circle around the Attenborough pitcher plant; the only sound the soft pitter-patter of raindrops.

"Where did Uriel go? I've never seen her so…" Perl broke the silence.

"Hey, look," Bear cut her off, pointing at the ground with one of his free arms. "The grass behind you. It's growing like crazy!"

"It's circling us," chirped Lyre, squeezing Bear's hand tighter.

Perl and the others watched as giant mushrooms, taller and wider than Bear, sprouted from the lush ring of emerald-green grass encircling them.

"It's a fairy ring," Opis said.

"Whoa," Tars said, staring up at the tree-like fungi.

"They're so lovely," Nan said, admiring the golden-brown mushrooms.

"Wait. You hear that?" Corvax asked.

"I can't hear anything," Tars said.

"Exactly. The woods have gone dead silent. No frogs, no birds, no bugs. Nothing."

"He's right. It's too quiet," Javan eyed the woods around them.

"Did you say fairies, Opis?" Perl looked down at the tiny jellyfish-girl standing next to her, holding her hand.

"Yes, the mycelium moves outward from the center. As the center dies, it forms a living ring from which the mushrooms arise," Opis said.

"Marasmius oreades," Javan said, recognizing the fungus.

"Correct," Opis replied. "And from these fungi—"

Before Opis could finish, from the tops of the mushroom caps emerged creatures. Half cherub, half insect; their soft, delicate bodies draped in strands of shimmering mycelium and teeming with bioluminescent spiders. The fairies peered down at The Nine, their bodies glowing like fireflies.

Enoogoo, with Tanda, took a few cautious steps toward the group as they stared curiously at the fairies.

"No one look into their eyes!" Opis warned.

Master Tanda spoke up. "Listen to Opis, Seers."

"But...they're so beautiful," Perl said. She couldn't help herself; one of the fairies stared right at her, its large oval eyes unblinking. Perl noticed its pupils were cherry-red faceted rubies, matching their plump lips. The spots on Perl's face and arms intensified, matching the fairy's radiance.

Sitting atop the mushrooms, the fairies began to rock back and forth rhythmically, humming a deep guttural melody. It reminded Perl of how Amanita sang in the arena. *"Not a song,"* she thought. *"A spell."* Perl took in a deep breath; the pungent smell of cloves and bitter almonds filled her nose. She felt her body grow heavy; warm.

"I said don't look!" A zap from one of Opis's tentacles snapped Perl back awake.

"Ow!" Perl winced.

Tars, Flax, Lyre and Bear didn't listen, however. The four of them were staring moon-eyed up at the mushroom fairies, swaying in sync with them. They pulled the circle this way and that. Opis stumbled trying to keep her footing.

"They're hypnotizing them," Perl said, recalling how the Under Kingdom arena had fallen under Amanita's trance.

"Stop moving!" Corvax said. "Everyone, snap out of it!"

"We need to use the Attenborough plant!" Javan said.

Bear began to hum, as did Lyre, mimicking perfectly the fairies' captivating sound.

Flax tried to free his hand from Perl's, but she held it fast.

"Flax no, don't let go!"

"But I...want to dance with them," Flax had an odd half-smile on his face.

Mycelium roots sprouted from the fairy's feet closest to Flax. The roots crawled up his legs and twisted around his waist. Like a net, it pulled him toward the fairy.

"SCREEEECH!" An ear-piercing cry from Master Tanda cut through the commotion.

Tars blinked, "W-what happened?" He, Lyre, and Bear looked at each other as if they'd just woken from a deep sleep.

"You were under their spell," Nan said.

"Ah, get it off!" Flax squirmed, tugging at the roots clinging to him. "Help me!"

"Hold still." Perl used the spikes on her wrists to cut the roots around the lizard-boy's waist.

"Guys," Corvax said. "They're changing."

The fairies had indeed morphed into something different. They grew more angular, bony; their pink skin now dark and blotchy. They hissed at the group; black fangs bared. Their eyes narrowed, filled with rage.

"Listen to me! Pay them no attention!" Master Tanda gave them the answer they needed. "Focus! Concentrate! Begin the incantation!"

The Nine tried to collect themselves and recited:

> *"Imagine an imaginary menagerie*
> *to grant all the wishes you wish,*
> *come guzzle greedily in captivating captivity,*
> *as I banish thee, for eternity,*
> *to a dungeon, everlasting."*

"Louder!" Tanda said.

As the nectar inside the Attenborough pitcher oozed to the top of the plant's lid, the fairy creatures stopped singing. They rose above their mushrooms, flying toward the pitcher plant, unable to resist its pull.

As they sang, Flax and Opis' electrical charges sparked and crackled and Perl's bioluminescence burned, sending a surge of energy through the group's joined hands. Javan and Tars' fur stood on end and Corvax and Lyre's feathers splayed out at attention. Arctic frost formed on Nan's crystalline wings; she ruffled them, releasing tiny snowflakes.

"Again!" shouted Master Tanda, circling above. "Again!"

The Nine repeated the incantation over and over; their chorus drawing the pitcher's sweet aroma into the air, luring the fairies to the plant's enticing nectar.

"It's working," Enoogoo watched anxiously from a low-hanging branch.

Perl and others sang out as the dark creatures fought each other, biting and clawing to get to the plant's milky, viscous liquid. One by one, they drank from the Attenborough plant's nectar and instantly dropped to the ground, twisting and contorting in pain. The glowing spiders scurried from their bodies and disappeared into the woods.

"Keep chanting," Lyre said.

As all thirteen dark fairies lie dying around the base of the pitcher plant, the carnivorous Attenborough drew the fairies' life-force from them. It pulled their ghost-like essences out of their bodies, sucking them inside. Once absorbed, the plant's lid sealed shut. The sides of the plant bulged out in places as a chorus of haunting screams was briefly heard, then all went silent.

"Thank Ever!" Bear and Tars said, breaking the group chant.

"Yuck," Nan and Lyre said, seeing the husk-like remains of the fairies lying in a scattered heap.

"It worked," Perl said. "We did it."

"Of course we did," Corvax crowed, as they dropped hands to hug and celebrate.

"So, they're gone for good, right?" Flax asked.

"A dungeon, everlasting," Javan quoted the incantation. "They're gone, alright."

Elder Enoogoo approached as Master Tanda returned to his arm. "Well done, Seers. Well done, indeed." The orangutan smiled from ear to ear.

Bear spoke up. "Those creatures came out of the ground. Was that the battle Uriel was talking about?"

"I am not certain," Tanda said, inspecting one of the mushrooms.

"Where did she go, Master?" Perl asked. "She missed it."

"Uriel sees all that you do, youngling," Enoogoo replied.

"Silence, Seers!" Tanda raised her voice. "The poison is here. Stay on guard."

"I'm sensing something," Opis announced to no one in particular. "The mycelium is sending out strange signals…"

"I feel it, too," Javan added.

Bear walked over to Opis, putting a heavy arm around her small frame. "You okay, Opee?"

"Shh!" Opis said, furrowing her brow. "It's becoming…"

"What?" Corvax asked.

"Unhinged."

The ground began to quake.

"Seers, move!" Tanda bellowed. "Away from the pitcher plant!"

"Behind me!" Elder Enoogoo said.

Corvax, Nan, and Lyre instantly took to the air as the remaining Seers ran, Bear scooping up Opis just as the clearing collapsed into a sinkhole, swallowing the Attenborough pitcher plant.

"The Lupuna tree!" Javan cried. "She's falling!"

The ancient tree came crashing down as the ground rumbled, crushing surrounding trees and hitting the ground with a sound like a thunderclap.

"Seers, close together! Air Seers, join us!" Master Tanda commanded.

"Why? What's happening?" Perl asked, pulling Fortis from its sheath. "We defeated the fairies!" Her spots illuminated her face in the shadowy undergrowth.

"Listen, something's coming," Javan said.

"What is it?" Perl asked.

Before joining the others, Corvax hovered above the sinkhole, looking in, his eyes peering deep into the blackness. "Bullet ants," he yelled down. "Big ones!"

"Not ordinary bullet ants," Javan said. "I'm sensing something more." The platypus-boy closed his eyes, concentrating. "Cordyceps."

"Ophiocordyceps unilateralis," Opis said. "Zombie ants."

"Zombies, ants?" Perl asked, "What are we talking about?"

"Cordyceps are fungal parasites. They fill the ant with spores, essentially taking over its functions," Opis said.

"It uses the ant like a puppet," Javan added. "Or in this case, a weapon."

"Arm yourselves with whatever you can find," shouted Tanda.

Perl had her trusty Fortis and Javan had his spurs, but the others were forced to grab sticks, rocks, or anything they could find to protect themselves. They closed ranks and readied themselves as the sound of scurrying legs and snapping jaws grew louder. From the sinkhole, a wave of oily black ants the size of goats came pouring out. Jutting from their heads was a stalk-like growth with a bulbous end.

"I've heard a bullet ant's sting feels like getting shot with a gun," Flax blurted out nervously.

"Well then," Bear slapped him on the back. "Nobody get stung, okay? Great!"

"The creatures are being controlled. You must sever the fungus stalks growing from their heads!" Enoogoo instructed the group, raising his blade high.

"Sever the fungus stalk," Lyre mimicked.

"Hold your ground, Seers!" the Master shouted, diving at a goat-sized ant nearing the Seers, ripping the mushroom stalk clean with her talons. The ant let out a shriek and staggered away.

The ants sprung from the hole, going directly after Perl and the others.

Three ants came at them, their large mandible jaws snapping. Tars had found a large thick piece of bark and he held it up like a shield, keeping the ants back. Flax jabbed at one of them with a sharpened stick, catching it in the face. The ant flinched but kept coming. Nan and Lyre dropped rocks from above.

"There's too many of them!" Bear shouted. He held thick branches in four of his arms.

The ants' wet stingers jutted in and out of their abdomens like daggers. Droplets of acid dripped from the stingers, scorching the ground.

"Fall back!" Enoogoo commanded.

"We're surrounded!" Tars said.

Master Tanda stabbed at their thoraxes with the horn on her head to stun them while tearing at the fungus stalks, yet more of the parasites continued to crawl out of the sinkhole.

"Look at that one!" Perl said, "It's covered in fungus!"

Opis charged up her tentacles on her head. She touched the ground with her hand, sending out an electric charge, creating a protective barrier around them.

The ant that was riddled in fungus was the first one to step on the electrified ground; it exploded instantly, sending a spray of toxic goo into the air.

"Nice one," Bear cheered.

"Ah, it burns!" Nan cried out. "The spores are sticking to my wings!"

Tars flicked off the spores on Nan with his tail. "They're everywhere."

"Fly, Nan! Flutter your wings," Corvax said.

"I'm sorry Nan," Opis said. "I didn't know."

Nan left the fray, vigorously flapping her wings to cool the burning sensation.

"Close in!" Master Tanda said.

"No more electricity!" Enoogoo said. Opis nodded; being so small, she knew she couldn't go face-to-face with the ants, so she did her best to stay behind the others and keep low.

The group tightened their circle as the waves of zombie ants swarmed. An ant sunk its jaws into one of Bear's arms. He screamed, trying to shake the thing free. Perl ran over and cut the ant's head off, which still clung fast to Bear's arm. Perl managed to rip the head away.

"You okay?" Perl asked, tossing the head aside.

"Yeah," Bear said, rubbing his arm. "But I'd much rather be home, enjoying a bowl of marmalade-covered tarts."

"We can't keep this up!" Flax said, bashing the leg of one of them. It fell over, unable to stand. Corvax swooped down, scooping up an ant. Before it could bite him, he dropped it into the sinkhole.

"Stay together!" Perl shouted. She sliced off one of the fungus stalks in one clean blow; the ant rolled onto its back, squirming.

"More trees are falling!" Javan said. "And every tree that falls is causing more sinkholes!" He fired quills at a pair of ants, stunning them briefly before Enoogoo brought his giant blade down, splitting the two ants in half.

Perl and the others looked around; it was a disaster scene as hundreds of trees lay fallen, broken; twisted like matchsticks. Giant craters were everywhere. And still the ants kept coming.

Nan had flown away to recover, but now she returned, carrying a handful of shield bark and sharp sticks. "Reinforcements!"

They grabbed the weapons and dug in; Master Tanda, Nan, Lyre, and Corvax in the air, the others standing their ground.

"Look! Out there! What are those?" Lyre asked, looking out over the treetops.

"What? I can't see where you're pointing," Flax said as the zombies pounded against their shields relentlessly, pressing the Seers up against the massive fallen Lupuna tree.

"Don't tell me more fairies?" Tars asked.

"I, I, don't think so…" said Bear.

A wave of pungent air blew in, filling the forest with a bitter, rotten stench.

"Ugh, I can't breathe," Lyre coughed.

"Good Ever," Enoogoo prayed.

"What is it?" Perl asked.

"The Army of Grigori," the orangutan said, knocking back an ant with a mighty thrust of his shield. "They've returned."

"Grigori?" Opis said, "You're certain? They haven't surfaced for thousands of years."

"You said an army?" asked Perl, puncturing an ant with her spiky elbow then slicing off the stalk from its head with a quick cut of her sword.

"An army of giants," said Javan.

"Giants," Perl repeated. She felt a pang of sorrow as she remembered Victr; how his face would light up as she regaled him with her tall tales of battling giants and slaying dragons.

"The Mother Trees are falling," Nan said. "If this keeps up, they'll all be gone."

Sweat poured and muscles ached as the nine Seers, Elder Enoogoo, and Master Tanda continued to battle. Many ants lie dead, but more came, crawling over the bodies to get to the group.

"Lyre..." Corvax weakly called over to his fellow Air Seer. Both were in the air trying to get a better look at the giants.

"Corvax!" Lyre flew over, catching the crow-boy just as he dropped to the ground. "Help, I think he's been stung!"

Opis rushed to him. "Corvax, are you okay?" She tried to steady the crow-boy as his thigh muscles spasmed.

"My leg, I can't feel it."

"I'm coming." Enoogoo sliced an ant's thorax in half, backhanded another one, and made his way over to Corvax. "Easy, now..." Pulling a silver vine from a pouch tied to his waist, he quickly tied a tourniquet. "This should stop the spread."

"But not the pain," Corvax choked out a laugh. He doubled over as it felt like molten lava running up his leg.

The others, exhausted and near collapsing themselves, held off the colony.

"That's it!" Bear hollered, angry at seeing Corvax hurt. Armed with weapons in every hand, he tore a path through the ants, cracking heads, smashing legs, breaking jaws.

"There's too many of them!" Nan said. "And now giants are coming, too!"

The ground rumbled as tree after tree fell, more sinkholes bursting open.

"The Grigori are coming!" Flax hollered.

"Master Tanda! How do we fight them?" Javan asked. "The Attenborough is gone!"

The great Battle Being flew up into a rain cloud, vanishing without a word.

"Master!" Javan stared at the others in disbelief. "She's left us."

"Should you follow her?" Nan asked Lyre, panicked.

"No! I won't leave you." Lyre said. "We stay and fight together!"

Perl stared wide-eyed into the distance like a deer frozen in its tracks. Through the scores of ants and broken trees, the giants marched towards them; dark silhouettes against the gray skies.

"Listen!" Enoogoo shouted. "Erotylidae!"

"What are Erotylidae?" Flax asked.

"Pleasing Fungus Beetles," Javan shouted.

"More Bugs?" Flax said, jamming his stick into an ant's side.

"We can't fight them all," yelled Tars.

The Seers held their ears as the buzzing chatter from thousands of blue beetles came roaring towards them from the depths of the rainforest. The sight of the massive blue swarm approaching triggered Perl's defenses. She ran over to where Lyre and Nan knelt next to Corvax.

"Quickly, everyone! Gather around!"

"You have a plan?" Bear asked, carrying Opis. "Should we run?"

"It's too late. We're pretty much surrounded," said Javan.

Perl looked around. All eyes were on her. "Okay. Close in. Real tight." The group pressed in around Perl. "Ready?"

Perl spread out her vampire squid cape, wrapping all eight of them in a spikey, tent-like dome. Seeing Perl transforming, Enoogoo guarded The Nine, hacking away at the attacking ants.

"Wow! You guys said Perl could do this, but wow!" Nan said, poking at Perl's taut skin.

Outside Perl's protective cape, buzzing noises and violent scuffling sounds could be heard. Perl briefly lost her footing as the things outside bumped and clawed at her cape. Bear caught her feet, holding her steady.

"It's getting louder out there," Javan said.

Tars looked over at Flax. "This is so weird."

"Rude, Tars," Flax joked, shoving his friend.

"Oh, I mean, not weird-weird. Amazing weird." The monkey-boy blushed. "Sorry, Perl."

Perl and the others chuckled, forgetting for a moment the danger that lie on the other side. Their joy amidst the chaos strengthened Perl's resilience; her spots intensified, lighting up the scene around them.

Some fifty yards off, the Grigori paused. Through the trees, they saw a strange orb glowing like a lantern. Around the orb, a chaotic scene unfolded; giant black ants clashed with wave after wave of blue beetles. The Grigori looked at one another, confused as to whether to engage.

"Cack-cack-caaack!" Master Tanda's peregrine cry rang out as she burst through the mist.

"For the Light!" followed Uriel, flaming blue sword in hand. Behind the two, an army of black bears, weapons drawn, came bounding through the woods, chanting in a deep, low hum.

The bears were large, muscular and ran upright. They wore the shining Hope-colored Natatory uniforms, their long mossy beards flowing as they charged. Many of the bears held giant baskets; as they approached, they released thousands upon thousands more of blue Pleasing Fungus Beetles. Once they hit the ground, the beetles immediately attacked the Zombie Ants, who turned to face their new enemy, no longer caring about Perl and the others. They attacked the beetles, biting them, stomping on them, stinging them, but were far outnumbered. The beetles crawled up the ants' legs, smothering them, chewing at the Cordyceps' fungal parasites. One by one the ants dropped, overwhelmed by the beetle army.

Horns blared and the bears let out a war cry, turning their forces toward the imposing giants, who stood nearly as tall as the surrounding trees. The Grigori marched toward the bears, roaring in anger at the oncoming threat. Thunder boomed like cannon fire, echoing through the jungle as the first waves clashed, led by Tanda and Uriel. As they collided, a great wind began to stir and the skies darkened; rain began to fall in sheets, turning quickly to hail. In the gloomy rainforest, the two armies pushed up against each other; scores of mighty creatures swinging their mighty steel, screaming, killing and dying, only to be replaced by another giant, another bear. The ground shook like an earthquake as they fought, and as the number of fallen warriors rose, so too, did the number of trees. The entire area looked like Hell on Earth; a tangled carnage of broken trees and bloody bodies; the ground pitted with black craters like gaping mouths ready to swallow anyone who got too close.

Amongst all the commotion, a dark, ghastly figure rose like smoke from one of the many sinkholes in the woods. The creature was large, angular; its four arms held up to the sky, with a pair of ram skulls floating above it. From two arms, opened veins sprayed out steady streams of blood, like fountains in some twisted nightmare.

Uriel plunged her flaming blue saber through the heart of a giant. She leaped high over another, taking its head off as she went. As she landed, another giant grabbed hold of her. It lifted her up to its chiseled face, its grip like a vice. The giant opened its mouth wide and was about to bite down hard when Master Tanda swooped in, clawing at the behemoth's back as she let out a cry. The giant dropped Uriel, roaring in pain. Uriel hit the ground and with one agile stroke, cut the giant's legs off at the knees. The hulking brute screamed, swayed, and toppled like a redwood tree, nearly crushing Uriel.

"Thank you, Tan—" Before she could finish, a voice like a razor sliced through her thoughts.

"Urrrielll!" The abomination spoke to her telepathically. Its voice was dry, cracking, ancient; as if the desert itself spoke.

Uriel stopped and turned.

"Azazel," Uriel replied in her mind as she readied her sword. *"Show yourself."*

The Beast emerged from the dark, wet forest, floating through the air. Uriel was a towering figure, but the thing coming towards her was twice her size. It hovered over Uriel; its jagged skull of a head was nothing but row after row of eyes that burned lava red.

"Corruptor," Uriel said aloud, gripping her longsword with both hands. "You are out of your cage."

Azazel's head fell back and it let out an ear-piercing scream, echoing through the trees. The thing took a long deep breath then exhaled, blowing an icy-yellow fog at Uriel. The moth over Uriel's eye disintegrated into dust. Uriel staggered backwards, coughing.

"Broken One." Azazel expanded its boney wings of decaying flesh, revealing Uriel's missing wing that it wore like a trophy draped across its back. *"I shall have the other."*

"Master?" Enoogoo, still guarding Perl and the others, heard Tanda's cry from the woods. Seeing the beetles going after the ants, the orangutan took to the trees, making his way to his dear master's voice.

Azazel threw the ram skulls at Uriel; the severed heads clamped onto her chainmail, biting and gnawing at her armor. Uriel's heart pounded and hail stones stung her face like tiny wasps as she fought off the skulls. She pried one off, tossing it into the air and splitting it in half with her blade. The other she knocked to the ground, crushing it under her boot.

"Watcher, you are no warrior." Azazel's red eyes flashed in the lightning; its head like a demented gargoyle.

"Back, back into the bowels to rot." Uriel swung, slicing across Azazel's long billowing gown, exposing swarms of horned vipers and serpents that crawled and buzzed around the Beast's torso.

"Shadu non val tok ess tu." Azazel waved its arms. Hearing the incantation, the Giants, as if hypnotized, formed a wall, pushing the bears to each side, clearing a path. The demon cocked its head; just a few hundred yards away it could see the glowing umbrella-like sphere where Perl was protecting her friends.

Uriel swung hard, severing one of the Beasts arms; dark blood splattered across her cheek. The arm hit the ground and turned into a snake, slithering up the demon's leg and up under its gown.

"Time on Earth has made you a worm," Uriel said, watching as the thing's bones and tissue began to grow back.

239

Azazel struck Uriel, slamming her against a tree with frightening force. Gasping for breath, Uriel tried but couldn't pry herself from the trunk, held fast by a dark spell.

"Mal don husk dey ull." Azazel floated down the cleared path towards Perl.

"Blind with only faith to see! At Ever's will come to me!" Uriel cried out, her voice like a siren.

High above the trees, a great ball of lemon-yellow light lit up the sky. The light grew more intense, as if the sun itself was about to burst. Fighting stopped as all eyes were drawn to the sky. From the radiant glow came three beams of light, hitting the ground directly in front of Azazel.

Three colossal golden bats appeared out of the sunbeams in glistening armor. The Light Beings flew at Azazel in a blur, attacking the demon's wings, ripping at them with their steel-tipped claws. Azazel countered, swinging its arms wildly, but the bats' echolocation allowed them to anticipate the demon's moves. They ducked and dodged, twisting and turning in aerial acrobatics around the creature. The golden bats backed the Beast up to the edge of a sinkhole. Azazel managed to get hold of one of the bat's wings. There was a loud screech as the demon pulled at the Light Being's wing. The other two went after Azazel's face, clamping down with their steely claws. In a tangle of arms and claws and blood, the four plummeted into the crater.

Released from the spell, Uriel's knees buckled and she went down, using her sword to force herself back up. The violent storm raged on, battering trees and opening more sinkholes. Uriel gathered her strength, sprinting between the raging bears and giants who resumed their fighting, making her way to Perl.

"Ever be with us," Uriel prayed, as she witnessed her Light Realm comrades' essences leave their bodies.

"I can't hold this any longer," Perl said, feeling her fingers cramping. "I have to let go."

"Corvax, can you walk?" Tars asked.

"No, but I think I can fly."

Bear handed the crow-boy his weapon.

"Ready yourselves everyone," Lyre said.

The Nine nodded to one another. Tars helped Corvax to his feet.

"Okay, Perly, let-her rip," Bear said.

Perl's vampire squid cape unfolded, reforming back into her arms and legs.

"I got you," Javan said, grabbing Perl as she staggered.

The Nine were not prepared for what they saw. Before them lie piles of dead ants, tens of thousands of blue beetles. Hail coming down in sheets. And in the distance, a full-blown war.

"The Bullet Ants, they're all dead!" Nan said.

"And look there! The Natatory Battle Bears!" Opis shouted, pointing. "The *Ursus* have come! Praise Ever!"

"I don't see Enoogoo," Bear said.

"Maybe he joined the battle?" Nan shrugged.

The group moved quickly past the ant corpses, the army of beetles still devouring what was left of them. All but Javan, who stood in shock.

"The trees," he mumbled. Pain like a dagger pierced the platypus-boy's chest. "They're all gone."

"Javan! Come on, we gotta go," Perl went back to Javan, the sound of the storm and cracking trees deafening. Bear, Opis, and the others kept moving, unaware the two had stopped.

"I...can hear their screams." Javan covered his ears, falling to one knee. "The Mother Trees…"

"Javan, please!" Perl pulled at his sleeve. "We need to get out of here."

"They're losing their children!"

"We'll help them!"

"This is what I saw. In my vision. This is the end."

"It's not the end," Perl shouted. "It can't be!"

The ground trembled, and an enormous crater opened up, separating Perl and Javan from the others.

"Perl! Javan!" The Seers yelled across the chasm.

"We gotta go back," Bear said.

The group split; some going left, some right around the giant sinkhole. Corvax, Nan, and Lyre took a straight shot over the giant sinkhole, but flying in the heavy hail and winds was difficult.

From the black pit Azazel resurfaced, the remains of a golden bat wing in its claws. It moved towards Perl.

"Oh, Ever," Perl muttered under her breath, seeing the dark specter. Her bioluminescence lit up; the spikes on her arms extending. "What is that?"

"Perl! Get behind me!" Javan readied his venomous spurs embedded in his hips.

Azazel came towards them. *"Un lum ta shell."*

Perl felt her body go stiff as a board. She tried to hold onto Javan but couldn't feel her fingers.

"Perl?" Javan saw the strange look on her face.

Perl went straight back like a falling tree. Panic washed over her; her eyes like full moons, staring up at Javan. "I...I can't move!"

"No!" Uriel felt Perl's fear. She sprinted, practically flying over the thick, slippery forest landscape. A number of giants tried to form a blockade in front of her, but she broke through them like a wrecking ball.

In her mind, Uriel called—*"Quantaa, come!"*

Javan fired. Spurs went into the Corruptor's chest, but barely stuck in the demon's rocklike breast plate. Azazel flicked a wrist, flinging Javan into a pile of dead ants.

Perl screamed. Her spots went supernova. The vipers hanging from Azazel hissed and coiled from her light.

"*Un lum ta shell.*"

As quickly as they lit up, Perl's bioluminescent spots dimmed again. Every breath she took became labored, as if she were breathing through a wet, heavy blanket.

Azazel moved closer. "*Un lum ta shell. The Chosen One is mine.*"

Through the hailstorm, the great Battle Protector Quantaa heard Uriel's call and came rocketing through the air. It hit Azazel with all its force, sending the demon flying backwards as if struck by a bolt of lightning. It slid to a stop some fifty yards away. Quantaa flew upwards, circling back around for another blow.

"Cack-cack-cack!" Master Tanda shrieked. The lizard-falcon emerged from the dark skies and flew beside Quantaa; the two of them dove like a pair of missiles towards Azazel.

The Demon rose back up. It raised its arms up at the two flyers just as they were about to strike.

"*Mal cha sinew!*" It bellowed, and instantly, Quantaa and Tanda froze mid-strike. Quantaa whined and Tanda shrieked; the two flapped their wings helplessly, trapped like fireflies in a jar.

With the two Light Beings restrained, Azazel was about to turn its attention back to Perl when Enoogoo swung down from the trees and came barreling at the demon, his sword in hand. Azazel hissed, waving its arms upward in a sweeping gesture. The great orangutan felt the plants and weeds grabbing at his feet. He tripped, hitting the ground as the vines crawled up his legs and over the top of him. Within seconds, he was entangled in the forest floor's thick, soggy mesh.

Bear, Tars, and the others were making their way back to Perl and Javan, the blasting hail and gusting winds forcing them to move cautiously around the crater.

Crawling his way out of the pile of ants, Javan spotted a blue flame moving like a blur through the sheet of hail, headed toward the dark phantom.

Uriel came up behind the demon at full speed. She leapt, her blue flame taking off one of Azazel's arms. The demon screamed, its severed limb twirling into the air, breaking the spell that held Quantaa and Tanda. The two Light Beings dove toward the ground then quickly banked, redirecting their path towards the Dark Being.

"Quantaa, attack! Attack!" Uriel yelled.

Quantaa's pair of mighty jaws clamped down on one of the Beast's wings, ripping at it. Tanda struck too, its razor-sharp talons scraping at Azazel's face. Blood poured from the demon's many eye sockets.

Uriel spun, ducked under an attack, and sliced off another of the creature's arms, yet watched as the first arm had almost grown back. The three Light Realm Beings fought Azazel with every ounce of strength they could muster, knowing this ancient creature would not die easily.

Wounded and distracted, Azazel's spell cast on Perl broke. Perl slowly crawled over to where Javan was hiding.

"Are you okay?" Javan asked. Perl nodded. Her body was sore and sluggish; as if she'd been sleeping for days.

Corvax, Nan, and Lyre landed beside them. They huddled next to a fallen tree, all of them drenched to the bone.

"Are you hurt?" asked Nan.

"No...but that..." Perl blinked through the downpour, seeing Uriel and Quantaa. "What is that thing they're fighting?"

"Azazel the Corruptor." Corvax said, rubbing his throbbing leg. "One of the first of the Dark Beings. It fell from the Light with The Ullen."

"We can't just sit here; we have to help them!" Perl wiped the rain from her face, pulling out Fortis.

Corvax shook his head angrily. "No, Perl. This isn't your fight."

"Perl, there's nothing we can do," Nan replied. "We have to protect ourselves right now. Uriel and Quantaa and Master Tanda will prevail."

Perl gritted her teeth; she was angry and scared.

"The others are trying to make their way around the sinkhole, but I think we should get back to the safety of the trees," added Lyre.

"What trees?" Javan spoke up. "Look around. We're surrounded by death."

Corvax put a hand on Javan's shoulder. "We need to stay together. We will find a way to—"

"It's too late! Amanita has released the poison! It's spreading as we sit here!" Javan shouted over the claps of thunder.

Perl had never heard such anger or desperation in Javan's voice; he had always been her calm no matter the storm. She felt helpless as she looked at the others. They had no answers, the warm rain streaming like tears down their faces.

"*Water.*" A glimmer of an idea popped into Perl's head. "What about the water?"

"What do you mean?" Corvax replied.

"Ever since I was little, water has been my conduit. I have a connection to it. I..." She paused. "I might be able to control it."

"You mean the rain?" Nan asked.

"Not the rain, but the water in the ground." She turned to Javan. "The trees are dying from the poison in the soil. I can try to pull out the poison from the groundwater and stop it from spreading."

"Pull it out? To where?" Lyre asked; Javan and the Air Seers looked at one another with concern.

"I'll absorb it," Perl shrugged. "I'll take it in, and then release it somewhere safe."

"This isn't stacking turtles or lifting a manatee out of the water," Javan argued. "It's poison, Perl. A lot of poison!"

"Do we have a choice?" Perl turned to the platypus-boy. "I'm not even sure it'll work, but I have to try. Amanita's killing the rainforest. If there's a chance I could stop her, I have to try."

"No," Javan shook his head. "It's too dangerous—"

"Hold on," Corvax interrupted. "We've seen Perl's telekinetic abilities." He looked at Perl. "This could work."

The winds picked up, the steamy wet rain swirling about them.

"Move back, everyone." Perl waved the group away. Javan was about to protest once more, but held his tongue.

Perl knelt, pressing her palms to the warm, wet ground.

Perl closed her eyes. She began to breathe slowly, rhythmically; the sounds of the storm and the fighting receding in her mind. She visualized the mycelium; billions of tiny strands connecting every tree and plant, spreading out across the rainforest in an infinite web.

The rest of the Seers had made their way around the crater.

"Uriel...Master Tanda...Quantaa," Bear blurted out. The tardigrade-boy was drenched to the bone and out of breath; he and the others looked just as miserable.

"Shh," Javan held a finger up to his lips.

Bear, Opis, and the others looked over at Perl.

"What's happening?" Opis asked.

"Perl is using telekinesis to connect with the water in the mycelium," Corvax said.

"She is trying to absorb the poison," Lyre added.

"Can she do that?" Asked Tars. Javan shrugged. "Well, the least we can do is keep her safe," Tars added.

As they had done many times in their training, the Seers formed a circle. All eyes were on Perl as the battles in the distance raged on.

Perl concentrated, controlling her breath. She could hear the low roar of rocks; smell the soil as every spot on her body began to glow and pulsate. Perl felt the earthy taste of the soil in her mouth along with something else, something rotten and sour. *"Amanita's poison."* Perl could hear the trees whispering, *"We are starving...we are starving..."* It was the same whispering Perl had heard when she and Amanita had made their blood oath.

"Like the moon I tilt the Earth, restoring balance. Water, come to me." Perl repeated softly. She imagined drawing the water inside the mycelial vessels up through her fingertips. Perl's arms began to tremble. She could feel the poison moving towards her. *"Water, come to me...come to me."* Perl's arms burned; her fingers felt like red-hot pokers.

As the Seers watched, the hail slowed to a gentler rain. The winds died down and from the dark clouds, a small patch of blue sky broke open above their heads. A thin shaft of sunlight beamed down, bathing the group in a golden light.

"I think it's working!" Flax said, recharging his scales in the sunlight.

Tears were now streaming down Perl's cheeks; the pain growing. Where her teardrops fell, white-capped mushrooms sprouted, popping up all around her like kernels of corn.

"You're doing it, Perl!" Tars spun his tail excitedly. Nan and Lyre hugged.

Perl cried out in pain; it felt like liquid fire coursing through her veins. The color was draining from her hands, turning an ashy gray.

"No, something's not right," Javan said. "Perl, stop! That's enough!" He ran over to her, grabbing around her waist while trying to pry her hands up. "They won't budge!"

Perl's entire body began to convulse. Her hands were black; tiny fissures ran up her arms.

"It's killing her! Bear, help me!"

"Let go, Perl!" The tardigrade-boy pulled with all his might, managing to get one of her hands out of the ground, then gasped. Webs of gooey black tar were pumping into Perl's hands, coursing through her veins.

"Mal don husk dey ull!" Perl screamed, throwing her head back as black clouds closed off the patch of blue, the wind and heavy rains resuming. *"Mal don husk dey ull!"* Perl's voice echoed through the forest.

Hearing Perl's possessed cry, a wave of fear ran through Quantaa. It whined, flying away from Uriel and Tanda as they fought Azazel.

"Quantaa, stay and fight!" Uriel commanded, but the great greyhound was filled with dread. He took off, through the clouds to the safety of the Light Realm. The demon Azazel was drenched in blood. Its face was all but torn away. Its arms were gone. Yet it lived. It laughed a wicked laugh, like the howling of the damned.

"It is done," it declared.

The Grigori Giants, under Azazel's spell, were no longer needed. As if hypnotized, they stopped fighting and crawled back into the craters. The Battle Bears, unsure what was happening, dropped their weapons. Some fell to their knees, exhausted; others assisted the wounded.

One of Azazel's arms regrew, and before Uriel could take it off again, it got hold of Tanda. The falcon-lizard squawked, clawing and batting its wings to escape its grasp, but to no avail; with a quick twist, Azazel snapped Master Tanda's neck, tossing her to the ground.

"No!" Enoogoo, still trapped in the jungle growth, felt his heart burst.

"Tanda!" Uriel saw one of Javan's spurs lodged in the Beast's chest. She could feel the boy's love coursing through the atoms inside the spur. "By love's pure Light I end you!" Uriel swung her sword, driving the spur deep into Azazel's black heart.

The snakes clinging to its body fell, writhing on the ground. Azazel bellowed, clawing at its flesh. It pried with fresh arms, cracking open its ribcage to try to pull out the spur. Uriel seized the moment, slicing at Azazel's neck, but the Beast managed to lean away, the blade grazing its neck and leaving a wound, but not a fatal one. Azazel flapped its wings, hovering over Uriel.

"Ullen's will is done." Its words echoing like shattered glass in Uriel's mind. The Beast flew into one of the sinkholes, returning to The Dark Realm.

"Perl." Uriel ran to the group. She saw Perl hunched over as if in a praying posture. Hundreds of white mushrooms climbed up and over her, smothering her.

The Seers ripped and tore at the fungi, which grew faster than they could get rid of them.

"Please Perl, you've got to let go!" Bear pulled at her hands, trying to release the dark mycelium's death grip; yet it pulled both of Perl's hands back into the ground.

"Perl!" Javan begged, seeing her sparkling green eyes turn black.

"Away!" Uriel rushed in, pushing aside Javan and Bear. The others backed up, giving her room. They looked with alarm at the great Light Protector covered in blood from head to toe, her bright armor scraped and dented. Where her beautiful moth always fluttered was an exposed scar, dark and jagged. Uriel waved her arm, "Solvo!" The connection broke, freeing Perl's hands from the Earth.

Perl, pale and unconscious, flopped backwards, thick black liquid dripping from her fingers. As soon as Perl's hands were free, the mushrooms stopped growing and the wind and rain died down. Bear, Tars, and Flax pulled them off the girl, stomping on the mushrooms, smashing them to pulp. The Seers huddled around Perl; the bright, cheerful girl they knew looked nothing like the broken, sickly sight before them.

"She's going to be alright, isn't she?" Bear asked.

"It was too much. I knew she shouldn't have done it," Javan said, wiping away a tear.

"Perl did what had to be done," Opis said.

Uriel placed her forehead against Perl's; it was ice cold. "Her mind is trapped in the Darkness."

"Perl, wake up," Javan said. "Please wake up."

"We must get her to Palo Santo." Uriel stood, carrying Perl in one arm, using her free hand to open a sparkling lavender portal to Greenheart.

Uriel stepped through the portal, followed by the eight Seers. Nan, who was the last to step through, paused to take one last look back at the devastated rainforest— Splintered trees, ant carcasses, and debris were scattered everywhere. Smoldering carbon hissed from the many open pits that peppered the landscape. The last of the Natatory Battle Bears trudged off into the forest, carrying their dead and injured into the mist. In the distance, Nan spotted Enoogoo hunched over on a fallen palm tree, his soft orange hair swirling in the wind. She smiled and was about to call out to him but stopped. The great orangutan was cradling his beloved Master Tanda, sobbing and gently kissing her head.

"Carbon levels have skyrocketed after a severe storm decimated half of the remaining rainforest, killing countless species of wildlife. Scientists warn this could mean the beginning of the end for human kind."

"Turn that garbage off," King Tobias said.

"We need to stay on top of world events, Brother," King Névenoé insisted.

"That's what our counselors at court are for. We are here to enjoy Sri Lanka! Relax already, it's our honeymoon!"

King Névenoé stared at the projection as the news anchor continued.

"Areas of the forest landscape are covered in a toxic black fungus that has yet to be identified…"

"Brother! You are killing the vibe," Tobias shouted.

"Fine." Névenoé switched off the broadcast. "Speaking of our council, what's the latest on finding the escapees?"

"Let it go, Nev," King Tobias said. "The scouting teams have lost over twenty of our men trying to scale those cliffs. Unless those mole-born are part mountain goat, they're all but dead by now."

"Don't you find it strange that there are still herds of reindeer surrounding the foothills?"

"Not particularly." Tobias took a bite from an apple.

"Where did they all come from? It's the Desertlands." Névenoé leaned on the balcony railing, looking out over the rugged landscape; their fortress being the highest point in the center of the small island.

"Maybe you should go back home and see. And bring back some venison for Kandy and I. Oh wait, you're terrible at hunting," Tobias laughed.

"I would have beaten you…"

"Boys, boys, you know I hate when you fight. Plus, it upsets Baby, isn't that right, Baby?" Kandy Vandenmire, heiress to her grandfather's steel empire, and namesake of Sri Lanka's capital city, lounged on an oversized satin pillow under a covered cabana, stroking the fur of her pet cheetah *(Acinonyx jubatus)*. The big cat wore a silk collar that matched her owner's bikini. "Explore the temple, take a boat out on Kandy Lake, just stop bickering! It's such a turnoff."

"Sorry, Sweetness." Tobias sat on the floor at the foot of the pillow. "Let me see if I can turn you back on, hmm?" He grabbed her foot and began nibbling on her toes.

"Speaking of temples, what's so sacred about that thing, anyway?" Névenoé walked over to the other side of the room, where a small but extravagant altar stood. An object was prominently displayed. It was a tooth, placed upon a tiny gold pedestal, enshrined inside a golden dome and surrounded by precious gemstones.

Kandy giggled, "Stop that, you bad boy." She pulled her foot away from Tobias. "The tooth is said to have belonged to some kind of Buddha. It was given to the monarchy in ancient times. Whoever possesses it governs the country. I only hang on to it to keep the superstitious locals in line."

"What type of gems are these?" Névenoé ran his fingers along the opalescent stones.

"Moonstones, aren't they precious? I love how they play in the light up here." Kandy smiled at Tobias, who was crawling up the satin pillow to lay next to her.

"Enough about stones, it's our honeymoon." He pushed the cheetah away. "I love to play in the light, too." The cat let out a low growl and jumped to the ground.

"Be nice to Baby, she's a delicate pussy cat…" Kandy giggled as Tobias tickled her.

"You don't like when I'm…nice," Tobias smirked.

"Hint taken," Névenoé scoffed, exiting under the arched elephant tusks framing the doorway. "I'm going to visit our fair queen."

In her extravagant glass-and-steel domed chamber, Mik rested on a chaise lounge made of zebra hide, examining the intricately carved gift from Gretar. *"I miss you, my love."* The new queen was surrounded by a literal jungle; plants and flowers of every kind packed the room; marble fountains filled with fish sprayed crystal blue water into the air; exotic birds chattered and spider monkeys sat in trees, grooming one another.

"Ah! Red Queen! There you are!" Névenoé entered the room, his voice echoing off the glass walls, frightening the monkeys, who scurried off.

Startled, Mik dropped Gretar's gift. The small nut rolled to a stop at the end of Névenoé's pointed boot.

"What do we have here?"

"It's a gift. For you, my King," Mik said, thinking quickly.

Névenoé reached down and picked it up. "How very…primitive," he said, eyeballing it closely.

"It's carved from a walnut, native to Mont Michel."

"Ah, Mont Michel. I recall you and Ivry's quaint little sweet sixteen birthday ball. I had hopes of marrying the both of you. Such a shame she died. And now it's you who has two Kings."

Mik hated both brothers with a passion, but knew she had to try to stay on their good sides; that is, if either of the wretched brothers had a good side.

"Speaking of home. I haven't heard from my father or my mother since we left the Under Kingdom. Could you contact them for me?"

"Oh, but you haven't heard, there's been an accident." Névenoé tapped on his tech device on his cuff. "I'm afraid your poor father's been murdered."

"What?! Murdered, how?"

He showed Mik the screen on his wrist playing the fake video.

"Bandits broke into his chambers the night we left for our honeymoon."

"Where was Snive and his team? What about mother? Is she okay?"

"It would seem the thieves got to Snive as well. But good news! Your mother is safe. She and Ruby will be staying with her sister in the north from now on. It's for the best."

"I can't believe he's gone." Mik's eyes welled with tears.

"I thought you hated your father."

"We were…just beginning to get along again."

Névenoé slowly opened the latch on the walnut, reading the inscription— *'You have my heart, you are my home.'*

The King looked up, cocking an eye at Mik suspiciously. She felt her cheeks flush.

"You? A romantic?" Névenoé said. "Hmph. I wouldn't have guessed that."

Shocked by the news of her father's death, Mik felt numb, trapped, yet she tried to keep her wits about her. "I have dreamed of marrying you ever since Ivry and I were little girls playing dress-up," Mik said. *"It was once true,"* she thought. *"A lifetime ago."*

"Perhaps I won't share you with Tobi. Perhaps I'll keep you to myself, hmm?" King Névenoé sat down on the lounge beside Mik, looming over her like a vulture. "One day it could all be ours." He snapped shut the delicate carved walnut.

The King leaned in for a kiss and Mik's body tensed up.

"Ours and ours alone." His lips brushed against her cheek. "If that is your wish, my fiery one."

Mik's Self-Slayer whispered to her— *"You will never get out of this marriage. Embrace your life as Queen."*

"No" Mik tried to shake that thought off, but it persisted.

"You deserve to rule. Take the spoils."

Névenoé grabbed hold of the back of Mik's hair and she surrendered to his kiss; a million thoughts racing through her head.

"What are you doing out of bed?" Gretar ran to take Sister Martha's arm, "Here, let me—"

"I'm fine. I'm fine. Stop fussing." Martha hobbled to her closet, wrapping a shawl around her blue robe. "I just had a bit of a chill. Did you get the ginger and mint for tea?" Turning back towards her bedroom doorway, she saw Dianna standing there. "No-no-no. What on Earth are you doing here?"

"I came back to get Amanita," Dianna paused. "She isn't who—"

"You should be in the mountain caves with the others." Martha wagged a finger, cutting Dianna off. "The children there need you."

"I know, but so many didn't make it out. We need to be here for them."

"It's true the Under Kingdom will be even more powerful now that it's united with the Graves." Martha sat on the bed.

Dianna stepped into the candlelit room, sitting beside Martha as Gretar poured water into a tea kettle.

"But look at you, you're covered in ash," Martha fussed, taking Dianna's hand. "What happened? Are you okay? What can I get you? Gretar, fetch me a warm cloth."

Dianna placed her other hand on Martha's. "Dear Sister, I am well. Gretar saved me."

"And for that I am thankful." Sister Martha's face grew serious. "But both of you need to go."

"We can't leave you here alone." Gretar said, steeping the tea with mint leaves.

"I am head of this burrow and have been for decades. I will be fine. And I am not alone. The Sisters that are still here will need my help to keep things running smoothly."

Gretar crossed his arms. "How can you continue to sew and supply food to those barbaric elitists?"

"Does the Brotherhood of the Quill on Mont Michel stop providing to The Golden Palace?" Martha said. "No. If they did, then all would suffer, the poor included. Our work in the shadows must continue. They need hope that a better world is coming." Martha squeezed Dianna's hand. "One that your Perl will surely bring. Your time in the underground is over. Your light is needed in the mountains now." Martha stood, taking the cup of tea from Gretar and placing a gentle hand on his cheek. "And you will see Our Lady of the Woods to safety."

"The mountains are treacherous. How will I ever find them?" Gretar asked.

"Dianna knows the Odina passageway."

Dianna nodded. "I made the journey once many years ago. We will follow the trail markings...if they're still there."

"Good, it's settled then. You will leave at dusk, when the temperature is low and the forest will conceal you. The well room passageway has been sealed off by now. You'll have to slip out through the coal room's exhaust vent. It's the only other route."

A few hours later under the cover of twilight, Dianna and Gretar scurried through the vent and made their way through the twisted forest, both of them covered head to toe in black soot.

"There," Dianna pointed as she shook the soot off her robe. "See that star etched in the sapling? Keep an eye out for more like that. We're on the right path."

Gretar turned back to look at the ominous Under Kingdom fortress, now far behind them. Toxic green fumes billowed from the gargoyles' mouths, wafting into the purple skies.

"Like sleeping dragons," he thought, the hairs standing up on his arms.

44 GLOBUS NATURA

The stained-glass windows of the Golden Palace were shrouded in black drapes and the entire island of Mont Michel was ordered to dim their lights. Only the towering 3D holographic videos played, honoring the life of Count Zell Graves.

Across the Narcissi social feeds, inside homes and businesses worldwide, the fake footage of The Count's brutal murder that had been planted by the Deathstalker Kings played on an endless loop.

The Countess Sarr, grief-stricken, had been shipped off to live out her days with her sister Monia, Duchess of the Last Ice Cap. Queen Mik and King Névenoé held court in the Palace, reigning over the Earth's supply of clean water, while King Tobias and his mistress Kandy Vandenmire ruled the world's tech energy from the Desertland's Under Kingdom. Various rumors spread about the kings, but all were quickly squashed by the brothers.

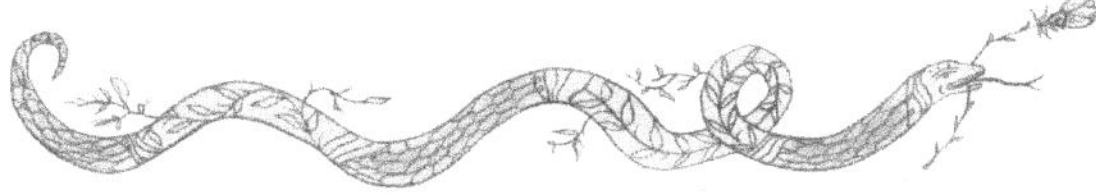

"In all my hundred and four years, I haven't seen the Globus Natura behave like this." Brother Ximu struggled to close the small door as brisk winds pushed inside the root cellar room. "The storm that damaged the rainforest has caused chaos in the natural order of things…"

"Here let me help you, Brother." Brother Basil set his large leather-bound book on the floor, placing his hands against the wooden door.

The two monks fought with the door as it rattled on its hinges. Butterflies, normally nestled in the delicate spider-webbed lace walls, fluttered wildly around the thirteen wobbling orbs. The usually tranquil waters in the pool that surrounded the open palms sculpture splashed onto the floor.

"One, two, push!" Ximu's long white beard flapped across Basil's face as the door slammed shut. Ximu fumbled through his robe pocket for the key, locking the door as it continued to rattle.

"This is bad, very, very bad," Basil stuttered.

"I fear we are at the dawn of Darkness, Brother." Ximu bent down, picking up Basil's book and handing it to him. "But for the rarest of circumstances, The Genesis Orb has always been in balance."

Brother Basil pulled out his feather quill, opening the book. "What shall I report?"

Ximu gently closed the book. "Sound the Evensong bell, call all Brothers to the chapel. We need to pray for The Chosen One."

"Perl. Why? What are you saying?"

"She needs our protection." Ximu said. "I can feel it in my bones." Brother Basil nodded; he and the other monks knew not to ever question the old monk when he had a premonition.

Basil hurried to the tower and struck the enormous bell, the sound reverberating across the island, summoning his Brothers to their small candle-lit chapel. Within ten minutes, the pews were packed shoulder-to-shoulder.

"Settle. Settle." Brother Jonathan rang the chimes beside the pulpit. "Brother Ximu has called a special meeting to bring us all together tonight so that we may send out the Bulwark Chant, to encircle The Chosen One with our protection."

Mumbling and murmurs filled the chapel.

"Let us first pray for our Brother Sebastian. We have not heard word from him since the escape attempt the night of the coronation. We pray that he, Dianna, along with the Forest Sisters of Elsewhere and the Odina tribe are safe and well." Brother Jonathan stepped aside, giving Ximu the pulpit.

"Praise be," the monks responded.

Ximu, voice heavy with burden, addressed the Brotherhood. "Word is Ever and Ever is the word, creating a Light that outshines any darkness." Ximu lit a small prayer candle.

"Praise be to all Nature."

"Wherever our Perl is, may she feel our love through the Bulwark Chant; verse twenty-one from the Book of The Awakening." Ximu stretched his arms out in front of him, palms toward the sky; the Brotherhood did the same. As they chanted, they lowered their arms turning palms to face Mother Earth, ending with the hands crossed over their hearts to honor the spirit that dwells within.

"Loammm"
(be thankful for the fertile soil)
"Doreaaash"
(be thankful for the Gift of Ever, given freely from the sea)
"Ummmeverrr Artemmm Infintummm"
(give praise to the Artist of All Things)

In a meditative state, arms moving seamlessly together; the monks continued chanting until the prayer candle went dark.

45 PINECONES

"I have extracted the poison," Palo Santo said, gently lifting Perl's head and wrapping it in a crown of ivy. "But because Perl is half human, her Self-Slayer was able to trap her in the Dark Realm."

Palo unwound the long vine of ivy that was connected to Perl, carrying it over to Nan.

"It's Perl's birth tree," Nan said, lowering her antenna so Palo could encircle her head with the ivy.

"Yes, it will help to bring her back to us." Palo wound an ivy wreath around each of the Seers, connecting them to one another and to Perl.

The eight Seers stood in a circle around Perl, who lay unconscious on a cloud inside Palo Santo's colossal glass greenhouse.

"I am here, Perl," Uriel whispered, removing her floral cape and draping it over Perl; the translucent lavender sparkling like diamonds in the sun-drenched room. A new leopard moth hovered over Uriel's missing eye, yet her severed wing, normally hidden under wraps, was exposed. Her armor was dented from the battle, and her ebony arms carried fresh wounds.

"Please, Uriel, if you would," Palo said, gesturing, "a conifer pinecone to each."

Using telekinesis, Uriel plucked eight pinecones from the great pine tree they stood near; each Seer took their pinecone as it floated over to them.

"The pinecone is the evolutionary precursor to the flower. Its spiral spine is in a perfect Fibonacci sequence," Palo said, placing the root end of the long ivy into a nearby water fountain.

"The pinecone is also an example of sacred geometry," Opis said.

"Indeed, all has been designed to perfection by Ever. Examine your pinecone, look at the base where the spiral becomes one; this is the center point. Press it to your forehead."

"On our third eye?" Asked Lyre.

"Exactly. The pineal gland in Perl's brain is pinecone shaped. It is the doorway to her consciousness, connecting the left and right hemispheres. The very seat of her essence within." Palo moved Tar's pinecone down a smidge, smiling.

"Thanks." Tars said shyly, his large eyes looking up at the Garden Nurse.

"Perl's gland is being obscured by the Dark Realm, making her prey to deception." Uriel stepped over the ivy vine, kneeling behind Perl's head and placing her hands on her shoulders.

"How do we open her pineal gland?" Javan said, staring at Perl. "When will she wake?"

Palo Santo went over to a towering cactus. Rather than needles, dodecahedron crystals sprouted from it. She plucked one the size of a cantaloupe.

"I want each of you to recall a beloved memory that you and Perl have personally shared. Focus only on that moment, do not waiver. Clear your mind of anything but that joyful moment." Palo nodded over to Uriel, then tossed the crystal into the air. Uriel held it telekinetically, guiding it over to Perl's body, where it began to slowly spin.

"That is how we open it, Javan," Palo said, wiping crystal dust from her hands onto her dress. "When she'll wake, I cannot say."

Palo blew into the air; a cloud formed behind each Seer. "Sit." Each of them took a seat on their floating cloud pillow. "Close your eyes." The Garden Nurse walked around the perimeter. "Find your happy, shared moment with Perl. Hold it in your mind, a constant state of pure bliss. From your subconscious, the ivy will carry your thoughts to Perl."

Palo looked down, stepping over a black and white spotted tail sticking out from a large hedge row. Parting the branches, she found Quantaa, heads lowered, looking forlorn. The greyhound was feeling ashamed for leaving the battle in the rainforest and abandoning Perl.

"It's okay, boy," Palo whispered to Quantaa, patting each head. She turned back to the meditation. "Let us bring our Perl home."

Smiles came across each Seer's face as they found their chosen moment with Perl.

Bear chuckled, reliving the moment he, Perl, and Opis tumbled out of the massive mound of wispy orange hair, looking like a bunch of orangutans. He had never seen Perl laugh so hard.

Flax recalled an earlier time in their Seeker training in Callowhorn; the pinecone reminding him of the day they juggled barrel-sized pinecones to entertain the baby porcupines. Perl, only twelve, wielding her sword, keeping their quills at bay, all while completely drenched in sticky plum juice.

Opis's mind was transfixed on Perl's face the day she had first called Perl, *'sister,'* watching as Perl's expression changed from lost and lonely to loved and accepted.

Tars thought of the campfire night before the Pompeius Games, when Perl filled her mouth full of marmalade-mallows, shaking her hair out big and crossing her eyes.

Nan held Perl's hands as the two girls spun in a field of singing sunflowers, falling down dizzy and giggling.

Lyre delighted in the moment of Perl telling her about finding her mother; recalling how Perl's bioluminescence glowed as she talked of Dianna braiding her hair.

Corvax saw the day he had given Perl the nickname "wildflower" as he listened to her go on about weeds. "*A dandelion is just as magical as a rose! I mean, you can make wishes on a dandelion's seeds. That's magic!*" Perl's big toothy grin, enchanting the crow-boy.

Javan was having difficulty choosing just one moment. His mind swirled from exploring the caves on Venusto, to rescuing Victr, to how Perl licked her dessert plate clean at Dragon Maw, to the time she had fallen asleep on his shoulder after a long day of training. His heart finally landed on the day they had reunited at Greenheart. Perl was wearing the rabbit-rabbit totem he had carved. He smiled at her, noticing her catch her breath as their eyes met. It was then that Javan knew, for him, this was true love.

The sun set and rose across the glass ceiling of Palo's greenhouse as the Seers held their meditations. Days came and went, and the passage of time could be seen on each Seer. Tar's mustache, which he preferred to keep trim, grew long, curling up in his lap. Javan's bangs fell to his shoulders. Flax shed his old scales; the new ones shining brightly. Lyre's feathers molted, while Corvax's jet black mohawk quill tips turned slightly grey. Opis grew two full inches. Nan went into a state of hibernation; Bear cryptobiosis. The ivy's roots drank from the fountain as Palo continually refilled the water. Uriel had not moved a muscle, holding steadfast to Perl's shoulders; as still as a statue. It was a timeless time, as the Garden Nurse flitted about the greenhouse caring for plants, feeding Quantaa, and keeping a watchful eye on the slow rotation of the healing dodecahedron crystal.

46 BLEMMYES

"Javan? Bear? Opis? Anyone, hello?" Perl wiped her filthy hands down the front of her Humor pants, leaving greasy black streaks. She stood up and looked around. The rainforest was dark and deathly still; black clouds blocked out the moon. "Master Tanda?! Where is everyone?" Perl shouted in all directions. "I pulled the poison back. I stopped the spread. It worked! Uriel? Javan?" Perl's voice echoed through the silent woods.

"What is going on? They wouldn't have just left me." Perl stepped around the carcasses of mutilated ants and splintered trees. She heard rustling in the underbrush not too far away.

"Who's there?" Perl said. "Come out! Show yourself!"

Perl struggled to see in the hazy. She tried lighting her bioluminescent spots, but surprisingly, they wouldn't glow.

"Here your light has no use, no light for thee," two garbled voices said in unison.

Perl froze in her tracks. "My blade has use." Perl pulled Fortis from its sheath. "Who are you? Where are my friends?"

"Those are two questions, and two are we."

A pair of identical creatures stepped out from the darkness. They were headless, yet each had a large face that protruded from the upper half of their chest. They carried long bows made from a tree branch with a quiver of arrows tied around their waists.

"Blemmyes left," the creature bowed. "And Blemmyes right," its twin bowed, both taking a synchronized step forward.

"Stay where you are," Perl raised her sword.

"Follow us to your friend from the realm of night." The Twin Blemmyes turned sharply on their heels, their rat-like tails flicking as they marched ahead down a rough path.

Seeing no other options, Perl followed from a safe distance behind the strange pair.

"Is this...the Dark Realm?" Perl called up to them.

The Blemmyes didn't bother to turn, but simply shrugged their headless shoulders, quickening their pace to a brisk trot. The trees, both the fallen and those left standing, were covered in thick fungus and mounds of tangled moss; figures trapped under the moss moaned as they passed. The air grew thicker with dust spores and fog. Perl coughed, struggling to keep up with the twins. The three came to an abrupt stop at the edge of a steep slope.

"Follow the light below," the one said, pointing down the hill to where a cave entrance opened up.

"No further do we go," the other added.

"I thought you were going to lead the way?" Perl asked. The two shrugged again. Peering at the dark entrance, Perl thought, *Why am I trusting these odd beings?*

"The fringe I remain with my twin," said one of the Blemmyes.

"The only way out is in," the other finished; the two pointing into the dark chasm.

"Comforting," Perl sighed heavily.

Laughter rang out from inside the opening. Perl took a few steps towards the cave. "Bear? Bear? Is that you?"

The Blemmyes nocked their bows and pointed them at Perl.

"Hey, easy. What are you doing?" Perl held up her hands in defense.

"To meet the power who knows no bound," one said.

"You must go underground," chimed the other.

"Okay, okay, I'm going," Perl side-stepped down the steep incline, keeping an eye on the pair until she reached the mouth of the cave.

"Let the path unfold."

"Your story will be retold."

The creatures lowered their bows.

"Wildflower! I'll race you!" A voice rang out from the pit.

"Corvax? Hang on, I'm coming!"

Perl entered the cave, half crawling, half-scooting on her behind down the sharp, gravelly descent until she reached level ground and was able to stand. Above her, Perl watched as the Blemmyes kicked and clawed at the dirt around the entrance, sealing it shut.

"Stop! What are you doing?"

"Sister, I am here." A shallow voice came from deeper within the cave.

"Opis?" Perl felt along the damp muddy wall for support. "I'm coming." Perl called out into the darkness, recalling the Blemmyes' words —

"The only way out is in."

"Opis, are you in here?" Perl couldn't see her hand before her face. She tried again to illuminate her skin; still nothing.

Laughter echoed in the dark cave. "Flax, Tars, is that you? Where are you guys? This isn't funny."

Perl squinted, seeing a faint light flicker in the distance. She held Fortis in front of her as she moved towards the familiar voices. The pitch blackness pressed in on her from all sides and made the hairs on her neck stand on end. Her walk turned into a full sprint towards the light.

"Whoa!" Perl skidded to a stop in front of a towering metal gate, blocking the way. She looked up and squinted at a sign above the gate— "Poison Garden."

A thick chain was wound around the gate, but it wasn't locked. Through the bars, Perl could see the light coming from around a curve up ahead.

"Okay, then," she sheathed her sword and began unwinding the cumbersome links. "What the—?" Perl jumped back. The chains had transformed into an emerald green snake; the cold steel now scaly skin in her hands. Perl dropped the reptile as it slithered through her legs and vanished into the darkness.

Pulling hard at the heavy iron, Perl opened the gate just enough to squeeze through. As soon as her foot touched the path on the other side of the gate the sky illuminated, revealing an overgrown garden with rows of tangled exotic plants as tall as redwoods. Hearing a muffled voice, Perl followed the path around a bend, and there at the end of a path was a thin, pale girl. She sat on a throne made of twisted roots teeming with multi-colored fungi. She held a leafy branch and was talking to it.

"Yes...no...we will have to see, won't we?"

"Amanita, is that you?" Perl thought she looked different, almost regal; she wore a long white gown made of shimmering moss with a high pointed collar that framed her alabaster cheekbones.

The girl ignored Perl, continuing her conversation with the plant. "You are so right, she is."

Inching closer, Perl saw that Amanita was talking to tiny naked, human-like creatures that crawled between the leaves on multiple arms and legs like insects. As Perl approached Amanita they scattered, hiding amongst the leaves.

"Finally. Those bumbling Blemmyes took long enough. We thought you'd never get here," Amanita said, shaking the branch, causing several of the humanoid-insects to drop to the ground and scurry away.

"And where is here, exactly?" Perl asked.

"Didn't you see the sign? Why it's my little toxic oasis."

As Amanita leaned back against her mud throne; golden scale worms and black larva wove in and around the packed dirt and twigs, making Perl's skin crawl.

"What have you done with my friends?"

"Silly Perl, you don't have any friends. No real ones, anyway. Unless you mean me, and I have done plenty."

Perl glared at Amanita. "We aren't friends, and yes, I've seen what you've done. Poisoned the rainforest." Perl moved cautiously towards the thin ghostly girl. "I heard the Seers' voices. Take me to them." Perl put one hand cautiously on Fortis.

Amanita smiled coldly. "Perl, you hurt my feelings with these outrageous accusations. After all, are we not blood sisters?"

"No, you tricked me into thinking we were. I know who you really are...Daughter of The Ullen." Perl stepped closer.

"You say that as if it's a bad thing," she smirked. "Oh, young one, there is still so much you don't understand."

"I understand that the Earth's ecosystems are falling apart, and hundreds have died because of you." Perl unsheathed her sword.

"Don't you mean...because of you?" Amanita waved her arm; a nearby branch whipped out, brushing its leaves across Perl's neck. "Allow me to enlighten you."

"Ah," Perl clutched her neck, feeling it instantly get hot. "What was that?"

"Gympie-Gympie, she's a stinger," Amanita laughed.

Perl felt like she'd been stung by hundreds of hornets. She scratched at the fine, brittle plant hairs embedded in her skin.

"Ah-ah! Careful not to rub it, you'll push the trichomes in even farther."

Perl's vision grew blurry. Amanita rose from the throne.

"Some call it the suicide plant because the pain is so bad you'll want to kill yourself to escape it," Amanita giggled.

"Stay back," Perl chopped at the air with Fortis. "Don't come any closer."

"Trust me."

"Why should I, Deceiver?" Perl could see Amanita had something in her hand.

"Because there's a fine line between poisons and cures."

Amanita held an open mussel shell up to Perl's face so she could see it. "I can take away the pain. Just ask."

A wave of agony ran down Perl's spine. "I don't want your…ahh," Perl fell to her knees, piercing the dirt with her sword to catch her fall.

Reaching down, Amanita plucked a chartreuse flower. "This is Hellebores, so stunning." She pulled a second flower. "And Opium Poppy. Plants have poison to protect themselves and if humans would only look, they'd find that venoms hold the blueprints for treating their ailments and diseases."

Amanita crushed the poppy, sprinkling the petals and pollen inside of the mussel shell. "You don't have to suffer, Perl."

Perl didn't know what game Amanita was playing, but knew she had to escape this torment.

"Yes, yes. Just make it stop."

Amanita kicked Fortis out from Perl's grip and into the thicket. "You won't be needing that." She bent down and ran the sticky mussel along Perl's neck, pulling out the toxic Gympie-Gympie plant hairs.

"The pain will linger for a while. Come." Amanita pulled Perl to her feet, tightly locking arms with her. "I'll show you more of my precious plants." She led Perl down a path with pendulous branches covered in golden flowers. "Careful, the Laburnum's bark and leaves contain the alkaloid toxin cytosine."

Though her neck still burned, Perl's vision began to clear. She ducked under some low hanging branches when she heard, "Come spin with me, Perl. The sunflowers are singing."

"That's was Nan. Where is she?"

Ignoring Perl, Amanita continued pointing out plants while dragging her along. "Over there is poison oak, and that's sumac, and of course everyone's three-leaf favorite, poison ivy. So many fall prey to her. Ironic, isn't it?"

"What is?" Perl asked, struggling to pull her arm free.

"Your birth tree is ivy," Amanita said, tightening her grip.

"How could you know that?"

"You still don't get it, do you?" Amanita tapped Perl on the nose. "You. Are. The. Poison."

"I think you have me confused with yourself." Perl shook her arm free, stepping back. "You're the one who poisoned the mycelium and destroyed all that rainforest. You, not me!"

"Did I, now? All on my own?" Amanita waved a boney white finger at Perl. "Your blood flows with mine, remember?"

"My blood has nothing to do with your destruction."

"You're half right, my half-human friend. I needed a touch more of...you." Amanita walked backwards down the path facing Perl. "Growing up, I had always thought Dianna was The One, and so I waited patiently. Did as I was told. But then, hello! You show up all full of light. So much so, you ignited a room full of dormant seeds in the nursery. Then I discovered that Dianna had been using your hair all those years to fertilize the crops. She wasn't magical at all."

"She's the most magical person on Earth."

"Perhaps. Who cares? Humans are a rotting breed. No matter, anyway. I swallowed your life-giving lock and killed Mother," Amanita said with an eerie grin.

"Liar!" Perl felt like someone had kicked her in the stomach.

"Burnt the olive trees and greenhouse to the ground." Amanita twirled. "She died slowly."

"She isn't dead. I would have felt it. But I'll kill you if you hurt her!" Perl came at Amanita, instinctively reaching for Fortis but finding an empty sheath.

Vines sprang from the trees, binding Perl's wrists and ankles.

"Oh, I like this side of you! So hostile, so angry." Amanita leaned in, whispering, "See? Your ivy is poison after all." The pale girl threw her head back laughing. "So poisonous that you cracked the realms."

"Let me go!"

"Don't you feel it? The venom has always been in your veins. But you've been brainwashed, told to believe that you are Earth's Savior. Think about it, Perl, of all the Beings you've met—wise elders, Light Realm warriors, ancients with far greater powers—Who are you compared to them? You're just an orphaned girl, half-human, with only a foot in their realm."

"No one's brainwashed me. If anyone's trying to, it's you." Perl struggled to free her hands, but the vines were strong.

"You're nothing but a pawn, child. Honestly, I commend them. They played you just right. They knew that war was eminent. Darkness at the precipice, fully prepared to inherit the Earth. They saw you as nothing more than a key to unlock the Realms, something they couldn't do because of Ever's *laws*. But you cracked open the realms to save your beloved monk. And now they leave you carrying the weight of the world on your small shoulders. Pretty cruel if you ask me."

Perl kicked and waved her bound arms. "Let me go."

"I am merciful," Amanita said, waving her hand, "to a point." The branches broke from the trees, yet the vines still kept a firm hold on Perl's wrists and ankles. The severed branch ends grew roots that walked like legs, pulling Perl along like prison guards.

"Where are we going?"

"You'll see." Perl watched as Amanita ignited her own bioluminescent skin; radiant light shimmering through every pore. "Follow my light that shines where no sun shines."

Perl's thoughts flashed to the day Papa Ximu held the barnacle from the whale and told Perl of The Prophecy. *"Maybe Papa interpreted the Book of the Awakening wrong. I'm not the only one with powers."* Perl looked at Amanita glowing; she was exquisite, otherworldly beautiful.

"The Ullen is the darkness within all. There is no salvation without The Ullen."

Perl tried to think. *"Where are we? What is this place? Is she my Self-Slayer?"*

"I am the yin to your yang, Perl."

Amanita could hear her thoughts.

"It is time to unmake the Earth and start anew. Humanity had its chance."

"You're wrong. There's hope for humanity. So many care and are trying to save the planet. If you just come with me to the Light Realm, I can—"

"And what?" Amanita turned sharply. "Pretend that this whole human experiment went right? No, Perl! Darkness is the root of light. Just like your vampire squid blood comes from the depths of the sea. The Light Realm doesn't want you to see that, Seer."

Amanita stopped at a tree that looked like Perl's treehouse in Greenheart, yet it was split down the middle. Growing up through the center of the tree was a branch from the rainbow tree in Tryfon's garden.

"All those names. All that death. And for what? To save the unworthy human species." Amanita waved her hand, releasing Perl's wrists and ankles from their bondage.

Perl stepped up to the tree, seeing Noaa's name inscribed on the bark.

"Your father isn't in the Light Realm." Amanita looked at Perl. "They lied to you about that, too."

"No, you're wrong."

"If your father was in the Light Realm, why hasn't he visited you? And why were you kept from your mother all those years?"

"Stop. You don't know anything."

"They don't want you to know the truth. Noaa sits with The Ullen. Now you must take your rightful seat as well."

"I know my divine truth."

"Stop living behind that mask, trying to please everyone who has only filled your head with false expectations and lies. You have been blinded to who you really are. Aren't you tired of living in constant fear of failing at this role, one that has been against your will?"

Amanita's words rang true; they buried themselves deep in Perl's subconscious.

"Tricksters wear masks to achieve their objectives, to use your Self-Slayer as a mind-killer." Perl heard Uriel's voice in her head.

"They are right about one thing, though. You can be the one to save humans from themselves." Amanita held out her alabaster hand. Blood dripped from the wound she'd cut to make the oath with Perl that day in the Sisterhood's grotto. "Come, let's go see our fathers together. Take my hand and surrender this burden."

Perl looked at her own hand; it was bleeding as well.

"Darkness is the true divine way. It is the root of Light," As Amanita reached out to take Perl's hand a drop of Amanita's blood hit Perl's thigh.

"Harmony is a color, silly. Seers wear Humor and Awakeners wear Hope." Opis's voice filled Perl's mind. Her thoughts turned to Bear, eating his jam rolls, his mouth slathered in sticky goo. Perl put her hands on her knees, looking at her filthy, greasy and mud-stained pants; the drop of blood soaking into the shimmering swirl of colors. Perl giggled softly to herself, escalating into a snort.

"What's so funny?"

"All of this. Me. You. But mostly me."

"I don't see what could be funny at this moment."

"I know, that's what's so funny."

"I said, take my hand, it's time." Amanita shook her hand at Perl.

The jingle-jangle of her bracelet's charms caught Perl's eye. There it was; Dianna's coquina clam shell. Perl snatched the butterfly shell, breaking the clasp. Perl clutched the bracelet in her fist, holding it to her heart. "She's alive. I can feel it." Perl laughed louder.

"She rots as we speak."

Perl stood tall, staring unblinking into Amanita's eyes. "I know what this is."

Behind Amanita, the treehouse tree and rainbow branch turned to ash, floating away on the breeze.

"Don't be so sure." Amanita was as still as a statue.

"You're afraid. You're lonely."

"You had your chance." Amanita's light gray eyes turned red. "You should have taken it." She smiled, her teeth sharpening into fangs.

"I recognize you. I see what you are," Perl said.

"You've chosen wrong!" Amanita wailed. Her jaw unhinged; demonic shadowy Self-Slayers swarmed from her throat, encircling her like a dust storm. "Humanity will end, and you along with it!"

"I accept you as you are," Perl said calmly. "Pass over me."

"Suffer!" Amanita whipped her arms; the Slayers came at Perl.

Perl's heart sunk as a black cloud began to swirl around her. She felt the pain of the Self-Slayers; having once been beings of the Light Realm, now turned to The Darkness upon their deaths. Succumbing to their agony was like fighting the pull of a tornado.

"My mind is focused, my heart is pure…" Perl repeated; she grew dizzy but held her ground. Ancient tongues in dialects she couldn't comprehend screamed out in agony around her. "Nothing will change the wave of my destiny!"

"Ullen be thy name!" Amanita shouted; a blast of energy knocked Perl off her feet and she fell down, down…

Perl blinked her eyes, tears streaming down her cheeks. The garden was gone. Everything was gone. She stood across from Amanita in a white void. The girl had transformed back into the Amanita Perl had first met; her hair painted in decorative florals, wearing her pinafore dress.

"I will decompose all that you bring to light." Amanita pursed her lips and smiled. "I am in the world."

Perl smiled back. "Then I love you."

The empty white landscape went pitch black.

In Palo Santo's greenhouse, the dodecahedron crystal floating over Perl's body shattered into pieces. The shards hit The Seers, breaking their trance-like meditation.

Perl sat up with a jolt, snapping the ivy vine that connected her to the other Seers. "Where am I?" She asked, seeing her friends and realizing she was lying on a floating cloud.

Quantaa bolted to his feet at the sound of Perl's voice, letting out a joyful howl.

"You are safe in Palo's greenhouse," Uriel said, leaning over to hug Perl. "You were trapped in the Darkness."

"Amanita was there. Or maybe she wasn't," she blinked, trying to clear her mind. "I'm...I'm not really sure." Perl noticed her friends were all wearing crowns of connected ivy. "I could hear your voices but I couldn't find you."

"We're just glad you're back," Javan said.

Perl smiled, "Why do you all have pinecones?"

"We were using them to bring you back by stimulating your pineal gland," Lyre chirped, gathering up the pile of molted feathers in her lap.

"The doorway to consciousness," added Palo Santo, "to draw your essence back to the Light."

Amanita's words came back to her in that instant; that she'd been brainwashed by everyone in the Light Realm, and that they were using her as their pawn. Sun beamed down through the glass ceiling onto Javan's adoring face. *It can't be true,* Perl thought. Quantaa licked her cheek, her face drenched in slobber; everyone broke into laughter.

"Thank Ever you're back," said Flax.

Nan blinked and yawned, still waking from her hibernation.

"What did I miss?" Bear stretched, emerging from his icy cryptobiosis state. "Perly-poo! You're back!"

"How long was I out?" Perl asked. "Judging by the length of Tar's mustache and Javan's bangs, I'd say quite a while. And Opi, you've aged."

The octopus-girl flipped her long tentacle hair. "Not as much as the old crow, I'd say."

"What, I'm even more distinguished now." Corvax ran his hand through the grey tips of his mohawk.

"Perl, how do you feel?" Javan asked.

"A bit sick to my stomach," Perl said, rubbing her belly.

"What's that in your other hand?" Uriel asked, as something shiny caught her eye.

Perl opened her clenched fist. "My mother's bracelet." The brass key, feathers, acorns, and shells slipped between her fingers.

"You didn't have that before, did you?" Tars said.

"Indeed, she did not," added Palo Santo; she and Uriel exchanged looks.

"How could Perl bring something back through the Realms?" Corvax asked.

"The dimensions are drawing nearer than ever to each other," Uriel said, inspecting the coquina butterfly shell.

"You mean humans and Light Beings?" Nan, asked.

"Yes, sweet Nan."

Conversation halted as Tryfon's ethereal voice filled the greenhouse. The Master appeared through a ray of sparkling light; the pleasant scents of jasmine, citrus, and pine wafted through the room. "It is good to see you all."

The Nine, along with Palo Santo and Uriel, bowed as Tryfon approached; his left head was a pink praying mantis, his right a beige and white barn owl.

"Human essences are the receptors of the Divine Mysteries."

Tryfon's long beard was a golden honeycomb buzzing with bees, who darted back and forth from the small garden of flowers sprouting from his shoulders. Flanking Tryfon were two Natatory Battle Bears that had survived the rainforest war.

"Love is the conductor, yet rebel spirits are vicious and cunning." Tryfon said, taking the bracelet from Perl's hand and placing it around her wrist. The broken vine magically grew back together. "The time has come for you to be the Mother Tree for humanity." Perl looked into Tryfon's soulful, tender eyes; his love washed over her like warm summer rain.

"Master, we must call a meeting with all of Venusto. Preparations need to be made for what is coming," Uriel said.

"The Nine will prepare at Natatory," Tyrfon said, tussling Javan's overgrown hair and patting Bear on the back. He gave a wink and nodded to Opis.

"Natatory? Now? They have not yet completed their training in Greenheart," said Uriel.

"The Apis Mellifera is the only insect that produces food eaten by humans." Tryfon said, as a honey bee landed on the tip of his fingertip. "Show them the unseen," he whispered to the bee. In seconds, the greenhouse transformed, illuminating the incredible patterns on flower petals as seen by bees.

"Wow!" Tars said.

"Amazing," said Lyre.

"It's so beautiful," said Perl.

"What's everyone—? Oh, you're seeing in ultraviolet light. Now you all know how I see the world every day," said Nan with a little laugh.

"No wonder you're such a giggle-mug," said Bear, smiling at the butterfly-girl.

"Rise, Nine, the brave Ursuses will lead the way." Tryfon lifted his magnificent sets of wings and the clouds they were seated on slowly vanished.

"Looks like we're already packed," Flax said, gesturing. Two wagons filled with their belongs were parked outside the greenhouse.

Perl noticed her sketchbook journal poking out of an overstuffed palm leaf bag.

"You will become Awakeners...for the great unearthing must occur to restore the balance of goodness in the world," Palo Santo said, pushing open a sliding glass door.

"All above is so below, so within is without," Tryfon turned, and as quickly as he appeared he was gone, vanishing into sparkling light. The buzzing bees from his beard stayed behind to discover the greenhouse's flowers.

The Battle Bears pulled the wagons, leading the way out to the main garden of Greenheart. Corvax, Nan and Lyre took to the air, following closely. Opis did a running leap, landing onto the back of the wagon. "You guys can walk. I'll take the free ride."

Tars gathered up his long trailing mustache, winding it into a ball to carry.

"We're on the brink of war," Flax said, slapping Tars on the back, "and you, my monkey-friend, are in serious need of a shave."

"Hey, not all of us got to come out of our meditation wearing a shining new suit of armor!" Tars joked; his large bulbous eyes sparkled with an array of brilliant colors, reflecting off Flax's scales.

Bear swiped a jar from Palo Santo's supply table and began scooping up the small bits of honey left behind from Master Tryfon's honeycomb beard.

"Bear, come on, really?" Javan rolled his eyes.

"What? It's like Master Tryfon wanted us to have it. So don't just stand there, help me!" Bear shook his jar at the platypus.

"Okay, fine." Javan took the jar. "I guess we shouldn't waste it." He quickly tied his overgrown bangs into a bun so he could see.

Perl paused, looking down at her mother's bracelet, rubbing the butterfly shell for comfort and a bit of luck.

"Her story gave you life. Her courage courses through your veins and it will guide you as you grow into the woman that you will become." Uriel placed her arm around Perl's shoulders and leaned down, pulling her in for a goodbye hug. "Draw strength from this."

"And you, you've been with me since birth. What part of your story is mine?" Perl asked, looking up into Uriel's violet eye; it sparkled even more brilliantly in the UV light.

She smiled. "The ever-unfolding, still unwritten part. The part guiding you to the truth."

"It wasn't just a dream, Uriel. Amanita was in my head."

"I know," Uriel said, kneeling down to look directly into Perl's green eyes. "And you will face her again."

"She said my father was in the Dark Realm."

"You have three hearts beating in your chest. What do they tell you?"

Perl paused. "No."

"Listen to that."

Perl hugged her Light Protector tightly, igniting the spots on her cheeks.

"I just hope there's some freshly-baked biscuits waiting for us at Natatory," Bear bounced past them towards the doorway, licking the honey from his sticky fingers. "You ready, Perly-Poo?"

Uriel stood, giving Perl a gentle nudge towards Javan. "She's ready."

Javan offered Perl his free arm; the other holding a full jar of honey. "You ready to explore Natatory?"

Perl took the platypus's furry arm, grinning a big toothy grin. "To the mountains we go."

The Garden Nurse slowly closed the glass door, watching The Nine trail the Battle Bears through the lush gardens. "Stay for tea?"

"Another time, my friend," Uriel replied.

"I thought as much," Palo said, watching as Perl and the others headed towards the floating mountain range in the sky. "Where will you go now?"

"To find Noaa."

Palo Santo latched the door and turned to face Uriel. "I see...and just how..." But the great Light Realm Protector was already gone.

The air was brisk; the sky pigeon grey, with dull clouds hiding the sun. Inside their sprawling one hundred and fifty room complex built into the mountainside, The Odina Brotherhood went about their daily chores. Outside, two Light Realm Protectors sat on a rocky escarpment keeping watch over the dwelling's newest arrivals.

"She's too close to the edge," said a Being with the head of a Tibetan Sand Fox; its crystal whiskers twitching nervously.

"Agreed," replied its companion, a portly Yak Being with wings made entirely of poppies, shaggy white fur, and lotus flowers growing from the tips of its six horns. The Yak fanned its wings, sending a gust of air towards a small girl who was walking along the top of the stone wall, forcing her to crouch to her knees to hold on.

"Get down from there you little tiger and come get a paintbrush," Sister Ursula said, as she and Sister Betty corralled the children into the circular kiva, The Brotherhood's outdoor ceremonial chamber.

"Lance, help her, would you please?" Said Betty.

"Yep!" Mixing crushed berries and beets to make paint, Lance put down his jar and hurried over to the girl. "Jump! I'll catch you!" He said, holding his arms out wide. She giggled and leaped and he caught her easily, squeezing the girl but accidentally knocking her goggles loose.

The girl winced, shutting her eyes and chattering her teeth. Even with the overcast day, the skies were still bright to the girl; the Under Kingdom escapees were adjusting to life above ground.

"Sorry, sorry." Lance quickly secured the dark goggles back on. "There, it's fine, you're okay." He gently put her down. "You can look now." The girl ran to Sister Ursula, yanking on her robe for a paint brush.

"This was a wonderful idea," Sister Betty smiled at Brother Sebastian. "It will surely help the mole-born to begin to express themselves."

"And perhaps it's time we lose the words "mole-born" from our vocabulary," Sebastian said. "Maybe we let them choose new names?"

"Yes, of course, you're right," Sister Betty agreed. "I love that idea."

Sister Ursula had given the small girl a few paints and a brush.

"Hold it like this, now dip and brush," Sister Ursula demonstrated. "Yes, good. See those? Those are birds, and that is a rainbow." Ursula pointed at the large decorative mural, filled with colorful trees, flowers, animals, as well as sacred tribal symbols. "You will add to the picture. Whatever you like, okay? Whatever you dream. Something that makes you feel happy and good inside," she smiled warmly at the girl.

Lance sidled up beside Sebastian. "So, what are our next steps? It's so secluded up here. How are we supposed to know what's happening in the world? We can't hide up here forever." The boy had taken off his heavy beetle armor, but kept his helmet on.

"It hasn't even been a full week. Let's catch our breath and let the children be children for a little while," Sebastian said, handing Lance a paintbrush. "That includes you, Featherstone."

The fifteen-year-old took the brush, smirking, "We still need to bring down the Deathstalkers. I can't stay much longer."

"Go paint something that makes you feel happy, beetle-boy."

"Fine." Lance joined the group of children doodling along the wall.

"What say you to a few stellar dendrites?" The Tibetan Sand Fox suggested.

"I concur. A splendid notion that will surely surprise and delight. The honor is yours," said the Yak.

Inhaling deeply, the Fox let out a long breath into the clouds, freezing the tiny water droplets inside. Shimmering crystals began to fall, drifting along like flecks of starlight.

"What on Earth?" Sister Betty held out her hand, catching a few flakes.

"What is this?" Asked a teenage girl.

The children began to chatter their teeth in panic, but stopped upon seeing the joy on the faces of Brother Sebastian and the Sisters.

"I can't believe it. It's snowing!" Brother Sebastian scooped up some powdery flakes that were beginning to accumulate on the ground.

"I've heard of snow, but I've never actually seen it," Lance examined a snowflake on his sleeve. "Incredible."

"No two are alike," said Sister Ursula, "like all of you." She cupped the chin of the little girl who had been climbing the wall. "How do you like the name, Crystal?"

The girl nodded and began twirling as snowflakes melted on her shaved head. She chanted her new name as she twirled in place. "Cry-stal! Cry-stal!"

Members of The Odina Brotherhood stepped out onto their balconies, taking in the wondrous sight. Many grabbed buckets, filling them; others threw snowballs at one another, laughing in disbelief.

Everyone in the kiva was playing in the snow, everyone except four-year-old Christopher, who was focused on his painting. His head darted up and down, up towards the jagged cliffs, then back again to the mural.

"Hey, Christopher, you want to play?" Brother Sebastian asked, holding up a snowball. "Oh wow, look at that. Very good! Is that a fox?"

Christopher shrugged his shoulders, then pointed up to the ledge several hundred feet overhead.

Sebastian squinted through the falling snow, "What, I don't see anything?"

Christopher tapped his paintbrush on his picture and pointed again to the ledge.

"The rocks?"

"No." Christopher tapped again and pointed, smiling; a look of pure joy on his face.

"He's most definitely captured your square head," The Light Protector Yak jested, snorting, flower petals shooting from its nostrils.

The Fox stopped making snow and glared at the Yak. He shook like a wet dog, spraying rain and slush at his companion. "Perhaps that's enough for one day." The last bits of snow clung to its whiskers.

"I do love the way the young ones catch a glimpse of us from time to time," said the Yak.

"Yes well, they still have shoshin," said the Fox.

"The beginner's mind," nodded the Yak. "Curious and full of wonder."

As the last of the snow floated down, the clouds broke, revealing brilliant blue skies. Sebastian stood behind Christopher as he continued to paint and point. The boy was growing a bit frustrated with Brother Sebastian for not seeing what he was seeing.

"What's the matter?" asked Lance, watching the two.

"I don't know. He's trying to show me what he's painting, but I don't see it," shrugged Sebastian.

"Well, that's no scribble," said Lance.

"I know, it looks like a…"

Lance looked up to where Christopher was pointing. "A…fox."

"Yes, but where?" Said Sebastian. "Do you see a fox up there?"

Lance nodded. "And some kind of…" Lance was entranced.

"Some kind of what, Lance?" Sebastian asked.

"Yak?"

The other children began to gather around Christopher. They stared up through their goggles, marveling at the two magical Light Realm Beings, smiles on all of their faces.

"What's happening?" Sister Betty asked.

"What are they all looking at?" asked Ursula.

"They're like Uriel," Lance said, recalling the moment he met the ethereal Light Protector. It was the day she has taken Perl, Dianna, and Sebastian through the portal to Mont Michel. He had never seen anything on Earth that looked like her; how she sparkled with an otherworldly light.

"Uriel's here?" Sebastian spun around, searching for Perl's guardian.

"No, it's just the two of them. They're magnificent beyond words." Lance waved up to them. "Hello!"

"Is that boy waving at us?" Asked the Yak.

"It appears as such," said the Fox.

"How can this be? It is an anomaly to have one witness us, let alone a dozen." The Yak called back. "Greetings, younglings!"

The children all waved, laughing at the Yak's curious voice; it sounded like the popping of bubbles.

"Where? Where?" Sebastian asked, slightly exasperated. A beam of light like liquid gold shone down from the Light Protectors to the children below. "Oh, my…I see them! I see them!" Shouted the monk, as the ethereal Beings materialized before his eyes. He and the Sisters fell to their knees, awestruck.

As the pair of Light Beings levitated from their perch, their flapping wings roared like a mighty waterfall and the air filled with the robust scent of sandalwood and sweet herbs. The Odina Brotherhood, who had been playing in the snow, stopped and stared in wonder. They, too, dropped to their knees, tears of wonder filling their eyes.

"Peace to you all," said the Fox. Each man, woman and child felt an overwhelming sense of love wash over them.

"Praise be Ever," said Sister Betty. "The Sacred Invisible…is now visible."

"Escape the snares of terra and become one." Sister Ursula quoted from The Codex. "My light breaks through not as sun, nor fire, but in the discourse of knowing the secret mysteries of nature."

"This is truly a sign. Can it be true?" Sebastian asked.

"Nothing is too good to be true," Lance said, watching the rocks and trees shimmer and sparkle with light from the luminous Beings. Lance smiled, realizing he was right where he was supposed to be.

"What are these?" Gretar asked. The pair had stopped to rest in the foothills after days of trekking through the forest.

"Reindeer." Dianna said. She stood, pointing, "Look! Do you see that sparkling ray of light, hitting the mountainside?"

"Reindeer." Gretar scratched his head. "There has to be thousands of them."

"Let me see those binoculars," Dianna said. Gretar pulled them from around his neck and handed them to her. "It's the Odina's complex. The light is showing us the way."

"Good, 'cause we're almost out of food. If we hurry, we can get there in a day, day and a half." Gretar said, breaking off a piece of bread and handing it to Dianna.

She didn't take it, her eyes glued to the beacon. Panning up from the mountain dwelling, she spotted the two glorious Light Protector Beings, wings spread wide, sparkling like diamonds in the sand.

"Praise Ever." Dianna lowered her binoculars. "Ha-ha! Perl has done it!"

"Done what?" Gretar had meandered away to pick a cluster of mushrooms. "What did you see?"

"The Light Realm is showing itself," Dianna said. "Look for yourself!" She handed him the binocs.

Gretar adjusted the lens, focusing. "Is that a hologram of a fox and some type of...buffalo?"

"That's no hologram...but perhaps a holy gram." Dianna giggled.

Gretar looked over at the woman. "I think you might be a little lightheaded. Here. Eat." Gretar handed Dianna the rest of the bread.

She took a big bite. "Now is the dawn of the great unearthing, my friend, and you are one of the first to witness it."

Gretar looked again. "You're telling me those creatures are real? And they're from the Light Realm?"

Dianna nodded, "I should know. I was once married to one."

"Okay, now I know you're dehydrated."

Two reindeer from the herd approached and knelt beside them.

"Whoa, what's going on?" Gretar said, taking a few steps back.

Dianna mounted the one closest to her, taking hold of its fur as it stood. "Let's go. We will be there in less than a day."

"Seriously? No way." Gretar said, bewildered as the massive stag nudged him with its antlers. "So, this is the Light Realm's doing as well?"

Dianna smiled, "Ever makes a way where there is no way."

"I trust you, Dianna." Gretar looked at the reindeer. "But can I trust you?"

The deer grunted, lowering its head.

"Okay. I'll take that as a yes."

Gretar cautiously pulled himself up onto the back of the reindeer. Trotting at first, the pair of reindeer soon broke into a full gallop, parting the great herd and making a beeline towards the mountain on the horizon.

A family of pink furry armadillos sat beside Perl, curiously observing the girl in her new Hope-colored uniform. Perl carefully balanced a rock atop a cairn tower, already twenty stones high. She was humming and singing a verse from the Nightingale's song:

"Take my wing in your hand
fly with me
to my hidden land,

under pines and waterfalls
twists and turns
I've planned it all…"

"There's the artist hard at work," Javan called out. "I've been looking for you."

"Ah!" The rock tower tumbled over. "I was just about to set a new record." Perl turned, giving Javan a playful side-eye.

A turquoise bead came loose from her braid, falling into the pile of rocks; the tiniest armadillo caught the bead on a bounce in its teeth and quickly brought it back over to Perl.

"Thanks, Pichi," she said, taking the bead. "And no thanks to you," she smiled at Javan.

"Sorry, but can't ya' just telekinesis the stones back up?"

"That would be cheating. Besides, doing it by hand helps me to better connect with nature. Finding each stone's equilibrium at its smallest contact point is like making the physically impossible, probable. Like the voice of Ever, it takes concentration, patience, and a willingness to—"

"You're doing it again," Javan smiled.

"What?"

"Talking like Divine Master Tryfon. Sorry, I mean your Dedo." Javan said, picking up a handful of stones to start his own cairn.

Perl sat down next to the armadillos to watch Javan as Pichi crawled up on her lap. "Go on then, let's see whatcha got."

"You see, it takes…" Javan placed his first stone on the corner of another. "…Confidence." He placed another, then another. "Knowledge of physical laws…" He stacked two more stones. "Focus, patience, steady hands, and knowing when…" He chose the largest rock to place on the top, "…to let go of things." He stepped back, admiring his work. "Ta-da! See? It's easy."

Perl didn't respond. She was inspecting the turquoise bead, watching how the color caught the light, and thinking about the old woman who had given her the box of colorful beads; a treasure the woman had been saving to give to her daughter, who had been killed in the arena games.

"I said, ta-da, easy!"

"All things seem impossible before they become easy." Perl braided the bead into Pichi's white fur that puffed out from under his pink dorsal shell.

"You, okay?"

"Yeah, sorry, of course you're an expert stacker, Land Awakener." Perl smiled up at the platypus-boy. "I was just thinking about my mom. I was hoping to go back home after Seer training ended. I haven't seen her since Victr's funeral." Perl pulled at a braid in her hair; several more beads came loose in her hand. "Probably time to take these out, but I just can't bring myself to."

Javan flipped his hair out of his eyes. "Coming here feels too fast. It's weird to hear you call me an Awakener, even if it's just in training. I've never made it to Natatory before, and I'm not sure I'm ready." Javan reached his hand down and Pichi hopped onto his palm. "But I'm glad we're doing it together."

"Me too." Perl patted the ground beside her. "Sit with me while I draw?" She picked up her sketchbook and pencil with the carving of a girl riding a whale on it; gifts from Uriel.

"Love to." Javan sat, curling the armadillo into his chest. He let out a heavy sigh. "I suppose next comes the not so easy task of balancing the Realms. In a way, they're each like a stone. Though individually unique, they rely on the others for support."

Perl nudged him, "Now whose metaphors are sounding like the Master's?"

"You must be rubbing off on me." Javan blushed; his bangs fell back down over his face.

"We will show humanity the magic in nature that has been right in front of them all along. With the world so in flux, hopefully they will be ready to see it." Perl brushed Javan's hair out of his eyes. "I'm glad you're here. It's nice to find something that is true and constant."

"I'll always be here for you."

"I know." Perl clutched her rabbit-rabbit pendent on her necklace. "I see you."

Flustered, Javan quickly changed the subject.

"So, what will you draw today, artist?"

Perl tapped her pencil against her lips, raising an eyebrow at him.

"No. Not me." Her gaze made him look away.

"Yes, you! And it's about time, too. Every other Seer has sat for me but you."

"Look around you, there are a million and one more amazing subjects up here," Javan scanned the Natatory horizon. "There! Look at those gigantic swans nesting on top of the yellow ginkgo trees, now that's worth drawing."

The skies turned a deep lavender as the sun set over the Natatory mountains, illuminating the swans. The little armadillo scurried down Javan's lap and over to its family, who were packing up their picnic to return to their burrow.

"You are more than worthy. Now just sit still." Perl cocked her head, studying the details of his profile.

Javan turned to look at Perl. "But I don't—"

Perl reached out and held his face. "There, like that. Now...don't...move."

"You—"

"No talking."

"Fine," Javan mumbled.

"Shh...an artist needs quiet stillness in order to recognize the Divine."

Resigned to the fact that he wasn't getting out of it, Javan shrugged his shoulders and smiled.

"Ah, there it is." Her eyes returned to the page as she began sketching and shading. "The love of Ever. It's in everyone and everything, everywhere, that's ever been created..." Perl bit her lip, looking up and back, up and back, finishing the final touches. She smiled to herself, pleased with her work. "So that we love nature and each other..." She held up the book for Javan to see, "Forever, evermore."

"Remarkable," Javan said, looking past the sketchbook and into Perl's emerald green eyes, the last bit of sunshine from the day reflecting in them. Perl smiled her big, toothy, ear to ear grin; the spots on her cheeks glowing.

"You like it?"

"I love it."

"Me too."

The pair laid back in the grass, their hands finding one another's. They stayed there for hours, looking up in quiet contentment at Earth; a delicate blue marble, spinning amongst a galaxy of stars.

Our first
Natatory
sunset.

Earth - Mont Michel & The Under Kingdom:

* *Perl: The Chosen One. Arrived on a whale to Mont Michel. Adopted by Papa Ximu. Daughter of Noaa and Dianna. Water Seer. Wielder of Fortis. Brave, curious, impulsive, lover of nature and her sketchbook. Has bioluminescence, telekinesis, sees humans' essences, can communicate with nature. Discovers new vampire squid powers.*

* *Papa Ximu: Head monk of The Brotherhood of the Quill. Guardian of Perl. Kind-hearted, even-tempered, loving, and wise. Perl sees all the monk as, "Spider-monks," their true essences.*

* *Brother Victr: Head cook for the Brotherhood. Dear friend of Perl. Big, strong, worrisome.*

* *Silvio Rossi: Brother Victr's little brother who died an untimely death.*

* *Brother Sebastian: Youngest monk, saved and bonded with Christopher.*

* *Brother Jonathan: Older monk, accompanied Victr and Sebastian on The Pilgrimage of the Truth.*

* *Brother Basil/Simon/Kirkwood: Run the Brotherhood's chapel and Globus Natura record keepers who assist Ximu.*

* *Regor: Perl's delivery partner and good friend on Mont Michel. Older, lanky fellow. Nervous giggle. "Goat-foot."*

* *Gretar: Activist. Member of The Ocean Conservation Coalition of Earthers. In love with Mik Graves.*

* *Dimitri: Mysterious old hermit who lives on Trash Island. Wild-haired, odd scientist. Apothecary. Formerly known as The Slaughterman, now a friend and teacher to Perl.*

* *Dianna: Perl's mother. 'Our Lady of the Woods' caring for the orphaned children rescued by The Forest Sisters of Elsewhere in the Under Kingdom. Widow of Light Realm Protector Noaa. Strong, kind, pure of heart.*

* *Sisters Martha, Betty and Ursula: Run the holy order of The Forest Sisters of Elsewhere. Providing guidance and food to the poorest of the Under Kingdom. Sew costumes for the wealthy elite.*

* *Lance Featherstone: Undercover Earth activist working in the Under Kingdom as the royal translator. Lives in the Slugabed Hovel. Smart, driven fifteen-year-old. Wears a stag beetle uniform.*

* *Christopher: Four-year-old boy rescued by the monks. Shaved head with scorpion tattooed forehead.*

* *Mole-born: Name given of the orphans rescued by the Forest Sisters of Elsewhere. Tattooed scorpion foreheads, ground down teeth.*

* *The Odina Brotherhood: Northern tribal holy order residing in a mountain citadel close to the Under Kingdom.*

* *Count Zell Graves: Chairman of the Oceanic Council/ Worldwide Waterways Committee. Overlord of the Golden Palace on Mont Michel. Husband to Sarr. Father to Mik and her deceased twin Ivry. Rich, powerful, ruthless, greedy, cruel. Member of the secret elite Under Ones Heel society.*

* *Countess Sarr Graves: Wife to Zell Graves. Vain, clueless, nervous, trivial. Adores her daughter Mik but is jealous of her. Going blind from overuse of Bella Donna.*

* *Mik Graves: Daughter to Zell and Sarr Graves. Last true redhead left on Earth. Founder of The Sisters of the Seahorse Initiative. Forced into an arranged marriage to the Deathstalker Kings of the Desertlands. In love with Gretar.*

* *Ruby: Mik's nanny. Buxom blonde. Devoted, loving, protective.*

* *Snive: Count Graves' weaselly, sycophantic assistant.*

* *King Tobias & King Névenoé Deathstalker: Rulers of the Desertlands and the Under Kingdom. Business associates of Count Graves. Born into wealth, arrogant, colorful. Members of the secret elite society Under Ones Heel. Control the world's technology.*

* *Kandy Vandenmire: Ambassador to the Southern Archipelago. Ruler of Sri Lanka. Prince Tobias's mistress. Business associate of Count Graves. Flashy, fiery, ruthless. Ex-rockstar. Has a pet cheetah.*

The Light Realm:

* *Ever: Creator of the Universe. Pure Light and Love. Ruler of The Light Realm.*

~Venusto~

* *Tryfon: The Divine Master of Venusto. Magical, ethereal, dreamlike in appearance. Compassionate, enlightened. The voice of Ever's love and light.*

* *Uriel: Light Protector. Eternal guardian of Perl. Stoic, statuesque, celestial, respected by all. From her endless battles, she is missing a wing and an eye. Has telekinetic powers.*

* *Quantaa: Two headed flying greyhound. Battle Protector. Powerful, obedient. Devoted to Perl.*

* *Grandmaster Olliv: Grasshopper-man. Head of Orientation and chaperone for incoming Seers to Venusto. Joyful, punctual. Repeats words. Drives the magical bagworm.*

* *Master Gichi"Gichi Manidoo Güzis": Seer Guide, "The Great Spirit Moon." Moon head continually moves through*

the lunar phases. Body of lush vines and arms and moonflowers. Walks on a multitude of hands.

**Master Tanda: Seer Battle and Strategy Instructor. Great marine iguana head and falcon body. Strong, fearless female.*

**Elder Enoogoo: Enormous orangutan, sings, loves and cares for Master Tanda. Assists Tanda with Battle training.*

** Palo Santo: Master Garden Nurse. Caretaker of the Greenhouse in Greenheart. Lives in a greenhouse in the sky. Ethereal, gentle, gracious. Mother to all nature.*

** Noaa: Biological father of Perl. Light Realm Being.*

**Light Protectors Tibetan Sand Fox & Yak: Overseers of the Odina Brotherhood.*

~The Seers in Greenheart~

** Javan: Platypus-Boy. Land Seer. Sweet, shy, concerned. Chestnut brown fur, long dark bangs. Clumsy out of water, but excellent swimmer. Electrolocation. Can shoot deadly quills. Of the Seers, he is the closest to Perl.*

** Tars: Monkey-Boy. Land Seer. Fun-loving, nervous, nimble. Large bulbous eyes with long mustache and tail.*

** Flax: Salamander-Boy. Land Seer. Cautious, jokester, energetic. Reptilian with solar-powered skin. Fond of raising his hand when speaking.*

** Corvax: Crow-Boy. Air Seer. Competitive, tall and muscular, serious. Black feathers, mohawk, cool gray eyes.*

** Lyre: Bird-Girl. Air Seer. Thoughtful, entertaining, supportive. Incredible mimic. Lovely plumage.*

** Nan: Butterfly-Girl. Air Seer. Sweet, upbeat, excitable. Excellent flyer. Arctic. Beautiful crystalline wings.*

** Bear: Tardigrade-Boy. Water Seer. Silly, light-hearted, friendly, resistant to extreme conditions. Caterpillar-like, chunky build, rumpled hair.*

** Opis: Jellyfish-Girl. Water Seer. Intelligent, outspoken, sometimes know-it-all. Thin, wispy. Translucent skin. Electrified tentacles for hair. Self-proclaimed "sister" to Perl. The smallest, yet, oldest of the Seers.*

The Dark Realm:

** The Ullen: Antithesis of Ever. The Most Fallen. Ruler of the Dark Realm.*

** Amanita: Daughter of the Ullen. Found as a baby and raised by Dianna. Same age as Perl, fourteen. Secret Under Kingdom arena singer. Shimmering white hair, alabaster skin, floral imprinted hair, steely gray eyes. The Deathcap.*

**Self-Slayers: Dark entities that attach to humans, feeding their minds with lies, corrupting their true essences.*

**The Backwards Man: An ancient Dark Realm Creature. Contorted. Monk killer. Fears humor and joy.*

**Surinam toad and toadlets: Dark Beasts that the Seers battle in the Half-Light Realm.*

** Whisper Wisps: Whisper evil into the ears of humans. Swarm around the Ullen's throne.*

** Blemmyes: Twin messengers. Headless with faces embedded in their chests. Exist between worlds.*

MELISSA (Greek for Honeybee) FLESHER
was born hopping from flower to flower,
climbing trees, digging in the mud,
and chasing butterflies.
A wonderer of nature and science,
she draws from both
when telling stories and making art.
PERL, THE UNEARTHING
is her second novel.

Melissa lives in Avon, Ohio
with her writer husband Erik,
her artist son Noah,
and loyal greyhound, Merlin.

@ melissaflesher
melissaflesher.com

www.ingramcontent.com/pod-product-compliance
Lightning Source LLC
Chambersburg PA
CBHW061143210726
48294CB00006B/1565